True North

ROSEWOOD RANCH SERIES

ALEXANDRA BANKS

WILLOW
HOUSE
Publishing

First Edition: May 2025

ISBN – eBook – 978-1-7637728-1-6

ISBN – Paperback – 978-1-7637728-4-7

ISBN – Hardcover – 978-1-7637728-5-4

For the hearts who just needed a little help to find their way. And a patient soul to wait for them.

Author's Note

TW –

This book contains difficult scenes and recounts. For the full list of trigger warnings please visit - https://www.alexandra-banks.com/ebook

The location and topographies of the places in this story have been fictionalized. They may not accurately represent actual location and terrain.

P.S The playlist is in the back!!

TRUE NORTH

Prologue

HARRY
SPRING OF 1972

The velvet teat rolls through my hands, one after the other. The milk hits the steel bucket with a ping. I can't hear it, but I know it does. "Burning Love" blasts through my headphones, the Zenith portable radio Ma bought me for my eighteenth birthday last month hangs from my worn jeans. The sun is just now comin' up. The birds no doubt starting their squawkin' as the small herd of Friesian cows mill over their fresh hay on the other side of the pen.

I nod to the tune.

The old milkin' cow shifts her feet. I pay her a glance, watching the bucket. *Hell, girl, don't kick it over. Not again.* Losing milk isn't an option. I wait for her to settle, hand tight over the rim of the bucket. She swishes her tail, slapping me in the face, before dropping her head into the feed trough.

"Steady, Mabes."

I take up my earlier rhythm, coaxing hot, frothy milk from her. Mable's udder is full—should get a half a bucket, I reckon. I relax as my song fades out and something grungy starts up.

Nice.

I return to nodding my head with the beat, letting my hands carry the same tune as the milk fills the bucket between my feet. I pause, turnin' up the volume. How is it songs can put you in a mood? This one makes me happy, excited. I let my thoughts wander to today and what it holds.

Prom.

Taking Lou, more specifically, to her prom. Dancin' never interested me, but she loves it.

I need it to go well. For the last part of the night.

The old cow lifts her head. I turn, too slow, to find what she's lookin' at. My old man's hand slams up the back of my head. The headphones fly onto the hay-littered ground. Stars creep into my peripherals. I jerk on the small wooden stool and shake it off.

Fuck.

I ignore him, setting my gaze on the udder in front of me. I can smell the booze from here. He never came home last night. So his mood tracks.

Lousy, damn—

"Answer me, you useless good-for-nothin'!"

My hands freeze on the teats. I suppress the urge to

strangle them between my palms in my wrath, but this old girl doesn't deserve that.

"Missed the question, sir."

"Ha. Sir, if you didn't walk around with your head in the goddamn clouds, Harrison, you would have half a clue what's goin' on 'round here."

I'm not going to bite.

Nope, not doing it.

"I didn't hear you." Stupid response, sure, but I can't answer a question I didn't catch.

"You shifted those bales? Weather's comin' in."

"I'll do it next."

"I'll do it next, what?"

"Do it next, sir."

"Better. I swear, boy, you are one useless son of a bitch." He wanders off, tripping over his own feet. My blood boils with the words he uses about Ma. I can't wait 'til the day I take her away from here. Find somewhere to make an actual home. Ma, Lou, and me. That old asshole can drown in his own liquor for all I care.

I pluck the headphones from the ground before Mable treads on them. Ma saved for months to gift me one birthday present. She should have kept the money for herself. But she's always looking out for her only child. One day, I will make damn sure every sacrifice she made for me in the last eighteen years is rewarded. Tenfold. Because it will be a cold day in hell when I turn out like my old man.

When each pass over the teats only produces a slow dribble, I grab the bucket and give Mabes a rub on the neck. I shift the stool onto the small rack overhead and untie her lead from the bar by the feed trough. She chews away, oblivious to the world, as I shut the gate behind me and head for the house.

A small two-bedroom weatherboard house with wood stumps sits in the center of the front yard, all that separates our small allotment from the road that leads into Lewistown. I walk up the back steps, careful with the old screen door. Taking my boots off, I carry the pail to the kitchen. No sign of the alcoholic, and I smile when I find Ma setting the table for breakfast. Lucky to make five-eight, her dark hair is twisted and pinned up, a little silver in the mix. Her fine features carry a weathering of fine lines. But her eyes carry more life than they should, considering the sorry existence we make do under.

"Mornin', Ma." I lean over, dotting a kiss to her hair before dumping the bucket on the small kitchen counter that is the centerpiece of this tiny kitchen.

"Mornin', love. How's Mabes?" She shakes a table-cloth out and watches it settle. With slow, quiet steps—that I'm sure she learned from needin' to keep outta the old man's way—she opens the china cabinet, sliding out two plates for breakfast.

"Two?" I ask. The eggshells we both walk on grind in my throat.

"Your father is asleep on the front porch."

"He can damn well stay there," I mutter. I hope he passes out for the rest of the day. God forbid he be sober tonight. I need it to go perfect. I'm not dealin' with him. Over my dead body is he gettin' anywhere near Lou.

"Grab the bacon and eggs, will you?" Ma asks. Her hands shake as she rests the plates on the table. A lifetime of the stress of living with the man who makes our lives hell most days of the week, now taken its toll. And I fuckin' hate it.

What I wouldn't do to change that for her.

I do what I can. Get between them when he's in a particularly bad mood. He's outta luck these days. I'm bigger than him. Stronger from carryin' the workload of two men. Last time he took a swing at me, he missed and fell on his ass. I didn't bother helpin' him up. Despite Ma's pleas for me to take care of him.

"Harry, those eggs are goin' to go cold quick."

"Shit, sorry, Ma."

"Language, my boy." She scolds me with a small frown. Even her discipline is gentle. How she ever ended up with Eddy Rawlins is beyond me. I thank my lucky stars every day that I take after my mother's likeness, personality, and features. I bring the food to the table and sit on my side as she sinks into her seat. Her thin hand brushes her dark hair over her forehead as she tucks it behind one ear.

"All set for this evening?" she asks, cutting her bacon. The mismatched cutlery, tarnished, makes for hard going.

"Think so. Can I take the truck? Pickin' up Lou."

"Oh, that makes my heart happy. She is the sweetest girl. A good head on her shoulders, make for a good wife."

I stare at her, mid-chew.

Did she find the ring in my dresser drawer when she was doing laundry or something? Changing the subject, I point to the eggs. "Nice and hot still."

She gives me a small, all-knowing smile and simply nods before returning her attention to her breakfast. With the last bite down, I pour her coffee from the small coffee jug. Adding a little of Mabes's offering for this morning, I slide it across the table to her. She takes it with a sigh.

"I'm serious, Harry. I won't be around forever. Louisa is wonderful. She's full of life, strong, and I've seen the way you look at her. Please understand, it's not every day you find that kind of love."

"I do, Ma." The words are heavy. I swallow the stone wedged tight down with my coffee. She pats my hand, giving me her please-consider-this look.

"Chores are waitin'." I stand and take her plate, dunking the both of them in the hot suds she has ready.

"Could you drive me to town later? I need more flour, sugar, etc.," Ma says from the table.

"After lunch, okay?" I look over my shoulder.

"Sounds good to me." She smiles softly at me. If she was allowed to have a license, she could drive herself. After I teach her to drive, I suppose. Maybe one day.

I wash up and head for the field. We need another few head of cattle sold this week in the store sale to cover next month's expenses and still give me enough to stack flat for our leavin'. Business was never something that interested me, but it's surprising what you can learn out of pure necessity. I'll work my fingers to the bone, if it means I can build a better life for Ma.

And hopefully, for Lou . . .

Ma wiggles the tie around my neck. I swear she cut off my air supply. I tug at it as she steps back, checking me over. Her hands clap in front of her face.

"Oh, darlin', you look so handsome."

"Ah, thanks, Ma," I mutter as heat floods my cheeks. Goddammit. Not the state I wanted to be in picking up Lou. She hands me the keys to the old buckboard truck.

"Oh, wait, I put something together for Louisa." She ducks from the front room to the kitchen, reappearing seconds later with a small cluster of wildflowers pinned to a silk ribbon in her palm. "You tell her I'm so proud of her."

"I will, Ma." I glance down at the suit I'm wearing— the product of Ma's thrift shopping with her skilled tailoring to make it more fashionable and a better fit. She rests her hands on my shoulders and tilts her head to the side. Silver lines her eyes. "I am so proud of you. No matter how things turn out tonight."

Yup. She found the ring.

I swallow as my heart kicks up.

"Well, isn't this cozy." The hard drawl snaps into the air a few feet away.

Ma stiffens immediately.

The slurred drawl tells me all I need to know. Hell, I can't leave her here with him like this.

"Go, Harry. I'll see you later." She forces a smile, ushering me toward the front door.

"I can stay, Ma."

She shakes her head fiercely. "No, this is important. Go."

Her hand squeezes around my upper arm as she gives me a stoic nod. Reluctantly, I walk through the door. It closes behind me, and I stand motionless for a moment, listening.

"You're up. Hungry, my love?" Ma placates him, the words muffled through the door. I wait for his answer.

"Starving, woman, bring a tray over to the box."

"Won't be long."

If she feeds him, hopefully he'll leave her be. I rush down the steps and head for the lean-to on the side of the house. The blue buckboard sits under the rusted sheet metal roof. I make a mental note to add it to the repairs list for this place. I slide into the driver's seat and fire her up. She rattles where she stands before I slide the stick into reverse.

The truck rounds the driveway backward, and through the window, I see Ma handing the old man a tray of food. He doesn't look at her, taking the cutlery and shoveling food into his mouth. Hope he chokes on it.

I make Lou's house in under ten minutes. Double-checking the small velvet box I have been hiding away for months is still, in fact, in my right pocket, I kill the engine outside her house. Nervous as hell, I grab Ma's corsage gift and walk up the path to her front door. Pressing a finger to the doorbell, I step back and slide my hands into my pockets.

A heartbeat later, the door opens, and my world stands over the threshold.

Lou's blonde hair hangs in pretty waves over her shoulders. Her bright green eyes lit up with excitement. Her prom dress, a long, floating pink one that reaches the ground. A shawl is draped over her shoulders. Cream. Silk? She looks a dream.

So damn beautiful.

"You're here," Louisa breathes.

And like that, my day got instantly better.

"Where else would I be, darlin'?" I smile at her, ignoring my thundering heart and the lightning rushing through my veins as she steps over the threshold and into my space. She floods my senses. Like she always does. The last twelve months of going steady have given me a focus and perspective I've never had before. I take my hands from my pocket, remembering the corsage. Damn, I hope it's not busted.

"Here, Ma made you something." I wrap my fingers around her thin wrist and slide the ribbon over it. Her eyes don't leave my face as I tie it around her wrist. She purses her lips, breaths stopped.

Her touch sends my head fuzzy. Where my fingertips graze her skin, something sparks to life. I turn her wrist over and inspect the final product. "She also wanted me to tell you she's proud of you."

Her face twists with emotion. The feelings Ma has for Lou go both ways. Another reason I love this woman so damn much. I drop her hand and crook an elbow. "Time to go? Don't wanna be late."

She smiles as her fine hand slides past my elbow and grips my bicep.

"Take me to prom, Harry."

"Yes, ma'am."

The glittering disco balls twirl overhead. Lou holds onto me as we sway on the dance floor. It takes everything I have to not kiss her in the middle of her entire class. Teachers watching. Friends milling about.

"Thank you for coming," Lou whispers in my ear as she leans into me.

"Anything for you, darlin'."

She leans back with a look I can't read and spins out of my hold. Snatching up my hand, she drags me through the crowd and out the gymnasium doors. The cool night air is an instant relief after the stuffy prom space. Lou comes to a stop on the sidewalk outside and spins back.

"There is something I want," she says, tilting her head. She swings our hands together between us. She's cute when she's coy. I pull her into my chest, and she giggles, looking up at me.

"What is it?"

She cups my face in both her hands, pulling my mouth to hers. Every cell in my body responds to her touch, her kiss. I want her, and she opens for me. Blood rushes south. I grip her face, sliding my hands into her hair behind her neck.

A soft sound slips between us, and she pulls back.

Heart racing, my gaze homes in on hers. It's hungry. Full of adoration and love. The way she always looks at me.

I close my eyes, swallowing hard. I wrap my fingers around hers, still on my face, and lower them. I sink to one knee, rubbing my thumbs over the back of her hands. Her brows drop, mouth agape.

"Ha—"

"Louisa May Masters, will you marry me?"

Chapter One

LOUISA
TEN YEARS LATER . . .

"Cut! Cut! Urgh, jeez, Brittany, pull yourself together." Annoyance curdles to shallow anger on our producer's face as our midday culinary anchor drops yet another bowl of batter, covering the floor. "Louisa!"

I pull the headset from my head and hug the clipboard to my chest as I rush to his side. "Yes, Marty?"

"Either that woman possesses the tactile skills of a toddler, or you ordered the wrong bowls."

I cringe.

It's not the bowls.

"Maybe she needs a break?" I ask in soft words, preparing to be in the firing line next. We've been at this Christmas baking segment for four hours. Britt was distraught when she got here; something about her boyfriend shipping out. Poor girl, that's got to hurt.

"Nope, I'm done waiting for this. We don't have the timeline to start again. Improvise." He flings a hand toward set.

"Improvise?" I barely let the word past my lips.

"Yeah, where you make shit up. Like half the people watching this crappy show are going to know the fucking difference. Give her a clean bowl. Go again!"

Shit.

I replace the headset and scurry onto set. Britt is on her hands and knees, tears scoring lines down her TV makeup. I drop to my knees to help. After four years of college and culinary school, my dreams of being in her position aren't looking as appealing as they once did. *Get a double major,* they said. *It'll be fun,* they said. Goddamn liars, the lot of them. I'll never land the chance to anchor a flea circus, let alone be the next Julia Child.

"Thanks, Lou. You don't have to . . . On a scale of one to *you're fired,* how angry is Marty?"

"He'll cool off. Are you okay?" I rest on my heels, and she does the same.

"I'll never get used to Toby leaving for tour." She swipes at her now-bleeding mascara, not doing herself any favors.

"Hey, hey. He'll be okay. I'm sure."

I actually have no idea about any of this military stuff. Heavens, I don't even know where the wars are in the world these days. I've been so occupied with my own harried life. Always keeping my eye on the prize.

The next Julia Child.

God, wouldn't that be something.

"*Now* ladies! Or do I need to send in the cleanup crew!"

Take a hike, Marty.

I glance back at the grump of a producer who's been running us ragged for months for his ratings. "Jesus."

"Sorry, Marty," Britt calls out.

"Don't be sorry, Brittany, be professional. Get the damn segment done. It's not a hard ask. At this rate, we'll be doing it live. We have less than ten to air."

"Ass," she mutters.

Marty is notorious for running timelines into the ground. It's not the first time a prerecord has had to be live because of his sloppy time management. With the floor clean and the bowl replaced, I radio for makeup and wardrobe. Britt disappears for exactly two and a half minutes and is back with a smile plastered on her pretty face in no time.

Safely behind the camera crew, the countdown starts. *On Air* flashes red over the entrance door. The clapperboard snaps. Britt starts mixing. That smile still in place. She picks up the spoon when the batter is done, and she has talked the audience through making it. Holding it over a prepared cake tin, she begins to scrape the batter into the tin. And then it happens.

Again.

I watch in horror as the bowl leaves her fingers, slamming into the cake tin, rolling over the counter, taking props and glass jars of spiced and herbed oils with it. You could hear a pin drop as we all hold our breath while the three tall glass oil bottles roll toward the edge of the counter.

Crack!

Crack! Crack!

Shit.

I drag my gaze to Britt's devastated face. Her chin wobbles, her hands still outstretched like she could stop the slow-motion disaster from happening.

"CUT! Fuck me, Britt. Greenroom. Now!" Marty throws his headset to the ground. Britt runs off in a fluster of tears. I pick up the gear and hang it over his chair.

This time, cleanup sorts out the mess as I run through the run sheet, hoping—no, praying—Britt survives Marty's wrath.

"Think he'll fire her?" one of the sound guys says, padding over to where I stand.

"Britt? No, she's the face of the show. You can't replace her without affecting the ratings."

He looks at me, chewing his bottom lip, hands in his back pockets as he rocks on his heels.

"You need something, Dylan?" I ask, feeling as awkward as he looks right now.

"Ah, yeah, so." He runs a hand through his hair, looking to the floor. "I was—"

"Masters! You're up! We're going *live*, people. Hustle!" Marty's voice booms through the set, echoing through the house seats that are used for other shows produced in the huge space.

Dylan stiffens and hurries back to his post, sinking into his chair with the look of a petulant child scolded for skipping school. *Okay . . .*

I snap my focus to the producer striding my way. The look on his face, all business, has my nerve up. Instantly.

"Up?" I ask, brows knitting.

"Get to wardrobe and makeup. You know this segment, you're subbing in today."

"I—" I choke on the air in my lungs.

"It's what you've worked toward for years, isn't it? Now's your chance. You've got five minutes."

I grip the clipboard to my chest, blinking as I try to discern if he's messing with me or deadly serious. But I'm not prepared. Wanting something badly and stepping up under duress are two very different things.

"Masters, now. We haven't got all day. Frigging hell, this is the last time I work with women. On the grounds on unprofessionalism, for one thing."

I shake my head. He's such an ass.

Not helping the nerves that are currently tossing javelins through my veins. I swear one pierced my heart.

He throws his hands up. As if to say *hurry the hell up.*

I drop the clipboard and run to wardrobe. The second I'm inside, the door shuts. Hands work me over. My old ripped jeans hit the floor. The sweater Mom gave me goes next. In under a minute, I'm standing in front of the long mirror in clothes I would never wear, looking so far removed from myself. If it wasn't for the hair, face, and hands that I'm currently turning over in front of me, I would have thought some other woman was standing here.

About to live out the chance of a lifetime.

Daytime television culinary anchor.

Holy shit.

Someone grips my shoulders, hauling me into a chair. Fingers pull through my blonde hair, turning it from its updo of necessity to blown and curled. Something like fine dust explodes over my face as the young woman in front of me taps, swipes, and shapes my face.

Two minutes later, when they swivel the chair toward the long mirror, my mouth gapes. Someone more like Miss America stares back at me. I've always been pretty, but this is otherworldly. They are miracle workers. At least if I screw this up, no one from back home will recognize me.

Always a silver lining.

Heels slide onto my feet and the door opens. Manny, the wardrobe director, gives me a push, signaling me to hurry up. I jump from the chair and clack down the long white hall back to set. Marty glances me over before a small mic and receiver are planted on my body. Rough hands turn me toward set.

It's now or never, Louisa.

I stalk my way toward the counter we have worked on for the cooking show for the last three years. I have to own this. I can recite this segment backward, so that shouldn't be a problem. Still, I'm always behind the camera, not in front of it.

Shit. Shit. Shit.

I move in behind the set kitchen counter. The camera rolls in. The teleprompter rolls in beside it. The green words hover. As if waiting for my signal.

The room falls silent.

Marty cups his hands under his chin, mouthing 'We are live.'

Oh great. Just great.

On Air flashes red.

My heart flings in my chest.

A stone grows in my throat by the second.

The clapperboard slams.

The teleprompter rolls.

My shoulders heave, hands clammy, as lightning buzzes through my body.

The last breath I took is lodged tight.

I open my mouth to repeat the words that rolled out of sight.

I try to swallow . . . and choke.

I can't breathe.

I grip the edge of the counter.

Darkness floods my vision.

I'm drowning.

An ugly gasping noise leaves my throat.

"Fuck!" Marty jolts from his chair, knocking it backward.

I lean on the counter. The teleprompter slows to a stop. Whispers start up.

I turn and slide down the side of the counter.

Hot tears tracking over the Miss America makeup.

I chug a sob before my face falls into my hands.

Chapter Two

LOUISA

The heavenly fragrances of Italian cuisine wind around me as the small older women in front of me opens the front door.

Mama's Place.

Lewistown, Montana.

It's surprising how the same this town is since I left over a decade ago. My parents moved on, but it always felt like home to me. Besides, I don't think I could face them now. My plans were grand. I was sure I would make it.

Almost did.

Shame, as petty as it can be, saw me pack up and come back to the last place that I felt safe. The last place I felt like myself. And free. Without expectations. The workload. Studying and long shifts. I worked my ass off in Cali for the chance at my dream. Nobody could ever say I didn't try.

All I want to do now is cook, earn myself enough to live a simple life for a while. That plan has me standing shy of the threshold of the only Italian restaurant in town. I loved coming here before I left.

"Louisa, bella, look at you! You got so beautiful!" Mama Mancini holds her arms open as if inviting me into a hug. I stand with one small overnight bag and my hand-bag. My worldly possessions rolled into a single overnighter. What do you really need to live a good life, anyway?

She ushers me through the door when I don't fall into the hug.

"Oy, I see how it is, tesoro. You follow me."

"It's so good to see you, Mrs. Mancini. Thank you for putting me up in the apartment, it's appreciated."

"Ah." She waves over her shoulder as she takes the steps slowly, hand tight around the rail. We ascend to the apartment over the restaurant. She unlocks the door and holds it for me.

"Thank you. Are you sure that rent you mentioned on the phone is enough? It didn't sound like much?" I ask.

The pittance she is asking for this spacious two-bedroom apartment took me by surprise.

"You can help out in the kitchen from time to time, hey? Your mama used to say you enjoyed cooking?"

"Yes, I do. I would love to, thank you."

"You get a job at Darla's Diner like you hoped to?" she asks as she turns on the light switch.

"I did, four shifts a week. Maybe some weekends, too."

"That's good. A woman needs to be busy. Idle hands . . ."

"I've heard that before." I smile at her. She is the sweetest.

She pats my cheek and takes my hand. Turning it over, she drops the keys in my palm. "You eat dinner with us a few times a week, hey? I could use some company other than *il marito*."

I tilt my head with a frown.

"Someone besides Mr. Mancini." She winks.

I chuckle and thank her as she makes her way down the stairs, slower than before. When she clears them without incident, I shut the door and turn the lock. Old Cali habit. Guess it's not as needed in Lewistown.

I lean against the door and close my eyes, letting my head fall back to thud on the wood. "A fresh start. It's only up from here, Louisa. You can do this."

I look around the apartment. The small green L-shape kitchen is in one corner with a weathered rectangular wooden table with two chairs. An old blue sofa that looks like it's seen better days sits on the other side of the room. Three doors dot the wall across from me. I'm guessing that's the bathroom and two bedrooms.

I pluck up my bag and walk for the center one.

Opening the door, I find a small bathroom. A white ceramic pedestal vanity sits under a small mirrored cabinet. Black-and-white tiles cover the floor, and a clawfoot bath sits under the only window in the room. No shower. How old-school Lewistown.

I try the next door, left of the bathroom. Bedroom one. The window overlooks the ugly metal roofs of downtown Lewistown. Trying the next one, I find a huge front bedroom. Soft, sheer lemon-yellow curtains flow over the open window. An old cast-iron canopy bed with ornate swirls in the headboard is the centerpiece of the room. A long sofa under the window with a small side table. I've never had this much space for myself.

Needless to say, apartments in Cali are tight.

I'm liking this change. More than I thought I would. I drift to the window, looking down on Main Street. Everywhere I look in the small one-horse town, all I find are snippets of memories of another lifetime.

Each one featuring him.

From the day I met Harry Rawlins, he was a force of nature. Always so few words. But the impact he had on me . . .

"Come on, Louisa!" Mom called from the driveway.

New school. New friends.

Yay . . . Not.

Changing schools at sixteen is nobody's idea of fun. Let alone mine.

"I'm going as fast as I can," I call down through my bedroom

window. Mom throws her hands up. In truth, I have been dreading this move. I don't make friends easily, and the thought of talking to strangers has me tied up in knots.

I run a brush through my unruly hair once more and swipe up my satchel before running down the stairs and through the front door.

In the car, Mom sighs at me before pulling out the drive. We make it to the new school as the bell rings.

Great, just great.

Next thing, I'm staring at the most uptight principal I have ever seen. His comb-over and knee-high socks are ridiculous.

"Miss Masters, you may go to class now. Your buddy will be along to show you around shortly. Don't make a habit of being late. Not the greatest start for a new student." His reprimand shines in his eyes as much as it's carried in his words.

"Yes, sir."

"She's a good kid, really—" The door closes behind me, cutting off my mother's plea. The principal's original take of me is spot-on. I'm not a straight A student. The core subjects do nothing but bore me. Guess that's what I would call it when I spend the majority of the class dreaming up new recipes.

Science is okay, at least I get to use a burner and boil stuff.

Not that it's edible.

I make my way to the locker that's to be mine. A bunch of girls stand nearby, their scathing gazes running the full length of me. They chuckle between themselves, most likely entertained by my hand-me-down clothes. One steps forward and opens her mouth to say something before someone snaps the group's attention. When *they all turn at once, like a pack of lionesses who just sniffed out a gazelle, I slide in by my locker, doing my best to ignore them.*

"Hi," one coos at whoever is approaching. I don't hear a response, but by the footfalls, I can tell it's a guy.

"How was your summer, Harry?" Another giggles.

Heavens above.

Harry doesn't respond, simply walking past.

He must be a year or so older than us. He is definitely a senior. His dark hair is messy, his deep blue eyes land on me, and he adjusts his backpack over his shoulder. Wearing jeans and a white T-shirt, his form is fully on display. Biceps, chest, and those legs. He either works out or works hard. My guess, by his calm demeanor, is the latter.

My face heats when his gaze lingers. A slight scowl tells me he wants to be here about as much as I do. The scoffs of the girls behind me see it flame red.

Shit.

"You Louisa?" he says, slowing down. "S'posed to show you your classes."

Um, okay . . .

"Ah—tha—thanks?"

I hesitate but grab my books as he keeps walking, not looking back.

Crap.

"Oh my god. Do you guys know each other?" one of the girls demands.

Seriously, how did they come to that conclusion from that interaction?

"I—"

The second bell screams overhead. I slam my locker shut and catch up to him. But all I can think of are those deep blues and that face. My stomach explodes with butterflies as he opens the door and nods for me to go inside.

"Meet you here after class. Don't go wanderin' off."

I haven't heard from Harry for over a decade. The last night I saw him, he dropped to one knee. And like a young, scared, desperate girl who felt the need to prove herself, I up and ran.

Home. Then to California.

God above, he probably hates me.

I did love him. As much as a seventeen-year-old girl could. That much I know.

But small-town plans were never mine.

I scoff a laugh at myself.

Look at me now. Back here. The big city drop-out.

Looks like Harry knew something I didn't. I hope things aren't awkward when I run into him. *When,* because this little town isn't going to let me out of seeing him. My heart races at the thought of who he became. What he'd be like now. Maybe he's married.

He probably is.

My stomach turns, sending an ache to my heart.

Dammit.

My alarm squawks at six a.m. My cue to dress and get ready for my first shift at the diner. I brush my teeth and pull on my jeans and a blue button-down shirt, hoping my uniform will be ready. I plan on changing when I arrive.

I grab my purse and keys and jog down the stairs. The restaurant downstairs is closed, chairs on tables. I unlock the front door, making sure to lock it behind me before crossing the street and heading to work. I pull my long hair into a ponytail as I walk toward Darla's.

I make it the three blocks to work to find two other women standing around out front. They are in peach uniform dresses. One pulls a drag on a cigarette, a rolled up white apron under one arm. They turn toward me in unison.

"Hi," I offer. "Louisa, first shift."

"Lisa," the brunette with the cigarette says with a small smile.

"Cynthia, hon. And welcome to your first day. You take the regulars, hey? No time but the present to learn their set-in ways." She winks at me.

I chuckle.

"Sounds good."

The door opens, a tiny silver bell chiming as it does.

The two women file in past the older woman in her peach waitress dress and white apron. "You must be Louisa?"

"Yes, ma'am. Darla?"

With a nod, she waves me in. "Come on in, hon. Your uniform is in back waitin' for you."

I beam at her.

So far, so good.

I walk in after the others. Cynthia turns back with astonishment over her face. "Hey! Weren't you on that cooking show a few weeks back?"

I freeze on the spot. My mouth opens.

Nothing comes out.

Shit.

Chapter Three

HARRY

"Hup-hup!" I ride behind the small mob of heifers. The old man is swayin' on his mount. Always tanked. Serves him right if he falls off and smashes his face in.

"Harry! Move them up."

No shit.

The only reason he's leading is because he's too drunk to notice when a beast straggles and gets left behind. Even in this small allotment of ours, he's useless. I wave a hand so he knows I heard but essentially ignore his order.

He's having one of his rare good days when he is capable of more than layin' on the daybed for hours. Ma pleaded with me to let him help. Although he's more of a hinderance, I know she would rather have him out of the house.

Less eggshells that way.

So, I'm more than happy to buy Ma a little parcel of relief from him. With the last heifer in the yards, I push my mare sideways and shut the gate, leaning out of the saddle. The heavy iron loop drops over the wooden post and I sit back in the saddle. Twenty head for the store sale. Should keep the roof over our heads for the next few months.

A far cry from the dairy we ran five years ago. We were too slow. Too outdated, with other farms upgrading to pumps and trucks. The old man couldn't come at that. *No use spending money on something we already do*, he used to hiss. So, we got left behind. Outpriced and needing a change.

Cattle ranching became the next logical step.

I wouldn't go back to milkin' cows if you damn paid me.

"What time the truck comin'?" the old man says as he sways atop his horse, plodding toward the gate.

"End of day. I can handle the draft if you want to do a perimeter check?"

He glances at the milling cattle. Their brown coats shine in the summer heat. But more importantly, they're hefty. The pastures I've spent three years improving have finally paid off. With this lot gone, I can put more into the business account to make a bid on a bigger place. Maybe even a sizable ranch, if I wait a bit longer.

Across the field, at the house, Ma pushes out the back screen door and stands on the top step. Tea towel in hand, she dries a plate. I wave a hand, and she returns the gesture. The silent check-in she always does when I work with Pa. As if she trusts him about as much as I do.

I can handle the old fool. The only person he's a danger to out here is himself. Inside the house is a different story.

Something thuds.

The cattle startle.

I search for the old man's hat.

Nothing.

Fuck.

Jumping off my horse, I climb through the wooden rails and walk to where the heifers have separated. Between hooves and covered in dirt, he lies, out cold. I knew he was drunk, but this is a new level. Even for him.

I roll him over with one hand and his head lolls. "Jesus Christ."

I stand up, heading for the rail. "Ma! Come grab the gate, will ya?"

She drops the plate and towel to the step and hurries to the yards, her worn long skirt hovering over the golden grasses as she goes. When she sees her husband lying in the dirt, her face falls. She grips the gate, staring for a moment before undoing the latch and standing ready to open it for me.

I talk to my old man, scooping his thin frame off the ground, and carry him home, following Ma as she walks ahead. I hope she doesn't think this is her fault. She's partial to giving him whatever he wants these days, if only to keep the peace.

God, how the fuck is this still our damn life?

She pads up the back stairs and pushes the door open. "On the daybed, my love. I'll clean him up."

"Let him sleep it off, Ma. You don't need to baby him."

"Maybe." The word is no more than a whisper.

Inside, the house smells almost like roast beef. The scent of seasoned veggies, herbed and cookin', tangles with the odd meaty fragrance.

"What's cookin', Ma?"

"I thought more food, hearty meals, might soak up the extra booze he's been taking in. A roast, etc."

"Always lookin' out for him." I kiss her forehead. "Don't understand why."

"One day, Harrison Rawlins, you will love someone so much, you would turn yourself inside out to make sure they're okay. With no regard to your own well-being. Then, you will realize you have something real. Something worth fighting for."

She pats my cheek like she's done for the past twenty-eight years. I force a smile. I had that. At least, I thought I did.

Louisa was my person. The one girl who had me in pieces with just a smile. For every second we were together, until the day she smashed my heart to smithereens. I still love her. Probably always will. We were young. But you don't feel that deeply, that completely, for someone if it's simply a fleeting phase.

When I don't respond, Ma tilts her head. "You'll find it again, I promise."

I can't even respond.

The phone rings, and she rushes to grab it before it wakes the old man.

"Oh hello, Evelyn."

Ma's best friend. I have the phone bill to prove it.

I nod a *see you later* and push for the back door. I haven't allowed myself to think about her since that night.

That doesn't mean she hasn't infiltrated my thoughts every damn day since.

I walk for the cattle yards, my mount still tied to the gate where I left her. She's a good mare. I should give her a name. But that feels too risky. Horses die. Get sold off. I can't go through gettin' attached again.

Hell's hounds, I'm pathetic.

Even my thoughts are runnin' scared with their tail between their legs.

Fuck me.

Been livin' under a storm cloud since she left . . .

Too much.

That's too much, Harry.

Snap outta it.

I untie Horse from the rail and lead her back to the barn I hand built around ten years ago. Trying to work out the loss of her with my bare hands. The debilitating pain of losing the other half of my soul when I was barely old enough to understand the gravity of what I was going through.

Understand just fine now.

Work is my salvation. I have spent the last ten years makin' something of this small allotment. Buying up the land around us to build the equity. Equity is king, they say.

I release the clasp on the girth and slide the saddle from Horse's back. She shifts on her feet. Sweaty, she flicks her tail. I dump the saddle on the rack I spent too many hours building and return for the bridle. Sliding the strap loose, I slip it over her ears and toss it onto a hook. I give her forehead a rub before hosing her off and letting her loose to her pasture.

"You really should give that poor girl a name," Ma says softly from the doorway of the barn. "You owe her that much."

I chuckle. "You two been talkin'?"

She offers me a small smile.

In this hard life, she wasn't granted many, so I take it like the gift it is.

"Going into town today?" Ma asks.

"If you need?"

"Yes, I think I'm all outta potatoes and flour. You could stop at the diner for lunch. The roast will keep for supper."

"You sure?"

I fight off the blush that's creepin' up my neck. I love my mother, I really do. But her cooking's never been her strong suit. And she is all too aware how often I frequent Darla's in town. Breakfast, lunch, and sometimes supper, if I'm feelin' like splurging.

"Oh, I'm sure." She pulls an odd face. "I know my cookin' doesn't even come close, hon. I'm not offended, I promise. You've always loved your food. Even as a little boy. Have no idea where you put it. Not an ounce of fat could hang around with all that muscle."

She rolls her lips together, like she wants to say something else, but won't.

I chuckle and lean on the barn doorway. "When you want to head off?"

"Give me twenty?" she says.

"Sure, be up to the house soon."

"Oh, and Harry, change out of that shirt. It reeks of horse and dirt."

Okay . . .

I shake my head at her and finish up by tidying the barn and putting out a couple bales of hay for the heifers. They make short work of it, and I head to the house to clean up for the diner.

That's new . . .

What is Ma up to?

I run a hand over the wood grain of the truck's dash. It may be old, but it's a classic. Plus, it's the one thing the old man gave me I don't resent or hate. I let her idle, waiting in my clean clothes as Ma makes her way down the front steps. She locks it and hurries to the truck.

"What's the rush?" I ask.

"Oh." She sits in the passenger seat and fixes her hair, holding a small mirror up that she fished out from her oversized handbag. Even for almost fifty, she's still beautiful. The deep blue eyes she gave me are lit up with excitement as she pats her brown hair with streaks of grey.

"Finished powderin' your nose, Your Highness?"

She beams but nods and pulls her seat belt over her chest. "Yes, let's go."

"What's got you all worked up?" I ask, backing the truck out of the driveway and shifting it into drive.

"Nothin'."

I raise an eyebrow as I glance at her.

"Never mind." She pats her bag and forces her face to a somber facade.

"If you say so."

She stares out the window. I drive us into town and park by the convenience store. Easier to cart the groceries that way. I kill the engine.

"You want me to come with you, carry the potatoes, etc.?"

"Um, no, I should be fine." She is out of the truck before I can crack my door open.

"Enjoy the diner!" she calls from a little way down the street.

What? Did she burn the roast altogether or something? I swipe my hat from the center of the bench seat and head up Main Street.

Folks say hi as I close in on Darla's. The doorbell chimes, and I look around my regular haunt, checking if my usual booth is free. It is. I pad toward it and drop into the seat, facing away from the counter. No need for people to see me. Or me them. I pluck the hat from my head and place it on the seat beside me.

The place is busy. Chatter, cutlery clinking, coffee pouring fills the air in the muddled mix of food establishment sounds that relaxes me. Ma was right, this is one of my favorite places. The waitresses move around in their peach dresses and white aprons. The joint feels like something from a drive-in picture.

"Your booth is up," Cynthia calls to another waitress.

Is it bad I'm here so often that I recognize each of their voices?

Peach falls in beside me.

"Coffee, hon?" she says, coming to a stop beside me.

The voice is new, but not unfamiliar.

I should make a good impression on the new girl since

I practically live here. I sigh and mutter, "Why else would I be here?"

Deciding that's not the first impression I want to make, I add, "Yeah, please." I look up. "And my regu—"

My gaze meets one I haven't seen for over a decade.

Shock fills her face.

The coffee pot in her hand slips. Glass and hot dark brown liquid explode all over the red and gray tiled floor.

I choke on air.

"Louisa," I rasp.

"Ha—" Her face breaks. She spins on the spot and hightails it behind the counter.

Fuck.

Chapter Four
LOUISA

"**Y**our booth is up," Cynthia calls.

Desperately trying to squash a short and very inappropriate conversation about television crew sex scandals with old Mrs. Hills, I punch in the amount on the till, pulling out her change and placing it in her hand. I glance at Cynthia. "Okay, thanks."

A dark head of hair and shoulders in an old work shirt are visible over the booth divider. He sits in the last booth by the back wall. My area. I grab the fullest, hottest pot of coffee from the hot plate and round the counter. Passing the booths, I check in as I go.

"More coffee, Errol?"

The old man beams at me, toothy smile plastered on his face.

"Thank you, sweetheart. You're a keeper."

"You doin' the keepin'?"

It's amazing how the accent blooms back to life once you're home. It helps that the customers expect it. Learned that on day one. The Cali accent wasn't doing me any favors. So, I dug deep, and that old drawl was still in there. Lucky me.

I pour the old man some more coffee, and I'm pretty sure his eyes are not on my face. I chuckle and squeeze his shoulder, making my way to the last booth.

The dark head of hair leans back in the booth, sending a hand through those dark locks. Wow. Now I need to check out his face.

Shit, Louisa. Stop.

I so need to get laid.

I check my apron pocket. The slip of paper from earlier, when I met Brad, is still secure in there. I smile to myself. Dating again will be a breath of fresh air.

Bradley Connors. I vaguely remember him from high school. He's quiet but seems nice. I ponder what to wear to our first date.

Closing in on the booth, I say, "Coffee, hon?"

The man mumbles something under his breath that sounds like "Why else would I be here," not looking up. That voice . . .

When I don't move the pot closer, he shifts on his seat.

"Yeah, please." Now he turns his head, eyes drifting up. "And my regu—"

Instantly, my stomach drops out, only to resurface as a bundle of knots on fire.

Air leaves my lungs and stays gone.

The coffee pot in my hand slips.

Heart flinging around my rib cage like a panicked, injured bird, I try to school the shock from my face.

Shock at seeing him again.

Shock at the sight of him. He's grown into something breathtaking. All hard angles and kind face. Those dark blue eyes . . .

"Louisa," he chokes.

"Ha—" My voice breaks.

I can't.

My hands tremble. I wring the apron between my fingers, trying as hard as humanly possible not to cry. I slam my shoulders back and slip over the sea of coffee, rushing behind the counter and into the supply room. The door slams behind me, and I slide down the wall.

"He's . . ." I pull my knees into my chest. It's like not one day went by. The feelings that I had for this man haven't changed one iota. At all. A hot tear carves a path down my cheek. I swipe it away.

Nope, we are not doin' this.

"I'm okay." I suck in a huge lungful of air. I knew I would run into him eventually.

Never in my wildest dreams would I think he would still have that effect on me.

And then, oh my god, he walked in.

Technically, I walked to him. Still . . .

And I—

I am rebuilding. Not sinking back into something so serious. I need to be me for a while. Not the girlfriend. Not Louisa Masters the career woman. Just me. Just Lou.

It's been a long time since anyone's called me that . . .

Only one person ever did.

And . . . I dropped a pot of steaming coffee at his feet.

I push to my feet, determined to have a do-over.

Let's do this again.

I can be friendly, right?

I open the supply room door, and Cynthia walks in with the mop and bucket. "You okay, love?"

I wipe my hands on my apron, like it needs fixin'.

"Uh huh." My voice is too high. She raises an eyebrow like she doesn't believe me. Heavens, *I* don't believe me.

"Your area's all cleared up. But you might want to service that booth. He's a regular, and a good one."

Of course he is.

"Sure, on it."

I blow out a breath and clear my throat, hands sweeping over my hair. Cynthia shoots me a sly look. "You look fine, Louisa. Go get him, tiger."

"Ugh, not helping."

She cackles and disappears around the corner with a mop and bucket. I walk through the swinging doors and to the counter. I glance around the diner. The end booth is empty. Shit. The doorbell chimes. The hat and the back of a work shirt slip through the door and vanish.

Double shit.

I pull off my apron and hunt for Lisa. I find her at a table in the middle of the checkered floor. I'm by her side a second later. "Hey, can you cover for me for five?"

"Sure."

"Thanks." I fly out the doors and spill onto the street. Desperate to find the hat, I swivel my head, searching for it.

People.

Hat . . . Wrong one.

Harry's dad's old buckboard truck sits by the grocery store. I run to the store and rush inside. The place isn't busy. Only a few people. I rush down the first aisle. Nothing.

The next one.

Nothing.

The nex—

I slam into a woman, her back to me as she reaches for a can on the top shelf.

"Shit! I am so sorry!" I try to steady her as she teeters on her feet, grabbing onto the cart by her side. She turns, a little dazed, and sets her gaze on me. The grin that grows on her face sends my heart racing. Not because she's happy.

Because she's Mrs. Rawlins.

Oh god.

Harry still drives his Ma to town?

I guess some things never change.

"Louisa! Heavens above. Look at you! It's so good to see you, my girl." She pulls me into a hug. I freeze for a moment, not knowing if things have changed. When she hugs me tighter, I realize they haven't. I hug her back. A moment later, she releases me, holding me at arm's length.

"Well, aren't you a sight for sore eyes. Evelyn told me you're back in town. Are you staying for good this time?"

"It's wonderful to see you, too, Mrs. Rawlins. I'm not sure what I'm going to do."

She tilts her head. "Well, I for one can say it hasn't been the same around here without you."

I chuckle. "Thanks, but I think Lewistown does just fine without me."

"Who said I was talkin' about the town?"

Oh?

Oh . . .

My face heats as I realize she means Harry. She smiles, it's so kind and loving, and now I feel self-conscious in my waitressing uniform. My gaze hits the floor.

"Actually, I could use a hand with these here groceries. My Harry went to Darla's to find himself something good." She pushes the cart along the aisle.

He found something, at least. Most likely the scare of a lifetime in the form of the last person he ever wanted to see.

I follow, not knowing what else to do. Stopping at the herbs and spices, she pushes to her tiptoes, reaching for the thyme. One of my favorites. Her fingers brush past the small bottle. I don't remember her being this small. Maybe she shrank a little with age. More likely I grew. The last time I saw her was ten years ago.

My mind wanders back to that night.

The devastation that wrecked her son's face.

The guilt that's eaten me since, for running off without explanation. It's the one thought that never leaves me. I wish I could take it back. Have a do-over on that one moment. The answer would be the same—I was seventeen, for goodness' sake.

I fold in behind Mrs. Rawlins and grab the glass bottle for her. She spins back and pats my cheek.

She does that a lot.

I chuckle. "What else do you need?"

She scrunches her nose up a little. "Well, if you're not in a hurry to go back to work?"

Ah ha! She knew exactly where I was. I wouldn't put it past her to have sent Harry to the diner herself. If there is one thing I know to be true, she loves her son more than the air in her lungs. Always has.

Knowing Harry, he never told her what happened before I left, only that I did.

"Potatoes and flour. I think that will do for the minute." She wanders off with the cart and I fall in beside her. I should be getting back. Pretty sure my five minutes was up about ten minutes ago.

We head for the checkout with the small list of items. She pays in cash, and I carry her bags. She makes for the old blue buckboard truck the Rawlins have owned ever since I've known them.

"I bet I could make much better food for my boys with some proper instruction," Mrs. Rawlins says as we reach their vehicle. She opens the door and squeezes the lever, shifting the passenger seat forward. I place the bags in the small space and step back.

"Sure, what did you have in mind?"

"Oh, something new age. I'm sick of eatin' the same old thing night after night. Could you come out during the week? I don't want to eat up your weekend. A young girl like you must have a thrivin' social life."

"Huh, not exactly. And I can do Wednesdays. It's my day off."

"Wonderful! Should I go back inside and grab some better ingredients?"

"I can bring some things." The door to the diner opens a little ways down the street and Lisa waves at me. Time's up.

"It's lovely to see you, Mrs. Rawlins. I'll be out Wednesday around lunchtime, okay?"

"Sounds perfect, sweetheart." She beams at me. "Please, call me Rosie. You're far too grown-up to be callin' me Mrs. Rawlins these days."

"Okay," I say with a chuckle. "Bye, Rosie!"

I round the truck, heading back to work. Past the pharmacy, I turn back and wave to Rosie. She rolls the window down and waves me off. I turn back and slam straight into something hard. Warm. All sandalwood and heady.

"Shit! I'm sor—" I look up and into the deep blues of none other than Harry Rawlins.

His jaw is set.

I step back and suck in a rapid breath.

He stands there, staring at me. All lines and angles. Gaze homed in on my face as his hands hang by his sides.

"Hi," I offer in a soft squeak. I flatten my immaculate uniform with my hands, not knowing what to do with myself.

"Hi." His tone is anything but friendly.

I guess I don't deserve anything more. Heavens, if the shoe was on the other foot, I doubt I'd be this put together.

"I ran into your mom," I offer to fill the loudest silence known to man.

He glances to the truck.

I wring my hands behind my back, trying to look anywhere but his face. My heart is clambering in my chest, sending my stomach into a flurry of butterflies. How does the man still have this effect on me ten years later?

He shifts on his feet, like he wants to be anywhere but here.

"I should head back to work." I go to move past him.

He plucks his hat from his head and runs a hand through that hair.

I stutter a goodbye and edge past him awkwardly. "See you 'round, Harry."

Without a word, he hesitates, but walks for his truck.

Well, that went well. I roll my eyes at myself. God, I am the stupidest woman alive. He's never been a man of many words. But that was strained, even for him. It's funny the way you can still know someone, to a certain extent, even after a decade apart. I push the diner door open, and the noise of busy and the scent of coffee reels me in.

My head is anywhere but at work.

This is not how I wanted to start my fresh start.

Consumed by an old flame. God, I'm pathetic.

Get a hold of yourself, Louisa.

The rest of my shift drags, and I occupy my mind with anything I can find. The last thing I need is to catch feelings for someone who can barely stand to be around me for less than five minutes. I wander home to the apartment straight after my shift. A small box of leftovers from one of the casseroles Cynthia whipped up sits in one hand as I unlock the front doors to the restaurant. Making sure to lock them behind me, I head upstairs.

I'm halfway through my meal when I remember the promise I made Rosie.

Dammit.

Maybe it will be fine? Harry will be outside with his work, right?

It's just cooking lessons. Rosie is a friend. That's all this is.

Besides, I have a date with Brad following the trip out to the Rawlinses' farm. So, I'll be keeping my distance from Harry. I finish the last of the delicious savory goodness and wash up the cutlery.

Tossing the container in the trash, I run myself a bath. Eager to wash away the sweat and grime from the day, I undress and slide into the hot water. Letting out a long, slow, and steady breath, I let my eyes fall shut.

It'll be okay.

It'll be fine.

"Moving on. Starting again. Fresh start . . . and all that," I whisper to myself as I sink under the water.

I may as well stay down for all my willpower is worth around Harry Rawlins.

The sooner I go on that date with Brad, the better.

Chapter Five

HARRY

Ma is pacin'. Glancing at the damn clock every few laps of the kitchen. I know what she's doin', and it ain't gonna work. Louisa Masters is about as available to me as a second moon landin'. I finish up my early lunch and wash up my plate. I have no intention of being here when she decides to grace us with her presence.

You think for a man who's spent the last ten years pining for this girl, I'd be happy to see her. But coming face-to-face with her was anything but a good experience. It brought back the memory of her runnin' from me as fast as she could. Not to mention the heartbreak that followed. It took me years to come back from that.

"Later, Ma. Enjoy your lesson." I grab my hat and stalk for the back door.

"You're not stayin'?" she calls out behind me.

Like hell.

I fly out the back screen door like the house is fire. I can feel Ma's gaze burnin' into my back. Guess I'll be getting an ear chewing for that later. I'm not meanin' to be rude. Just don't need another round of Louisa in my life right now.

I have to focus. I'm so close to getting us off this tiny-ass farm and onto a ranch. In three months, give or take a few weeks, I'll be in the position to make my move.

Hell will freeze over before I let Louisa glide into town and wreck my life again. I round the side of the house to where I parked the truck. Fences on the southern side need attending to. I'll start on them first. That'll take a few hours; she should be gone by then.

Here's hoping.

I run the buckboard to the barn and load it up with the post hole shovel and crowbar, post rammer, toolbox, and three fresh coils of wire. Nothing like keepin' your hands busy to clear your head. Ma's sentiment. Works every damn time.

Tracking the vehicles across the fields, I hop out to work the few gates on the place as I go. Reaching the southern boundary fence, I let her idle at a stop as I sweep my gaze up and down the long run of sagging posts and wire. So much for a few hours.

The old man told me it needed fixin'.

This needs replacing.

Dammit.

Lucky for this old fence, I now have the perfect reason to spend hours with my hands busy. I kill the engine and grab the toolbox from behind the driver's seat. Snipping the wire, I watch as the entire line sags even further when the last bit of tension goes.

Four hours later, my hands cramping from repetitive use of the wire cutters and pliers, I call it a day on the fence. With all new posts rammed into the soft earth and two new wires along the long stretch to hold it in place until tomorrow, I toss the tools back into the box alongside the leftover posts.

Sliding the toolbox back behind the seat, I push the seat back and climb in. I rest my head back on the low bench seat backrest and close my eyes. Balling my hands tight and flinging them open, I coax the blood back into my hands. As feeling returns to my fingertips, I turn the engine over. She rumbles to life.

The drive back is slow. I'm killing time.

I'm well aware that this is me being a coward. Or standoffish. One of the two.

I'm sure Ma will have words ready and waitin' for me when I get back to the house. When I finally reach the barn, I jump out and haul the fencing gear out, in case Ma needs to go somewhere between now and when I make it back to that fence.

It's only when I turn the truck for home that I catch a glimpse of a small yellow Datsun in the driveway.

Surely, Louisa isn't still here?

I grind my jaw, weighing up my options.

I'm guessin' she's going to be around for a while, since she got a job at the diner. I should be polite. She is doing a nice thing for Ma.

I pull up by the house and turn the vehicle off, making myself climb out and up the stairs before I lose my nerve. Walking into the kitchen, something heavenly engulfs my senses. Louisa leans over a large pot. Ma is chopping beside her. Neither woman looks up. The old record player is on. The two women sway to an Elvis tune.

I can't help the smile that stretches over my face.

For the briefest second, I let myself think this is my life. Coming back from ranchin' work to these two.

My chest aches.

I punch the thought down and clear my throat.

"Oh hi!" Louisa says, looking up from the pot. The wooden spoon, still in her elegant hand, continues to stir like it's second nature.

"I—" I say. Ma winks at me. "Hello, Louisa."

I shove my hands in my back pockets, not knowing what to do with myself. Lord above, how am I nervous and angry at the same time?

"You want to try?" Louisa holds the spoon up from the pot. Steam billows up from a thick red sauce.

"I should—" I turn on my heel.

"Come here, my boy. You *have* to taste this, we've been slavin' over this here stove for two hours. Show Louisa the respect and hospitality you were raised to have."

Heat flushes my neck. I drop my gaze to the floor. Ma may be a small lady and comes with a heart of gold for those she loves, but lord above, she gets the last word when I step out of line.

As I, apparently, am now.

"Yes, ma'am." I look to Ma with an apology.

With a coy smile, she shakes her head. I walk to where Louisa stirs the pot again. "Let me have it."

Her eyes light up as she pulls the spoon out of the pot. It drips, and she swipes it over the edge with quick precision. It's heading for my mouth a heartbeat later. I lean in. Her scent mixes with the fragrant sauce and a stone grows in my throat. I choke on the last of the air in my lungs. The spoon meets my tongue.

I close my lips around the hot wooden spoon. Instantly, flavors spring to life in my mouth. She takes the spoon back, slowly. Her green eyes are on my face. Now her chest heaves like she's the one who just had something hot shoved in her damn face.

I swallow the mouthful down.

My eyes drift shut. I'm drowning in the most incredible flavors.

"Do you like it?" she asks softly.

I open my eyes. Lips parted, I can't pull my gaze from hers.

She frowns, then schools her face. "Do you . . . do you want some more?"

Body rigid from being this close to the only woman I

have ever loved, ever wanted, I try to move. To tell her no. To tell her it's fine.

I can't do either.

"Oh! Hon, you're going to be late for your date!" Ma gasps, her hand coming to rest on Louisa's shoulder.

Louisa startles and spins back to face Ma. "Oh, goodness, I lost track of time! I have to go."

She unties the apron, her fine fingers expertly working the knot undone. I watch as they press against the small of her back. Heart hammering, I can't do anything more than simply stand there. Barely breathing.

She moves quickly, giving Ma a quick hug. "Same time next Wednesday? We can do the fresh pasta to go with that sauce. You did such a great job, Rosie."

Rosie?

What the hell?

That's a bit friendly.

Like the dope I am, I stand there, wordless, as Louisa rushes away from me for the second time in ten years. Running toward another guy.

This time doesn't feel any better than the first.

The last of the sun's rays disappear over the horizon as

the old man stirs. It only takes three minutes before the cuss words and raised voice start.

Fuck me.

I make a point to be in the kitchen as he wanders around waiting for a plate of food to materialize at his place. Head of the table. Head of the family. Like he deserves that title.

More like the ass of the family.

Bitter, nasty old shit he is.

"What you lookin' at?" he hisses at me, fingering tobacco onto a paper before he licks the edge and rolls his smoke.

Ma hates it when he smokes in the house. He does it when he's in one of his moods to spite her. His messy bed hair is oily and plastered to one side of his face. Ma gently sets a plate of food and cutlery at his spot on the table.

"Eat something, Eddy, you'll feel better." Ma gives him a pleading look. Her hands wring through the apron covering her skirt.

"Ah, probably tastes like dirt." He pushes it away.

My hands fist under the table as Ma sits in her spot across from me. Her gaze stays stuck to her plate. I eat the food she prepared and make sure to clean the plate.

He puffs away on his tobacco like it's his last meal.

Wouldn't that be somethin'.

"I'm taking the truck. Boys are having a game tonight."

How on earth he can keep track of anything in his alcohol-induced hazy days is beyond me.

"Fill it up on the way home, will ya?" I ask.

"You run it dry again?!" he hollers.

Knew that was a bad idea the second the words left my mouth. Ma stares at me. I stare at her for a heartbeat before dragging my attention back to the man who's supposed to be my loving father figure.

"Yeah, while I was busy makin' a living and keeping a roof over your sorry ass."

He jolts from the chair, unsteady as usual.

"Harry," Ma whispers, shaking her head.

She wants me to keep quiet. Let things go. Let it be.

I'm done with his bullshit.

So, I stand and fold my arms over my chest. I'm bigger, taller, and not riddled with the aftereffects of the drink.

"You think you're some big rancher now, do ya? Couldn't make a rag out of cut cloth. Go ahead, brag all you want. I bought this land. Started this family!"

"And drove it into the goddamn ground when you lost interest." My words are guttural, harsh. "Go to town, take your fill. The only thing you're good for is holdin' down a bed, anyway."

He takes a swing at me, and I lean back as he stumbles forward and crashes into the china cabinet.

With a little luck, the truck won't make it home.

It's when I turn back that I realize my mistake. Tears

stream down Ma's face as her gaze is stuck on her shaking hands between her plate and the edge of the table.

Fuck.

She's probably thinking he's gonna take this out on her when he gets back. That somehow, it's her fault I ran my mouth.

The old mongrel deserves more than the railin' I give him. But that's not a luxury I can afford when the consequences affect the only person I have left in my life.

Louisa's smile springs to mind with that thought.

I push it away.

Nope, still down to one person. It doesn't matter how much my stupid damn heart still aches for Louisa, she's not mine. Most likely never will be.

What woman in their right mind would volunteer to be part of a family like this?

"Not wastin' my time here with you two ungrateful ingrates," the old man says, swiping up the truck keys from the hook by the door and pushing through the front door. The engine roars and gravel flings at the house as I look to Ma. "I'm sorry."

She shakes her head again. This time, she looks up and tries to force a wobbly smile. I wish she wouldn't bother tryin' to protect me anymore; that role has definitely flipped between us. And I will put myself between her and that monster any day of the week.

"If I—" She pulls in a ragged breath and tries to

compose herself. "I would give you a different life if I could, my boy."

My nostrils flare, tears burning the back of my eyes. I know she would.

She tries to every day.

Berating herself.

Being submissive to him to keep the fuckin' peace.

All for me.

But I'm done with these eggshells. With this pandering to a man who doesn't deserve the family he's been gifted.

Done.

I briefly consider cutting the brake lines the next time the old man needs the vehicle. But the fear of being caught and leaving Ma all alone squashes that erratic thought.

Any chance I have of seeing Louisa again would evaporate.

So, we stay stuck in this pattern, until life grants us the miracle of change.

I'm so late.

My first date back home with Brad the accountant and I'm fifteen minutes late. I check my wristwatch again and wander to the front window. The parking by the curb outside the restaurant, which is bustling with patrons, is occupied. He's probably already here.

I grab a light sweater just in case, and I walk out the apartment door and lock up. Padding down the stairs, the delectable fragrances of all things Italian cuisine float up the greet me. It's absolutely heavenly.

Picking my way around the full tables, I find Mama Mancini waitin' on a table, her hands full with an over-sized pepper grinder. Her small frame looks ridiculous holding up the gigantic wooden utensil.

"Let me," I offer, filing in beside her.

"Oh, Louisa, your date is still not here?" Her worried eyes glance from me to the street outside.

"Most likely outside." I hold the grinder up and smile at the couple seated at the table. "Pepper?"

They both nod. Pretty sure these folks run the craft store down by the convenience store. I crack pepper over each plate until I get the *that'll do* hand signal from each.

"Where else do you need me, Mama?" I ask, turning to face the old Italian lady who's already done so much for me in such a small amount of time. Letting me stay in her apartment at such short notice. The recipes she slides under my door when I mention loving a particular flavor or dish.

If ever there was a godsend, this woman is it.

A horn honks outside. A red car slides into a parking spot that freed up.

Okay, so I'm not the only one late.

Mama Mancini's brows drop at the same time mine do, when we watch Brad sit in his car, not moving.

He's not even coming inside?

Okay, then. I wave to Mama and push through the restaurant's front door.

"Hi, sorry I'm late." His voice wobbles when he leans over and calls through the open passenger window, and his eyes flick from my face to straight ahead looking through the windshield. Annoyance lances my veins but dies out quickly as I see his hands white-knuckling the wheel.

"Um, hi."

He nods stiffly.

He's nervous. A small smile wants out over my face, and I school it back.

"You look nice, Louisa."

Well, that's something, at least.

"Thank you," I say softly as I drop into the low, plush bucket seat of his car. By the smell of it, it's pretty new. It's nice. He leans back into his seat and starts the car.

"Where are we going?" I ask, trying to recover from the last minute.

"Movies."

One word. Great. Not the best start to a date. But I've had worse. California isn't exactly known for its chivalrous men. This one might take a while to thaw. This rates about a three on the shitty date scale. And I've been on least four "ones" before. I can salvage this. I think . . .

The last time I was at the Lewistown drive-in was with Harry. So many great films failed to hold our attention there, the moments always stolen by the both of us not being able to keep our hands off each other.

Nonetheless, we got our dose of movie culture there, and some must have sucked us in. I still remember the one-liners. Those nights were some of my favorites with Harry.

"Did you eat before you came?" I ask.

"No, you hungry?"

Starving.

After smelling Mama's cooking while getting ready and then being immersed in it before he came, my stomach is tight with hunger.

"Yep, but whatever you want to do is fine."

No way am I going to be known as the whining date. Lewistown is small. People talk. My reputation here is stellar. I intend on keeping it that way. My mind drifts back to the cooking I did with Mrs. Rawlins—Rosie. I wonder if she's tried any of the other combinations we talked about.

She was so happy there in her kitchen, stirring, chopping, talking, laughing. I know she doesn't have the best life. Harry always tried his best to take care of her, with his father being out of action and all.

". . . seen it before?"

I snap my head to Brad. His eyebrow is raised. That was a question? He must have asked me something.

"Seen what before, sorry?"

"*Empire Strikes Back*? It's the movie we're seein'."

Oh brilliant, nothing like a sci-fi movie to put a girl to sleep. "No, I haven't. Is that what's showing?"

"Yup, for the whole month. Awesome, hey?"

"Sure." I stare out the window. So now, I'll be bored and starving. I have half a mind to ditch and walk back home. But I need to move on, start making a life for myself. And dating is a part of that.

We pull into the drive-in, and Brad parks by the small box to connect his red rocket to the movie system.

Moving about like a rabbit in the fox's den, he constantly glances back to where I sit, as if I will poof out of existence like one of the characters in those films. The huge white screen above the fence oscillates with hazy static. They must be starting soon.

The speakers of his car crackle with the connection and I wind my seat back. If I can't eat or enjoy the movie, I can at least have a nap. It's sweet Brad is making an effort. He chats to some guys as they walk past with snacks, then disappears.

Okay . . .

Ten minutes later, he returns. His arms are loaded with snacks, hands gripping two drinks with straws.

Brilliant work, Brad.

My stomach grumbles.

I lean over and relieve him of the drinks as he sinks into the driver's seat.

"Thanks, Louisa."

He doesn't look at me, handing me two packets out of the four he's carrying. So, I watch the screen burst to life with the opening scene, some sort of probe coming from a spaceship.

Anything would be better than a sci-fi movie. Documentary. Thriller. Adventure. For a date, if Brad was smart —which apparently, he is not—a romance would put him in good standing to progress this here occasion.

"Have you seen this one before?" I ask.

"Yes, please don't talk during the showing."

His eyes don't leave the screen.

I roll my lips. Guess who never left high school.

I open the snacks and eat as quietly as I can. With a full stomach, I relax and try to take in some of the movie. But honestly, I'm lost as to who is who and what is happening. So, writing this night off already, I wrap my arms around my chest and pretend to watch the film.

But it's not the spaceship on the screen I see, or the character with his laser pointed at the enemy already. The only face I see is one that's held my mind captive for the last ten years. Those deep, dark blues that see right through me.

See right into the guilt I've housed since that night.

Running off on Harry . . . For so long I have wanted to tell him how sorry I am. I mean, I was the minute I made the street curb. But I was more scared than anything else.

Scared I'd stay in this small town and not even have the chance to follow my dreams. I've seen what small towns do to big dreams. And it ain't pretty.

No, it's more like what I'm living now. But at least I had the chance. I gave it my best shot. That, I will never regret. I let memories of Harry drag me under as the movie plays on. The days we spent in the sun in his fields. Walking along Little Casino Creek in the summer, barefoot. That one night in the back of his truck, under the stars and a full moon, when we almost lost it all to the overwhelming pull between us.

Something shakes my shoulder. Hard.

I jolt up off the seat. "What?"

"Movie's over, Louisa."

"Oh." I run a hand through my hair. "I fell asleep."

"Yup." He forces a smile and starts the engine. The large screen above is white again and cars are pouring out of the drive-in. "I'll take you home."

"Thanks."

We drive in silence all the way back to the restaurant. The lights are on inside. Mama and Pa Mancini sit at one of the center tables. I'm guessing they're tallying the night's income. I gather my things.

"Did you wanna come up?" I ask with a small smile.

"Sorry, I'm wiped."

I huff an incredulous laugh. "Yeah, okay. I have an early shift, anyway."

"Want to go out next week?" His eyes turn soft as he leans in. *Are those puppy eyes, Brad?* Urgh.

"Maybe. I have a lot going on. Let me get back to you."

"Sure. Night."

I lean in for a kiss. He freezes, his Adam's apple bobbing. I peck a kiss to his cheek, muttering, "Thanks for a nice night."

Well, that was painful.

Why does he have to be so cute? Maybe he's not boyfriend material. But I won't write him off yet. Because unlike the dead-in-the-water date, he may be able to fulfill another need I have.

One with less strings.

What guy isn't up for that?

The familiar dark head of hair sits in the last booth on the end in my section. I snatch the coffee pot from the machine and take my time getting to Harry Rawlins. The man who occupies my head when he absolutely shouldn't. Not after what I did to him.

Guilt drives me forward, and I'm by his side a heartbeat later. "Coffee?"

He looks up. And unlike this scenario the first time, I have a firm grip on the coffee pot, even with those blues staring up at me. That jaw. The way his hair falls around his face. A girl could get hot and bothered by that there alone. His hands grip the plastic menu, and I've never wanted to be an inanimate object more.

"Yep, and the eggs and bacon. Late breakfast."

"How's your ma?" I ask, filling his mug with coffee.

"Fine."

"Just fine?"

"Yes, Louisa. Fine."

I roll my eyes at him and make my way back toward the kitchen to put in his order. By the time I make the counter, the butterflies that took flight when his eyes met mine have graduated to fire-breathing dragons.

Damn you, Harry Rawlins.

What does a girl have to do to get this man out of her system?

Possibly Brad . . .

But the thought makes my stomach flip. The dragons are replaced with heavy iron knots, and I shake the thought from my head. *How about abstinence, Lou?* Sounds much better than awkward Brad.

I sigh and work another few tables before Harry's order comes up. The small bell on the pass dings, and I grab his plate. Maybe we should have this out. Hauling this guilt around is doing nothing for my conscience.

I place the food in front of him and plop onto the bench seat on the opposite side of the table. He picks up his fork and stares at me.

He raises a brow. "You needin' something?"

Yes, you out of my head.

"I want to apologize . . ."

His head hangs, hands still gripping his cutlery. A long, heavy sigh rolls through his lips. "I don't wanna talk about it, Louisa."

"Well, I do."

His head snaps up.

"Jesus, woman, let it be. Diggin' up the past ain't going to do either of us any good. So, if you don't mind, I'll be eatin' alone."

I frown, studying his stern face for a moment before rising with the scraps of my dignity. "We will be having this conversation, Harry. You can't stay angry with me for the rest of our lives. We both liv—"

"You done?"

My mouth gapes.

Screw you. "See you 'round, Rawlins."

He grunts and shovels food into his mouth. The temporary moment we shared in his ma's kitchen is obviously long forgotten. Out the back, I hunt down Lisa and beg her to swap out our sections. I need this job, but I do not need his moody bullshit.

"Sorry hon, tips are too good. I ain't swapping, got three kids to feed. Maybe you could convince Cynthia?" Lisa's face is all empathy.

I can't ask her to swap when she needs the money more than I do. It's not right.

I wander to the front of the diner. Cynthia is pouring more coffee for a couple of her regulars. "Hey Cynthia, would it be possible to swap areas, even for a week or two?"

She turns back, pot in hand. "Why you wanna go and do that?"

"It's just that—"

Her gaze snags on the last booth and the dark head of hair visible over the bench seat. "Ah, I see the problem. You know what? My daddy always said you should face your problems head-on. Now, what kind of a friend would I be if I let you run from yours?" She smiles at me.

Ugh. "I tried. Said problem refuses to engage."

She laughs. "Hon, you two will work it out."

"No, we won't. We can't when he refuses to talk to me. Let alone look at me half the time."

"You ever wonder why that's still happenin'?" She walks back behind the counter with her pot, leaving me staring at the back of that dark head of hair. And the knots from earlier sink, bursting to life as a flutter of butterflies break free of their chrysalises.

Shit..

So much for movin' on.

Chapter Seven

HARRY

The bank manager on the opposite side of the desk leans back in his chair. It creaks under his surplus weight as he crosses his arms over his chest. "You'll need a substantial down payment for a place that size, Rawlins."

"Yes, sir."

I have more than I need. A decade of scrimping and saving has afforded me that. *Us* that. Ma will be coming with.

"Well, if you're good for the down payment, and I assume you'll be selling some of your current properties, there are several auctions for properties in the local area coming up. What exactly are you lookin' for?"

"Ranchin'. Something that'll carry around a thousand head through the winter. Not too close to town. I want sizable land, not joining allotments."

"Hmmm." He slides his glasses up his nose and pulls out a file. I wait as he flips through pages until he finds what he's searching for. He plucks it out and holds it away from his face. "This here sounds like what you'd be after. Twenty thousand acres, mostly mountain country, over forty percent productive fields at the base. And the two surrounding ranches may also come available in the next twenty years, no kids to hand it down to. You know how it goes."

He hands me the paper.

Typed-up specs and a description of the land cover the whole page.

"It looks about right," I say, handing him back the paper. "Where is it?"

"About an hour out of town, out on old Hillview Road. Big old sign that's fallin' down, you can't miss it. But Harry, you won't be the only one interested in this ranch. The auction will be tight. At least, that's my prediction."

"But if I bid, I'm good for the mortgage through the bank?"

"I'll need to tally the final numbers, but I think it should be doable. However, if it goes over what you have available to you in the way of finance, you're gonna need one hell of a year to cover the first mortgage payment."

I can't flatten the grin claiming my face. This is every-thing I have worked so hard for. For years. "Yes, sir."

He stands and shakes my hand. "Tell Barb out front

you want the address for the ranch on Hillview, she can give you a rough map."

"Won't be necessary, thanks again."

I give him a brisk nod and walk out of the only bank in Lewistown, more determined than I have ever been. I am so close.

Back at the truck, I sit staring down the street, letting her idle. I may just pull this off. And if I can get the ranch profitable in the first few years, save like I'm used to doin', maybe other investments would be an option. My gaze snags on blonde hair blowing in the day's crazy wind. The short shorts she wears accentuate those long legs, sending warmth to my core.

She's talkin' to the accountant.

Why is she talkin' to the accountant?

Louisa is animated, smiling as she touches his arm. He doesn't respond. I lean back in the seat and watch them like it's my God-given right. I glance at the time on the town square tower clock. It's a little after four.

Louisa is off work now.

She walks around a parked red car and climbs into the passenger's seat. The accountant drops into the driver's seat. When the car starts and they pull out and head for the town lake, I shift the old truck into gear and turn her toward the outskirts.

Hillview Road sounds pretty damn good right now.

The busted sign arching over the entrance sways in the breeze like the posts are rotted off at the ground. The owners of the ranch still live here, so I kill the engine and glance around, trying to make out what I can.

One run-down old barn.

One large but worse for wear homestead. No yard. But a bunch of ancient trees surrounding the house. Like loyal knights standing at attention. The old weeping willows sway on either side of the house, a few in the front and at least one huge one out back. The yards are too close to the house. No round yard. No stables.

The bank manager was right to say this place would need a stellar year to cover the mortgage payment. Hell, it'll take me a whole six months just to fix what I can see, and I haven't even set foot on the place yet.

I rub a hand over my head and blow out a breath. I'm not afraid of hard work or long hours. And if it means a better life for Ma, then I'm all hands on deck. I take a few more minutes to look around and make a mental list of what needs fixin'.

On the way home, I decide to keep this under my hat for now. I don't want to get Ma's hopes up. Or have the conversation about the old man a second before I have to. Ain't no way I'm taking him with. One of his buddies can take him in. It's time we washed our hands of the old bastard.

It's about dark when I make it home. The lights are all on and Louisa's car is in the driveway. What the hell?

Shit, it's Wednesday.

How the hell did I forget?

And why is she still here?

I pull up in a flurry of gravel, killing the engine as I push out of the vehicle like a rattlesnake slid up onto the seat. Taking the steps two at a time, I burst through the door.

Yelling finds me before I have the chance to lay eyes on either Ma or Louisa. I rush toward the sound. The second I find Ma, my insides crawl with lava. A vicious welt tarnishes the side of her face. Her arm is held out, crossed in front of Louisa. Who stares, wide-eyed and shaking, at my old man.

Fuck.

Judging by the determined look on Ma's face, she's been doin' her own yelling. My hands curl to fists, breaths burning their way over the raw sound leavin' my throat. I glance at Louisa. Her eyes flicker to Eddy, as if assessing what's going to happen next.

The old man drags his glare to me. "Well, if it isn't the get-about. Where the hell have you been? Why's the bank manager ringin' me?" He takes a step forward.

He's sober.

Fuck.

"Harry, take Louisa home," Ma says, fear warring with determination, its filthy remnants lacing her voice.

Ignoring her, I step into his space. "What did you do to her?"

"Never did deserve a girl like her. Making sure she knows it."

I turn to Louisa. "You alright?"

She nods, her eyes not leaving mine.

"Please, Harry, take her home. I'll be fine." Ma stares straight at the old man. There haven't been many times she's stood up to him. Louisa, apparently, was worth the fight.

I step up, towering over the mongrel as I say, "I ought to end you where you stand. But, for some godforsaken reason"—I glance to Ma—"today is not that day."

He shakes his head and leans back like he's about to take a swing at me. I step out of his way, and he falters onto one knee before pushing to stand.

Guess all that alcohol had permanent effects.

I walk to where Ma still holds Louisa behind her. "You sure about this, Ma?"

She tilts her chin up, looking into my eyes with a forced smile. "I'll be fine. Take Louisa home, my love." She turns back. "Please, hon, don't take anything you heard tonight to heart. Please."

I hold out a hand to Louisa. Hers, fine and soft, slips into my own, still shaking. I lead her from the living room to the kitchen. Now I see the mess. The upturned pots.

The freshly made pasta flung around the room. Flour over the floor and counter.

"Jesus . . ." I mutter.

"I need to—" Louisa darts to the counter, picking up her handbag. I bundle her out the door and down the stairs. When we're outside, I blow out a breath. That's not what I wanted her to be a part of. Or witness.

Shame and regret heat my face. I hunch my shoulders over for a moment and close my eyes.

I should turn right back around and knock the old man off his block. I shouldn't leave Ma there. But she insisted. And by the looks of Louisa, she can't take another argument. Much less one with Ma involved.

I open the vehicle door for her, and she slides in, not saying a word. Clutching her bag to her chest, she stares ahead as I slide into the seat and turn over the engine.

We are halfway through town before she speaks. "Will she really be okay?"

Her eyes find mine. Tears shine and fall as she looks back through the windshield. She doesn't wipe them away.

"I don't know."

I really don't. Any moment of any day he could decide to snap. Be too drunk to know what he's doing.

"I was so scared. He—"

I pull over by the restaurant and kill the engine. "Best to forget anything 'bout Eddy Rawlins, Louisa."

She turns on the seat and waits for me to look at her.

When I do, her face scrunches up. "Rosie." She blows out a breath. "She was protecting you. Your dad said such horrible things. Telling me to run far away from you." Her face twists with the statement. Tension hovers between us as a stone forms in my throat. But she continues. "Your ma, she fought for you. Telling him to stop. God, the way that woman loves you, Harry . . ." Her voice breaks.

I can't look at her.

I just can't.

My old man got one thing right. Louisa should stay far away from me. There is no way in hell I'm lettin' her live through this disaster of a family. That would be beyond damn selfish. I won't put her anywhere near it. I couldn't. It would take the last bit of strength I have left. The tiny sliver of restraint I've had around him would disappear if he ever laid a hand on her.

"You should go," I say, not lookin' at her.

"Yes." She sniffs, wiping her face. "Go back to Rosie. Tell her I'll see her next Wednesday, okay?"

I snap my head to her. "Louisa—"

"I made a promise, Harry. I'm not breakin' it. I'll pick her up and she can come cook with me here if I have to."

I don't know what to say. My throat burns and the bridge of my nose prickles as the woman before me blurs. She'd do that for Ma?

"Sure, she'd love that," I finally say, hoping the wobble in my voice isn't as noticeable as it feels.

"Night, Harry." She pushes up a smile.

It's a sad one. Showcasing her big heart. The same one I fell in love with all those years ago. And there's another chink in my armor. The first was in the diner when she wanted to apologize for old hurts and running off on the night of prom.

Louisa Masters always had my heart wrapped in hers, but it's moments like these I can't shake off. These are the single moments that stand out that I can't ignore. Instead of acting on them, I store them away. Push them down, where light can't touch them. So they have no chance of blooming back to life.

She does deserve better.

And I can't guarantee I can give it to her.

Not yet.

When she's safely inside, I turn on the truck and head back toward the outskirts. But instead of driving home, I park by the lake. Dropping the tailgate, I sit facing the water. The slap and swoosh of the small ripples moving across the water with the night's light wind calms my racing heart and tapped-out nerves.

It could have been a lot worse.

He could have hurt Louisa.

Ma could've been hurt worse. Hell, she has been.

Louisa could have brushed her hands of Ma. That would break her heart. She sure likes havin' her around. In all honestly, I'm glad Ma has someone. She needs more than only a son to talk to. Her friend Evelyn will never visit. She's too aware of the situation to brave the storm.

I lie back on the tray as the stars make their way slowly across the sky. Night sounds fill in around me. I suck in a long, deep breath. If only I could freeze time right here.

When the cold boards set an ache between my shoulders, I sit up and jump off the tailgate. I drive home, slow. Maybe Ma will be in bed. Maybe he'll be back in town with his buddies. Here's hoping.

A flash of blue and red lights catches my attention half a mile from home.

Fuck.

I push the old girl faster.

The police lights light up the old house like the damn county fair. I fly into the driveway. Behind the trooper vehicle, the ambulance sits, doors open.

Fuck. Fuck!

I was gone too long.

Ma.

God, if anything's happened to her . . .

I fly out of the truck, leavin' it idling, and lunge up the steps. An officer stands inside the door. He stops me, his hand on my shoulder, as I make it across the threshold. "I'm sorry, son."

Chapter Eight

LOUISA

The service was short. Few people came. Harry stood as still as stone as the preacher man said his piece and they lowered the wooden coffin into the ground. I can't even begin to imagine how he is feeling. The last words to his—

I stifle a sob. My heart breaks for Harry.

His jaw feathers when someone tosses dirt onto the coffin, now low in the earth.

Fine fingers squeeze around my own. I glance to my side, where Rosie stands, tears streaming down her face. Her black hat shrouds most of her face. The black dress I found for her at the thrift store hugs her figure. It's the least I could do.

"If anyone would like to say some words for Eddy?" the preacher man asks.

The small crowd shifts but doesn't answer.

Harry's shoulders rise and fall evenly as he turns and walks away.

"Oh, Harry," Rosie sobs.

"If you would like to join us for the wake later at the tavern." The preacher's words are halfhearted, a final statement.

Murmurs rise as the rest of the crowd disperses. I turn and hug Rosie. She shakes as I rub her back. The ache that grew in my chest for this woman the second Harry told me what happened blooms to life again.

"Can I take you home, Rosie?"

She holds me at arm's length. Her face breaks as she tilts her head. "Evelyn is taking me home with her. I don't think I can go back there. Not just yet."

"Okay, but here"—I pull from her grip and pull out a small notepad and pen, scribbling down my number—"is my number. Please use it if you need anything. And if you're up to it. We can still cook, if you want to keep busy and all."

She scrunches her face, patting my cheek. "I would love to, hon."

"Good, we'll make something amazing." The last two syllables are weak with emotion. It's all I can do to not cry again.

I mean, he was a miserable old man and made her life a living hell. But he was Harry's father, and I'm sure he'd been a good man at one time. He would have had to, for a woman like Rosie to have married him.

I walk with her back to the truck. Harry sits in the driver's seat, turned outward, heels resting on the running board. The brim of his hat rotates through his fingers.

"I should find Evelyn. She should be here somewhere. You two make your way back. I'll see you later, my love." She nods to Harry. He returns the gesture as the hat stills in his hands. "And you Wednesday, Louisa."

"Sure, Rosie." I hug her again; I can't help it. I want to protect her, the way she did for me before . . .

She breaks from my hold a moment later and walks for Evelyn's car. I wait until she is safely inside and the car drives away.

"Thank you for coming, but you didn't have to." The voice behind me is raw. I have to compose myself before I turn around.

When I do, Harry's deep blues are stuck on mine instantly.

"I wanted to," I utter. I don't move closer.

God, all I want to do is protect his heart from all this. Like he should have had his entire life, instead of a father who tormented him. It's my guess Rosie stayed because financially she'd no other choice. And now?

"Come on, you should get back to the diner." Harry stands and rounds the hood, pulling my door open.

The diner is the last place I want to be right now. But after my shift ends in about two hours, I have an afternoon of Brad.

I almost forgot about the buffer I'd created. My Brad buffer. Who is supposed to be the wall between me and none other than the man in front of me. And currently, I'm wishing I never put it there. But I slide into the seat and stay quiet on the way back to the diner.

Five minutes later, Harry pulls over in front of the diner. He stares at his hands gripped around the wheel as we idle, parked in an awkward silence.

"Well, thanks for the lift," I say, feeling stupid as hell the second the words leave my mouth.

Harry clears his throat and hops out. A moment later, my door opens. Taking it as my hint to leave him be, I slide from the truck. The thought of leaving him, though, doesn't sit right. We might not be friends, or even on the same page right now. Despite the fact we can't seem to get out of each other's orbit, my heart aches to leave him this way.

"If you need anything," I utter, popping to my toes to kiss his cheek.

My nerves are shot.

My words weak.

But he simply nods and closes the door behind me as I walk down the street. I turn back at the diner entrance, glancing at the old buckboard. He sits back behind the wheel, staring at his hands again. Pushing through the doors, I make my way into the back and change.

My mind is a scattering of Harry, Rosie, and the life I left behind ten years ago. The what-ifs of if I hadn't run halfway across the country from it all. What would things look like now if I'd stayed put when he dropped to one knee?

"How you doin', darlin'?" Cynthia slides into my space with a soft, empathetic smile.

"Oh, hey, I'm fine."

I'm the last person this small town should be worrying about. Harry and Rosie need their support, not me.

"Well, if that changes, you know where to find me."

"Thanks, Cynthia. How was the morning?"

"You know, the same old, same old. Not much changes in this town, hon."

I chuckle. "Guess not."

The entire reason I left was because of that very sentiment. Now, being back here, I'm not sure whether that's a bad thing anymore. I promise myself I'll check in on both Rosie and Harry in the next few days and set my focus on the last few hours of my shift and my afternoon with Brad.

The weekend rolls around, and I'm at the small lake in the center of Lewistown. It's pretty. And it is currently lined with stalls and families out for the afternoon. Brad's been part of the community initiative for years, apparently. And now, by extension, so am I. His family owns the accounting firm in town, and they have a charity drive for locals every year. They own shares in many of the businesses around town—some they even own outright, or so he told me on the drive out here.

Even Mama Mancini has a pop-up stall, with her baked Italian goodies drawing most of the crowd. Who could blame them? Her food is something straight out of Little Italy, and as divine as a bite can be. I stand behind the stall taking gifts for the children's ward at the hospital.

"Here you are, sweetheart," a familiar voice says, handing over a box with a toy truck inside. I look up from the clipboard home to the list of names and donated goods to find Rosie.

"Oh, hi! Thank you." I move around the table, folding her into my arms. She smiles and returns the hug.

"How are you?" I ask as she steps out of my hold. I look her over. She looks okay, the same Mrs. Rawlins I've always known, her demeanor and dress unchanged. "How's Harry doin'?"

"Well, you know my boy, keeping himself busy. Always a fence to mend or something to build."

I tilt my head with a sad smile. I know Harry. But I was gone for ten years. So, I know him only as well as my absence over the last decade affords.

"He would love to see you, I'm sure. Are you still coming for our Wednesday lesson?" Her eyes search mine.

"Of course, wouldn't miss it. I can pick you up. We can cook at my place, if that's easier?"

She pats my hand. A knowing look that only time and experience brings covers her face. "You come to us, darlin'. I'm not afraid of my own house."

"Are you sure? Harry can drive you in if you're not comfortable driving with me?"

"No. Sweet pea, I know you're tryin' your best to protect this old lady. But I'm fine, really. See you for morning tea Wednesday. I'll bake something and put on the pot, then we will cook."

She waves me off as she follows Evelyn toward the next stall. I watch her go, still awestruck at the strongest woman I've ever met.

"Louisa, where do these go?" My thoughts are ambushed by Brad. I spin back to find him with his arms full of wrapped gifts.

"Oh, shoot. In the bin for lucky dip, hey. Who knows what's in them."

He gives me a stiff nod and drops the presents into the large plastic bin behind him. When he turns back, his gaze wanders in the direction Rosie went.

"She doin' okay?" he asks.

"I think so."

He comes to stand beside me and shoves his hands in his pockets. "Did you want to go for ice cream after this?"

I meet his gaze. The brown eyes searching my face are

hopeful. He's sweet, if not a little standoffish at times. I should make more of an effort.

"Yeah, that would be nice. Maybe we could drive out to the lookout after?"

"Why?" His brows furrow.

Um, because that's what couples do?

Hang out, look at the stars.

Snuggle up and make out.

"Oh, it's just a thought."

Brad's mother, Dot, wanders over. "That's a wonderful idea, Louisa! Honey." She turns to her son and straightens his collar, and I have to look away as light crimson crawls up his neck. "You two young ones take off. Ice cream and the lookout sound perfect."

Brad feigns an awkward smile as she pats his face like a little boy. I roll my bottom lip through my teeth, if only to keep the giggle wanting out of my throat down. We walk back to his car and climb inside.

"Sorry about my mom, she gets like that about girls."

Girls?

How old are we?

"It's fine; it's sweet. At least she cares."

"Yeah, tell that to every girl in this town she's harassed to go out with her only son. God, it's so embarrassing. I'm not . . ."

I place my hand over his resting on his thigh. "How about we get out of here?"

His hand slips out from under mine in one swift

motion. His face reddens for the second time in five minutes. "I don't really do personal space."

Is he kidding?

"Oh, okay." I sit up in the passenger's seat and run my hands over my shorts, which now feel way too tiny. All of a sudden, feeling self-conscious, I wind down the window. Did it just heat up in here? I feel like the salacious woman trying to seduce some innocent guy who's never been touched.

Maybe Brad hasn't?

California was many things, frigid not one of them. The small-town country girl I was before I left lasted about six months before I fell headfirst into the life lessons I'm sure city girls learn way earlier than I did.

When we pull up in front of the ice cream place, I wait for my door to open.

But it doesn't move. Brad just waits by the store's front door, hands in his pockets, eyes darting around as if someone might see us. I sigh and push out of the car, making my way to where he stands. I grip my purse by my side, adjusting its long strap over my shoulder.

Ordering our ice cream, we find a booth and eat in silence. *Pretty sure this is not what your mother had in mind, Brad.* You know what this guy needs? Some life experiences of his own. I lick the ice cream from the round scoop and hold his gaze. His eyes widen. I fight the urge to burst into hysterical laughter.

I shouldn't mess with him.

But, ugh, he is such a prude.

No physical contact.

No small talk.

Scratch that—no talk, period.

"We should head to the lookout before the stars start coming out. That's the best part, you know, watching them pop into the sky one at a time."

"Okay. You finished?"

"Yep." I wrap the last of my cone in a napkin and place it on the small plate on the table.

"Do you know any of the constellations?" Brad says all of a sudden.

"A few, you?"

"Most of them. It's kind of a family hobby."

Ah, of course he does.

We drive the ten minutes to the lookout, the highest point in the geographical makeup of the outskirts of Lewistown. Brad kills the engine, and we sit on the warm hood of his car. He is more animated now that we are doing something he's obviously interested in.

I have hope.

I lie back on the hood and slide my hands onto my stomach. It's so peaceful out here. And the last few weeks of my transition back to this small town seem to fade out as the first star does, in fact, pop into the darkening sky. I grab Brad's shirt and pull him backward. He lies beside me, glancing at me every few seconds, like I'll vanish if he doesn't check back.

When the sky darkens, he points to the first cluster of stars gracing the sky. "See those there?"

The wind picks up a little and it's cool. I shuffle closer. His warmth is nice. I follow the line of his pale arm, past his manicured fingertip to the blanket of inky blackness overhead. The bunch of stars he's trying to show me look familiar.

"What are they?" I ask.

"Ursa Major." His arm moves, finger pointing to the next set of stars. "This one here is Hercules."

"Oh, there you go. I didn't know that. Never took the time to learn them."

"They are tricky when you first start star watching. But once you see them. You see them, you know."

Yeah, I know. Like people. Or a person. It's like the day I really saw Harry, I could never unsee him. He cannot *not* exist to me. I sit up in a panic. I'm literally lying on some other guy's hood, pickin' out stars, surrounded by all this nature and beauty, and my mind is still stuck on damn repeat over Harry Rawlins.

"Brad?"

He sits up. "You need to go home?"

"No," I say and grab his shirt. Before he gets the chance to pull from my hold, my lips are on his. He stiffens, then relaxes. I run my hands to his jaw. He makes a small groan as his hands land on my hips.

His mouth is still closed.

His eyes are probably open.

I break away.

Brown eyes, full of surprise and wonder, stare back at me. "Louisa, I want to—"

I pull his mouth to mine.

The grimace shuddering through my body is involuntary. It's like kissing a sibling. Hands press against my breasts. Now he gets into it? Seriously?

I push away and hold him at arm's length. "Brad, I—"

"I know, this is so special. I can't believe what's happening. My mother's right, you are so lovely."

I cringe on the inside.

Things are going from awkward to plain awful.

There is no chemistry here. No spark. No *anything*, really.

"We should go," I say, sliding off the hood.

"Sure, you need your rest. Up early and all."

I don't work Sundays, but I'll keep that fact to myself.

We ride back into town in silence. Brad looks pleased with himself. I suppress the urge to roll my eyes at him. I'm about to make a break for it and wrap up the night when he leans over. "Night, Louisa."

His eyes close. He leans over the seat, his face so close. I dot a kiss on his cheek. "Night."

I climb out of the car and go to shut the door when he says, "Oh, there's a dance on next weekend. Would you like to go with me? I'm not sure about the dancing, but there'll be a crowd and a cookout."

He doesn't dance. Figures.

I should say no. I should shut this down before he gets any other bright ideas for dates. Just my luck, he finally thaws, and I'm not interested.

The rumble of a pickup rollin' through the quiet street snags my attention. I look up to it, and that blue buckboard of Harry's squeals to a stop at one of the few intersections in Main Street.

He doesn't notice me.

I hope.

I bend down, meeting Brad's gaze, and force my best smile. "Sure, what time will you pick me up?"

"Seven okay?"

"Perfect, see you then."

"Yeah, sure."

I stay low, hanging in Brad's car as the rumble moves past and fades. I'm a coward. I know. But the one thing I won't do is start something I can't finish. Harry's been through enough. And a huge part of it is my fault.

I stand tall and shut the car door before pivoting and heading inside. Mama Mancini waits for me, sitting at a front table. I'm not three steps into the restaurant before she waves for me to sit.

"Bella, what are you doin' with that poor boy?"

Boy?

Guess I'm not the only one who has noticed it, then.

"Just hanging out." I look out the window as Brad's car pulls away from the curb.

"You want to know a secret, *bambina?*"

I chuckle at the way she refers to me as a baby. "Of course."

"*Al cuore non si comanda.*"

"What does it mean?" I ask.

She pats my hand. Her focus wanders toward the kitchen. The sounds of Papa Mancini still cleaning up drift through the restaurant, tangling around us as if to drive home the point I am sure she is about to make. I can tell by the look in her eyes.

"It means love will not be commanded. You cannot control your heart, bella. It is boss."

Is that what I've been doing? Trying to tell my heart what to do, to feel something it doesn't, trying to change its mind? I guess I was. Trying to protect myself and Harry. It's the only thing I can do for him, if he won't even talk about it.

"I want to keep things simple, Mama. I just came home, it's not—"

Her hands land on one of my own, gripping it tight. "Time does not matter to the heart, it skips ahead and it falls behind. You have to work on its terms when things are *this big.*"

I swallow, dragging in air. Harry and I have always been too big. That's why I ran in the first place. Scared of the monumental force that is Harry and Louisa.

I still am.

Chapter Nine

HARRY

Ma's been humming' all damn morning. I swing the axe into the split post, splintering it into pieces. The smells coming from the kitchen are divine. I knock the wood from the block and set up another log. Sweat flies from my arms and forehead as I bring the axe down again. I know who's inspired all the cookin' Ma's been obsessing over.

Louisa.

"Harry!?"

I drop the axe into the chopping block and wipe my brow.

"Harry, Louisa is pulling into the driveway. Can you help me move the table?" she calls, moving down the hallway toward the back door.

What? Why?

"Why we movin' the table, Ma?"

I stand, hands hanging by my sides, arms buzzing from the exertion, veins popping along my forearms. My bare chest is covered in sawdust from an hour of chopping and splitting wood.

My shirt is tucked into the back of my jeans, my boots covered in sawdust. I'm filthy.

The screen door pops open, and Ma's gaze finds me. Her brows lower. "Harrison Rawlins, you're beyond dirty."

"Workin' has that effect."

"Goodness me, put a shirt on." She turns to leave but spins back around. "No, actually, clean up first, then I need you to move the big old table in the dining room."

"Give me a sec to tidy up this lot."

I turn back to my pile and bend over, stacking the wood and kindling. We haven't eaten in the dining room since I was a boy. What's gotten into her today? The door pops open again. "I'll be up in a minute, Ma. Hold ya horses."

A light, amused huff filters through the back door.

I spin back to find Louisa at the top of the steps. The morning sun lights up her blonde hair. Her glittering green eyes rove over me before she meets my eyes. "Need a hand to clean up?"

I push my shoulders back and toss the log still in my hand onto the pile. "Nope, was about to head inside."

"Right." She descends the stairs like I invited her to.

I turn back to the pile and finish stacking the wood.

The tap at the hose whines and I stand in time to find water rushing toward me. Planting my boots into the ground, I brace myself as she hoses my face, my neck, and my shoulders. The water trickles down my chest and stomach and soaks my jeans. The cool water is heaven on my burning arm muscles.

Not letting on either way, I follow her gaze as she steps closer, hosing off my chest. The stream sinks lower, water splashing over my hard stomach. Louisa's hand loosens around the end of the hose as she opens her mouth to say something.

Nothing comes out. Her arm drops as her tongue sweeps over her bottom lip and her eyes lift to mine. Fire inches its way across my heart, filling my thundering veins with something close to lava.

Footsteps track toward the back door inside. Ma.

"Har—"

I shake my head like a dog. Louisa drops the hose with a squeal and flings her arms up, her hands protecting her face as she puts space between us. I can't help the smile splitting my face as she cowers away from the water droplets hurtling from my hair.

I chuckle. It's hearty and warms my heart, something I haven't felt in years. When she's far enough away to be out of my range, she stands up and crosses her arms with a shaky laugh. Her eyes are stuck on me when Ma pushes through the back door.

"Harry? The table."

"Yeah, Ma, comin'."

She looks between us and then to the hose still pouring water over the ground. "Clean up before you come inside. I don't want mud gettin' trudged through my house, you hear?"

"Yes, ma'am."

Louisa shudders a breath, as if coming back to reality, and turns back, turning off the tap. She hovers for a moment. Her shoulders heave, her face carrying something I haven't seen for over ten years.

Need.

"I should . . ." She flies up the stairs, and the back door slams behind her. I stare at the ground where she stood. The sliver of hope, of happiness we had fades. The vision of her getting out of Brad's car the other night, trying to hide from me as I drove past, floods my mind. The memory burns.

It's like the thing hanging between us is so raw, so real, she's afraid of it.

Or embarrassed by it.

I, for one, am sick of trying to figure out which. She's right, we should talk about this. I want to know either way. Pined ten years for this woman. And if the look on her face right now is anything to go on, she isn't exactly indifferent to me either.

I hose off the rest of the sawdust and tug my boots off. Rolling up my jeans, I pad up the back stairs and make a beeline for my room. The rusted, old metal single bed I've had since I was a little kid sits in the middle of the room. A wooden dresser and a chair I built are the only other items in my room. It's all I need.

I close the door almost shut and peel the wet jeans from my body, hanging them over the varnished chair. The small window in my room in the back corner of our little weatherboard house faces the barn. I pull the second drawer open, tugging out clean jeans and a work shirt.

Dressed, I run a hand through my still damp hair. I pluck fresh socks from the top drawer and wander to the kitchen. Louisa and Ma sit at the table, sharing the heavenly baking my mother spent over an hour making early this morning.

"Hungry, my love?" Ma looks up as I pull on a sock.

"Gotta shift the heifers, fix the southern fence, wire's snapped."

"Do you need a hand?" Louisa looks up from her teacup, the good ones Ma's only ever used once in my lifetime.

Looks like Ma's pulling out all the stops today. I would love to know why. Maybe Louisa could help me shift the heifers, we could talk.

"You any good on a horse?" I ask, cocking an eyebrow at her.

"I can ride well enough. What do you need?"

"Will only take about half an hour. Easier to shift them with two people."

"Sure, can I finish up here?" She looks to Ma.

She ain't askin' me.

"Hon, I will make a start on the new recipe. I think I have that much sorted." Ma beams at her.

"Okay, great. Meet you outside in a bit?" Louisa asks me.

I give her a nod and swipe an apple from the bowl on the counter and head for the back door and my boots.

With my well-worn boots on, I pluck my hat from the hook by the back door and push it onto my head. The cream work shirt hangs over my body, and I roll up the sleeves before tucking it into my jeans. In the barn, I saddle up Horse and the gelding I broke in last winter.

Louisa appears in the doorway as I move to lead them out. She has Ma's boots on and my old hat. Where on earth did she find it? Ma must have stashed it away somewhere. "This old girl will be yours," I say, handing her the reins to Horse.

"Hey, lovely," she says, rubbing the mare's face with a hand. "What's your name?"

"Doesn't have one." I swing into the saddle.

"Harry, how could you not name her?" Louisa scowls at me but bounces up into the saddle like she's been doin' it every day for the last ten years.

I simply shrug and push the gelding into a walk, out into the field. Horse trots along behind, and they catch up. Louisa reins her back to walk beside me and the gelding.

"So, who are we moving?" she asks, glancing around the fields like she might catch a glimpse of the herd.

"Over the rise, to the north. If we lope, it'll go faster."

She gives me an unreadable look but pushes Horse into a lope, leaving me behind. I sit on the gelding, hands on the pommel for a moment, just watching her ride away. Her blonde hair spills behind her like a goddamn golden waterfall, her curves rockin' with the gait of the mare.

Shaking my head, I push the gelding into a lope and catch up. I make it to them when they slow down for the gate just up ahead, at the foot of the rise. I step the gelding sideways and lean down to unlatch the gate. Louisa walks through first and I follow, closing the gate behind us.

"How's your ma doing?" she says softly, like that's not the question she wanted to ask, but the one she was brave enough to.

I stare ahead. "She's fine. Despite the fact he was her husband, she mourned the man she loved years ago. Her words, not mine."

"She told you that?" Pretty green eyes meet mine.

"Yep." It's all I can say. And I get it, I do. Because I went through a similar process losing the loving father I once had. Not the same relationship by anyone's standard, but a loss, nonetheless.

"Harry," she says, reining Horse to a halt. "Are you—"

She breaks eye contact, staring at the rise. She sucks in a breath. "Do you need anything?"

"Nope, just to get my work done." I push the gelding for the gate. This time, I dismount and work the wire gate as Louisa and Horse walk through. She smiles down at me, those dark lashes and pink lips makin' it hard to breathe.

I mount up and push the gelding into a lope, leaving her behind. As if distance will save my heart from this woman. Horse thunders up beside us seconds later. Louisa is shaking her head at me, but the smile wrapping around her face takes the last of my lousy breath.

"Come on, Harry, smile. It's a great day. We will make it one!" She gives me a mischievous look and nods ahead. A beat later, she gallops away, popping out of the saddle, her hips, ass, and waist on full display. *Goddammit, Louisa.*

Like a freight train, it hits me why I wanted to make thirty minutes alone with her. To find out one way or another where the two of us stand. Now, with her full of life and beaming at me, her body doing things to me I have pushed down for years, I can't bring myself to think about askin' anymore.

Denial is better than rejection.

And this man can't take being told no by this brilliant girl more than once. So, like a complete coward, I stay silent as we herd the heifers to the next field over. Louisa stands in the stirrup irons, whistling and waving them on like she fuckin' belongs here, sending a tightness constricting through my chest.

When the heifers are settled, we walk home on foot, horses at our sides. But even as we wade through the soft Montana grasses, my mind wanders to where we could be if this moment was our reality. Our lives together. The sentiment I have been haulin' around since the age of seventeen.

"Lou—"

"I know what you're gonna say, Harry. And give me a break—it's been a while, and Cali ain't exactly known for its cattle herding gigs."

I snort a laugh. The image she put in my head with those words cracks me up. But that was nothin' near what I was gonna say.

"Oh my god. Harry Rawlins . . . did I witness an actual *laugh*?"

Her face is fake horrified, her hand slapped over her heart.

"You'll keep, darlin'." I try to scowl at her but only manage to make her laugh harder. I can't help the chuckle tumbling from my mouth as she doubles over. Poor old Horse doesn't know what to do, shying one moment, sniffing her curiously the next.

Those two are a sight.

We walk home, Louisa periodically giggling whenever she looks at me.

This woman is so happy. She is like literal sunshine

when she's in a room. Lighting everyone around her up. How could I ever deny Ma that kind of thing in her life? And even if I have to put space between us to make sure Louisa and Ma's friendship remains, I will.

'Cause, right now, I'm stuck between needin' to know if she still feels any semblance of what we used to have between us and making Ma's life the best it can be. And I won't risk anything more.

Timing's not right.

Maybe I'm just a coward.

Maybe I'm hiding behind doing the right thing . . .

Either way, I won't give this girl one iota of a reason to run off this time.

At home, Ma and Louisa get stuck into the cookin', and I retire to the small corner of the house where I tally the cattle in my record book and balance the ledgers. Half distracted, I scratch out this month's numbers. The aromas drifting through the house are makin' me hungry. And when lunch rolls around, I can't stay stuck to this chair a moment more. I move to push out of the old chair, but a bowl of something steaming and smelling like heaven appears on my desk.

"You oughta eat," Louisa says, folding her arms over her apron.

I lean back in the old captain's chair and meet her gaze. "Thanks."

She offers a smile. "Your ma sent me in."

I huff a laugh. Of course she did.

"She asked me to stay for supper. Is it too weird?" She chews her lip. I break eye contact. If she had any idea what that one gesture did to me . . .

"Why would it be weird?" I ask plainly.

"I don't want to be here if it makes you uncomfortable. Helping with chores is one thing. Eating together is . . ."

"It's fine. Don't over think it. I mightn't even be here for supper."

"Oh." Disappointment floods her face. "You're goin' out?"

"Maybe," I say, shoving off the seat and standing. I need some air. That look on her face.

She backs up, giving me space. "Okay, sure. I better get back."

Louisa disappears through the living room and into the kitchen. And despite my head screaming at my heart, I follow her.

"Oh, hon! What have I done wrong? I swear, it doesn't taste the same as yours . . ." Ma says, worry lining her voice when I walk in.

There's a small silence as Louisa taste tests the sauce from a spoon. Then, "Oh, Rosie. This is wonderful!"

Ain't how I would describe whatever this is.

But, hell, at least Ma's happy.

Chapter Ten

LOUISA

With Harry disappeared to the barn, Rosie and I whip up a storm of dinner items. Some Italian dishes I'm slowly learning from Mama Mancini, and some from my time in Cali. A far cry from her meat-and-potatoes repertoire the Rawlins have lived on for years. The end result is a feast fit for a household of people.

With only the two of them, I guess I should stay. The day has flown by with all the chatter, chopping, stirring . . .

Rosie seems happy. And I'm glad I could put a smile on her face. She deserves that and so much more. As the sun sets over the western mountains, the back door slams.

"Oh good, now, maybe we can set the dining room

right." Rosie drops her knife and wipes her hands on her apron, darting toward the footsteps coming down the hallway. I test the seasoning on the dish I'm almost finished making. Flavor bursts across my tongue. *Hmmm.* Yep, that's great. The brown butter and sage chicken dish is ready.

I remove it from the heat, resting on a ceramic potholder, and move to the oven to check Rosie's beef braciole. The heavy cast-iron pot bubbles away. The lid cracked a little. I lift the round top and let the fragrant steam wash over my face.

Oh my goodness, she did so great!

I make a small slice into the largest one. The meat is cooked.

Perfect.

I turn off the heat and toss some couscous into a bowl, adding boiling water. The greens we have been slicing are ready for steaming. I set them up and set the timer. Harry appears, leaning on the doorframe. He's filthy. Dirt and hay litter his work shirt and jeans. His hat, still on his head, dips. "You got a minute?"

I freeze, timer still in my hands. He could get anything he wanted just lookin' like that. Heavens above.

His socked foot brushes over the top of the other. His boots have come off. Some things never change. Rosie's always been a stickler for the boots-off-inside rule.

"What do you need?" I finally say, and he looks up.

Deep blue eyes bore into mine. My heart flips. The timer clatters onto the counter.

"Table. Need to move it."

"Oh, of course," I whisper. Heat flushes my cheeks, and I duck my head, removing my apron and rounding the kitchen counter. I follow him into the space that hasn't been used as a dining room for years. With the table pushed against the wall, and the chairs stored under it, Eddy had used the space for his single lounge and television set. A small side table and ashtray still sit by his old chair.

"You know, this old thing can go to the barn. But can we move the table. Set it up with the chairs?" Rosie says, scanning the room.

"The old chair's gonna have to go first, Ma." Harry grips the headrest and all but tosses it toward the hall. The small side table is thrown onto it before he turns back to me. "Table first. You grab the chairs."

Oh, okay.

Harry grips the long edge of the table and picks it up like it weighs absolutely nothing and drops it in the middle of the room, under the low-hanging decorative light. Breaths shattering in and out of my lungs at the sight of him manhandling the enormous piece of furniture, I shake my head to catch myself and pluck up a chair and set it at the head of the table.

Rosie helps, and we have six places set in no time. She

disappears and returns with a washcloth, giving it a once-over. The old hardwood gleams. It's beautiful. The chairs are a bit worn, but the dining suite transforms the entire room. The timer sings, interrupting my thoughts.

"Shoot, that's me!" I rush to the stovetop and turn the gas off. The greens smell almost as good as the rest of the meal. I drain them and toss them into a white ceramic bowl, seasoning with olive oil, salt, and pepper before scattering a layer of slivered almonds I toasted earlier over the elegant stems and bushy heads.

"Where do you want me, Louisa?" Rosie perks up, leaning on the counter.

"This is your kitchen, you tell me what you want." When she hesitates, I add, "But we are ready to plate up."

"Goodness." She meets my gaze. "This all looks so amazing. Thank you for sharing your extraordinary talent with me, sweetheart."

"Of course! I'm glad I could give you something useful. Especially now . . ."

She rounds the counter. "You listen to me." Her head dips, her frown intensifying. "Don't you go feelin' sorry for me. Or that son of mine. We won't have it. This life is too short to be poutin' over the little things. So, we are going to enjoy the wonderful food only possible because you're here. And we are going to make the most of the company." Something rogue flashes through her eyes as she pats my arm with one hand and releases me.

"Well, in that case, let's eat this stunning meal before

it gets cold." I turn and grab three plates and cutlery. She takes them from my hands. I find a tablecloth and follow her, laying it down before she can deposit her load. We pad back, collecting the dishes and potholders.

With the food laid out and places set, I step back beside Rosie. "You did it. It looks like something you'd be served in a restaurant." I wrap an arm around her shoulders.

She leans into my shoulder with a sigh. "It most certainly does, sweetheart."

"Something smells good, Ma." We both look toward the door to the living room, coming off the hall. A freshly washed Harry stands in clean jeans and a T-shirt. His hair damp from his shower. My gut flies into my lungs and sticks. I purse my lips as he studies the table. The food.

"You can thank Louisa for her patience and talent." Rosie breaks from my hold and unties her apron. "Thanks, Louisa." His words are raw, and quiet. "For doin' this for Ma."

"You said that already. But . . ." I move toward the table. "You're most welcome. She deserves so much better than what she was dealt."

He clears his throat and pads for the table. Pulling out a chair on one side, we both start as Rosie rushes into the dining room. "No, no. You're the head of the table now, my love."

Harry chuckles.

The sound is like a slap to the chest. He moves to one

end and pulls out a chair but hesitates. I look to Rosie. Her glare is pinned on her son. And it's a warning.

"Here," he says quietly and pulls out the chair on the other end, nodding for me to sit.

"Oh, thanks," I utter, dropping into it. It's an old captain's chair. The arms are worn of varnish, the seat solid hardwood but the backrest is slatted and shaped to fit the body. Delight floods Rosie's face. And when Harry makes it back to his and drops into it, she smiles. Really smiles, hands clasped in front of her face.

"Eat! Please, don't wait for me, I still need to wash up." Rosie darts off toward the small bathroom in the eastern side of the house. Harry clears his throat.

"Grace?"

"Who?"

He huffs a laugh. "We're sayin' grace, Louisa."

"Ah, sorry." Heat flushes my neck and face. Sitting at the other end of the table, at least we won't be joining hands. But the thought of touching Harry right now sends even more crimson flooding my face, my body reacting at just the thought. With just him and I in the room.

"For these and all his mercies, may his holy name be praised," he says, softly.

"Amen," I add.

"Amen." He looks up. "We waitin' for Ma?"

"We should. She worked so hard on this."

We sit in silence that's not at all comfortable. *What is taking Rosie so long to wash up?*

"Finish all your work?" I ask, trying to fill the silence slowly deafening us.

"Nope."

"Oh, was there a problem?"

"Nope. Ranchin' work never ends, is all."

"Of course, sorry."

"Maybe we should eat?" he says, glancing at the doorway. Rosie's place sits empty, her plate empty. I swing my gaze to the untouched food that's no doubt going cold.

"I'll go and check she's okay," I offer and push from the chair. I wander through the house to the bathroom.

"Rosie, are you okay?"

Muffled steps move toward the door. It swings open a second later. Her brows lower. "You oughta be eatin'."

"We're waiting for you."

She smiles and pats my arm. "Of course, where are my manners? Give me a moment, will you?"

"Sure." I head back to the table and drop into the captain's chair. "She's coming."

Harry nods and starts loading up his plate. "You gonna tell me what all this is?"

He doesn't seem too worried about the ingredients, by the rate he's shoveling large portions of each dish onto his plate. Rosie appears and places candles through the center of the table. She picks up her plate and takes a little of each dish. Setting it down, she lights the candles.

Harry's face hardens as his mother ignores his glares.

"You're not eating with us?" I ask.

"Oh hon, my old head is about to split. I'm not used to cookin' for hours a day. You two young things enjoy each other's company." She winks at me and grabs her cutlery and heads for the hallway. She's eating in her room?

I stare at her retreating back, mouth agape. Her hand hits the light switch as she passes the wall, leaving us sitting at the table with only candlelight.

She totally set us up.

When I feel Harry's glare home onto my face, I snap my attention to him.

"I—"

He holds a hand up. "Just eat, Louisa."

I clamp my mouth shut and take the closest dish. Just enjoy the company. Her words were hints. But I never thought she would pull a stunt like this. Was this entire cooking lesson gig just a charade to wrangle Harry and I into the same space?

I huff out a breath in disbelief. I didn't even see it coming.

But I can't be too harsh on Rosie. She's the sweetest woman to ever walk this earth, and I know what she did came from love. I just don't want her to be disappointed when her plan fails. Because by the look on this moody man's face, he's less impressed by this little maneuver of hers than I am.

So, being the problem solver I am, I decide to lighten the mood.

"So, Harry, you come here often?" I ask, my face serious, feigning the overacting serious face you'd see in one of those flicks at the drive-in.

His hard face flinches. Hands gripping the cutlery as he rips a mouthful of meat from the tines of his fork, he chews, face stern, then swallows before the stone cracks and he chuckles. "You didn't just say that."

He swipes up his glass and washes down the mouthful.

I hold both my palms up, looking like something from *The Godfather*. The last film we'd seen together before prom. In my best dramatic Italian accent, I squeeze out, "What can I say, I was set up."

He half chokes on his water, setting the glass down too hard. I can't help the laughter shaking my shoulders. We crack up over the food. I press a hand over my mouth, trying to stifle the laughter. "Oh, Harry."

"That's my name, don't wear it out," he says like Danny from *Grease*.

I double over, barely missing the edge of the table. He nods his head and rolls his shoulders back, sliding his fork behind his ear. I toss my head back, my stomach aching from the uncontrollable laughter.

So, he does get out. At least, he's seen that film.

And all of a sudden, the thought of Harry taking someone else to the drive-in movies sucks the air from my lungs. My laughter chokes out. And when I meet his gaze over the candlelight and long table, my breaths shallow out.

Panic rolls the swallow I just took into a sob. I tamp it down. Drawing in a long lungful of air, I steady my racing heart, trying to ease the ache in my heart. Harry's smile falls and he dips his focus to his plate. Retrieving the fork from behind his ear, he stabs food onto it, his teeth snapping the morsel from it.

I train my focus back to the food and finish it up as quickly as politely possible. Following it down with a glass of water, I set my cutlery on my plate.

"I should really go home." My words are harsh against the silence stretching between us. And I flinch when they land, sending Harry's eyes up to mine.

"Yep." He drops his cutlery and stands.

I follow suit, collecting my plate and walking it to the sink. "Can I help you put the food away?" I offer.

"I think Ma can handle it, Louisa."

He gives me a suspect look, with one eyebrow raised. Does he think I'm trying to prolong this all-day visit? The one I hadn't planned on?

Hell. I was supposed to meet Brad after lunch. Dammit. I'd forgotten all about it. So caught up in being part of this little family for just a moment.

"I'm sure she can." I grab my bag and give the kitchen a glance. It's still a fair bit of clean up.

No, you know what, Harry can help her.

I stalk toward the front door. I slide on my shoes and push through the door.

"Hey?" a gruff voice calls from behind me. "Thanks for

dinner." He nods and turns on his heels, disappearing into the candlelit dining room, his tall figure no more than a moving shadow looking outside in. With a sigh, I drift down the front steps and across the grass to my car. Inside, she's still warm from the long day in the sun. I fish the keys from my bag and turn them over in the ignition.

The car croaks through a whine but doesn't start.

Dammit!

I try her again.

Same thing. No start.

I slam a hand on the steering wheel. The last thing I want to do is go back inside and ask for Harry's help. I groan, letting my forehead slump against the wheel.

"Screw you, Betsy. Of all the times to give out."

I pluck up my bag and shove through the door. I slam it and march back inside. Harry and Rosie are cleaning the kitchen when I burst through the front door. They snap their heads up to me in sync. Harry tosses a tea towel over his shoulder and takes a bite of chicken, leaning on the counter as if waiting for an explanation.

"My car won't start," I say.

Harry raises an eyebrow, turning to Rosie.

She holds her palms up over her shoulders. "Hey, wasn't me this time."

He studies her face before turning back to me. "Need a lift, then?"

"Please."

I swallow. The last thing I wanted was to be in close quarters with Harry Rawlins. My heart—no, my soul—can't take that. It has absolutely no self-control around this man. It's taken a literal Brad barrier to keep me from being sucked into his orbit. He's like a stinkin' magnet. And I'm the woman who is programmed to be pulled into him. I'm positive he and I together can only be negative.

The tea towel hits the counter as he swipes up his truck keys and pulls on his boots.

"Thank you again, Louisa." Rosie's smile is so wide, happiness radiating from her in spades. Maybe this is all worth it. Maybe.

We slide into the pickup, and Harry fires it up. He reverses away from the house and shifts it into drive without a word.

"Rosie looks happier," I say, breaking the thick silence.

He nods. The cab is flooded with his scent. I tilt my head and close my eyes. It's too much. Too many memories flooding in, just being in this seat. The vehicle bumps along the road. I force air in and out of my lungs. Close proximity with him has always messed with my head.

"She is," he finally says.

I open my eyes and give him a small smile. I'm happy for that, at least. When my gaze doesn't leave his face, he glances at me, brows lowering.

"Spit it out, Louisa."

His hands grip the wheel tight. I rub my finger over the strap of my bag. I look through the windshield, hoping the darkness will swallow this thing hanging between us.

But my insides explode and send my head spinning when he pins me with those deep dark blues. "Ain't askin', darlin'."

Chapter Eleven

HARRY

The look of pure devastation on Louisa's face is like a knife through my gut. What'd turned out to be a night of surprisingly warm moments has been turned on its head by yours truly. I never could control my reactions around this woman. No better than the teenager I was. Lightning flashes miles away. Thunder growls a moment later.

Green eyes tighten as she hugs that damn bag to her heaving chest.

"Ain't askin', darlin'," I grind out.

Her face hardens, the prettiest scowl twisting those stunning lips. If she wasn't throwing out the I-hate-Harry-Rawlins daggers straight from the very green eyes that hold my mind captive every single night, I'd pull this truck right over and take her face in my hands and slam my mouth to hers. Inhale her. Devour her. Wipe the pouty little look right off her face.

"Fine, you want to know what I'm thinking?" she bites out.

"Yes, ma'am." I keep my face straight, despite the amusement soaring through me right now. The wind picks up, jostling the vehicle.

"Why are you bein' so nice to me? Why is your Ma bein' so nice? After everything I put you through, you're just indifferent now? The first time I saw you, the day at the diner, you hated me. Now? You just *don't*?"

Hated her?

What the hell?

I slam my foot on the brake and slide the truck over to the side of the road. We stall out with a jerk. I slam the brake on and am out of the driver's door a second later. I walk down the dark dirt road, breaths heaving from my lungs.

Gravel snaps under my boots as I stalk as far from Louisa as I can. Before I turn around and say something I shouldn't.

Like, *I never hated you, Lou. I damn well love you, woman. Always have, always will. You can't just turn something that strong off. It doesn't work that way.*

Thunder claps again, this time closer.

The passenger door opens and shuts. Swift footsteps close in behind me.

"Harry!"

I stop and close my eyes. I won't leave her in the dark. The vehicle is safe. The side of the road in the dark ain't. Her little fiery huffs meet me before she rounds me to stand face-to-face. She folds her arms again.

Guess it's now or never.

"What are we doin'?" I breathe.

"You're drivin' me home, you ass."

I hang my head, losing a breath. Misty rain closes in around us.

No escaping now.

"I mean this." I wave a hand between us, closing my eyes like a coward.

"*This?*" she huffs, and I open my eyes as she takes a step back. "There is no this, Harry."

Her words are soft. Sad.

I grind my jaw shut. Nothing's changed for me. Not a damn thing. I still think about her every minute of every godforsaken day. Have since the day we met. Even during the ten years we were apart, she was never far from my mind. Now, with her standing in front of me, it's harder than ever to rein in the feelings I have for her. To stop from giving in to the things I want.

"So that's it, then?" I manage.

She just stares at me now. Her chin wobbles, and she shifts on her feet.

"I'm seeing Brad. You're in the middle of—" She glances behind me, as if whatever she is thinking about could be seen in the darkness hanging over the middle-of-nowhere gravel road.

I step closer, unfolding her arms. Her breath hitches, sending my nerves electric. "Lou?"

I haven't called her that in ten years.

Her eyes flick up to mine. Her nose crinkles like she's tryin' not to cry.

Fuck.

I need to know if this is one-sided. Because the last time we tried this, we ignited something that felt eternal. So all-consuming, it had the potential to ruin us both. And it almost did. We were too young.

We ain't young anymore.

Blood thunders through my veins, the humid air popping them to the surface. My hands grip her upper arms. I press my forehead to hers. *Please, darlin'.*

"I can't do this . . ." she whispers, pulling out of my hold.

"Can't or won't, Louisa?" My tone is harsher than I mean it to be. But the toll of wanting someone, pining for them for so long, has me wound up.

I'm desperate for her.

My shoulders rise and fall in quick succession as choppy air burns my insides.

She steps back. "Can't."

"That's bullshit, and you know it!" I close in on her.

She snaps her head up, chin tilting in defiance.

God, I love her this way.

"What the hell would you know? You never left. You stayed here and did the same thing for a decade. I didn't have that choice. I had to leave. I had to take chances. I had to be scared."

"You had to, or you wanted to? 'Cause from where I was standing, you leavin' looked a whole lot like runnin'."

"You asshole." Her palm meets my face a second later. I close my eyes, molars grinding, as the sting burns its way through my cheek. The burn sinks low, igniting the heat low in my core. My cock twitches with her assault.

"Oh no!" she gasps. "Harry, I'm sorry."

A trembling hand presses lightly on my cheek. "I am so sorry. I shouldn't have don—" She cuddles into my embrace, hands gripping my T-shirt. I dip my head into her hair. I breathe her in.

Fuck, I deserved that.

I know exactly why she left. It took me a while to figure it out in the aftermath of her walkin' away ten years ago. But I understand now, she had to get out. There was nothing here for her. The only thing she would have had was me.

No career.

No independence.

I've seen it hundreds of times. It's like a small-town epidemic. As much as it burned that only having me wasn't enough to keep her here, if we'd traded places, honestly, I would have done the same thing. I take her arms and pry her away from me.

"I'm glad you got out, Lou. I just wish I'd had the guts to go with you."

Her face looks like she was the one who just got slapped. Her eyes are wide, her mouth agape.

"You—" she starts and snaps her eyes to the ground, now turning muddy from the rain falling around us. Her hair wet and dangling over her now soaked top has my breaths quickening.

"If you'd asked me, I would have gone with you."

"But your ma?"

"I was never thinkin' straight around you, Louisa May. Reality probably would have sunk in a few weeks later, and I woulda come home. So, I guess the end result would have been the same. Least this way, we might be granted a second chance."

The hope rising when her breath stalls out is agonizing. The overwhelming need to kiss her pushes me forward. I take her face in my hands, moving in until our breath mingles. She swallows, opening her mouth to say something.

I hover, waiting for her.

It has to be her choice.

This time, she comes to me.

I'm hard, straining against my jeans, blood bounding through my veins, thundering out any rational thought. I press into her, nudging her nose with mine. A small whimper leaves her lips. The sound alone almost brings me to my knees.

"Harry," she breathes.

"Yeah, Lou."

"I should go home."

The stone forming in my throat chokes out any response I might have thought of, and I put distance between us.

"Right." I run a hand through my soaked hair, letting fresh air burn into the depths of my lungs. I step back and wave a hand toward the truck. She turns awkwardly and walks for the vehicle. I follow, holding back. Her wet clothes cling to her elegant curves. Not helping my aching cock any.

Dammit, Louisa.

She climbs into the seat, and I release a low growl at my own stupidity. Too fast. I moved too fast. I don't have a thing to give this woman right now. And she's sending me crazy. Her words sayin' one thing; her body, her eyes, her actions sayin' something else entirely.

We drive into town in silence. After the few minutes it takes to park and kill the engine, she shifts her bag to one hand, the other on the door handle.

"Thanks for the lift."

We both notice Brad at the same time, hovering by the restaurant doors. Hell, this guy's got it bad. Almost as bad as me. The fact Mama Mancini hasn't let him up means something. It's almost as if she's not on board with the whole Brad situation.

Smart woman.

"I should go," Louisa says.

"Yep." I start the pickup and nod toward Brad. I swear she cringes as she pushes the door open and steps out.

Fuck me.

We were so close.

******

The last thing I should be thinkin' about right now is Louisa damn Masters. The auctioneer rattles off the redeeming features of this old ranch. I've been here since before the crowd arrived. Walking the lots, inspecting the structures. Met the owners—well, I guess sellers, now.

She's a fixer-upper, but for what I'm tryin' to build, the exact ranch I want. The old couple gave me a brief rundown of the seasons they've had, like the rest of us here in Montana haven't lived through them also. Bill, the old cowboy, showed me over the yards, his system, and pointed out the water points and such.

Despite their age, they've kept this place runnin'. It's admirable, especially since they had no kids to take the helm when old age caught up with them. I swore right there and then, that won't be me. Which brings me to glance at the long table under one of the old trees by the house.

Mama Mancini and Louisa are catering for the auction today. She surprised me, walkin' in with an armful, makin' her way to set up. Guess it's right she's here. I've kept this under my hat, so to speak, from Ma. Don't want to get her hopes up. But having Lou here has me determined. No matter what happens between us, she makes me want to be a better man. Always has.

The yodel of the auctioneer pulls my thoughts back to the action unfolding in front of me. The crowd is drawn closer, automatically moving as one toward the man with the voice, throwing numbers up quicker than lightning in a dry storm.

"Hup, can I get three eighty?" the auctioneer throws toward the mass of grumbles under hats.

A hand goes up. An older man, with a handlebar moustache.

Jesus.

"Three eighty-five?"

I raise my hand with a nod.

"Now we're away. We have three eighty-five, can we have a three ninety. Three nine zero."

Handlebars raises his hand.

My heart pounds. Everything is moving so fast. The desperation I feel after seeing the ranch and talking to Bill is crippling. I shake my hands out. Warmth moves in by my side, despite the morning sun. I look down to find Louisa.

"You're bidding?" Her green eyes meet mine.

I nod and snap my focus back to the auctioneer.

"Four twenty, do we have four hundred and twenty thousand dollars?"

Handlebar raises a hand.

Fuck. I'm getting close to the top of my budget.

"Does Rosie know?" Louisa whispers.

"Nope."

"What's your top line?" Louisa asks, determination over her face.

"Four eighty."

She chews her bottom lip. "And you're sure about this, Harry?"

"Yes, ma'am."

"Can we make four fifty?" the auctioneer squawks.

Handlebars shakes his head and rolls a paper through his hand. Hope springs from somewhere deep. I raise my hand. But a young guy in front of me raises his at the same time.

Dammit.

Louisa's hand slips into mine.

"Four sixty?" The auctioneer's gaze swings between me and the other guy.

I raise my hand.

"Four ninety, last call." The young guy moves forward with a hand in the air.

Fuck.

That's it, I'm out. I lost it.

"Dammit," I growl, dropping my shoulders.

Louisa's hand slips out of mine as she says, "Four ninety-five!"

Chapter Twelve

LOUISA

"Lou, no. I'm out." Harry's worried eyes pin me to the spot. Another face of Harry Rawlins that tugs at my heart. After the other night, I thought I'd seen the whole of him. And this here has me just as worked up. But not because of him—*for him*, this time.

"Not yet, you're not." I walk up beside the young guy still bidding, tossing him a sweet smile.

"Sweet Jesus, woman," Harry rumbles from behind me.

"Do we have five hundred?" The auctioneer glares at me as if I'm intruding on some secret boy's club by simply standing in the crowd.

"How much do you want this?" I turn to the young guy, now wringing the flyer about the ranch between his hands.

"It's a commission piece to me."

"So, you're not a rancher?"

I check out his clothes. A clean white shirt, dress pants, and loafers. It's probably some investment to him. It's not that to Harry.

"Here's the thing. This here bit of land is special to someone really important to me. How about you catch the next one, buddy?"

"How about we war this out and see who comes out on top?"

His gaze narrows, and he looks back to the auctioneer. Luckily for him, he's about to leave empty-handed and find something that'll be less hassle. This place makes most fixer-uppers look like the Taj Mahal. But important to Harry is important to me.

"Five oh five!" I call out.

The ruddy-faced auctioneer looks puzzled, but to his credit he continues. "Can we get five oh six?"

Living in Cali was an experience in life lessons, and the one I learned most prominently? How to save. I have life savings that would put most working males to shame. And if I can help Harry with it, I will.

I pin the young guy in the clothes that have probably never seen a dirt road let alone a ranch before with my best I-dare-you look. His hands fly up in surrender.

Harry crowds behind me, his chest heaving at my back. I raise my hand, one finger in the air.

"Sold! Five oh five to the little lady."

Side glances and grumbles move around us as the crowd slowly disperses.

"Congratulations?" the auctioneer says as he stops in front of Harry and me.

Harry pulls me away a few feet, dipping his head. "Lou, I don't have five oh five. The bank isn't going to go any further than four eighty with the down payment I have."

His eyes burn into mine. But I see the way he's looking at this old place. He wants it like I wanted freedom all those years ago. So, I step a little closer, resting my hands on his shoulders as I whisper, "You don't. But *we* do."

His face is shocked as he lifts his head.

"I have some savings. You can pay me back later. Or whatever. Besides, I figured I owed you one after . . ."

"Making your own life choices does not equal owing me. Let alone money, Louisa."

I cup his jaw with my hand. I can't even help myself.

"No, maybe not. But you want this. And I want you to have it. Hey, what are friends for?"

I wander back to the auctioneer. "Harrison John Rawlins is the name you're going to need for your paperwork. How soon do you need the funds?"

The auctioneer looks over my shoulder as Harry comes to stand behind me. Shaking his head with a smile, the auctioneer takes down Harry's name. "Should be around a month before anything official changes hands."

He holds out a hand and I step aside. Harry shakes his hand. The auctioneer walks away, heading for the food stall.

I worry my bottom lip through my teeth.

Did I really just do that?

Harry stares at me, eyes wide and lit with wonder.

"Lou . . ."

Laughter bursts through my lips. I press a hand to my mouth then let it fall as I still. "You did it, Harry. You got the ranch!"

He scoops me into his arms, swinging me around. The hearty laughter rumbling from his throat tightens mine. His scent tangles with my already shot nerves from the auction.

Heavens, it's exhilarating and terrifying all at once. And for some reason, it felt like this is something I had to do. I have a feeling about this old place.

If anywhere felt like home, this would be it.

Maybe Harry'll let me visit occasionally.

My hands shake when he lets me down. Only days ago, this close, we were fighting about us. The connection we have. Have always had.

Harry's hands still grip my arms, my body pressed to his when gravel crunches under shoes.

"Harry?" The voice echoes around my head.

Familiar.

We both turn at once to find Brad holding a clipboard.

Oh shit.

I stumble out of Harry's arms and dip my gaze to the ground.

"Bradley," Harry grunts.

Harry calling him Bradley sounds hilarious. Or maybe that's the nerves. Or the insane chemistry between Harry and me that still has me in its vise grip. I try to stifle a giggle. And fail. I slap a hand to my mouth.

What the hell is wrong with me?

I should go help Mama Mancini before I end up with my foot in my mouth. I excuse myself, telling Brad I'll see him tonight at the dance. Brown eyes follow me as I move in behind the catering table.

"You win, bella?" Mama asks, excitement lifting her features.

"Yes, he bought the farm."

Mama pulls a surprised face, and I realize the words that left my mouth.

"I mean, Harry, he—"

She holds up a hand. "I'm happy for you both."

"No, Harry bought the ranch, Mama, not me."

"Uh huh." She slices up the dessert slab she spent hours on last night and places the small pieces onto paper plates. Her smile doesn't fade as she starts to hum, going about her work.

"What?" I tilt my head and frown.

"I'm wondering how long it is going to take before you understand, bella."

"Understand what?"

I am not sure where she's going with this.

She points her cake knife to where Brad and Harry stand, talking. Harry's arms are crossed, his body facing Brad, but his eyes are on me.

It's as if he's not taking in a word the accountant says.

"Ah, now she is starting to get it . . ." Mama holds a plate up to me. "For the new ranch owner." She turns me with her hands, pushing me out of the stall. I can't go over there with one plate and hand it to Harry. I'm supposed to be dating Brad.

Now, seeing them side by side, I wonder what the hell I was thinking.

I divert with the plate, deciding now is not the time to go choosing something I have no idea whether I can commit to. Hell, I don't even know if I'm staying in Lewistown for the long term. Getting my life together was the plan. Finding some kind of normality was as far as I was thinking.

I wander toward the old homestead. The old trees flanking the house like dutiful soldiers grow on me immediately. Gosh, this place is something else. I run a hand through the green veil of the first willow I come to and let the ancient tree swallow me whole as the curtain falls behind me. I pad toward the trunk and turn, leaning on it.

I pluck the sweet morsel from the plate and take a bite.

Good lord, this is incredible.

All of Mama's food is.

I close my eyes and imagine, for a minute, what my life would have been like if I hadn't run when Harry dropped to his knee. And for the first time since that night so long ago, I let the daydream consume me completely, letting this facade of friendship I've been holding up crumble.

Brad takes my hand as we walk from the car to the old community hall. The music inside is loud and twangy. It brings back so many memories. Every single one . . . Harry is in. Guilt twists in my stomach as we approach the doors, where a man stands taking entrance fees. Brad drops my hand before anyone can notice and fishes money from his wallet.

"Have a great night," the old man says with a nod to me.

Walking inside, Brad puts a little distance between us. I try not to take it personally. I know he doesn't do public affection. And I find myself wondering why he dates at all. The crowd is lively. A bunch of men and women dancing to the two-step beat the good country folk of Montana love so dearly.

I spot the girls from work and lean over to Brad. "I'm going to say hello to Lisa and Cynthia."

"Sure, I'll grab us some drinks."

I nod and smile, walking for the only two friends I have in this small town. They wave when they see me coming. I rush to their sides.

"Wow, things really do stay the same in this town." I chuckle and look around.

Cynthia's husband, Steve, leans over and wraps an arm around her middle. "Oh, I don't know, I think the ways things are . . . they're pretty good." His blond hair is messed up like her hands have been traveling through it. They probably have.

Three kids zoom toward us, squealing and yelling. Lisa spins around toward the noise automatically.

"Now, y'all get outside. Stay out of the way of the cars. Michael, look after your brother or I'll tan your hide!" They tug on the skirt of my dress, like it's some sort of dare, and dart away, running through the crowd.

"Sorry, doll. They're always a little dippy when we're out. Hence, we barely leave the house." She pulls a cigarette from her purse and lights it. She waves to her husband who is behind the band. He gives her a smile and waves back, then waves to me as he returns to his work.

"So, where's sad Brad?" Lisa says with a smirk.

"Oy, be nice. He's gettin' the drinks." I glance toward the bar. He stands there, ordering.

"I will never understand why you're wastin' your

precious prime with Connors." Lisa stumps her half-finished cigarette with her heel.

"Hey, sometimes it's the quiet ones." Steve winks at me.

Good lord.

I spin back and watch the crowd shimmy to one side, tapping their heels and then toes to the boards. From the corner of my eye, a cowboy hat catches my attention. Standing in the doorway, Harry looks around as he hands over his entry fee. Only yesterday I saw him at the auction, but it feels like a month has passed. He's dressed in his good clothes. Dark jeans and a crisp white shirt. His good hat sits on his head, and a leather necklace I recognize from . . .

Anxiety peaks through my core, sending hot waves through my body, ending up all over my face. And it's only when he steps aside and lets a smaller figure through that I shift on my feet, letting the heat waves peter out.

Rosie is dressed in her Sunday best, her dark hair up, a small evening bag hanging off her elbow. She smiles at the man at the door and pats Harry's arm. He leans down to listen. A second later, his eyes snap to me.

Oh no, Rosie Rawlins. Your setups have run their course.

I excuse myself from my friends and make my way to the bar. I need a drink. I need to be anywhere but near Harry Rawlins. I have a tendency to let dreams and whims run rampant when I'm near him. I don't regret helping him out with the ranch auction, but business is one thing.

This thing between us is another thing entirely.

And if I'm honest, even if we can be friends, I value having him in my life. I can't lose that. I don't want to. Or Rosie. So, I do what any girl would do when she's trying to forget a guy. I cling to another one.

I slide my arm through Brad's and give him my most sincere smile.

He startles and glances at where our arms are linked. It's so innocent, it's preposterous. But he slides out of my embrace with a grimace.

God above.

All of a sudden, I'm conscious of every pair of eyes looking our way. I feel like I'm forcing this thing at every turn we take. With the need to avoid my past and the one man I don't trust myself with, I'm humiliating myself.

"Shall we dance?" I ask, trying to save face.

"Ah, I don't really dance." Brad swallows, glancing at the crowd, now moving at a sane pace, couples coupling up.

"Please? One song?" I give him my best puppy-dog eyes.

"One." He walks for the dance floor.

I can feel heated stares at my back. Most people probably wondering how I managed to make the uptight accountant dance when he clearly doesn't.

He stops, tentatively resting his hands on my hips. I wind my arms around his neck.

"This is nice." I smile.

His face is stone.

"Brad? Are you okay?" I study his face as the music hits the melodic chorus, the lyrics whining something about starstruck lovers.

He sways side to side. I look around the huge old hall. And my instincts are right. People are staring as the crowd seems to form a circle around us.

Now, I'm starting to feel something like Brad is. Harry sits at the bar, dark hooded focus drilling into the piece of wood floor I stand on. Brad stiffens as he takes in the scene around us. He clears his throat, pulling back.

"I'm sorry, I can't do this." He snaps from my hold and stalks for the exit.

"No . . ."

His back disappears through the door and into the dark night.

The music crescendos. Every set of eyes that had been not-so-subtly focused on us before now stares right at me. Heat rushes my face. There's nothing quite as painful as being the small-town spectacle. I try to make my feet move. I need to get out of here. Panic floods in, seizing my limbs, sending my hands shaking. Breath burns as I try to choke air into my lungs.

Tingles inch over my fingers.

No.

The floor swims in my vision.

The last time this happened, I'd just flaked on national television.

Everything slows like molasses in winter.

Warmth wraps around me.

His scent folds in as strong arms press me into a wall of chest. Lips dip by my ear.

"Breathe, Lou."

Harry.

Oh god.

"Harr—"

"I got you. Keep movin' to the music, okay?"

His hat dips, covering us both. My safety net from prying eyes and wagging tongues.

Lord above, what will people think. One guy walks out and I'm in another's arms a moment later.

Shit.

This is not what I wanted.

I wanted normal.

Quiet.

Peace.

To be hidden away . . .

I clutch Harry's crisp, clean shirt and slam my eyes shut. His hands hold me to him. I choke through a sob, letting the last ten years thunder through my heart. The aches and the sadness. The loneliness I felt when I left. The humiliation I felt when everything fell apart in California. The shock of seeing Harry again after so long.

After my body lets go and the shock wears off, I push out of his hold a little way. The music has stopped. A fine hand rests on my forearm. I turn to find Rosie.

Her worried face tilts. "Sweetheart, are you alright?"

I nod. "I—I'm okay."

"Take her home, Harry. I'll be fine here."

"No, I can walk," I insist.

"You're not walkin'." Rough hands grip my arms. "I'll take you home. Or anywhere else you need to go."

Rosie pats my cheek and walks back to her friends.

Harry takes my hand and leads me toward the doors. I follow, not game to look back. I can't even face the girls from the diner. That can wait 'til Monday.

Outside, in the truck, I sit in silence as Harry turns her over and pulls out of the parking lot. It's only six blocks from the hall to the restaurant. I really could have walked.

"Thanks for the lift," I say, my words almost monotone. I'm starting to think that's the only phrase I can manage around this man. The stress of the anxiety attack has me exhausted. That, and the fact I feel like a compete idiot. Losing it in front of the entire town.

"Sure." He stares through the windshield as we come to a stop sign. His hands grip the wheel tight. His jaw is set. He's probably just as embarrassed about my episode as I am. I continually disappoint him.

"You know what? I'm going to walk. I need the fresh air." I push the door open before he can drive on.

"Louisa," he pleads.

I shut the door and walk down the centerline of Main Street, clutching my bag to my body. The pickup idles behind me. I stalk my way toward the restaurant. Three blocks, and I can hide away from the world.

A door opens and slams behind me.

"Louisa!"

His long stride comes up fast. His hand grips my wrist. I stop, air burning through my lungs, blood barreling around my veins like a speed racer.

"Lou, please. Look at me."

"You should go back to the dance." I don't turn back. I can't.

"No."

I huff an incredulous laugh. Always so damn defiant.

"I told you, I'm fine. Go and have fun," I toss over my shoulder, eyes set on the street in front of me.

"I am. I mean. I was—"

I turn back. "Watching me fall apart in front of the whole town is fun?"

His face turns serious in an instant. "That's not what I meant."

"Tell me, Harry. What do you mean? No, hang on." I hold a hand up. "Tell me what you *want* me to do, so I can do it and move on with my life."

He closes the distance between us and takes my face in his hands. My body is alive the second his skin touches mine. Shoulders heaving, I study his goddamn handsome face.

"I want you to stop fighting me. I—" He sucks in a breath and tilts his head up to the inky sky. "I want this hot-and-cold bullshit between us to pick a fuckin' side. I want . . ." His gaze drops to my mouth. His thumb brushes over my bottom lip.

My insides melt to nothing, and I can barely breathe. But I manage, "What?" The word is harsh, desperate.

But he tightens his grip, eyes burning. Something painful takes over his face.

"What do you want, Louisa?"

Chapter Thirteen

HARRY

I press my forehead to hers, closing my eyes. I can't look at her when she inevitably rips my heart out for a second time. But she doesn't breathe a word.

I push back, hands on her face as it falls with desperation and she says, "I want you in my life."

Pushing onto her toes, she brushes her lips over mine. I could just lean in, fall a little further and blur the lines between us. It would be so easy. But as much as her confession clears some things, she hasn't given me any reason to take her word that we're anything more than two people who can't stay away from each other. Nothing concrete.

So, we're back to friends?

Like the type of friends you call when you are short a dime to land the ranch of your dreams.

And the thought that she's tellin' me what I wanna

hear turns the acid in my gut to ash. Is this even real? And is she gonna hang around long enough for it to work? Once bitten, twice shy. Even though every cell in my body screams to sweep her up and take her word as truth.

"You say that, bu—"

Her finger presses over my lips. "The things I wanted never lined up before, Harry. I was always forced to pick one or the other." Her worried green eyes search my face. "But I . . ."

A horn blasts through Main Street.

Hell. The old buckboard is blocking the through traffic. Hilarious as that is for Lewistown on a Saturday night.

"Hold that thought. And Lou," I say as I release her and make for my vehicle, still looking over my shoulder, "outta the middle of the damn road, woman." I force a smile, ignoring the raging torrent of flame licking my insides for the last few minutes, and turn my attention to the truck. Three cars are lined up behind it, waitin' to get wherever they are going.

I shove the old girl into drive and make for the curb where Lou stands. She watches the traffic drive past before hugging her bag to herself. Her light hair blows around her shoulders. The summer dress she is wearin' ends only shy of her knees, giving the perfect view of her long, slender legs. The curve of her hips. Those breasts that have kept my mind occupied late at night for over a decade.

I kill the engine and return to stand in front of her the way we were before the interruption.

"Which part we up to?" I whisper.

She presses a hand to my shirt over my heart, her eyes studying the rise and fall of it over my chest. This close, she infiltrates every sense. Her skin under my touch, her fragrant cinnamon-and-vanilla scent flings memories back to the surface like something smashed me wide open. Broken parts and all.

"The part where I tell you how the things I want don't line up. Or at least, they didn't before. I don't even know what does anymore or what will."

No, no. This indecisive bit is getting old.

"So which part doesn't fit with this?" I wave a hand between us.

She opens her mouth to respond, only to close it a second later. Her eyes tighten.

"I-I can't think straight when I'm around you." She pushes out of my hold and walks down the sidewalk.

Feelin's mutual, darlin'.

But that's the way it's supposed to be, isn't it?

That's how you know it's real.

"Louisa May Masters, stop walkin' away from me. I swear to god."

I catch up to her and grab her wrist. She stops, her fiery stare burning into me. I take the other wrist and step forward. She steps back. I move forward, sending her back until she meets the oversized window of the craft and gift store. I pin her to the glass, both wrists by her hips, my knee between her legs.

I'm done with this cat n' mouse.

"Stop thinking about all the things that could go wrong, Lou. Get outta that head of yours and for once listen to your heart."

My breaths plunge and rise in choppy waves. I press my body to hers. She whispers my name, and it takes every inch of self-control I have not to implode right here and now.

"I don't know," she chokes, looking off into the distance.

"Don't know what?"

"Where I belong! Or what direction I'm supposed to take."

Hell's hounds. My heart aches for her.

"Look at me, Louisa." I palm her face, letting my thumb drift over her bottom lip. We are so close, our breath mingles, her small pants crashing into my heady, burning ones.

She sucks in a ragged gulp, and her green eyes swing back.

"Right here"—I point to my chest—"this is where you belong. You need a direction, then I'm your true north. Trust that."

Her breath stops.

I dip my head, brushing my lips over hers. "That's all you need to know."

God, how long have I waited to kiss this woman? Too fuckin' long. My body is electric with her in my hold. My cock hard as stone, I'm burning for her. Her effect on me will never waiver.

"Say somethin'," I breathe.

Tears well in her eyes.

Dammit.

"Harry, what if it doesn't work out? It's a small town. What if—"

I slam my mouth over hers. Those words, they're mine. I swallow them down, extinguishing the sentiment they hold. The thoughts I am sure are ramping up in that incredible brain of hers are whisked away. She slides her arms around my neck, and I run my tongue against the seam of her lips.

She opens, and I sweep in, loving her like I've waited ten whole years for this.

And I have.

We both have.

Heat licks my spine, sending my cock harder, my hold on her tighter.

I break away, remembering where we are.

Louisa stares up at me, lips swollen, chest heaving.

"Harry, I—"

I nudge her nose with my own. "I should take you home."

"Okay . . ."

I brush my fingers over her cheek, tucking the waves

of blonde hair behind her ear. Her lips part, as if my simple touch has her drowning.

Not just me, then.

Even after all these years.

To my surprise, she starts walking for the restaurant. I follow her after a beat, watching those hips sway with every step. Her long blonde hair falls in waves down her back, swinging in time to her elegant stride, the hem of her dress skimming the back of her thighs.

Hell.

If she wasn't the only woman in the world I've ever wanted, this could be highly inappropriate. When she slows at the locked restaurant doors and slides her key into the mechanism, I catch up, wrapping myself around her.

I have no intention of going upstairs tonight, but I sure am going to make the most of this moment. Louisa's hand stills on the door handle as my lips graze her neck. She spins in my hold and takes my face in her palms. Dipping, I kiss her with everything I have. Like the floodgates that have been held back for so long have finally burst with a hard, all-consuming motion.

Louisa breaks the kiss. "You should probably leave," she utters.

"I should." The words are a rasp.

Now that I have held her, even the thought of walking away and leaving her for a moment burns. I don't want to go home. Hell, Ma's probably wondering what's takin' so long.

"Harry," she says, hands resting on my collarbone. "You told Rosie about the ranch yet?"

I straighten. *Way to change the subject, darlin'.*

"Nope. Not yet."

"Oh, I thought. Well, maybe I could give you two a hand to settle in? Help Rosie set up her new kitchen. It's kind of exciting."

I shake my head, huffing a chuckle. "She would love that. But it's a state secret 'til next month, okay?"

"Sure. Night, Harry."

She pushes through the doors and turns back to lock them up. As she ascends the stairs, I stay standing on the sidewalk like a lovesick fool. Remembering the last best memory I have of her here.

"You have to take me to Mama's. It's not a real date, we're not really goin' steady without the table for two by candlelight, Harry."

Louisa's head rests in my lap. I sit against the headboard of the truck parked at the lake. The stars overhead shimmer, and I still can't believe the most amazing girl I've ever met agreed to a date.

Now, apparently, we're going steady.

My head is spinning from the thought.

She considers herself mine.

Fuck me.

"What's so good about the Italian restaurant, Lou? We could eat anywhere."

Anywhere I could afford, that is.

Her head pops up, and she twists her body to face me, palms bracing her as she wriggles closer. "It . . . how do I explain it . . . It's not only about the food; it's like an experience. The smells, the sounds, the soft lighting. It's like being eternally in love."

Instantly, her cheeks redden. And the smile pushing up on my face sees it deepen.

"It sounds like a place for couples. Weddin's and shit," I offer. But when her face falls, I know I've taken her vision of the old place and shattered it all over the ground.

"Never mind." She lies back in my lap.

Her eyes close. I take in her breathing as it quickens then settles. I brush her hair back behind her ear, her disappointment at my response twistin' like wire in my gut.

Ain't havin' it.

I lean down and dust a kiss to her temple. "How does Saturday night sound? Table for two at Mama's?"

Her eyes fly open. She scrambles into my lap, hands gravitating to my jaw like they always do. "You mean it? Can . . . Your mom won't mind you spending the money?"

She won't know.

God knows I can't afford anything fancy, but for Louisa May, I'll find a way.

"Thank you, Harry. Mama's place is so special to me. It's the first place that felt like home when we came to town. And you're gonna love it. I know it."

The widest grin stretches her beautiful face. And that's when I feel it. The overwhelming tug at my heart telling me there isn't a damn thing on this earth I wouldn't do for this girl.

When the cool night breeze finds me, I turn away from the restaurant's doors and head for the pickup. Hopefully Ma will be ready to leave.

The music is still blasting throughout the old hall rafters when I pull into the parking lot. Brad's red car still sits where it was when we left. I have half a mind to give the loser a piece of my mind. He must be as bright as a bag of rocks, thinking his behavior's anything but questionable. Leavin' Lou in the middle of the dance floor amid a panic attack. He never checked if she's okay. Or manned up to make certain his date was taken care of. What the hell is wrong with the guy?

I walk inside, scanning for Ma.

I find Brad.

Sitting at the bar with two of his buddies, laughing like he hasn't a care in the world. Well, he's about to get one. I stalk my way over to his seat.

"Hey, dickhead! You treat all your dates like lepers?" I swing his chair back with one hand. He startles, spilling his lemonade over his iron-creased stonewashed jeans and loafers. The sickly-sweet aroma of it floods the area.

Fuck me.

His buddies stare, white-faced, not moving.

What the heck Louisa ever saw in this weedy ingrate is beyond me. And after tonight, there will be no more Brad. He can find some other poor girl to flake out on.

"What the hell, Rawlins!" His voice is too high, his face laced with annoyance. Like he's the one who's inconvenienced by the events of tonight.

"Stay away from Louisa. Your little tryst is done and dusted, you hear?"

"What gives you the right to tell me who I can date?"

I scoff a laugh. "*Date*? That's what you call that pathetic show of ditching a girl midway through a dance?"

His chin tilts up and he puffs out his scrawny torso, his striped short sleeves pressed into a crease billowing over his thin arms. "Where do you get off—"

I grab his collar and lean in, my face inches from his.

"You're done, Bradley. You left her standin' on the damn dance floor. You're done." I shove him and he falters backward on the seat.

"Okay!" His hands shoot up in the air like he's in a goddamn hold up. I turn to walk away. "Fine, she's all yours, Rawlins. Too loose for me, anyway. Always wanted to be touched. Ugh, it's not proper."

I spin back. My fist connects with his pasty jaw a split second later. He flails backward. The chair plummets to the floor and he slams into the wooden floor. His buddies shoot out of their seats and put space between us. Neither of them offers Brad assistance. Figures.

"Harry?" The small and very familiar voice snaps me from my tunnel vision. Ma's hand rests on my forearm. "I think I'm ready to go home."

I turn back to her. She offers me a small smile and nods.

"Right." I stalk for the doors, Ma trailing behind.

Not even an hour after I finally break through that Louisa May Masters wall, and I'm a moody possessive hothead already. And the feeling of helplessness, of overwhelming need . . . of the absolute desire to fall headfirst into her has me in a vise grip. Like it did a decade ago.

I've always felt too much.

It has a history of driving me to do emotionally rash things. Like proposing on prom night. And punching pasty accountants.

The upside . . . it lets me read people.

And I count it as a gift.

But, hell, fuck me.

Chapter Fourteen

LOUISA

Mama Mancini transfers the large pot to the burner. Her grip falters and it drops with a bang. I glance up from the chopping board, waiting to make sure she's okay. Today we are working on a red sauce recipe she had handed down to her from her grandmother. Culinarily speaking, it's a huge deal. And the fact she's sharing it with me makes me so grateful and beyond excited.

"You like this kitchen, bella?" Old eyes peer over the pot at me, her hand stirring at a rhythmic pace.

"I like being in it with you," I send back over the top of the pot.

"Good, good."

I crush the garlic and dice the onion as instructed. When I'm done, I scrape the tiny morsels into the pot. We stand, watching the bubbles pop in the surface of the sauce as the fragrant scents of herbs, garlic, and something so very Italian infiltrates every inch of the old kitchen.

The front door opens, sending the small bells jingling. It's a little early for the lunch rush yet. I lean backward, poking my head around the door to see who it is.

I find a cowboy hat as it slips off a dark head of hair. I snap back straight and press my hands to the wall, letting my forehead meet the wallpaper.

"Oh, now I know who it is." Mama smiles at me.

Dammit. I'm that obvious. I can't help it.

And it's my own fault. Because I knew this would happen. This is what I ran from last time. The flood of every emotion I feel at the sight of him.

"Go, go! I will save you some. And the recipe is in your folder already." She taps the beige folder under the counter I have been saving the recipes she teaches me in.

"Are you sure? I should stay and clean up."

She waves a hand at me. "Papa can help me clean up. You go, while I'm still young, bella."

I chuckle. That saying, *while I'm still young*, is her favorite.

I untie the apron string at my back with fumbling fingers. I round the counter and walk into the restaurant front room. Harry holds his hat between his hands at his waist. His face lights up with a smile when he meets my gaze. My heart flings against my ribs.

"Hey," I breathe.

"Hi," he rasps.

"What—what are you doing in town?"

"Bank. Just at the bank. Had some more things to sign."

"Oh, good. How's it coming?"

"Well," he says, but his jaw ticks. "I mean, it's on track. We move in next week."

"Yay! Oh my goodness, that's so exciting. Are you . . . excited?"

"You mean for all the long days and millions of things I have to fix? The barns, the fencin' . . ." His eyes drop.

"You want to go somewhere?"

"What you thinkin'?"

"Let me grab my purse and we go out to the lake?"

"Sure, Lou."

"Great, I'll only be a sec." I bound up the stairs and pluck my bag off the small wooden kitchen table. I do a quick check in the mirror to make sure I don't have red sauce on my face and grab some chewing gum. Unwrapping the gum, I sail down the stairs and pop it into my mouth as I halt before Harry.

"You hungry?" he asks.

"Sure, I could eat."

"How does burgers and shakes by the lake sound?"

I chuckle and swing my bag over my shoulder. "Is this a date, Harry Rawlins?"

He smiles at me with his megawatt smile, deep blue

eyes lighting up as he grabs the door and holds it open for me.

Be still, my heart.

With a bag full of burgers and fries between my legs, I hold two large paper cups with chocolate shakes. Harry drives us to the lake. Being midweek, it's deserted. Perfect.

The last time I was here, the community function had this place buzzing. And Brad was hovering. I never heard from him after the dance. Probably for the best. I don't need more complications in my life. Harry, the diner, the restaurant, and my own peace of mind is more than enough.

He shifts the truck to park and kills the engine. I hand him his shake, and we hop out of the vehicle. We're on the far side, furthest from town. We could be naked and no one would know.

I scoff internally at the thought.

Harry puts the tailgate down and we sit on it. I put the bag in between us, opening it up, and hand him his food.

He bites into the burger without a word, his focus scanning the water.

"You're quiet." I glance at him before biting into my own burger.

He swallows, taking a sip of his shake.

"I'm filtering through all the things I have wanted to say to you over the last ten years. Tryin' to find one that doesn't sound ridiculous."

I sip my drink and set the cup down beside me.

"Well, tell me something I missed."

He scoffs. "Could take a while."

My heart flops.

I missed so much. I missed him. I missed the years that formed him into this man in front of me. And he missed mine. We can never get them back.

"Pick one, Harry. You have god knows how long to tell me them all, so just start with one." His eyes pin me, tightening like whatever's trapped his mind hurts.

"I was proud, I *am* proud of you for leavin'," he finally chokes.

My mouth gapes. "But I—"

"No, you did what was best for you, Lou. I was an idiot if I thought what I, we, had back then was enough." He shakes his head.

My heart aches watching him beat himself up for his past decisions. God, I have made some doozies. That's half the reason I ended up back here. I slide off the tailgate and push between his legs. His head lifts, his eyes finding mine.

"I thought I would find what I needed on the other side of the country, Harry. I couldn't have been more wrong."

His Adam's apple bobs. He blows out a breath and grips the edge of the tray. "Your turn."

"You want me to tell you something from the last ten years?"

"Yep." Blue eyes pin me down where I stand.

"Okay . . . I wanted to be the next Julia Child." I chuckle as the words leave my mouth.

He frowns. "The who?"

I crack up. Of course, only Harry Rawlins would have no idea who she is. I dot a kiss to his cheek and whisper, "A culinary goddess who gets paid to be on TV."

Strong arms wind around my waist. His mouth hovers by my ear. "The only goddess I ever met is standing right in front of me."

Electricity skitters over my skin. My stomach bottoms out as lava glows to life low in my belly.

"Well, maybe she shouldn't have run away . . ." I pant.

"I still would have loved her, anyway," he says, the words raw, gravel.

It's like a hit to the heart.

I push up and meet his gaze. I knew we thought we were serious back then. Just teenagers. But to hear the words from him now . . .

It's both devastating and healing at once. *Would have.* Not does.

I fold my arms over my chest. "It was a lifetime ago."

"Lou," he says softly.

"No, it's a decision I have been tortured by for the last ten years. I know we were kids. But I never saw it as something premature. I still don't. That's why I had to . . ."

"Had to what, Louisa?" He slides off the tailgate and closes the space between us.

"Why I had the Brad buffer. Dammit, Harry, I have no control over the things you do to me. And that's terrifying. Because if I let you in, *really* in. There's no coming back from that. If you walk away, I drown."

"Hey!" His hands grip my upper arms, dark gaze burning into me. "You described the exact way I feel about you. Except, I couldn't leave. I didn't want to leave. Still don't. Tell me, Louisa, runnin' on your mind this time?"

No. Of course not.

I open my mouth to respond.

He goes to break away. I grip his jaw. "No, we're not doin' this. This bit where every time I need a minute, it reads as a failure. It's part of who I am. It takes me a while with this stuff. These feelings. Was the same at the dance. I need you to be patient, please?"

I can see the way he is trying to protect himself. And hell, I don't blame him. Not one bit. I did run. I broke his damn heart. And that's one thing I will never forgive myself for. Not ever.

"I won't hurt you again, Harry. I'll break my own heart before yours. That much I can tell you."

His chin wobbles. He shakes his head.

He's not getting it.

"I can't take what I did back. But I *can* make it up to you."

"Lou—" He presses his forehead to mine. His jaw clenches as he growls through a choked-up breath. "I ain't worried about me. And you have nothin' to make up for."

Then why is he shaking his head?

"But I thought—" I start.

"No. Don't you dare break that big heart of yours. I'll take whatever you give me." His lips push to my own. My hands wander into his hair. Heat sinks in my belly. We have always been fire on fire. His lips trail my neck, and I tilt my head back, drowning in his touch. My panties are wet with need for this man.

"How about we start again. You and me on the ranch. We make a go of it. Find out what happens when we give in to this thing."

I suck in a ragged breath. "Harry . . ."

His head pops up. "Yeah, darlin'?"

"Are you serious?"

"Well, you do own part of it." He chuckles.

With a soft laugh, I grab his face, pulling his mouth to mine. I let it hover shy of touching. "I do."

He quirks an eyebrow but doesn't miss a beat. "Well, as the new owner of a ranch, it's only proper you come out to inspect. And maybe, as the new owner, you should be stayin' out there, too."

"Is that a fact? And where will I sleep?" I nip his bottom lip.

"Anywhere you want. I hear the barn is cozy in the winter."

I cackle, slapping his shoulder. He dips, kissing me hard.

Hungry.

I open for him, desperate to have him everywhere I can. He tastes like chocolate and that definitive Harry scent. All woodsy and manly. The ache in my heart from his earlier words drops to my core, lighting a fire. Sending my center liquid. I ache for him all over as I let my hands wander over his toned body, his neck, the valleys and peaks of his chest. Over his hard stomach, only stopping when I hit the button of his jeans.

"God above, Louisa, you have no idea how much I have wanted this. How long I waited . . ." His lips trail kisses down my neck, dusting pecks over my collarbones before hot kisses land on the top of each breast. I gasp at the sensation of his mouth on me.

God, we really do go from zero to one hundred.

It's like neither of us have any control over this.

The thread strung tight between us has a life of its own. One growing bigger and more beautiful every day we spend together. I can only imagine what it would look like, feel like, after years of being with this man.

Chapter Fifteen

HARRY

Ma fusses over Lou in the old ranch kitchen. They are busy unpacking boxes, working out where they want things to go. I like seeing them together. They are like two peas in a pod. Does somethin' to my insides watching them.

"Where do you want your big pots, Rosie?" Louisa asks, pulling two from a deep box.

"Oh, hon, under the sink, you think?" Ma studies the bare-bones kitchen, hands on her hips. Louisa bends, placing the pots where instructed, and takes her next order. I've never seen my mother so animated. So determined. It's good. It's better.

"Harry, could you grab the last few boxes from the truck?" Ma tosses over her shoulder, arms deep in a box herself.

"Sure." I unstack the chairs and set them around the

old hardwood dining table on the other side of the large kitchen dining area, on the hearth side. I slide the captain's chair in at the head of the table. "Lou, give us a hand?"

"Yeah, gimme a sec." She finishes sorting cutlery into a drawer and rounds the counter. Ma smiles at us as we cross the threshold onto the porch.

Lou glances back. "It's so great to see her happy, Harry."

"Sure is."

We walk to the buckboard parked under the closest old tree. When we're out of sight, I crowd her against it.

She huffs a breathy laugh and slides her arms around my neck. "I'm glad you're happy, too."

"Got everything a man needs. Hard work, sunshine . . . woman."

My gaze drops to her mouth as it curls into a sweet smile. I dip down to claim her lips as mine, but a fine finger halts my progress. I look up at lit green eyes.

"I'm not moving in with you, mister," Lou rasps, then offers up a sad smile.

"But you are part owner . . ." I lean back, still wrapped around her.

She chuckles. "That is not why I helped you at the auction. Besides, Mama Mancini needs me. And I don't —" She rubs a thumb over my jaw. "I need my own place for a while. To ground myself. You know what I mean?"

I nod.

But the lump in my throat renders me speechless. I want her everywhere. I want her beside me on this ranch. I want to build a life with Louisa. And if it was up to me, there'd be no waitin'.

"This is not me running, I promise. Okay? And we can see each other every day, like we do now. I need to make something for myself, too."

Her eyes are pleading.

How can I say no?

How selfish have I been, thinkin' of only what I want?

Hell, it's the reason she ran in the first place. I never once asked her what she wanted—I assumed. Like I did with the ranch offer. I'm a goddamn fool.

"If that's what you need, darlin', I'll give it to you and anything else."

Her worried face tips up with a glimmer of happiness. And she sends her hands through my hair before pulling my mouth to hers. I sink into her like it's a place I never wanna leave.

She opens, and I take it all.

A small voice clears a short distance away.

Louisa pushes back.

I hold her steady, turning around. "Jesus, Ma."

"I thought you must have gotten lost, or have those boxes been long forgotten?" She smiles, her eyebrows raised. The mirth covering her face is priceless. Lou's face reddens as if caught with her hand in the cookie jar.

"Sorry, Rosie," Louisa says, manhandling a box from

the buckboard and into her arms. I follow suit and walk the last box into the house. Ma stays out in the yard, staring up into the trees. The old branches are gnarled and twisted like they have weathered one too many storms. From the kitchen counter, I watch as she talks to herself, sending whatever prayer she's sayin' up into the great canopy of the tree.

When she returns to the kitchen, her face is sad.

"Talkin' to the trees now, hey?" I say, opening the box to find linens wrapped around her most precious porcelain china. She pats my shoulder before diving her hands into the box to retrieve her most worldly possessions. "My son, Mother Nature is always listening. I'm simply askin' a favor."

"Sure, Ma."

I don't ask what the favor is. Hell, probably best if I don't. It's not like we're churchgoing folk. Never have been. But I'm sure she believes there's something out there bigger than just us. I hope she's right.

Louisa's words float back past my mind. *Not moving in with you, Harry.* I'm a little disappointed she won't be here from day one. But mostly, I'm annoyed at myself for assuming what she wanted. For not even bothering to ask.

I make a mental note to correct that as soon as I have the chance.

The sound of eighteen wheels braking shatters the comfortable silence we have been toiling away in. Damn, I almost forgot the cattle are coming today. What's a ranch without a herd?

"That's my cue, ladies. Lou, can you give me hand in an hour?"

Louisa looks up from the floor where she sits arranging baking dishes and trays. "Course, where do you need me?"

I can't help the smile blooming with her words.

"Yards behind the barn, say, forty minutes? Horse will be waitin'."

"Harrison John Rawlins, you ought to give the poor girl a name. You owe her as much." Ma's always had a soft spot for the mare.

"Horse and I will be ready in forty," Louisa says, standing as she dusts her hands on her jeans. I grab my hat from the hook by the front door and shove it on. With a quick dip of my brim to the best women on God's green earth, I shoot out the door and head for the yards.

The semi pulls in and starts its reverse for the loading ramp. The dusty brakes squeal as the tail of the cattle crate hits the wooden posts precariously holding up the fallin' down ramp. Its rails bow as the semi rolls forward a little, and the driver hits the brake.

Two decks is all it took for my herd at the allotments to be transported to the ranch. And now that they are here, I realize this number of head is nowhere near enough.

"Mornin'." The semi driver comes up beside me as I

look over the cattle milling in the crate. He leans on the side, plucking out a paper and a wad of tobacco. He rolls it as he glances at the old yards. "These old railin's seen better days. Name's Ned." He extends a hand. He's not much older than me. I shake his firm grip and turn to the yards.

"Same everywhere on this old place. Everything needs fixin'."

He laughs. "Good thing you came along, hey?"

He slaps me on the back.

"Yeah," I say with a chuckle and slide the rear crate gate open, pinning it back. Ned climbs up the side of the crate, opening another interior gate. My cattle—heifers, steers, and a few old cows—wobble their way down the dusty ramp. I swear the only thing still holding it up is the dirt inside it.

When the last beast is off the trailer safely, Ned files in, shutting the gate behind them. I crawl through the rail and walk through the herd, checking them over. He climbs onto the top rail of the yard. His ripped jeans and holey shirt match his tattered hat. He chews on a stalk of grass, the smoke long gone.

"Not too bad for a starter herd. But this big old place is gonna need more to earn its keep, Harry."

Harry. Like we're friends.

"Yeah, I'm seeing that."

"You'll find bigger lots of breeders over in Great Falls.

Sales are every Wednesday." He spits the stalk of grass to the ground.

"Right." I make my way back to where he sits and lean on the closest upright post.

"You need someone to show you around the chaos, let me know. The auctioneers have favorites. But, hey, you managed to snag this place. So you should have no problem."

"Yeah, well."

As if it's her cue, Louisa, Horse, and my gelding clip-clop over to where we are.

Ned pulls his hat off immediately, sitting up straighter before jumping down from the railing. "Howdy, miss."

"Hi," Lou says. A strange look twists her face as her gaze finds me. Horse stops behind her, nudging her shoulder, alongside the gelding. "Ready, Harry?"

"I should get on with it, then," Ned says, looking between us. Louisa's attention hasn't left my face.

"Yeah, thanks, bud."

The semi growls back to life and pulls from the loading ramp. Louisa's eyes widen as the end posts sway. "Wow, that needs some love."

I chuckle. "This whole place does."

"Luckily, she has the best rancher I know." She winks at me and pecks a kiss to my cheek. The semi clears the ranch entrance, turning wide onto the dirt road.

"Ma okay?"

"Yep, lyin' down for a rest. So, the afternoon is ours."

She rests a hand onto my chest but nods behind me. "And theirs."

It's the first time on a horse on the ranch. It's surreal. I worked so long for this. Now, it's happening, and I feel nervous, sure, and behind already all at the same time.

"Saddle up, cowboy; let's move some cows."

She hands me the gelding's reins and swings onto Horse before lookin' down at me. Eyes full of excitement and wonder, Louisa trots for the gate. I swing into the saddle and follow. She leans down, opening the gate, and we walk through. Taking the gate from her hand, I throw it shut. The mechanism rattles but takes, holding it closed.

"Where are we takin' them?" Lou calls out from the other side of the yard.

"South pasture. It's the only one that's still fenced."

Louisa howls a laugh. "Oh, Harry. It's too much."

I chuckle as I open the gate leading to the pasture. I take the lead and walk through, hoping the herd remembers their routine, even in a new environment. Sweet little hup-hups sweep over the cattle. I turn in the saddle to find Lou waving and trotting back and forth behind them, moving them out of the yard.

She's a goddamn natural, this woman.

An hour later, I round the herd and trot to the back. The grass is thick, lush, and evergreen. The mountains are a few miles away, leaving the pasture in its shadow. The perfect spot, accentuated by the odd copse of trees dotted throughout the large holding paddock. A deep stream runs along the perimeter of the pasture as if a border between the flat and the mountain.

Louisa's skin is flushed with the midday sun. The old hat of mine on her head has my insides doin' a jive. Her blonde hair sways over her shoulders with every long stride Horse takes.

"Fancy coolin' off?" I ask, nodding to the stream.

"Shouldn't we head back?" She lifts the hat, wiping away sweat from her brow.

"Or we could take a swim in the stream? Be a shame to ride all this way out here only to turn around again."

She trots over to where I sit on the gelding, leaning forward, both hands on the pommel.

"Harry Rawlins, are you trying your luck?"

How does this woman read my damn mind like a book?

"Yes, ma'am."

She chuckles. "Well, okay, then." But to my surprise, she bursts Horse into a lope, heading for the stream. I send the gelding after her at a gallop. Her hand holds the hat on her head. I race up beside her. The smile that splits her face will keep my memory happy for the rest of my life.

Lou pulls Horse to a halt and swings out of the saddle before I can pull the gelding up. But she stops at the water's edge. Breathless, she turns back as I swing out of the saddle. But the mirth in her eyes moments ago now turns into something much, much deeper.

I pad to where she stands and pull my hat from my head, letting it fall onto the grass. I slide hers off, and it joins mine a heartbeat before I crash my mouth to hers. Her hands wind around my neck, traveling up into my hair. Her lips are soft, velvety. Her body molds to me. Her scent winds through my senses, my body ignites, sending my cock rock-hard. I grip her face, tracing the seam of her lips. She opens, and I dive right in.

Her elegant features are incredible under my fingertips. I trace one hand down her neck, eliciting a whimper. I swallow it whole and let my hand wander to her collarbone. Louisa's hands tighten in my hair.

I come up for air.

"Dammit, Lou, I'm burnin' up here."

Her eyes are strung out, her breathing choppy and fast. Her fingers tremble as they leave my hair and trail down my neck, over my pecs, and back up to my jaw.

"You have me in cinders, Harry Rawlins." The words are choked out, like those choppy breaths are more hindrance than help.

"What can I do to ease the burn, darlin'?"

"Touch me, everywhere."

Lightning, consuming every inch of me, implodes. I grab her, tugging her onto my hips, and walk into the water. I don't care that my boots are wet. My jeans are soaked, then my shirt. Leavin' any logic I might've had on the shore line, I walk until we are ribs deep in the water. Louisa wraps her legs around my waist and leans back in the cool water, arms out like a goddamn snow angel.

The soaked shirt is transparent now, clinging to her perfect curves. The angles of her throat, the soft pulse of her neck, the jut of her elegant jaw. My breaths burn, and now I feel it. More than before. That invisible tug between the two of us which sprang to life the day I laid eyes on this girl.

This woman.

That day at the diner. For a moment, back then, I thought she was a mirage. One of my many dreams of the only woman I ever wanted.

Now, right in front of me, she waves her arms over the water's surface, her hair fanning out behind her. The rise and fall of her breath wrenches mine so tight I can barely draw air.

"Lou," I rasp.

Her arms still. She lifts her body off the water, arms sliding around my neck. Water runs down her slicked hair. Droplets hang from her nose and eyelashes. She's never looked so beautiful.

So edible.

"Yes?"

My heart stutters. I can't form the words I was sure I needed to say before. I'm hungry for her. A man's never been so desperate. I send kisses over her neck. She leans into me, a whimper passing through her lips.

"Take it off, please. Harry."

I growl, nipping the flesh where her neck hollows out before her collarbone. Her hips wriggle around my waist. "Off, please."

I pluck the buttons of her shirt loose, one after the other. When the shirt is peeled away, I toss it onto the shoreline.

Louisa's greens meet my blues, her hands disappearing behind her back. Her bra disappears under the water as she tugs it from her shoulders and her hand rises from the water, the lacy offering in her upturned palm. "Yours."

A cheeky smile blooms over her face.

I rest my forehead on hers, taking the lacy piece from her hand and tossing it aside. I close my eyes and try to steady my breathing. The Louisa in my dreams is nothing compared to the woman in front of me.

Fine hands grip my jaw, and her lips brush mine. "If we start this, I don't think I can stop."

"Darlin', it never ended for me."

Something like worry claims her face. "No, I'm sorry. I shouldn't—"

"It's done. We're movin' forward."

"But—"

"Kiss me, Louisa May."

"Har—"

"I ain't askin, darlin'."

An incredulous laugh slips past her lips, and she

brushes her nose past my own, lips nipping my top lip. I capture her bottom one with my teeth. Her breath hitches.

"Everywhere, Harry."

"Sweet Jesus, woman. You're expectin' a lot of a man." I shake my head, feigning seriousness.

She slaps my chest and chuckles, but it dies out when my gaze holds hers.

"How about I show you all the places I found in my dreams when you weren't here . . ." I lower my head and run kisses over the tops of her breasts. She arches into my touch. Her hands grip the opening of my work shirt, pushing those perfect fuckin' tits into my face. A growl rumbles through my throat. I pluck a hard, pert nipple up with my teeth.

"Har—" The little cry following her halfhearted attempt at my name sends lava coiling through my veins. My cock throbs with the need for her. One arm around her hip, I let the other trail for the button of her jeans.

"Harry, please, out of the water. I want to see you. Touch you. I can't here."

"Hold on." I stalk toward the shoreline, droplets cascading from her perfect naked form as I rise from the water. She studies my face as we cross the pebbled threshold out of the water.

I lay her on the thick, swaying grasses. Kneeling between her legs, it hits me how much I've needed her. And how much I have to make up for.

I'm all fumbling fingers and nervous chatter as I pry the wet shirt from Harry's shoulders. God, this is not my first time. Why the hell am I so nervous? It's like I'm a love-sex virgin. With the only sex I've ever had being for fun, or a casual arrangement, the overwhelming emotions that have me on tenterhooks doing this with Harry are insane.

Like it's weighted so much heavier than anything else. It's too much. And nowhere enough. I can't get close enough to him. The mountains stand over us, hiding us away from the world. The sounds of the running stream do absolutely nothing to take the edge off this burn I get from the slightest look from him.

I run my hand over his chest. The toned dips and valleys steal my breath. His dark hair, wet and shaggy around his face, he pushes back with a hand. The biceps in his arm flex, the forearm following suit as he runs a finger behind the opening of my jeans. My body aches for his touch.

"Everywhere, cowboy, remember?"

"We waited this long, there's no way in hell I'm rushing this."

He wants to savor this.

Of course he does.

The man of few words takes things slow. He's an enigma. A man out of his time. Something stoic. Nothing like the fast-fling fakers of the Cali scene. Hands sweep me up as he lays his shirt underneath me. Apparently, I weigh nothing. Not to Harry Rawlins.

"Everywhere starts here," he rasps, dotting a kiss to my forehead. He tracks his way down, crawling over the top of me. Water drips from his skin, dotting over my bare stomach, each drop sending the lightning in my veins skittering faster. Strong arms hold him above me as he reaches my neck, my collarbones, and then to my right breast. When his mouth finds my hard nipple, I arch into him.

So desperate for him.

I ache everywhere. The pounding blood in my veins sinks to my clit. I wriggle my hips. I need him. I want to feel him.

My nipple slips from his lips with a pop as he travels to the left breast. It's all I can do to sink my hands in his hair as my heart rattles around my rib cage like a runaway freight train. I'm so nervous. So worked up over him. It's like nothing else before.

"And here," he rasps, his warm mouth brushing over my ribs before his breath tickles my belly button. The moment it travels further south, heat floods my core, sending an agonizing throb into my center.

Wet jeans.

No good.

"These are comin' off," he rumbles.

Yes, they are. I lift up, and he makes short work of my tight jeans with rough hands. The movement jostles my breasts. A small, raw noise climbs up his throat. Hearing him, seeing his hands on my body, I couldn't care less if I never took another breath ever again. Tears burn the back of my eyes. I scrunch up my face, desperate to stifle the overwhelming emotions that come with losing myself to Harry.

Eyes shuttering closed, I draw in a ragged breath, hands gripping the soft grass beside my now bare hips. Warmth descends over me, cold, wet denim touches my hip bones, and a hand slides behind my neck, another scooting under my shoulders.

My back leaves the grass. I open my eyes as I'm lifted up, coming face-to-face with deep blues, deep, heavy brows, all angles and dark hair.

The air that's been precariously inflating my lungs disappears.

"Har—"

"You need to tell me what's goin' on in that head of yours."

I huff a shaky breath and briefly close my eyes, letting my hands wander over his broad shoulders enroute to his neck, arriving among the damp, dark locks that will always steal my breath. "It's nothing, I just . . ."

Drawn-down brows rest against my forehead.

"Spit it out, Lou."

My hands tingle.

God, please no, not now.

My chest tightens.

As if reading my body better than I do, his thumbs caress my cheeks. "Breathe, Louisa May. I got you. Ain't gonna let a damn thing hurt you ever again."

I suck in air, fighting off the emotion that's clawing at my insides. I'm trying to tell him what he means to me. I don't understand why my stupid body is having a moment. At all.

I swallow back the remnants of flailing negative thoughts that are no use to me at this moment.

"Us."

"What about us?" he rasps.

"It's too much," I whisper, cupping his face with my hands, "and not enough, all at once. I can—"

His mouth crashes over mine.

I let him devour the last word for a moment, then my brain catches up. I need to say this.

"I can't control myself around you. I have no control of this. It's autonomous."

He raises a brow. "Smaller words, darlin', the blood is nowhere near my head right now."

I chuckle and it turns into a breaking, happy sob. "This thing between us, it's like an invisible force. I can't see it. But hell, Harry, I feel it. I feel *everything*."

"Same. I ain't goin' to question it. Not this time 'round."

I pull his mouth to my own. He opens, and I am taking what my heart wants, finding out what I missed for so long. I settle on his lap, knees digging into the grass. The ridge in his jeans is bliss against my aching core. He leans back, snapping up a nipple in his mouth. I arch into him, still not close enough. Palming my ribs, he runs a finger under one breast.

"Please . . ." I whimper.

I'm off his waist and lying on the grass a second later. His cool, damp hair tickles my stomach as he shuffles backward between my legs. Big hands push my thighs wider. I palm my breasts, needing sensation everywhere.

"Sweet Jesus, Lou," is all I hear before his tongue runs the length of my wet center.

I'm up off the grass, hands in his hair, instantly. His mouth works my soaked pussy like he's been doing it his whole life. His gorgeous hair is silk between my fingers. The fire he's building with every lick, every suckle is going to burn me alive.

"Harry, plea—Oh God!"

He takes a long, languid draw on my clit, and I spiral.

Two rough fingers plummet inside me. I clench around them as the ache becomes too much.

"I've waited a decade for this sweet pussy, Louisa. And, fuck, it was worth every godforsaken lonely day I went without you. But now, I wanna see that beautiful face of yours fall apart."

Short pants leave my lips as his mouth finds my clit, lips tugging before his tongue swirls around it. I cry out as the spiral escalates, sending pure bliss imploding through my core, every inch of me trembling. Harry's deep blues watching me is too much. I come hard and fast. Tears burn and fall. I choke on the useless air lancing through my lungs.

I tumble back down to earth, sobbing uncontrollably.

Harry is on his knees, wrapped around me before my next battered heartbeat thumps. I let ugly sobs assault his chest.

"I'm sorry," I finally choke out. His skin is wet with my tears, his body still wrapped around me. He holds me at arm's length, gaze searching my face, and I force a wobbly smile. "I'm sorry it took me so long."

I chug another sob and suck back the tears.

A soft smile blooms on his face. "Better late than never."

I chuckle, wiping my face dry.

"Come on, we should get back." He pushes to his feet, his jeans bulging, still damp from the stream.

"No." I grab his hands, holding him to the spot.

He looks down at me as I push to my knees. He's not getting out of this that easily. I meant it when I said I wanted him everywhere. I pluck the button of his jeans open and lower the zipper.

"Lou . . ."

I press a finger to my lips.

I need to taste him. I want to see if I have the same extraordinary effect on him that he has on me. I tug the wet material down. The pants hardly budge. I look up with begging eyes. A rough hand slides into my hair before it cups my cheek, his thumb pushing into my mouth. His lips twitch, breaths coming quicker, rougher than before.

"A little help," I say, pulling at the denim.

He leans back a little, his stare never leaving my face. Like he's afraid if he pulls it away, me on my knees before him will simply disappear. Maybe he's dreamed of something like this, only to have woken up alone.

For so long.

With the achingly sad thought, I tug harder, and the jeans move down. I send the boxers down to where the denim rests on his thighs, revealing his hard length. I can't take my eyes off it. I'd wondered, from time to time. When I couldn't sleep, sometimes late at night, I would fantasize about what it would have been with Harry.

Now, it's right in front of me.

My mouth waters at the sight.

I grip the bulging length and swipe my thumb over the tip. A shudder rolls over his body, his hands snapping to my face. I look up.

"Louisa." My name is gravel, barely audible.

His deep blues drill into my green as I slide the tip into my mouth. His head tilts, jaw clenching. His eyes are hooded, desperate, the shade now deeper, grounding and darkening by the second. His legs tense as I pull up, sucking the tip. I take him as deep as I can.

Loving the way that every inch my mouth travels makes his face move that tiny bit.

His tongue darts out, licking his lips. My face is taut with dried tears. I don't care. All I want to see, to feel, is this man. This stoic, incredible man who waited ten years for me.

I swirl my tongue over his tip before letting my teeth grace the now leaking opening. It's salty and delicious. I run a hand up the inside of his muscular thigh, wandering my fingertips over his balls, one then the other.

The groan rattling his chest is intoxicating.

I trace circles around one, taking him to the back of my throat. With as much pull as I can manage, I slide back up. His body trembles, hands gripping tight in my hair. I do the same motion again until he quakes where he stands.

"Stop, Lou, 'less you want it all," he pants.

"I want it all, Harry," I say, not letting up on my assault of lips, mouth, and hand. Rough hands pull my face away, holding me back as I kneel. His eyes slam shut, jaw twitching as a growl rumbles up his throat.

"Goddammit, woman," he utters.

I pump him hard with my hand, desperate to see him fall apart.

And he does.

Hot ropes of white land on me, sliding over my breasts. The warmth of it caresses my nipples. I'm mesmerized by the sight of him. Clenched, angled jaw. Deep blue, lust-drunk eyes looking down at me as his fingers grip my chin, tilt my head up, and force my eyes to his.

His face is wrecked, a war between pleasure and emotion cracking it six ways to Sunday. His breathing is a choppy rasp.

I push to my feet, taking his jaw in my palms as I sink my mouth over his. His fire meets my own, as if being spent all over me is only the beginning.

I break the kiss and study his expression. "No turning back now, is there?"

"I hope not," he breathes.

How could we? This force of nature that is *us* keeps pulling him and I along.

Both of us helpless to pull away.

I don't think I will ever want to . . .

Ma doesn't seem to have noticed our half-day absence. If she did, she doesn't say a word. She sits at the dining table, mending some item of clothing. Never stops.

Louisa left not long after we made it back, midafternoon. It's empty without her here now. I understand this is not what she planned. But my heart can't stop reaching for her, regardless.

"I need a drivin' lesson," Ma says out of the blue.

"What for?" I ask.

The second the words leave my mouth, I regret them. Her focus on the work in her hands intensifies. The old man never permitted her to drive, claiming she would never be home if she had a means of getting herself places. Old bastard never relented, not in all the years they were married. Not even when she would have been better off drivin' him when he was drinkin'.

I won't be him.

"When?" I ask.

Her gaze pops up from the needle and thread in her hand. "You don't look too busy now."

I chuckle.

"Sure, I have a little time before I need to get back to fixin' every run-down bit of this place."

"Good." She drops the darning to the table and makes her way to the front door, pushing on her floppy hat and sliding on her weathered boots. Shaking my head, I follow, planting my own hat on my head and tugging on my boots. By the time I get to the old buckboard truck, she's in the driver's seat, hands on the wheel.

Like a kid with a new toy.

I drop into the passenger's seat and shut my door. "What's got you wantin' to be drivin'?"

"Well, we're much further from town now. I can't be askin' you to take me in like we used to. Plus . . ." She glances to me briefly before rendering her focus back to the dusty windshield.

"Plus?"

"You won't be wantin' me around all the time. You two need to—"

"You two? What are you talkin' about?"

"Louisa and you need space for a proper start." She nods her head, as if cementing the idea.

"Ma, Louisa and I, we're . . ." I don't know what we are. I know what I want. I still haven't gotten up the nerve to ask her what she truly wants. I had ample time to do so today. Did I do it? Nope.

I shake my head, as if that will dislodge the thought along with my cowardice. I've never possessed the ability to think straight around Louisa Masters.

"We can talk while I drive," she suggests, nodding to the gravel road before us.

I grunt a response and point to the ignition. "Turn it over. Make sure it's in neutral first."

She nods, her hand gripping the gear stick. I place my hand over hers, wobbling the stick side to side to show her it's in neutral. She turns over the ignition, and the old girl rumbles to life.

A smile lights up her face like she won the best prize on the planet. It's the little things with Ma. That's what makes her so endearing. I smile at her as she grins at me. With a chuckle, I point out the speedometer and the brake, the pedals, and so forth. She nods with every new piece of information.

"Right, press the clutch in, and shift her into first." I wave at the pedal, then the stick. She pushes the clutch all the way in. Her leg shakes with the pressure. It's not an easy truck to drive. Old and stuck in its ways, some days it takes a little manhandling. Her hand pushes the stick to first gear.

"Good, now put a little pressure on the accelerator while you ease off the clutch, slow like."

"Uh huh." She purses her lips, attention swinging from the windshield to her feet as she shifts the pedals. The engine roars a little, and we move forward with a jerk.

"Steady, let her roll."

Her foot pops off the clutch and we jolt forward, but to her credit, she doesn't freeze up, just accelerates. Like she's been payin' attention every time I drive her somewhere. I wonder how long my mother's wanted to learn how to drive. How long she was denied this small privilege.

We travel along the ranch's gravel driveway slowly. We make the entrance, and I pull the wheel 'round, helping her steer onto Hillview Road.

"This is good. I think I'm getting the hang of this." She pushes the pickup faster. It whines, needin' to shift up gears.

"Clutch in, shift into second."

The clutch depresses, the roar dissipates, and the old girl slows while Ma finds second. Her foot pops the pedal, and we surge forward. She picks up the pace, the widest grin on her face.

"Now, lesson for lesson." Her voice is serious, like we're in grade school.

I roll my eyes and stare out the window.

"You're never too old to listen to your mother, my boy."

I can't help the smile growing on my face. But I owe my mother more than I could ever repay, so I drag my eyes from the mountains and fix them to her.

"Fine, shoot."

"About you and Louisa."

"Ma," I utter in protest. I don't need to talk about Lou right now. If I do, I'm likely to end up with a raging hard-on while sittin' in a confined space with my mother.

"No, I want you to know this. I won't be around forever."

I lean into the old seat and turn my body toward hers. Talk of her not being here does something to me that I hate. We have been through so much. I can't imagine her not having the chance at finally being happy.

"Don't say that."

She chuckles.

"We all die eventually, Harry. If I go before my child, I'll consider myself blessed."

Her words grate against my heart. I hate this conversation already.

"Anyway. I want you to know . . ." She hesitates as if weighing the words. "A good woman is the makin's of a man. There are some things you can't do in this life alone. Those things, essentially, mean the most. Like a happy life. A full life of love and companionship. But it's more than that. It's like, how do I say it . . ."

She glances at me, making sure she holds my attention. "Your life, your dreams, are like a big ship. An ocean liner, or an exploration ship. One of those ones from the days of the first explorers. She's your captain. You, her first mate. You're mighty strong by yourself. *With her,* you'd be unstoppable. There is nothing a good pairing can't overcome."

The last few words are too quiet. I can't help but think she's learned all this by making mistakes. By living the opposite of what she is speaking about. Her analogy sits heavy in my gut, like the anchor she forgot to mention. Now, I realize that's because the unsettled feeling I've had since the day Lou walked away from me outside the high school gymnasium is exactly what she means. I've been drifting.

Lost at sea.

Sure, I sunk myself into work and building up the family business to buy a ranch. I've never had much focus after that milestone. As if the goal was compensating for what I lost ten years ago. A consolation prize.

And now I have the ranch, I realize how big and lonely this life will be if I have to do this alone. The truck lurches over a pothole in the road. Ma gasps, hands white-knuckling the wheel.

"Next left, turn in and send her right 'round. We'll head home."

She smiles and lifts one hand to her forehead in a sloppy salute. I chuckle. Never before have a mother and son been so close. I swear, the only silver lining—and there is always one of those, I believe that—to come from the horrendous life we led in the old man's house was that it brought us together in such a profound way. Nothing will ever match the devotion Ma carries for me.

And I for her.

The second the thought rings through my mind, I'm a liar.

Because there is one woman I can't live without.

And she ain't in this truck.

Wednesday is here, and Lou is back. I meet her in the driveway, her with an armful of groceries for Ma to turn into some mouthwatering morsel and the prettiest smile I've ever laid eyes on. I, however, can't stick around. I have the sale in Great Falls at noon. If this ranch stands any chance of making it through the next twelve months, we are going to need breeders.

A couple semi loads of them, at least.

I wave Ma goodbye through the front window as I shove on my hat.

"You're not stayin'?" Louisa asks, disappointment claiming her face.

"Need to be at the store sale over in Great Falls. I'll see you later."

"Oh, sure." She offers me a small smile.

Drivin' the hour and a half to Great Falls, I mull over Ma's words from the driving lesson last week. For the first time in my life, I let myself dream big. Like bigger than growing a profitable ranch. Maybe other investments. Other income avenues. Others have done it. If I can make the first ten years good ones, then I'll have equity.

Today I spend the last of the capital from the allotment sales. A little I had leftover as a nest egg, just in case.

I ponder a fifty-fifty split. Half stock, half investment down payment.

The thought sparks something that fires off by itself. The hope and excitement it brings fills my heart. It lights me up.

Damn.

Lewistown is no big fare, to be sure. Most small businesses turn over a profit in town. At least the owners claim they do. The drive flies past, and I find Ned leanin' on the gate to the sale yards, waitin' on me. I park and walk to where he is rolling a smoke.

"You oughta give that up, bud," I say in lieu of hello.

He blows a cloud of smoke to the side, with a grin. "Was hopin' you'd make it, Harry."

"Can't have you buying up all the quality stock."

He turns and heads through the gate and I follow. I

haven't been here before, having only used Lewistown's smaller market for the allotments.

"Nah, I only transport 'em, buddy. I like the work, don't like the stress of ownin' a ranch."

"That so."

"Hell, you've got your work cut out for you on the old ranch. Holler if you ever need a hand, hey?"

"I'll keep you in mind. Maybe roundup time."

He shoots a smile my way as we file into the sale house. Its round, fenced off pound is circled by stands, like a small grandstand outfitted for buyers. Just beside the gate the cattle come through, a platform juts up. Two men stand discussing whatever is on the clipboard hovering between them.

Chatter echoes around the space. Ranchers fill the space, shakin' hands and chuckles happening all around us.

"Busy place, Ned."

He nods, finding a seat and dropping into it before rolling another smoke. "Yeah, I guess. This is nothing to the all-breeds sales in spring. Can't get a parking spot for miles."

I sit down in awe, imagining this place overflowing with stud ranchers. That'd be somethin' to see. The auctioneers call the start of business, and I watch in fascination as the room quiets so quick you could hear a pin drop. Hooves over damp earth move next.

A herd of twenty or so young red heifers trot into the

pound. The hammer falls, and the auctioneer bursts into a yodel I barely understand. It's nothing like the auction of the ranch. I study the crowd, seeing how it moves, the faces they make as they take in the herd. Ned nudges my shoulders.

"Nobody ever wants the first lot. If you want a cheap lot, this it'd be it."

"What are they up to?"

"Still too low for a profit."

"So, that would be to my advantage?"

"Yep."

I raise the bid card in my hand. The auctioneer snaps his focus to it. Pointing to it instantly. A few more bidders raise their cards. The price moves up a little.

The second auctioneer scans the audience.

"Do we have fifty? Can we get a fifty?"

I raise the card. Fifty cents a pound. Times the weight of each heifer, say around five hundred pounds. Only a quarter of my budget. I wait until the crowd doesn't offer anything else before raising again.

"Fifty, buyer five eight three nine. Sold!"

The hammer falls again. Two men on horses ride into the pound, ushering the small herd back through the gate they came.

"See, too easy." Ned leans back in his chair.

"I still need another eighty head. A handful of bulls."

"Shoulda got better seats. You're gonna be here a while, Harry."

"You be around later to haul them back to the ranch?"

"Yeah, bud. I'll be haulin' all day between your lots and whoever else's buys I can wrangle to load."

Ned rises from his seat. The next lot walks into the pound. Cows and calves. A heavier set breed.

The auctioneer starts up, his yodel now fully warmed up.

Here we go.

Chapter Eighteen

LOUISA

I swirl the dark icing around the top of the triple-layer chocolate cake, like I'm Van Gogh putting the finishing touches on a masterpiece. I am a hundred percent certain it will taste like one. So same, same. Mama Mancini's eyes follow the spatula, never leaving the task.

This cake right here is her legacy, and she is giving it to me. Well, the recipe and the technique, at least. It smells divine. I can only imagine how incredible it will taste. This is the second layer of icing, the first being a crumb layer, and she cuts no corners. Thus, nor do I.

The bell to the restaurant chimes. Her focus breaks. I stifle the urge to breathe in my first useful lungful since I picked up the spatula.

"You want me to see who it is?" I ask.

"No, no! You ice, I'll entertain."

Entertain?

She's expecting company?

I send the spatula round for one last swipe, leaving a swirl that looks delectable. I drop the utensil in the sink with the bowl of icing and stand back.

Wow, she's a real beauty.

I take the recipe in Mama's handwriting from the counter and slide it safely into my folder. I'm not losing this one. A familiar low chuckle comes from the front of the restaurant. I glance at my wristwatch. Almost six. The last of the sun's rays splinter through the front glass of the establishment, scattering its brilliant light over the red-and-white tables and chairs and glinting off the black-and-white tile floor. It's serene.

"She won't be long," Mama says, rounding the corner as she waltzes in.

"You set me up, too?" I raise an eyebrow at her.

"Bambina, I have no idea what you talk about?" She smiles, then pulls a silly face.

I duck my head around the door.

Harry sits at a table for two, his hat under his chair, hands on the table by the cutlery flanking his plate. The other side of the table is now sporting a fresh place setting. Every other table is bare, seeing it's the one day of the week the restaurant is closed.

"What did you do?" I whisper at her.

She chuckles, swiping up a tea towel and diving her hands into the hot, soapy water in the sink. She washes the icing bowl and sets it to drain. I pull the tea towel from her shoulders and dry it up.

"No, no. You and the cake have a date."

"You've been talking to Rosie?"

"Bambina, the whole town's been talking. You two are the only ones who aren't seeing what's happening."

That's not entirely true.

My mind flies back to the other day at the base of the mountains. The ride home. The unspoken things exchanged with the smallest of looks as we swayed our way back to the homestead on horseback.

The spatula hits the draining rack. I reach to pick it up and she slaps my wrist away. "You go. Or will I have to take your place?" Her brows shoot up, the cheekiest smile blooming on her kind, wrinkled face.

"Alright. But we don't need a village to figure out what this is between us."

"Oh, *mia cara*, you have neither the choice in that nor the heart to tell a soul no. Go on now!" She waves me off. I untie the apron over my dress and fold it before placing it on my folder under the counter. I slide the cake plate from the counter and into my hands. It's heavy.

Stepping into the dining area, I hold my breath as I walk the cake to the table. Heart thundering, I set it in the center of the table. Harry clears his throat and stands. "Lou."

I meet his gaze, and my body vibrates with nervousness.

Dammit.

One little escapade into the mountains and I'm a puddle around Harry Rawlins. It takes a beat to steady my nerves enough to say, "Hey, hungry?"

"For cake?" His eyes darken, dipping to my mouth.

Yeah, me neither.

"Sit! Sit!" Mama squawks at us as she pulls out the linen from under each place, setting mine down on my lap. Harry catches his before she can do the same for him, dropping it beside his plate.

"Mangia! Eat, it's only good fresh," Mama insists.

"Good, good." She pours water into our glasses and lights a small candle. This is feeling more and more like a date with each passing moment.

The front door chimes again. Papa Mancini waltzes in, in golf shoes and outfit, and he greets his wife with a hug and a peck to the cheek. He winks at me as she takes his hand and drags him back to the kitchen.

Harry chuckles. "Does this seem like a setup to you, too?"

"Subtle, aren't they? If only they knew . . ." I flash wide eyes at him.

I take the cake knife and sink it into the center of the cake, pulling it down to make the first cut. It cuts like a hot knife through butter, the texture absolute silk.

Sliding a slice onto his plate, I suck the icing from my thumb. Looking back up, I find Harry's eyes stuck on me. He hasn't moved. His hands nowhere near his cutlery.

"You don't wanna taste it? It took me hours, *literally*."

"I—"

"Well, you two! We will see you tomorrow. Lock up for me, will you, bambina?" Mama pats my cheek as her husband walks past. They are out the door not a moment later.

Oh yeah, definitely a setup. What is it with this town?

That is the second time this has happened. First with Rosie and the meal at the old place, now this. Seems they all think we are none the wiser to this thing between us.

Remembering the cake, I wedge a bite from the first slice and hold it out to Harry.

His brow raises, mirth lighting up his eyes. "You feedin' me now?"

I huff a small, tight noise and spin the fork back around, biting the cake from it a second later. Harry tracks the movement, surprise stretching his features. My eyes flutter shut the instant the rich velvetiness hits my palette. A soft moan slips out.

Holy Mary, mother of—this cake is a life experience.

"Lord above, woman, you keep making those little noises and this cake is going to end up on the floor."

My eyes snap open.

I find Harry's darkened eyes locked onto my lips. He shifts on the seat, as if he's no longer comfortable where he sits. His hands grip his cutlery as his jaw clenches.

With him, I'm totally alive.

Simply by walkin' into the room, he raises me up.

I lower the fork slowly, digging it into the dark choco-latey goodness. With my gaze locked onto his, I take my ever-lovin' time to part my lips and slide the fork onto my tongue, then bite down.

Harry glances through the oversized windows of the restaurant. Then, as if deciding something outright, he stands, hauls me to my feet, and sweeps me into his arms. His corded forearms hold me to him as he nods to the cake. I twist and pick it up, cradling it in my arms.

Without a word, he heads for the stairs, climbing them one by one to my apartment. His eyes burn into mine as his Adam's apple bobs. His grip turns too tight as we push through the door. A few long Harry strides and my ass hits the surface of the small kitchen table.

Harry snatches the cake from my grasp, depositing it by my side. I want to run my hands through his hair. Sink into his kiss and surrender to his touch everywhere. But he stands back, chest heaving, body so rigid that, if you didn't witness the last few moments between us, you would pick him for angry or upset.

I know better.

I know what we do to each other.

How the burn takes over.

"Harry," I whisper. "Come here."

He shakes his head, so subtly it almost doesn't regis-ter. "Ain't movin' a muscle."

"Why not?"

He tilts his head before closing his eyes ever so briefly. A groan leaves with his next breath.

Deciding I have waited long enough for this man, I pull the shirt from my body and toss it at his feet. I want him.

At least, I *think* I'm ready for this.

His gaze snaps to mine.

The fire in his eyes could turn even the hardest element to ash. I let my hands wander to the clasp on my jeans, flipping it open.

He takes a step forward, boots scuffing over the floor as it creaks. His attention flits from the cake to me. A heartbeat passes, and his rough grip surrounds my face, his body pressed between my legs.

He claims what's his.

It's all I can do to tame my desperate heart, to slow my rapid pulse. Sliding my hands into his hair, I curl my fingers around his locks, tight. He lowers me to the table, his rock-hard cock grinding into my center. The pressure is bliss against my aching clit.

He pulls back when I'm lying before him. The meal in front of the man.

My hands fall from his hair to my sides, breaths heaving as I lay waiting.

"We doin' this here, darlin'?" Harry rasps.

"Anywhere, I don't care."

His jaw feathers before he tugs at the jeans hugging my hips, darkened blue eyes staring down at me.

I want to see him.

Touch every toned ridge. Every hard line.

I snap up, sitting on the end of the hard surface. I draw my knees up, pressing the soles of my feet to the edge. Letting my legs fall open, I lean forward and pluck the buttons open on his old work shirt. He stands, stoic, rigid. His gaze never leaves my face as I bare him, first the shirt—he toes off his boots—then the jeans and boxers.

I hold my breath as I trace a finger over his jaw, down his neck, and over his bounding pulse point. Lower, I send my hand over his toned pecs, before tracking a digit over his corded bicep and forearm. God, I love these.

Harry's breaths turn erratic when I brush my hand lower, finding his rock-hard length. It's warm, velvety, and makes my center coil into itself with the lightest touch.

A low groan splits his lips as I rub a thumb over his tip.

That sound . . .

I release him and lie back.

It takes him a beat to realize I'm once again spread before him. The ache in my center is so intense. Implosion imminent. Harry's dark stare flicks back to the cake.

I can't wrangle the burning breaths in my lungs as something sinister flashes through his eyes.

"Having trouble choosing which to eat?" I ask.

Harry leans over the table, bracing above me on corded arms. His teeth nip my nipple before scattering rough kisses up my neck and claiming my mouth.

I open for him, but he breaks away.

"Who said I had to choose, darlin'?"

I glance at the cake. When I turn back, his hands are sliding under my back. The bra hits the floor. The panties follow.

"What are you up to, Harrison Rawlins?" My words are threadbare.

"Close your eyes, Lou."

On a shaky breath, I do as I'm told, letting my eyes flutter shut.

The table creaks as he leans in again. Something cool swipes over my nipple a second later. The earthy tang of chocolate floods my senses.

He *didn't*.

I crack an eye open.

"Closed, Louisa," he growls.

The same cool, silky sensation covers my other nipple. It dots in places over my belly and lower still on my hips.

He hovers above me, and I'm tempted to open my eyes again. The rich icing tingles against my skin where he swiped it. I wriggle on the table, desperate, needy. My core aches, my clit is consuming me, reducing me to one point.

"Harry," I whisper. The word is wobbly, weak, and strung out.

"Patience."

The table creaks again as he leans over me, to the cake, I assume. His shadow above me disappears, and a rough hand grips my hips. I can't help but roll them under his touch.

A low growl echoes through my apartment.

A thud tells me he is on his knees.

"Come on, let me open my eyes. Please . . ."

"The only thing you're opening for me right now are these pretty thighs."

He pushes my legs wider. His hot breath hits my center, and I lose a whimper.

"Har—"

The cool icing hits my clit and sweeps through my folds.

Oh. My. God.

"Jesus Christ," Harry drawls. His raspy words falter as if sticking in his throat. "I'll be back for dessert later."

The table wobbles a little as he rises to stand. A hard bite closes around my nipple, and I snap up from the table, unable to stifle the cry rattling up my throat. Harry's hardness presses into my thigh as he sucks and licks the icing from one nipple.

"Heavens abo—"

"Keep 'em closed until I tell you otherwise."

He bites down before licking the nipple, soothing it. I rock my hips into him. My entire body is on fire. My heart hammers, sending the echo to my head.

Harry moves to the next nipple. "So fuckin' delicious, Louisa May."

Lord knows if he's talkin' about the cake or me.

Knowing this man, both.

My nerves flare. My body wants this. My heart and mind are borderline undecided.

Still.

I can't escape the insane chemistry between us, yet I can't fully give in to it either.

"Dessert time," he murmurs.

My breath hitches as he descends my body, placing one chaste kiss to my skin at a time. It takes every inch of willpower I have to keep my eyes closed.

I grip the edges of the table, my hands desperate to hold something. Harry nudges my thighs, sending my legs wider for him, and I moan. My body burns for his touch. The throbbing in my clit drowns out every last sensation.

"Harry, please . . . I'm going to—"

"Open your eyes. I want you to watch me take my fill."

His tongue runs the length of my soaked center. I cry out, arching from the table. My hands sink into his hair as he looks up, those deep blues holding my attention. Barely shifting the air in and out of my lungs, I'm a trembling mess as I widen my legs further for him.

"Fuck," I rasp.

Something dark flashes through his gaze.

My insides melt. When the undertone doesn't leave his eyes, my liquefied core flips the misshaped lump over in my gut. Teeth cinch over my clit. My head falls backward, hair dangling down my bare back, hands snapping on the table behind me, bracing against my inevitable demise as Harry suckles my clit. His hot tongue forms circles over my bounding apex as he sinks two fingers into my wet center.

I hiss, a hand snatching at his hair.

I shake. Each breath is more useless than the last. He works me over with purposeful, slow precision. Like we've known each other's bodies for years.

A stone forms in my airway.

We don't.

We haven't.

Instantly, the air merely sustaining me peters out. I shift on the table as the emotions I have kept at bay for so long break free of the dank place I shoved them, soaring into the light. Harry takes a long, hard pull on my clit with his lips, fingers thundering into me. I come hard.

The thoughts splinter and crash out around my mind, dissolving to nothing. My hips rocking, he coaxes me through every last wave of bliss.

God, this man.

Always taking his damn time.

Always paying attention.

This. This is why we're too intense.

Why being everything to each other is dangerous. Like we climbed in this hot rod of a relationship and floored it, throwing caution to the wind.

I slump backward, lying on the table. The emotions that soared before bliss crash down on me like a concrete blanket.

A strong arm sweeps my back up and off the wooden surface. Harry tugs me, hands gripping my hips, to the table's edge.

"Jesus, Lou . . ." he growls.

His erection looks painfully hard.

I want to cross that line, I really do. But my head is not moving as fast as my heart. I shake my head, with a breathy moan.

"What is it?"

I drag in a wobbly breath, and it takes every bit of nerve I have left to lift my eyes to his.

"I-I can't."

I want to. God knows I want to. But I know when we do this, I will be careening off this cliff, headfirst, at a million miles per hour. If I end up moving somewhere else, then what happens to us?

To Harry? I—

He cups my jaw with one hand, dotting a kiss to my forehead. As he pulls back, he brushes my hair behind my ear. "Waitin' never killed a man. I waited ten years, Lou. Take your time, darlin'."

"I'm sor—"

He moves to one side, coming back with a handful of cake and the cheekiest grin I have ever seen on his gorgeous face.

"You gonna feed me?" I ask, a giggle almost drowning out the last word.

"Something like that," he drawls.

Cake squishes over my lips. Icing shoves its way up my nose. I gasp, mouth agape. He loses it, bending over with a cackle.

"Oh. My. God. That's it, Harrison Rawlins. You are getting it now!"

Swiping up two handfuls of the silky cake and icing, I lunge at him. He moves too slow. I coat the side of his face and neck with it. He swings around, catching me with one arm. I scream, trying desperately to pull from his strong hold. He chuckles into my ear, edging me closer to the table. To the cake.

"Uh uh, no way. It will take me days to wash the icing out of my hair, Harry."

"Not if you have help," he growls into my neck.

He turns us as one, pinning me to the table. I slam my eyes shut, holding my hands up in a desperate attempt to hold back the chocolatey assault. The earthy cocoa scent shrouds the space between us as he plucks up a handful with his free hand, rubbing it over my face and into my hair.

"Oh! You!"

The heartiest laugh rumbles up this throat. "You look kinda dirty, Louisa May."

I grab handfuls of his hair and drag his mouth down. Icing cakes my face. I don't care.

I taste him.

He sinks into the kiss.

Rough hands pull me to his hips as he wanders around the apartment blindly. "Bathroom?"

I point to the middle door, and he pads for it. Letting me down, he runs the bath. I trail a finger through the icing on his neck, tasting it when I reclaim my finger.

Lots of steam and too many bubbles later, I'm lifted into his arms. He steps into the bath. We sit, Harry at my back, relaxing into the hot, soapy water as the chocolate melts from our skin.

Mama Mancini's chocolate Italian cake is some kind of aphrodisiac.

A coincidence? I think not.

I chuckle to myself and lay my head on Harry's shoulder. A kiss dots to the crown of my head.

This right here is heaven.

"Can you stay?" I ask when the silence floods the small bathroom space.

"Sorry, Lou. Early start."

Of course. Ranchin' never ends.

Just like this thing between Harry and me. Ever present. All-consuming.

"A little longer?" I ask. Heavens alive, I'm beggin' now.

"I'll stay and snuggle. Whatever you need, you ask, and I'll make it yours."

I turn my head back, planting a kiss to his jaw. He folds his arms around me, and I'm caged in as bubbles slop about the bath. "Good to know."

Chapter Nineteen

LOUISA

The bustle of the restaurant hums along. After an eight-hour shift on my feet, the last thing I wanted to do was be servin' food again. But Mama was desperate, her two waitresses both called in sick, so I rested my weary feet for a beat and grabbed an apron. The pepper grinder gets heavier with every set of patrons I serve. By closing time, I'll be dead on my feet for sure.

The space is illuminated by table lights, soft lamps hanging three-quarters of the way up each wall. The harsh light of the kitchen pours through the open doorway. No service porthole door for this place. Mama and Papa like to see their patrons enjoy their hard work. They consider each person who dines here family. It's an amazing place. An amazing family to be part of.

Like a second home, almost.

The Mancinis created that. With every dish. Every gesture. Every conversation they have with the people who come through their doors. Tears prickle behind my eyes. It's been so long since I felt this at ease in a place, this wanted. Cherished.

I promise to whoever is listening that this is what I will create one day for the people who find themselves in my life. In my home. Wherever I end up.

And I am caught in the overwhelming feeling of never wanting to leave.

The thought surprises me, snapping me from my reverie.

"Bambina, order up!" Mama calls through the pass. I finish the pepper for a couple I assume are on a date. He looks nervous, she looks bored. I suppress a chuckle.

"Is there anything else I can get you?" I ask.

"No, we're good. Thanks." The girl throws me a faint smile.

I turn on my heel, heading for the pass. Two bowls of Mama's linguine wait, steam swirling up from the delicate pasta. It smells like heaven. What I wouldn't do to slide to the floor somewhere out of the way, off my aching feet, and inhale a bowl of this creamy goodness.

Mama glances over, her hands still working on the meal she is preparing. "Table twenty, bambina."

"Twenty, thanks." I swipe the bowls from the space and head for the table by the window. Halfway across the room bustling with happy diners, I make out the occupants of table twenty.

With an internal eyeroll, I make my way over.

"Here you go, Mama's special linguine. Did you want pepper? Extra parmesan?" I ask.

Brad's awkward stare holds me for a millisecond before his date speaks up. "No, none for me, thanks. Bradley?" she asks, her voice light and sweet.

Bradley, indeed.

Hope she knows her date is a flake in every possible department.

He clears his throat, focus stuck on the food. "I'm good."

Of course he is.

"Sure, holler if you need anything," I say to the poor girl, giving her my best sympathy smile. She tucks a piece of dark hair behind her ear and returns the smile, albeit small.

Mama's voice drifts over the crowd once more and I am heading for the pass for another round. The night passes quicker than I realize, and when the last patron crosses the threshold and onto the sidewalk, Mama leans against the doorway to the kitchen, tea towel in hand, something like curiosity in her eyes.

"What is it?" I ask.

She sighs. "Not much, bella. Just—"

A crash rings out from inside the kitchen. We both hurry to the source of the noise to find Papa on his hands and knees, a full pot of spaghetti now spilled over the tiles, his shaking hands attempting to sweep it back into the colander it came from.

In this moment, they look so frail, so old.

This is their life's work, but it is evident, more and more each day, they are getting too old for the pace and workload this restaurant demands. I hit the floor on my knees and help Papa usher the last unruly strands of pasta back into the colander. Dark brown eyes topped with bushy eyebrows find my own.

"I don't know what happened. It slipped."

He rests back on his knees, hands shaking as they come to rest on his lap. Mama is by his side immediately, hauling her love to his feet. I clean up the mess as she sits him down at a table in the next room. I hear her soft words. Even though I don't understand them, I can read the tone, the love that laces them. The tenderness and concern.

They are too old for this.

They can't give it up.

I place the colander in the sink and mop the floor to a shine. An idea hits me as I swipe the head of the mop from tile to tile. I bite my lip. It's a crazy thought. Definitely a leap for me, and possibly not even an option for Mama and Papa.

Leaning the mop on the counter, I wring my hands through my apron. Mulling the idea over, I approach the table they sit at.

They both look exhausted.

"Mama, can I talk to you about something?" I ask softly.

Papa pulls the chair out beside him, and I sit. Mama folds her hands, one over the other, on the table in front of her.

"Do you have plans for the restaurant? I mean for the future?" The words come out in a rush. My heart hammers in my chest.

They exchange a look before the old lady's face turns to me. "What did you have in mind, Louisa?"

Not bella.

Not bambina.

Shit.

I crossed a line.

Nerves rack my body as a weight descends, hunting out the last of my air.

Papa tilts his head, brows lowering. "You can tell us, *mia cara*. As much as we love this place, we understand it will not be ours forever. Is that what you mean, huh?"

I nod lightly.

"I mean, I'm not your daughter. I don't even work here. But I had this thought . . ."

"She had a thought, *mon amore*, now I am intrigued." Mama's face is hilarious.

Her amusement, the adoration filling her eyes, lightens the ache behind my breastbone a little.

Laying my palms flat on the table, I look at them both

before saying, "If I work here every night, learn every recipe and the business side of things, would there be a chance you would sell the restaurant to me somewhere in the future?"

I hold my breath the instant the last word passes my lips. My gaze alternates between the two people who have felt like my own parents since day one. The silence ratchets up the tension.

It's a stupid idea.

I mean, they probably want to hand it over to some relative of theirs. I'm not even Italian, for goodness' sake. Loving a cuisine doesn't make you a master of it. I am such an idiot. Heat flushes my face.

Mama rises from her seat. Her cool hands cup my face, and I look up at her. My heart is doing its best to break through its confines.

I force a breath in.

A breath out.

"Is that what you want? To be here, for who knows how long? You don't have other plans?" Her words are soft, her eyes now laced with concern.

I know I have been indecisive the last few months. My plans have been anywhere else but grounded, but this place, this food. These people. They are solidifying in my heart. For the first time since my big dreams were shot to hell, I'm excited about something. *Sure* about something.

"Yes. It is."

I must look like a desperate fool, but it's not for the

reasons most people would think. They say it can only take a moment for a person to realize where and what they want in life. I look around the restaurant as the silence between us grows. The Mancinis exchange another set of unreadable looks only they can interpret.

A warm hand slides over mine. I turn to Papa. He says, "How about this. Since our life's work is going to have to support us in our retirement, we let you work here for a discounted buy-in. Then, in six months' time when we make the move to a new life in Florida to be closer to family, you can buy out the remaining equity."

I open my mouth to respond.

A buy-in.

They are letting me in?

Holy shit.

It's more than I would have expected.

"Yes!" I jolt from my seat and wrap him in a hug. "Heavens, thank you."

Mama hugs me from the side. Her fine hand squeezes my shoulder, and I turn to find her eyes lit up. "Bambina, you have much to learn. But we are thrilled to put our legacy into such capable, loving hands."

"For a price, Mama." Papa chuckles.

She slaps his shoulder. "Shush, you. The girl must do this the right way. Plus, this old lady comes with hefty retirement plans."

I release them both and step back. "What are we talking for the buy-in?" I spent some of my savings on

Harry's ranch. I'm praying what's left will be enough for the buy-in. I can keep working at the diner to sock away the rest. If worst comes to worst, I can ask the bank for a small loan to take over in six months.

"I think five thousand ought to be plenty. We can sort the rest out after your time." Mama looks to Papa, as if confirming the fact.

He simply nods.

"You sure this is what you want, Louisa? That's a lot of hours. The diner, then your nights spent here," she says.

I know she means less time for Harry.

But I have finally found my direction, and I'm not losing it now. I still have Wednesday and Sunday off. That's basically a weekend right there. It's six months, not forever.

"I'm sure," I finally say.

Mama wraps me in a tight hug. "This place has been waiting for somebody to come along and see it the way we do. I'm glad it is you, bambina." With a peck to the cheek, she releases me. "Come on, amore mio, leave this young girl to her dreams. This old lady is dead on her feet."

We bid goodnight after the Mancinis do a last cleaning sweep of the kitchen and lock up. I tread up the stairs, exhausted but excited at the same time. It's the first time in a long time I have felt that expansion in my chest.

It's something like hope.

Chapter Twenty

HARRY

Fencin'.

Because it's the only thing that helps me get out of my head. After the other night with Lou and the damn chocolate cake, my mind's been doin' three-sixties on repeat.

Everything from dragging her home to the ranch and not letting her leave to granting her the space she asked for. And everything in between.

I strain the top wire like my life depends on it. Arms flexing, I ratchet the tension on the strainers, pumping the iron handle one more time to give the wire tension akin to a finely tuned instrument. The old wooden post to my right creaks a little.

Just right.

I'm mullin' over where to go next with Lou. Tryin' to

grapple with the fact that the one woman I have ever loved, ever thought about, is still hesitating when it comes to us. To a life here in Lewistown, on this ranch with me.

I can't say I blame her. Hell, I fought hard to secure my *something* to spend my life workin' on, and I know she is desperate to find that for herself.

I'd been torn between her happiness and the life I always thought we'd have. But when I imagine her unhappy, even if it's being by my side that causes her that, I am willing to stomp on my own heart to protect hers.

So, I'm fencin'. Hands workin', mind a little slower, the knot in my gut a little looser. Me and fences have always had an unspoken agreement. I fix, maintain, and build them, they give me back my peace, if only for a little while. It's a good trade-off. A productive one. Nothing a little sunshine, fresh air, and fresh blisters from wrangling wire to solve a man's problems.

I pluck the pliers from my back pocket and secure the last length of wire, winding it back on itself and looping it around the taut length before twisting it back 'round. As if the fence is offering up the solution along with its completion, a notion comes to me.

Something so out there, it may just work.

I've always had Ma to help me find my direction. Maybe I can be that for Lou. Until she finds her feet and makes a concrete decision. The realization that this could go either way for me sinks in like the stone that slipped into my gut.

Just like that, this man needs another fence to fix.

Sweet Jesus.

Ma putters in the kitchen, humming to herself. Louisa's late. Which is not like her at all. Especially when it comes to Ma. I can tell by the way she talks about my mother and the care she takes, Lou is fond of her. They have a bond.

"Harry? Louisa should have been here an hour ago. Pop up the road and see she didn't break down, will you?"

Her gaze is fixed on me as I cart and stack wood into the living room, restocking the wood rack at the hearth. The days have started cooling off, and with fall only a few short weeks ahead and Ma feeling off so much this month, I won't leave having her end up in a cold house to chance. Tossing the last log into the rack, I rise and dust my hands on my jeans. Glancing the clock, my eyes widen. Hell, she is late. Lunchtime was two hours ago. Worry snakes through my body, laying its ill-fitting heat through my veins.

"Jesus, Ma. Why didn't you say somethin' earlier?"

"She's a capable girl, I thought she was running behind. But two hours is unlike her."

"I'll say."

I grab my hat from the hook by the front door and slide my boots on.

"Make sure you find her and bring her here!" Ma calls out behind me as I stalk through the door and cross the front yard to the truck. I fire her up, reversing from the parking space and sending her down the driveway like a man on a mission.

Gravel flies up behind the truck as I push the old girl as fast as she'll go on the potholed dirt road. Hands white-knuckling the wheel, I scan the road ahead for any sign of Lou's yellow Datsun.

Twenty minutes later, a small figure moves along the side of the road. I squint my eyes, tryin' to make them out. A few minutes later, I roll to a stop beside a flushed Louisa, haulin' two bags of groceries and her handbag. The smile that finds me when I lean over and push the passenger door open sends my heart straight into my throat.

"Hell, Lou, what are you walkin' for? You break down?"

Without a word, she dumps the bags on the center of the bench seat and slides on in. Her head slumps back to the back of the seat and she sighs, long and low. Her skin is flushed from walking in the midday sun, despite the cooler temperatures this week. Sweat glistens on her neck as moisture trickles down between her breasts.

She turns her head to face me, her eyes bright. Her lips parted, she says, "I thought you'd never find me."

She breathes a small chuckle and turns her head back to the resting position. It's all I can do to stare at her. Louisa exerted and out of breath is sending every last drop of blood south and all rational thought flyin' from my head.

I clear my throat, hoping it'll ease the need that is rapidly escalating. "How far up is the Datsun?"

"Too far," she breathes.

"Need me to take a look at it?"

"Later." She waves a hand at me, closing her eyes. "Take me to the ranch first, these ingredients are not going to last much longer. Plus . . ." Her head turns, and it's now I notice the low-cut top, the skirt grazing the tops of her knees. Her green eyes are laced with something I imagine mine are, too. "Rosie is waitin'. I hope she's not too annoyed by my tardiness."

"Tardi—" Fuck me.

"God, I am so hot from carting those bags. Who woulda thought food would be so stinkin' heavy?" She fans her chest with her hands.

I shove the truck into gear and turn her around. With the windows down, the breeze must be helping. The flush of her skin fades and she smiles at me while I drive.

"So much better," she says softly.

Her skin is a wash of goosebumps as I pick up the speed, her nipples hardened to peaks behind that low neckline. My cock aches from just taking her in like this. Out of breath, nipples that are just callin' my fuckin' name as her eyes stay stuck on me, occasionally drifting along my arms to my hands gripping the wheel.

"You gonna keep lookin' at me like that, darlin', this old truck is gonna have to pull over."

Her tongue darts out, licking her bottom lip. When they part again, her hand wanders to her neckline, pulling the material from her skin to cool down.

"I have a better idea." Her words are light and suggestive.

"I'm all ears, Lou."

Without a word, she moves from her seat and comes to sink onto my lap. The truck swerves as I slow down and look past her. "Sweet Jesus, woman, we wanna get there in one piece."

"My thoughts exactly. You and me, as one."

I almost lose my grip on the wheel. Darting my gaze to hers, I frown. "But the other night—"

Her mouth crashes down to my parted lips. She kisses me briefly before leaning back. I slow down and pull the truck over. "Lou . . ."

A finger presses over my lips.

"I have something to tell you."

"You do, hey?"

The prettiest smile blooms over her face as she says, "Uh huh."

"Spit it out, then."

Leaning back further onto the steering wheel, she studies my face, not saying a word. Her hands grip the hem of her shirt, pulling it from her body. It hits the truck's footwell, and I can't take my eyes off her. Those hard peaks I was admiring a moment ago are bared next. The heat in my core turns to a raging wildfire.

"Touch me, Harry. I want your mouth on me. Hands on me. Fingers, teeth. Whatever you can give me. But keep drivin'."

"Yes, ma'am."

I shift the old girl into gear and pull back onto the dirt road. Lou runs her hands through my hair, I nip her hard peak, tugging it through my teeth. She whimpers, arching against the steering wheel. I steady the truck as it takes a slight detour to the left and glance up at the gorgeous woman on my lap.

"Hell, we shoulda pulled over for this."

"Not yet, please."

She grinds on my lap. Her wet center soaks through my jeans as she moans with the friction between her sweet pussy and my rock-hard cock. Her hips roll and her lips find my neck, brushing up under my ear, and I groan.

Grip tighter on the wheel, I resist the urge to pull over, strip that pretty fuckin' skirt from her hips, and sink balls deep into this incredible fucking woman.

"God, Harry. When we're together, it's like nothing I've felt before," Louisa whispers.

Shivers skitter up my spine, sending the ache in my cock painful. "That's because no one else was ever supposed to touch you." The words are rough, claiming. Her mouth gapes, her eyes the darkest shade of green I have ever seen them. Choppy breaths leave her parted lips, falling onto my face.

"Fuck it." I slam on the brake and haul the truck to the side of the road. Plucking Lou from my lap, I lay her on the bench seat. Her desperate expression doesn't change as I hitch her skirt up and slide her soaked panties to one side.

"Harry, please . . ." The words are almost a cry.

Sweet Jesus.

Arousal slicks her thighs. Her pussy glistens, and I spread her legs as wide as the small truck cab allows. Instead of diving right in to where she is hungry for my touch, I grip her ankle. One sandal-clad foot resting on the steering wheel, I dot kisses from her ankle, along her delicate calf, to the soft spot behind her knee. She squirms on the seat as I nip her there. Her hips roll upward, affording me a much better view of the pussy I am desperate for.

Lou comes first.

In every way.

Always has.

Always will.

I reach her inner thigh, and she whimpers. "This here is my favorite damn place, darlin'. The ways I have fucked this sweet pussy in my dreams. Eatin' it whole until you come all over my face, legs wrapped around me. Is that what you want, Lou? You want me to make you come so fuckin' hard, make you fall apart?"

She snaps up off the seat, hands gripping my face, mouth claiming me. She opens, and I dive in, a tangle of tongues and teeth. Gripping her hips hard, I drag her toward me. Breaking the kiss, I kneel on the running board beneath the door opening.

"Mine, Louisa May. Not Brad's. Not some guy in Cali's. This was, is, and always will be mine," I growl. "Play with those pretty fuckin' tits for me, Lou. Roll 'em through your fingers, tug on them. Now."

Her hands tremble as she arches off the seat to release her bra. Her perfect goddamn breasts have my throat closin' over. I snap my gaze from them and run my thumb over her clit. It's the slightest touch. Cruel, when she is dying for me like this.

Her hands still, now only lightly holding the soft flesh of her lush, round tits.

"Play, Louisa. You don't get touched until you do," I rasp.

I want to watch her. I want her hot center wrapped around my digits, her pussy on my tongue, while I suckle her throbbing sweet bundle of nerves between my lips. I want her to know I am the only man on this earth who can do this to her.

Make her know pleasure so fuckin' good.

Make her come this fuckin' hard.

I will be the last man to ever claim this pretty little cunt.

I growl, and she bucks her hips toward me.

"You can do better than that," I growl.

She rolls one nipple between two fingers. Her breathing shatters. With the small mewl that slips past her lips, I almost lose my load to my boxers.

That's my girl.

"More," I snap.

"O-okay . . ."

Now both hands tug, squeeze at her soft flesh and tease her nipples. The cries that follow are something I'll store away for the rest of my life. Fuck me, this woman is stunning.

Devastation to a tee.

I send a flurry of kisses over the inside of one thigh, pushing it back further, widening her legs as much as I can. My rough palms hold her knees apart as I grace the other thigh with another cluster of kisses. This time I bite down close to her pussy. Her wetness brushes over my stubbled jaw.

"I can—I can't breathe . . . Harry."

Fu-uckk.

I glance up to make sure she is, in fact, breathing. Her

chest snaps up and down so rapidly I'm sure each of those useless breaths burns. "More, darlin'?"

"P-ple-ase. Please."

I'm taking my sweet fuckin' time. Making her wait. Making each time I touch her mean something. I'd be lyin' if I said a little of it wasn't outta spite for the ten years this woman made me wait. But who am I tryin' to fool? I woulda waited another five decades for the chance to do this.

I sweep her clit with my thumb, watching as even the smallest touch I make sends her reeling.

I want more.

Like the addict I am, I crave her—that's never been any different. I run a hand from her knee to one velvet pussy lip, teasing the wet entrance with slow up and down strokes. She wriggles her hips, chasing the touch.

"You desperate for this?"

One of her hands lowers from her breast, fingers brushing, hunting for her clit. Her mouth opens on a whimper. I bat her hand away.

"Mine, Louisa May."

I dive right in. One long, languid sweep through her wet center. Her legs fold around my head, as if she can't stand the thought of me being anywhere else right now. With two fingers, I tease her entrance as I suckle her clit.

Her legs begin to shake, caging me in further. I send my tongue around in erratic swirls. Lou's hands fly from her breasts, gripping anything she can find. One groping the seat's edge, the other the top of the backrest.

I sink two fingers into her.

"Harry!" My name is followed by a jumble of incoherent words as she bucks off the seat.

I clamp my teeth down around her clit before sucking hard. Her pussy strangles my fingers as she comes.

So fuckin' hard.

She's a twisted mess of limbs, trembles, and messed-up hair as her head tosses sideways. The sight is too much. My balls tighten and the sensation of losing control floods in.

I grip my cock the best I can through my jeans, but it's too late. As Louisa writhes against my face, I shoot hot, sticky ropes of release into my boxers.

Another thing I barely have control over when it comes to Louisa May Masters.

When she realizes I've inched away, her orgasm fades, and she sits up. Fine hands search for my head, prying it up. Green eyes find my own. "You okay?"

"It was a happy ending for us both," I rasp.

Delight fills her features. "But—"

I push to stand from the side of the truck. "I'll get you cleaned up. Ma'll be worried sick by now."

"Harry, no." She grabs my hand. "Please, let me love you, too."

"Think that particular horse bolted, Lou."

"Oh—ohhhh. Two happy endings. Sorry, I get it now."

She giggles, blush flooding her pretty features.

I narrow my eyes at her. "As much as I could see you naked all day, Ma might have a different opinion. Clothes, Lou. We need to get back."

She scooches over on the seat, pulling her clothes back on. The rest of the drive home is filled with comfortable silence. As the ranch comes into sight, Lou slides a hand into mine. Her words are quiet when she says, "You're not the only one who dreamed about what we would be like, Harry."

Chapter Twenty-One

LOUISA

Rosie stands at the kitchen counter with me, but her usual fire is dimmed today. She stirs the pot of red sauce, her hand shaking more than usual. I move closer to where she stands.

"Are you okay, Ro—"

Harry waltzes in after changing his clothes and doing a bit of bookkeeping. He dots a kiss to the crown of Rosie's head and snakes a hand behind my neck while his mother isn't looking, planting one to my jaw before winking at me as he strides out the door.

Cheeky man.

Rosie could have turned back and seen us.

It's not that I am ashamed of what lies between us. More the fact I don't want Rosie to get her hopes up. Or make it awkward for her in her own house. I am all too

247

aware three's a crowd. Ma's friendship is too valuable to me to ruin it by moving too fast, only to crash and burn.

"Do you think it needs more herbs?" A soft voice pulls me from my inner rationalizations.

"Hmmm. Let me try."

I pull the cutlery drawer open and grab up a teaspoon. Diving it into the sauce, I take a small portion and blow on it as it steams. I take a tentative taste, the hot liquid touching the tip of my tongue. Something is missing . . .

"Maybe a little more paprika. Just a touch. Otherwise, it's delicious."

She offers a soft smile, swiping at the paprika and dousing the bubbling liquid with a few shakes. I stir in it for her with the large wooden spoon. The aroma wafts through the kitchen, and now it smells perfect. Rosie takes a fresh teaspoon, repeating the tasting procedure. She takes a small taste, and her eyes light up for the first time today. "You're right. My gosh, Louisa, this is deli—"

Her face crumples, twisting in pain.

I discard the stirring and still. Something like dread curls in my gut. I could tell she was off from the moment I arrived.

The spoon falls from her hand, clattering on the wood floor.

She falters and slumps against the counter. I grab for her.

"Rosie!"

Her eyes are strained and fixed on my face. Her mouth opens to speak.

She gasps, clawing at my arm as I lower her to the floor.

No.

No. No. No.

God above, please no.

One hand falls away from my arm, then her palm pushes into her chest. She slams it over her heart, like that will dislodge the pain. Her face and neck are now reddened with strain.

I look around.

Harry is long gone.

I can't leave her.

"Harry!" I shout toward the window as I sink to my knees, trying to hold her up as I desperately hunt for something to help her. The phone is on the other side of the kitchen. The Lewistown ambulance is at least an hour away.

I cup her face in my hands as tears burn my eyes. "I'm going to get Harry, okay? Just stay here and breathe slow, deep breaths."

She nods, a shallow movement that fades out my last bit of hope. I take off through the house and burst through the front door. The truck is here, he can't be too far.

I sprint for the barn. "HARRY!"

I fly into the dim, hay-littered space.

It's empty.

No Harry.

"HARRY!"

I take off toward the old yards. Tears stream down my face, blurring my vision. This is not happening!

Shit, not now. Not when they just made a fresh start.

I stumble over the uneven ground in my house shoes as I cut through the field to the yards.

"Harry, where are you?!"

He bursts around the back of the barn, rushing toward me, terror contorting his features. He all but collides with me. Covered in dirt and grease, he grabs my arms. "Louisa?"

My face crumples, my head tilting. "It's Ma. Please hurry, she collapsed. I think it's her heart."

"Dammit," he growls, taking off toward the house. I take off after him. I can't stop the tears flowing down my cheeks. My heart thunders, panic clawing at my insides. I groan, pushing it down.

Not. Now. Louisa.

We are *not* doin' this now.

I hesitate, the rough grass prickling under my feet. With every breath, I will the hideous effects of anxiety back down.

Time and place.

And this ain't it.

Semi-composed, I take off at a run for the house. The gravel bites my left foot. I don't bother looking down.

Fear for Rosie drives me forward.

By the time I make it back to the kitchen, I realize I have lost a shoe, and Ma is lying on the sofa. Harry is pacing, the phone receiver in one hand, the other running through his messy hair. The long spiral cord stretches out and collapses against the wall with every lap he takes.

I limp to where Rosie sits and sink onto the side of the sofa. I swipe at my face, trying to dry it off. Her eyes are closed. Her breathing is steady but too shallow, and she looks so small. Her fine hand slides from her side, wrapping around mine.

"Promise me you'll take care of him for me."

"No, Rosie, please . . ." I force the words past an impending sob.

"I'm handing this ship over to you, my girl," she gasps.

I shake my head, dislodging welled-up tears.

Her expression turns pleading.

I nod. "I will, I promise. I got it."

The smallest smile moves her lips, and she closes her eyes. Harry appears by my side. "Ambulance is on its way, might take a while, though."

Rosie opens her eyes at the sound of his voice.

He leans over, taking one of her hands. "How's the pain, Ma?"

Her breath hitches, and she winces.

That's not good.

"Ma?" Harry drops to his knees by the sofa, both of

his hands now wrapped around her frail one. "Hold on, please."

Her head shakes, as if saying no. And when she turns to her son, a tear glides down her temple, soaking into the worn fabric beneath her.

"Water," she rasps.

He bolts to his feet and rushes into the kitchen. Rosie's gaze finds me.

"I did it for him—my boy," she whispers, taking my hands in hers.

"Did what, Rosie?" I say, matching her soft tone, barely audible.

"I had to." Her face breaks, but she schools it back. "This is my penance. He never would have let you two have any of this. He wasn't going to let Harry have . . ." Rosie glances toward the kitchen.

Who? Eddy?

Rosie Rawlins, what did you do?

I sit frozen, perched precariously on the side of the sofa. Harry starts his way back to the living room but halts halfway when he notices his mother clutching my hand.

"I know it wasn't right, but it was *necessary*." A tear slides down her cheek.

"Oh, Rosie."

"Promise me, Louisa." Her eyes are pleading.

She doesn't voice what that promise is, but I know she

means keeping what happened with Eddy a secret. To save this life Harry wants to build for us.

I bury my heads in my hands for a moment, working through long breaths. Footsteps pad toward us and I lift my gaze.

Harry lowers to his knees by her side and helps her sip the water. Rosie swallows and lays back down. He tilts his head, his brows lowering as his mouth wobbles to a thin line. His Adam's apple bobs before he says, "What are we talkin' about, Ma?"

"Your father."

"Fuckin' hell, Ma. Not now," he breathes.

I guess there really is nothing greater than a mother's love. She made a sacrifice so great, so terrible, for the chance for her only child to live the life he wanted. That kind of bond between mother and son is only something you imagine exists in fairytales.

Tears course down my cheeks, and when Rosie drags her eyes from Harry to meet mine, it's all I can do to force a smile. I can't blame her. Everyone thought it; she was simply the soul brave enough to do it. I hug Harry's shoulder, and Rosie winces again, her breaths quickening.

She is dying right in front of us, and there is absolutely nothing we can do. Rosie grabs at her collar as Harry runs a hand over her hair. "It's okay Ma, you'll be okay. Those trees of yours have been listening. You've done your bit. Carried your load well. Just rest . . . *Please*."

I sob into Harry's shoulder, trying so hard to stifle the pain of watching Harry lose his mother. Rosie's eyes fall shut. A small whimper leaves her lips as she rolls into him. He leans in, hugging her tight. He rubs her arm, talking softly to her. I wrap myself around him, not willing to let go.

After all she went through, they went through . . . For time to be cut off. It's—

Rosie goes rigid, then slumps.

Harry leans back, desperately searching her face.

"Ma," he rasps.

Oh god.

She stills, her hand wrapped in her son's.

Harry's head sinks to the sofa beside her, his body shaking so badly the sofa moves.

"Oh, Harry." I curl around him, nestling my face into his shoulder. A long, painful groan reverberates from him. I chug through sobs. He rises to his knees, resting Rosie's hand over her stomach, and turns to slump against the sofa.

On my knees by his side, I wait.

He stares ahead, his body still trembling, hands shaking in his lap. I take them and slide onto his lap, wrapping myself around him, like I can protect him from the agony that just found him.

He chugs sobs into my hair. His hands find my hips and grip tight. I hold on, hold against the pain ravaging his heart.

I'm handing this ship over to you, Rosie said. What on earth does that mean?

Her family?

Harry?

A renewed sense of protectiveness washes over me. Followed by something stronger still—unconditional love. For this man. This family of two who fought so hard to make the most of each day, despite the shitty hand they were dealt. If Rosie Rawlins had the strength to weather that monster of a husband of hers and protect her son all these years, I can do the same.

Harry draws a shaky, long inhale. I lean back, untangling myself from around him. When those deep blues finally hit home, I see torment and grief warring each other.

"You loved her well, Harry, you did so good by her," I whisper the words, thumbing his cheeks in a fruitless effort to dry away the constant stream running down them.

He simply swallows.

He's too still.

Shock is setting in.

I tilt my head, forcing the sob that wants out of my throat all the way back down. I promised to take care of him, and it's exactly what I am going to do.

"I'll put on the kettle," I say softly, rising from his lap.

His body jostles a little as I leave, but his stare stays

pinned straight ahead. My heart cracks clean in two for the only man I will ever love.

Huh.

The realization is like a slap to the face.

I grip the edge of the counter and take in a much-needed lungful of air. Shaking out the haze threatening to pull me under, I pluck up the old kettle and fill it at the sink. Turning the center burner on, I set it down and leave it to boil.

Down the hall, I take out a blanket for Rosie. Harry still hasn't moved when I return. I cover her up, folding her hands over her chest and making sure her eyes are closed. I run my fingers over her dark hair, letting the tears fall silently for a moment.

The kettle squeals, and I spin back to make the tea. As I'm pulling mugs from the cupboard, the faint oscillation of a siren fades in.

Too late.

Minutes later, a knock rattles the door. I pad to it and let them in, giving them a brief rundown of what happened. One of the men simply nods. The other walks outside to use his radio.

I cross the living room to where Harry sits and kneel by his side. "Harry? The ambulance is here. Let them see to her?"

Dark eyes snap to mine. A groan falls from him as he staggers to his feet. Without a word, he stalks for the back door.

It slams behind him.

The two halves of my broken heart shatter to smithereens.

Chapter Twenty-Two

HARRY

The wire burns my palms. I can tell by the blisters and the dank stench of seared flesh. My hands are numb. My mind has my heart all cut up. Every second, new and agonizing thoughts fill my head. Some are *what-ifs*. Some are the dreams and hopes that, after yesterday, died along with my mother.

The moon is my only light, the soft sounds of lowing cattle in the field behind the homestead letting me know I'm not dreaming. This is the brutal reality that found me less than twenty-four hours ago. The grief sears through me.

"Harry?"

The lilt of her voice tangles through my dulled senses.

I tug at the wire. It flings from its hold. Another strand cut and loose. I haul on it with my body weight as if it's responsible for every rotten thing in my life.

"Harrison Rawlins, you are gonna hurt yourself . . ." The voice is soft and carries on the night's tempered breeze. Grass crunches behind me. Something soft and warm lands on my shoulder.

The wire falls from my hands.

An elegant shape wraps around me from behind.

Louisa.

"What are you doin' out here?" Louisa says softly.

A stone lodges in my throat so tight it burns.

Her head presses against my back, her warm breath washing over my spine. My hands hang by my side as tears burn down my cheeks. They quickly disappear in the constant breeze. My tortured soul simply offers up more, drenching my cheeks and stubbled jaw.

Louisa hasn't left my side since they took Ma away. I can see her heart breaking alongside my own. It's written all over her face. But I can't find it in me to comfort her. As if, if I do, that means this is real. I'm already drowning, gasping for air. I don't want to take Lou down with me.

My ship is sinking.

It's a sure thing.

A wobbly sigh brushes my back before her arms slip away. She moves to stand in front of me. I force myself to meet her gaze. Her chin wobbles, but her hands cup my face.

"Come back to bed, Harry."

I let my focus drift to the mangled fence. The wires I cut and tried to manhandle from their sagging posts.

"I can't," I finally breathe.

She means the big, empty bed I sleep in while she lies on the sofa.

Yeah, no thanks. Hard pass. "You should go. You have work in the morning."

Her brows lower and her mouth falls to a thin line. "I am not leavin' you, you hear? Not now, not ever. Most certainly not for a shift at the diner."

Her words are fierce, as if she fought long and hard to gain this position and isn't budging.

"Suit yourself. I need to finish this."

"Then I'm helpin'." She glances at the dilapidated fence.

In one of my old work shirts for a nightie, her bare legs are awash with goosebumps. Her long blonde hair is mussed and hanging around her shoulders.

"Go back to the house, Louisa."

She picks up the pliers and closes them around the top wire, just behind the point it's secured to. She tugs at an angle, and it slips back and through.

"Louisa . . ."

"I ain't leavin'. If this fence is what you need to fix, then we fix it."

A shiver racks her body, but she sets her jaw and stands a little taller.

"Dammit, woman. Go back inside. I ain't askin'."

"Neither am I," she bites out, stepping into my space.

After a moment of the world's most ridiculous stand-off, in the middle of a field in the center of nowhere, only hours before sunrise, I look down to the only woman who's ever held my heart captive. Now she is standing at my side, fighting for me in my darkest hour, my lowest point.

And I couldn't love her more.

"If you say so, Captain." I pluck the pliers from her hand and fold her into my chest.

The tool falls to the ground when she says, "I do, Harry. I do."

Coffee sits in the mug between my hands. I sit in the chair at the head of the table while Louisa flips pancakes. I don't feel like eatin'. She insists I must eat. So, blueberry pancakes, my favorite since I was five, are sizzling away in the pan.

The sun is still rising over the mountains when a pile of pancakes appears in front of me. Lou drops into the seat at my left side and dishes up a hearty serving I'm sure would feed an entire corps of Marines. I ain't complaining. This beats her not bein' here. Beats doin' this thing alone.

"Here, syrup." Louisa leans over, passing me the glass bottle of maple syrup.

My hand folds over hers, halting her movement as I pin her with my gaze. I want her to know how much her being here means to me. How much I wish this could be our normal.

Our life.

"Thanks, darlin'," I manage, my voice rough from last night.

"I wouldn't be anywhere else." She offers me a soft smile before returning to her plate. She looks tired. My old work shirt is still the only thing covering her body besides panties.

As if reading my wandering eyes, she straightens.

"I'll go get changed." She moves to stand.

I cover her hand with mine for the second time. "Don't."

"Harry . . ." she pleads breathlessly.

"I need you to be you right now, Lou. Not worryin' about what's the done thing. Or how things will turn out tomorrow or next week or even twelve months from now."

She chews her bottom lip, dropping her focus to her plate.

I know that look.

There's something she's not tellin' me. And I don't know if I've got the heart to hear her out today.

To my surprise, she simply sits down and takes a bite of her breakfast. I do the same, not tasting a mouthful, even though I am desperate for some sort of distraction from the only other sensation in my soul—grief.

"I meant what I said earlier," Louisa says between mouthfuls.

"Which part?" I bite the portion from my fork.

"I'm staying."

I freeze mid-chew.

She looks back to her food, cutting another morsel of fluffy pancake before stabbing it with her fork.

I swallow hard. If she is stayin' because of what happened with Ma—

"I need to tell you something. But I'm nervous, and I don't know if it'll pan out?"

I set my cutlery down on the plate.

Now she has my attention. "Well?"

Her expression falls, and my own softens.

"I have—" She shifts on her seat and glances to the ceiling. "I made an offer on the restaurant."

I lean back in the chair.

Now *that* I didn't see comin'.

I stare at her. Louisa's been hot and cold with this old town since the day she blew back in. Almost as much with the folk who live here. And with me, well, it was touch and go for a while. But the restaurant, that's a huge commitment.

She would be stuck here.

"Say something, Harry." Her hands are tight around her cutlery, and I swear she's holdin' her breath.

"You mean, Mama's Place? In Lewistown?"

She huffs a strained laugh. "Yes, one and the same."

I'm shocked in the best way possible. A jumble of words tumbles up my throat. None are good enough. So, I simply say, "Come here."

A heartbeat later, Louisa May is on my lap. I can't handle the way she is lookin' at me right now. Hope tangles with something like worry in those pretty green eyes. "I don't know the first thing about business, so I'm kind of hoping you'd help me out there."

"You want my help to run the restaurant? When do you take over?"

She tells me of the conversation she had with the Mancinis, and I take in every word. Pride swells. Only to be overshadowed by the overwhelming realization that Louisa is stayin'.

For good.

Life is ironic. I lose one great woman in my life, the one who stood by me for the last twenty-eight years. Now I have a shot at spendin' the rest of my days with the only person to ever hold my heart indefinitely.

Absolutely and completely.

"It feels like bad timing now, with Ma and all," she whispers.

I shake my head.

"No, Louisa, perfect timing doesn't exist. I'm living proof. Besides, Ma would've wanted this for you. For us."

Us.

Lou's face blanks, and I fear I've gone too far. Fine hands cup my face, soft velvety pink lips brushing over mine as they mouth the word *us*.

I crash my mouth into hers with the intensity of a man who's felt too much and needed for too long. I haul her onto my hips as I stand. But when she loses the world's biggest yawn, I rest my forehead to hers.

"Bath and bed, little lady. You've done more than your share of takin' care of this man for one day."

"Only if you come, too."

"I highly doubt we'll both fit on the sofa."

She shakes her head.

"No sofa?"

"No sofa," she breathes, green eyes flooding with depth, stealing the air from my lungs.

Abandoning the pancakes, I pad to the bathroom. Depositing Lou on the vanity, I run the shower. While heat and steam shroud the small space, I relieve her of the old work shirt. Standing now in only her panties, she has me hard as fuck. But one glimpse of the purple bags under her eyes, and I usher her into the steaming water.

When we are both washed and I find Lou another of my clean shirts, I sweep her off her feet and tuck her into the right side of my bed. Like she goddamn belongs there.

I pad to the window and draw the curtains closed. Turning back to climb into bed, I find her sound asleep. I crawl in behind her and wrap my body around hers.

A small, soft noise leaves her lips as she wriggles

backward, closer to me still. Burying my face in her hair, I thank whatever supreme being Ma used to talk to in the trees that I have Louisa in my life again.

This time for good.

My heart aches with the loss of my mother, and I hug Lou tighter. It's surreal she isn't just down the hall like she's always been. It's as if life decided I couldn't have too much of a good thing. I couldn't have Ma *and* Louisa.

That Ma will never see us together, never witness the life I plan to build with Lou, stings. Tears soak the pillow, and I let them fall. I cling to Lou. My life preserver.

Sleep tugs at me, and I go down willingly. The world will have to wait.

Chapter Twenty-Three

LOUISA

The crowd of people who have flooded the cemetery for Rosie's service is a testament to her wonderful soul. Evelyn stands by Harry as I read the eulogy. Every line, every sentiment jotted down was offered up by the folks of Lewistown. She was loved dearly.

"Rose Elizabeth Rawlins, Rosie, was . . ." The words sound too monotone, a disservice to her spirit, but I read on. The page of Ma's life story I have studied on repeat since it was put together is too rote. ". . . a loving mother who devoted her last breath to her family, Rosie . . ." I glance up at Harry.

He shifts on his feet. Tears cut down his face, moisture glistening on his jawline. Evelyn leans in, squeezing his hand. A stone grows in my throat at the sight. My heart is a mangled mess at the sight of my Harry, heartbroken. As if I can, I speak faster hoping to shorten his pain. "She will be so missed, but never, ever forgotten."

My throat closes over as tears blur my vision. Small, huffy breaths leave Harry. The preacher gives me a nod when I manage the last line and scramble from my spot to get back to Harry's side. The crowd sways where they stand, sniffles and sobs splitting the cooling fall air. As if the loss of this great woman brought its own cold front.

Harry's hat hangs in his hands.

His head bowed down, his throat works with every breath. I slide in beside him, wrapping my arm through his.

What I wouldn't do to take away the pain eatin' him up. The coffin lowers, and we step forward to throw flower petals and dirt over it. Harry falters forward, plucking a handful of dirt from the pile and scattering it over the wooden surface.

I take up a handful of yellow wildflowers I found on one of the hills at the ranch. Unfurling my grasp, I watch as they float down into the now motionless resting place of Rosie.

Ma.

I chug through a sob and roll my lips together, trying and failing to tamp down the sorrow fighting its way out.

"Bye, Ma." Harry's raw and tortured words see me look up. He stands close, and his arm winds around my back. I rest my head on his shoulder.

"We should get to the community hall for the wake," I

say softly. I need to make sure everything is in place. Mama Mancini's been helping me for the past day and half to ensure there is enough food and drink. Evelyn organized everything else.

We turn back and wander through the cemetery toward the truck, and Harry makes a detour. An old oak shades part of the southern end of the cemetery, and he pulls me toward it.

"Where are we goin'?" I utter.

"Not to the wake, that's for damn sure."

"Why not?"

"I ain't sittin' around, small talkin' my way through folks feelin' sorry for me. Or Ma."

"I don't think that's really the intention . . ."

"Ain't doin' it, Lou. There's no use rehashing what's done."

"Then where do you want to go?"

I lean against the tree. Harry stops in front of me, plucking his hat from his head. It spins through his fingers, the brim turning over and over like he's always done. "Home."

"I have a shift tomorrow. Early." It's a six o'clock start. It takes an hour to get to town from the ranch . . .

Harry stares off into the depths of nowhere, jaw clenching. "That tiny apartment isn't your home, Louisa, and you know it."

I do.

I have for a while now.

"What about when I work late at the restaurant? My little old Datsun isn't exactly reliable."

"Then I'll drive you. Or you take the truck, if I'm not usin' it."

"I can't ask you to do that . . ."

"You can and I will. I ain't askin', Lou. We're doin' this. I won't stand to lose one more thing."

I look up into the canopy of the old oak. Its dark green leaves move with the breeze, each one dancing like it has no care in the world. Closing my eyes, I rest my head back against the rough bark. With a deep, steady inhale I feel all the way down to my toes, I let the vision of what Harry is saying take over.

For the first time in my life, I'm in the right place, in the right moment. The pieces of my life I've been juggling precariously for years are slowly, carefully falling into place. The old tree at my back groans when the wind picks up, the branches swaying and leaves hissing.

Emotion drowns my senses.

I know it's Rosie.

Her and her talkin' to the trees.

Even when we were teenagers, she would say her prayers out in the fields, her words carried away by Mother Nature, not God. For these parts, even then, it was a bit odd. But her wisdom and love outshone anything else. As the breeze winds around the old trunk, wrapping me in its embrace, I know for sure it's her.

"Harry?"

"Yeah, darlin'?" His words are grounded this time, his gaze pinning me where I stand.

"Take me home."

He hesitates for a heartbeat, but when I push from the tree, closing the space between us to rest my palm over his heart, he understands.

"Yes, ma'am."

His large, rough hand closes over mine on his shirt before he pushes his hat onto his head and leads me home.

The restaurant is bustling. I guess with folks still in town for Rosie's service, it's to be expected. People I don't even remember strike up conversations as I try my best to alternate between cookin' and waitin' tables.

Upstairs, my bag is packed. The few possessions I have are bundled up and ready to go. Harry is following me home tonight, to make sure the Datsun gets there. After breaking down last time, he worries every time I drive her further than the town's outer limits.

"Louisa, a moment, bambina?" Mama says, coming up behind me. I finish up with the table I'm clearing and follow her back to the kitchen, arms loaded with dirty plates and cutlery. Depositing them onto the counter by the sink, I wash my hands and lean against the counter.

"How are you?" Mama's eyes are tight, concern lacing her features.

"I'm fine. Thanks again for letting me out of the apartment lease. I need to be where Harry is right now . . ."

Mama shakes her head. "We understand. Whatever we can do to help, just ask."

I offer her a soft smile, glancing at the crowd through the pass.

"Louisa, if your plans have changed, we will understand."

"Nothing changes with the restaurant, I promise. Only my living arrangements."

She leans in, patting my hand as she says, "Okay, bambina, okay."

With that, she wanders to the dining space, checking on patrons, clearing away. I turn back to clear the counter before helping with orders. I don't want to back out on the restaurant. It's something I can immerse myself in. Something to keep me grounded. I have wanted that feeling for so long.

When the last happy dinner customer has left satisfied, I lean on the front doorjamb, taking in the small, intimate space. Life happens in this little restaurant. Loved ones catch up on quality time. Conversations happen—the good, the easy . . . the hard.

The occasional proposal.

It's nice to be part of something so central to the people of Lewistown. It's almost as if Mama's is the beating heart of the small town. Where Lewistown converges to find its soul. I sigh, letting my eyes close, trying to ignore the ache in my feet.

A voice clears from the sidewalk.

"You two need a moment?" the rough, familiar voice quips.

I open my eyes and push off the doorframe. Harry folds me into his embrace. I sink into him, letting the long day melt into his sturdy embrace.

"You makin' eyes at this old place is kind of adorable, Lou."

I push back and look up.

His arms still hold me close, his eyes lit up with mirth.

"For your information, Harrison Rawlins, the only time I 'make eyes' is when you're around."

"Is that so," he says softly with a chuckle, leaning in, his lips brushing past my ear as he takes a swift, light nibble. My body instantly presses against his again. "I think it's time to go home, Lou."

Untangling myself from his tight hold, I yawn. "Sure is. Wait a sec while I lock up and grab my stuff?"

"How about this. You lock up, and I'll grab your bags."

"Bag. There's only one."

He chuckles, dotting a kiss to the crown of my head as he walks inside and up the stairs. I finish as fast as I can and close up. Harry stands at the front door, waitin' as I say my goodbyes and head out. Locking the front door and leaving the back for Mama to take care of, I follow Harry to the truck.

"I thought you're following me out?"

"Nah, I want you close. Besides, we can do it next week."

As if he read my mind, I sag with relief. I am too exhausted to drive across the street, let alone an hour home.

Home.

It sounds more right every time I say it.

Placing my bag in the back of the pickup, he holds my door open. I hesitate on the sidewalk, taking one last look up to the window that was my apartment. At the almost deserted Main Street of Lewistown I have been living in for months. It's silly, really. I mean, I'll be back for my shift at the diner in two days.

Still, it's a significant change.

Warmth folds around me from behind. Stubble sweeps over my neck. "Come on, darlin'."

I spin in his hold, and he sweeps me up. I hum as he deposits my weary body on the passenger's seat. He fills the doorway, arms resting on the roof of the truck, head dipped. "One last question . . ."

I look up at him. The angles of his jaw are tight. His eyes are fueled by intensity as he studies my face. Throat working, he swallows. He opens his mouth, but slams it shut again.

His eyes close, and I need to know what is goin' on in that head of his.

"What is it, Harry?"

He taps on the roof with a finger before pushing off suddenly. "Nah, forget it, was stupid. Let's get you home."

He shuts the door, and my gaze is stuck on him as he rounds the front of the vehicle, opens his door, sinks into his seat, and fires up the truck.

Okay . . . What's that all about?

I figure I should let it go, maybe ask later. As the truck travels past the little town's outskirts, I lean against the window. Sleep drags me into its abyss.

Chapter Twenty-Four

HARRY

Lou is out cold. One side of her face squished against the window, each breath coming steady and shallow. I roll the old truck into the ranch, pulling up by the house. She doesn't wake when I kill the engine, and I sit there for a moment, taking her in. I thought I knew what I wanted when we were young. But the woman she is today, and what lies between us now, makes the first go we had at this seem like nothing more than puppy love.

I glance to the darkened house.

No lights on.

Ma isn't here anymore, keepin' the home fires burnin' while I'm away. It pangs like it has permission. My breaths shorten, and I shift my focus back to Lou. I can only imagine my misery if she wasn't here with me at this time. I can't say I'd be strong enough to move forward.

I am eternally grateful I will never have to find out. Shaking myself from the reverie, I pop the driver's door open and round the truck. Slowly, I crack Lou's door open. She murmurs something incoherent and rolls away from the door as it moves, opening wider.

"Come on, darlin'."

I pick her up and carry her to the house. She curls into my chest.

"Harry?" My name is a mumbled whisper.

"Yeah, Lou?"

"We home?"

"Sure are." I step onto the front porch and turn to the side, awkwardly grabbing for the handle with one hand while still carrying her. She sucks in a waking breath and opens her eyes. I stand still before the threshold as the door swings open, knocking against the wall.

Lou glances between me and the doorway. "Put me down, please, Harry."

Something like regret seeps through with each word.

Puttin' her down is the last thing I wanna do right now. She wriggles in my hold, and I relent, her feet meeting the porch. Her arms slide around my neck, and I dip my forehead to hers as she tries and fails to stifle a yawn.

"You can carry me over that threshold on a different day, Harry Rawlins. Not this one."

"If you say so, Captain."

She gives me a quizzical look before dotting a kiss on

my lips briefly as she turns away and glides over the imaginary line. It's all I can do to watch her go. Into her home.

Our home.

And hell, if she doesn't belong here, all is not right with the world.

Lou looks over her shoulder, her gait slowing en route to the kitchen. "You coming inside?"

Damn straight, woman.

She hits the lights and puts the kettle on, puttering around the kitchen as I hover in my own house like a fool, struck. It's then I remember her bag. I wander outside into the cool, dark night and tug it from the tray of the truck.

On my way back, I stop by the old willow in front of the house. Its curtain of green waves gently in the breeze, its soft hissing mesmerizing me where I stand. The stars overhead shine like I swear they never have before.

The whistle of the kettle pulls me from the ethereal state. Through the front windows by the dining table, I see Lou. She plucks an overhead cupboard open, taking out two mugs. The door creaks as it falls open when she tries to close it. I make mental note to fix the kitchen as soon as I can.

Walking back inside, I find her sitting on the old counter, mugs of tea on the surface, waitin'. I close in on her and drop the bag at the foot of the counter. She leans back, head tilting to the side as she glances to the mug at her left.

Mine.

"You look tired, Lou."

She picks up her tea and blows into the steam before taking a cautious sip. "Hmm, I'm okay."

She passes me the mug left, and I take it. The heat of the tea descends all the way to my stomach. Lou puts hers down before tapping the counter.

"Before I forget." She claims my hand, pulling me toward her. I nestle between her legs as she says, "Thanks for the lift."

Her green eyes study my face. With every inch they take in, they darken further. Her lips part as her hands take my jaw and slide down my neck.

"Wasn't a lift, Louisa May. I was bringing you home. There's no goin' back."

"Good," she breathes.

Ain't no need to tell this man twice.

I slam my mouth over hers, tugging her forward on the counter with a rough hold. She opens for me like it's the most natural thing in the world. I take what she offers up. Fine hands tug at my work shirt. I lean away from the counter as she pulls the shirt up and off. It's barely hit the floor before she starts on my leather belt.

I close a hand over hers and she pulls away, breathless.

Lips swollen, chest heavin', she stares at me.

I can't help the way one corner of my mouth pulls up at seein' her like this. For me.

Hell, it's all I've thought about for the last ten damn years.

"Har—"

"We haven't talked about this, Lou."

"What do you mean?"

"How we gonna do this. Plans, you know."

Her brows lower for a moment before her mouth pops open a little. "Okay, well, I'm on birth control. Living in Cali, it was . . . a prerequisite, I guess."

My gaze flicks up to hers.

A prerequisite . . .

For her to . . .

Heat floods my center, spilling over into my veins.

So other men could—

Her hands claim my jaw as it feathers. I'm not as naive to think she's never been with a man before, but thinkin' about her, tangled around someone else. Someone *not* me. My mind is short-circuitin'. My hands grip the counter either side of her.

"My love"—Louisa directs my face up so I'm looking right at her—"the only thing that matters anymore, and right now, is you and me. You hear?" Her face is stern.

My love.

A stone explodes into my throat.

Lord above, I'm an idiot on legs over this woman. And

I am going make sure I'm the last man she will say those two words to.

Ever.

"Loud and clear."

The sweetest smile blooms over her face. "So, still wanna talk?"

"Nope."

I snatch her off the bench, pulling her onto my waist. She giggles, her body pressing into me. That's all it takes to get me rock-hard.

"Help me unpack?" she asks.

"Now?" I growl.

"I can't very well sleep in Rosie's room. And your sofa is kind of terrible."

I see where this is going as I rub my jaw with a huffy laugh. "You realize that only leaves one bed, Louisa May."

"Does it?" she says, feigning innocence. She slips down to her feet and steps back, mirth lighting up her stunning greens.

"Yup."

"In that case, I guess you will have to be the ultimate gentleman, since we're not—"

I grab for her and smash my mouth to hers. With the tea cold and long forgotten, I walk her backward toward the hallway, real slow, as I deepen the kiss. Her hands wander through my hair, and lord above if that ain't one of my favorite places for her hands to be.

Breaking the kiss, Lou takes my hand, leading me to

the master bedroom. She stops short in the doorway. "You sure about this, Harry? About us?" Green eyes, worried, connect with mine. I wish to hell she would stop second-guessing every decision she makes.

"Woman, I swear to god."

"Well, if you swear, and to . . ." She points upward. Cheek lights up her not-so-tired-anymore face. "Oh! My bag, I need it."

I slide back down the hallway in my socks and pluck up the overnighter. When I get back, Lou is sitting on her side of our bed.

Our bed.

Fuck, I like the way that sounds.

I hand her the duffle bag that should be an overnighter, not an *all my life's possessions* bag. She needs roots, this woman of mine. I fully intend on giving her them. Along with anything else she asks for.

She places it beside her and pulls out a small pair of sleep shorts and a tank top. The thought of her wearin' those around this old house has me harder.

Dumping out her clothes, she organizes them into the dresser by the window, shifting my clothes aside. The moment really sinks in.

"All unpacked." She turns back to the sleepwear she left of the bed. No panties.

I collect the bag from the bed, but there's something solid and heavy left in the bottom. "Forgot something."

I widen the handles, peering inside.

A blush claims Lou's face as she tugs her bottom lip between her teeth. A shy, breathy huff leaves her lips as she grabs for it.

She misses.

Now I *have* to know what's in here.

I swing the bag away from her and leap to the other side of the bed.

"Harry!"

She crawls over the bed. Fuckin' *crawls*. Hair draped over her shoulders, breasts swelling over her top. Arms held out, she grabs for the bag a second time.

I turn my back on her and pluck out the hard item.

"Oh my god," she whines against my back, hands now gripping my biceps. Her forehead meets my spine as a little moan slips through her lips.

The hell?

A plastic cock-shaped object is in my hand. Hell's hounds, I have seen it all now. I hold it up, inspecting the vein-covered plastic implement.

Sweet Jesus.

Louisa tries to grab it, coming around my side. "They are everywhere in Cali. Women have needs, too, Rawlins. This is not the Dark Ages."

This is what she uses when she needs release? *Fuck.*

With a heady chuckle, I coax her to standing in front of me.

"Grant a dyin' man his last wish."

"*That* has you dyin'?" She chuckles and slowly brings herself to look at me.

"Fuck yes, I wanna watch you do that. See your sweet pussy swallow this thing whole."

"I—" She seems out of breath. "You have to do it, I can't. Not with you lookin' at me like . . ."

I toss the bag to the floor and maneuver her to the bed. She sits as I come to stand between her legs, punching the small power button. The vibrator hums to life, and Lou shakes her head as if fighting the blush that's deepened and consumed her face. My body is alive with tension as I send the tip of the vibrator brushing over her nipple.

She arches where she sits, like an addict after a fresh hit.

"Sweet Jesus," I rasp, sending the tip across to the other nipple.

What a way to spend our first night here.

Nothin' will ever get this man more riled up than the sweet, small sounds outta this woman's mouth. As I run the plastic gizmo over her stomach and let it drop between her legs, she gives me one of those pretty sounds.

Her legs widen automatically, eyes falling shut as her head drops back. Bracing with her hands, she leans back, her perfect damn tits pushing toward me. Like the desperate man I am for her, I dive right in, needin' every tiny morsel she will give up.

I rip the bodice of her top down, exposing her sweet flesh. My belt half undone, my chest bare, I lean down, claiming a pert nipple between my teeth. Nothin' will ever taste as sweet as my Louisa May.

"Plea—" She writhes under my touch, center circling against the buzzing instrument still in my hand. "Off. Take them off . . ."

Dropping the vibrator, I rip the material from her shoulders. She doesn't protest as I tear the flimsy material clean away from her body. The white lacy bra I find underneath sends the last of my blood roaring south.

Lou braces further back, lifting her hips. "Off!"

Yes, ma'am.

I thumb the soaked strip of material between her legs. A soft whimper tumbles from those pretty, kiss-swollen lips.

"Woman, you are a sight for sore eyes. So fuckin' wet."

Her hips wriggle impatiently.

I slide the panties down her long legs, nice and slow. The way I've wanted to for as long as I can remember. It's better than I imagined. The soft material under my calloused hands, her silky skin sliding past my knuckles as I lower the white satin.

Laid bare for me, she is more than I deserve.

She's stunning.

Drippin' wet . . . for me.

Mine.

"Up." I jerk my chin up, indicating up the bed. She moves backward, her eyes never leavin' me. I swipe up the vibrator. With my cock straining against my pants, I kneel between her legs. "This is what gives you what you need, Louisa?"

I press the trembling plastic into her clit.

"Ye—Yes, mostly."

That changes now.

I snap my eyes to her wet center. Her fingers grip handfuls of bunched-up duvet. I move the vibrator south, letting it sit at her entrance.

Nothing has ever felt more wrong.

This cold thing's been inside her.

I tug at my belt, sliding it from the loops, and toss it to the floor. Shoving my zipper down, I hold the vibrating wand still as I tug my jeans past my hips, taking my boxers down with them. My painfully hard cock springs free.

Lou's lips part, her breathing picking up pace.

Atta girl.

"Harry, I can't."

"I'll just have to warm you up first."

I sweep the vibrator past her clit before letting it sink into her glistening pussy. She arches, those perfect fuckin' tits bouncing as she moves with a choppy rhythm.

Fu-uck.

My cock leaks at the sight.

My last thread of control snaps.

Tugging the vibrator back, I throw it on the bed.

With a bruising hold, I grip her hips and turn her over. Lou scurries toward the headboard on her knees.

I close in on her and fist her hair, and she turns her head back. Eyes wild, she spreads her legs. Each choppy breath she takes hits my face before I claim her mouth.

Ten fuckin' years.

That's how long my damn patience is.

And it just wore out.

"I ain't askin, Lou."

I nudge her entrance as she nods with short, quick movements, her strung-out little moans the only audible noise leaving her lips.

I slam up into her.

Back arching, pressed into the wall, she cries out. Her hand finds mine at her hip, fine fingers squeezing my rough hold.

Her heat swallows me whole.

My chest caves.

I pull out in one long, agonizing stroke.

<h1 style="text-align:center">Chapter Twenty-Five</h1>

LOUISA

Too much.

Too big.

One stroke of Harry Rawlins, and I've melted into oblivion.

He pulls out, ever so slowly.

My body trembles from the loss. The air in my lungs reduces to nothing but cinders. Mouth gasping, I wriggle back an inch. How can he give me that just to take it away? I cant my ass up.

"No, Harry . . ."

He slams into me again.

Harry fills me up, consuming me entirely. Like no one else before. Emotion clogs my airways. I hold onto his grip like he's the last lifeline I have.

Who am I kidding . . . he absolutely is.

"Mine, Louisa May. You always have been."

A sob breaks through, falling through my trembling lips. I suck back the emotion. I want this. I want him. I want this life.

No.

Not want.

Not anymore.

Now, it's pure *need*.

I can't imagine another life worth as much as this.

He slides out. The fist in my hair shifts, turning my gaze to his again.

"This right here, darlin'? This is what stays. You and me. You feel lost, you come find me. I'm your true north. Always have been. Understand?"

I nod.

He slams into me harder, shaking his head. "Nope, I wanna hear you say it."

"Harry," I pant. "Right here, you're my home."

His mouth crashes over my parted lips. With every thrust, I tighten around him more and more. Each puffy breath burns as he releases my hip and his hand sweeps up my stomach, squeezing my breast. I lay my head on his shoulder.

"Fuck," he growls. "You have no idea—"

He swallows hard with a heady groan.

I find those deep blues, and they are devastating. Flooded with love, need, and something so surreal. It's the fire that makes him Harry. It bores into me. Finding my wandering soul and lighting it on fire. Now he's part of me, like I have been part of him since our first innocent kiss as high school sweethearts.

I can't breathe.

He waited so long.

Tears burn behind my eyes.

Jaw clenching, he drops his head, lips brushing my ear. "Breathe, Louisa May, we're right where we're supposed to be."

I fold my hands around his as he takes up a caressing rhythm. Warm kisses dust down my neck. Rough hands slide over my skin, coming to rest on my hips. "I want to watch you. I want to see us joined, Louisa May."

I nod, sucking in a shaky lungful.

He pulls out. I curl into myself at the loss. Harry sits against the headboard and holds his arms out. I walk on my knees, moving over his lap, knees on either side. He brushes my hair from my face, tucking it behind my ear.

"God above, you're so fuckin' beautiful."

His Adam's apple bobs.

I huff an amused sound, rolling my lips together as I press my palms to his chest.

"Come on, Lou. Show me what your stunning face looks like when it falls apart."

I rise, and he lines his fat tip up with my entrance. Still, even after being nailed to the wall, he's too big. His chest rises and plummets as I sink a little way.

Jaw clenched, his hands snap to my hips. "Sweet Jesus, woman." The words are no more than a low growl.

Heavens, this man.

I pause, only an inch or so onto him.

The stretch is everything.

Harry is everything.

I want to sink so low there is no way to tell where I start and he ends. So we can no longer be pulled apart. Leaving no possible way for life to separate us ever again.

I need this man in the worst way.

He leans forward, clamping a nipple between his teeth, and I have no control over the way my body sinks onto his. His raw rumble fills me up, taking over my soul, shredding it and ravaging every morsel of self-doubt, every sliver of uncertainty over where I belong.

His grip turns feral, bruising when I take up the rhythm between us. Lips parted on threadbare breath, I search the face of the man in front of me as it falls to pieces. His face tugs into something so desperate that catches me off guard so badly, emotion flares behind my eyes, flaring my breathing hot and fast.

Nope, I can feel whatever this undertow is, but I am steering this ship. I close my eyes, forcing my emotion into something I can give.

I cant my hips, taking him deeper, and his head falls back, hitting the headboard. Delight courses through my veins at the thought of turning this burly, stoic man to putty.

I love it.

Leaning down, I dust hot, wet kisses over his collarbones, tracking them upward, laying a trail up his throat as it works under the touch of my lips. I nip his jaw as I rise.

I plummet back down, claiming his mouth.

He thrusts up, and I can't help the whimper that spills out. He devours the sound, pushing off the headboard. Hands gripping my face, he sends his hips up, thrusting hard as I rock my hips.

Deep blue eyes burn into my own as he sends me spiraling, thrusting so deep. Again and again.

"Harry," I whisper, hands planted on his chest.

"Yeah, darlin'," he rasps.

"Where have you been all my life?"

A choked chuckle tumbles from his face before it twists into something tortured. His breathing disintegrates into choppy bursts. His hands grip down hard on my hips, and I still over him, eyes searching his.

Briefly closing his eyes, he says, "Waiting right here for you to find your way home."

He thumbs my cheek, moisture coating his fingertips. I didn't realize I let the tears slip. He kisses me hard, and I break apart in his hold. But when he leans back and his brows fall, I wait for the next Harry Rawlins revelation I know will blow me away.

And he does when he says, "You never left this man any other choice, Louisa May."

In this moment, I wish I could change the last ten years. Take it all back. Stay rooted to the spot that night he dropped on one knee. What I wouldn't give to take back all the hurt I caused him. The long, lonely years he lived through.

"No." He runs a hand through my hair. "I can see those cogs turnin'. Don't you dare feel bad for having a life. I wanted that for you, still do."

"I—"

His brows rise, as he dips his head as if reminding me to choose my words.

"I don't deserve you," I finally breathe.

"Yeah, you do, Lou. You just took a while to realize it."

My face falls.

Only Harry would know the self-consciousness I deal with, the anxiety that holds me hostage every time I want something. He is the one good thing I've never let myself have. Not in the last ten years. As if my heart knew how good a man he is. Screaming for me to stay away, unless I ruin him, too.

I scrunch my nose up to stave off tears.

Good lord, I'm a mess.

I put it down to the last few months. Nothing about it's been easy or drama-free.

As I settle into studying Harry's gaze, I'm hopeful for the future, down deep in my heart and soul. The kind of hope that lets you know, whatever happens in life, I will be okay, because I will be with him.

I will have him by my side.

No matter what.

Before emotion takes me under and sucks me in an undercurrent I can't escape, I palm his face. His rough stubble is heaven under my fingertips.

"Well, in that case, I will spend the rest of my days showing you how much you deserve this woman and this life you want so much."

He chuckles and pulls my mouth to his.

"You're on, little lady."

I wriggle my hips, my only weapon left after his confession. His blues darken immediately, and his tongue is wanting in. I rock my hips, and the bliss grows instantly.

"Fu-uck, Lou."

I rise to my knees until his tip only just remains inside me. This right here, the way his face is all strung out, the sweet agony of having him *right there*, I'm savoring it.

It's only when fiery blues find me do I lower, only a little. A half snarl leaves his lips as rough hands snap to my hips, and he slams me downward.

"Ahh—Har—" Eyes closing, my head falls back as I arch into him. The whimpers keep fallin' as he thunders up into me, his pace unrelenting.

His lips close around a nipple, and the mewl falling from my throat is raw.

Feral.

"Deeper, Louisa May?"

I nod my head furiously, not able to breathe a word.

Harry shifts, grabbing me around the waist. He kneels before resting back on his heels. I'm still above him, but he is impossibly deep. I can barely rise all the way up.

"Fuck *me*. So damn tight."

It's all I can do to stay upright on trembling legs as he thrusts hard. I grip his shoulder with one hand, the other fisted in his hair.

I open my mouth to say something, I don't even know what, but every last syllable, thought, evaporates with each new, harsh thrust. Harry's all hard stomach, muscular legs, corded forearms. I'm a puddle of something unrecognizable in his hold.

Lightning fires, short-circuiting each nerve in my body as he hits something so deep. There is no air left. I gasp, desperate for more, not caring I'm drowning in him.

I cry out when his hand leaves my hip and his thumb brushes over my clit.

Oh god.

"Lou, come for me. I need to feel you fall apart."

"Ha—"

I choke on a thin inhale.

His thumb continues to run circles over my clit as the bonfire in my core roars to life.

With a growl, he sucks my nipple. Hard.

I explode around him, hips bucking into his harsh thrusts. Back arched. My hand, still in his hair, tightens, white-knuckling his messed-up brown hair. His mouth parts as he winces, but his lips curl up the tiniest bit as I cry out.

He's taking in every shape my face takes, every sound I make, every movement. He's mesmerized.

Like I'm his true north, and he refuses to let his eyes wander, to lose focus. Never wanting to lose his way ever again.

I won't let that happen.

I tighten around him further, taking up the rhythm, desperate to give him back what he's given me. It's more than a release, it's my heart and soul, the days I have left to live. The happiness, joy, love, and anything else I can give. It's his.

It's ours.

Harry takes my face, dragging my mouth to his as he meets me thrust for thrust.

"I love you, Louisa May Masters," he breathes. His forehead meets mine, and he growls, low and heady, as hot ropes flood into me. I ride him through his release, wanting to draw out every last ounce of his pleasure.

Starting now, this man has my utmost attention.

His breathing settles as he leans back with his palms flat on the bed behind him. The sweetest smile pops over his handsome face.

I lean down and kiss that smile, dusting my lips over his.

"For the record, Harrison Rawlins, thank you for waitin' on me."

Something like disappointment flashes through his eyes, but he runs a finger between my breasts and up my neck before tugging on my bottom lip.

"Sure thing, darlin'."

Chapter Twenty-Six

HARRY

"You good with a stick?" I ask as Louisa slides behind the truck's wheel. The dawn's light seeps around the broad mountains to the east. I pluck the collar up on my jacket and throw Lou's extra coat onto the seat beside her.

"Yep, no problem." She fires up the old girl like she's been doin' it forever. I shut the driver's door and lean through the open window. The weather is coolin' off more, and I need to ride out to check the herd. Lou's workin' a shift at the diner and then one at the restaurant. It's gonna be a late one. "I'll see you later, sweet man."

Dotting a kiss onto her forehead, I step back as she drives off, making her way to town. My days are long on the back of a horse, but they pale in comparison to being on your feet all day and half the night, trying to keep her dream going and scratchin' out a livin'.

Hardest workin' woman I've ever known.

Sorry, Ma.

That sees me pause. The next cold breath sends an ache spreading through me like it had fuckin' permission. It hurts. The absence of her. The things she will never be here for. I readjust the hat on my head, swallowing past the lump in my throat. The wind picks up, changing direction, buffering against the old worn hat on my head.

I can almost hear the words right outta Ma's mouth.

Now, don't you go feelin' sorry for me, my love. Things are just as they're meant to be.

The old trees surrounding the house creak as the wind wrangles its way through their old branches.

I clench my jaw, stuffing the splinter of pain back down. Ma wouldn't want me pining over what could have been and things that may never have been. So, I stalk my way toward the barn. The cold earth and dead grass crunch under each step. The gelding nickers as I walk through the door into the slightly warmer space.

I make quick work of saddling up, and I swing into the saddle and turn the gelding for the mountains. A few steps from the barn doors, I hesitate, looking back into the dim space. The Winchester hanging by the side of the weathered doors snags my attention. My gut flips.

I recognize the feeling, and it ain't one I make a habit of ignoring. I trot to where it hangs and pluck it from the wall. A small bag of bullets hangs on a hook where it was. I snatch them up, too, and tie them to the side of the saddle before swinging the rifle over my shoulder and pulling the strap tight.

Past the barn and yards, I head for the foot of the old hills that have stood here for generations. They have witnessed the rise and fall of every man who's tried to tame their surroundings and feed their families.

The secrets they could tell.

I push the gelding into a lope and tuck my chin in, shoving my hat on harder. The wind's icy fingers sneak behind my jacket occasionally, and I make good time to the lazy blue giants. The first remnants of snow have started to show on the higher terrain. I'm not goin' that far. Not today, at least.

I make the first pocket of the climb, and I swing out of the saddle to give the gelding a rest. He's breathing hard from the ascent. The small herd I pushed out this way a month ago shouldn't be too far away. If they are smart, they'll be on the lower ridges, protected from the wind and the cold. And close to water.

I check the ground for any sign they've been here.

I squat down, brushing a hand over the short, frost-burnt mountain grass. After a few minutes of doing the same, I shift debris to find the round outline of a cloven hoof print. A few steps toward the rise, I find a ton more. They were here. By the manure droppings to my left that are still warm and wet, very recently.

I pull up into the saddle and push the gelding up the rise, following the tracks. I tug my collar up. The higher we rise, the sharper the cold. I shiver as we spill over a ridge and onto a plateau.

The large green span flanks the side of the mountain, and I find a small cluster of the herd grazing away contently. I trot around them, taking stock of their numbers and condition. By my count, it's only a third of the cattle I sent out here.

When every beast counts, this is not what I needed to find.

"Fuck," I growl, rubbing a hand over my jaw. The stubble Lou's been hinting needs to be shaved barely registers on my cold fingers. I turn the gelding toward the rise and push him into a lope. We race toward the trees, tracking south.

The wind whips around. The horse tosses his head. The rifle slaps at my back as we make a bumpy path through the dense, woody trees. Light snowfall lets me know we're getting higher. The fallen debris is too much, and I slow the horse back to a walk. Then I hear it.

Howling.

Howls.

Multiple.

Dammit.

I rein the gelding to halt and listen.

The coordinated calls of the wolves echo through the trees from my right. The pack must be higher up to the south. I ride toward their call. My gut tells me the sound is anything but good.

We push through the dense timber, making slow time, but when the calls pierce the air around me, I slide the reins into one hand and pull the rifle from my back. The mountain makes a sharp drop, and I ride down it. It's like an old stream, winding around the side of the mountain. The perfect goddamn place to herd a bunch of cattle, if you're a wolf.

I follow the depression around the next bend.

What I find makes my blood boil.

A small herd, around twenty head, stand trapped. Flanked by the pack. Six in total. The wolves have already killed. Five of my herd lay mutilated on the ground. This is more than survival, they're playin' with them. Probably figure they'll eat whatever doesn't make it out of their ambush.

Too clever for their own good, filthy mutts.

I study them for a moment, still as can be. The gelding's ears are pushed forward, his back curled up. Two smaller dogs are to the left and right, a larger one taking point. One stands back, as if he's backup or too fuckin' special to get his paws dirty.

But the middle two are the biggest.

The gelding shies to the left.

A stick cracks under his hoof.

The wolves spin back. A few are still homed on the cattle.

The gelding steps back. I push him forward.

The low, feral growl of the biggest wolf vibrates

through the mountain around us. I cock the lever of the rifle.

I'm gonna have to be quick.

I got five shots, six wolves.

I'll be lucky to put down two.

The odds are not in my favor. Or that of the other prey animals on the side of this mountain.

The center wolf steps forward, head down. He snarls at me. I raise the rifle and look down the barrel. I take note of the dogs on either side of him.

He growls, lunging for the gelding.

The trigger gives way under my finger.

The rifle cracks.

The wolf slides to the ground.

I shift to the left.

Aim.

Squeeze.

Crack.

The whines and howls following have the four left high-tailing it up the side of the mountain, disappearing into the trees. The gelding shifts on his feet, bobbing his head.

Poor little man, too much excitement for him.

I swing out of the saddle and give him a rub before taking the reins over his head and in one hand. I walk to the first beast.

One of my herd cows.

Fuck.

She's still alive, only just. Lyin' in a pool of her own blood as it turns stiff on the frozen ground.

"Sorry, girl." I lift the rifle and shoot her point-blank. No need for her to suffer. The next two are dead, the last two not so lucky.

A small heifer and a calf, a little bull, lie gurgling in their own blood, their throats shredded. They won't last, but I won't let them suffer, either.

"Fuck me." I take my hat off, shoving my hand still holding the reins over my head. "Dammit!"

Reloading, I tap the last two.

Jesus fuckin' Christ.

"What a damn mess," I mutter to the gelding as I swing into the saddle.

I heard the remaining cattle down the hill. It's slow going and they are skittish, rightly so. Poor things. We reach the small bunch I found first, and I let them settle in and lope around, doing another once-over.

I wait a while to make sure they're not gonna spook and take off back up the mountain. Two wolves down, four to go.

The house is dark again when I finally make it back to the

flats before the fields between the barn and the mountains. The gelding and I are both exhausted.

I never found the remaining four wolves. Their day will come.

I estimate the loss, mentally calculating the deduction as I sway in the saddle, almost home. The loss of the breeding cow is the greatest. She would have produced calves for years. Closing my eyes, I let the long day melt from my shoulders, imagining coming home to Lou. The house lit up. Inside, the amazing fragrances of her cooking, everything warm and homey.

A fire crackling in the hearth.

Whiskey burnin' down my throat as I toe off my old boots.

I let the twilight dream take me down . . .

The ruckus of family.

Little ones running amuck under her feet, her belly swollen with our latest addition to the Rawlins clan.

The gelding tosses his head, slapping me out of my wishful thinkin'.

Making it over the rise, the homestead comes into view. The house is dark and the driveway empty.

No truck.

No Louisa.

It smarts like nothin' else.

I want her here.

I want her beside me. If the house is dark, it should be because she's on the horse beside me.

"Hup!" I push the gelding into a lope in a hopeless attempt to catch that last dream. My rational mind gets the better of the stray hope, reminding me we lost five head. Our herd is too small already. The first mortgage payment comes due in a few months. The chance of this place turning over enough for both of us to work the ranch and have no external income is slim to none at this point.

We fly into the barn, and the gelding slides to a halt over the hay-littered ground. I'm out of the saddle and snatching the tack from his back a heartbeat later, all but tossing it back to the hooks in the run-down tack room.

The ranch is far too big for one man to work. I'd need at least another four men to cover every acre of this old place. But I can't even afford the keep of the one man who lives here.

"Fuck!" I slam a hand into the side of the barn. The gelding jerks his head up. Cursing under my breath, I slide a rope around his neck and hose him off before tucking him away in his stall. At least he's safe from the wolves.

I mix up his grain feed and dump it into his side feeder before replenishing his water. After I'm done, I tidy up and pad back to the house. My legs ache from hours in the saddle. The stress of losing good cattle and trying to piece this puzzle of working the ranch from the ground up has my shoulders bunched like nothing else.

I tug off my boots and toss my hat to the hook as I

walk through the front door. The darkness greets me, and I remind myself Lou will be home in a few hours. Exhausted, I flop onto the old sofa and pull the whiskey decanter from the old coffee table Ma found in town before—

I fill the small crystal glass too full and slam it down. The heat snakes down my throat and I drop back, letting my head fall on the back of the sofa.

I have no idea why I thought I could do this.

Maybe the old man was right.

Playin' rancher and being a rancher are not the same thing.

The numbers alone are enough to balk any man. Even with a good year, the numbers only just add up, especially if you're needin' men to do the work.

Groaning, I slide farther down the sofa and pour another whiskey, this time a little smaller.

It warms me from the inside out, and I stare into the unlit fire.

Hunger pangs in my stomach.

Food would help.

I bet one meal of Lou's would fix this thinkin'. I can't cook to save myself. I push out of the sofa, slow. Padding to the kitchen, I pull the refrigerator door open. A casserole bowl with lid sits in the center with my name on it in Louisa's handwriting.

Harry. Eat, my love.

I'll be home as soon as I can.
L xx
P.S. Heat it up in the oven, 10 mins (preheat to medium heat).

I rip the lid from the container, and the smell of the tender vegetables and marinated meat hits me. My mouth waters from the smell of it cold. I can only imagine what it tastes like hot.

I move to the oven and set it like she said. Deciding to shower while I wait for it to preheat, I make short work of washing the day's disaster off. I slide old sweatpants on and forgo the shirt, still hot from the shower. The oven is ready when I head back into the kitchen, and I set the casserole dish onto its middle shelf.

Fifteen minutes later, I'm blowing on the spoon I chose to shovel the food down fast. It smells divine. Tastes even better. Before I know it, I'm swiping a finger down the side of the bowl to get the last of the sauce.

"God above, this is good," I mumble, slipping my finger into my mouth.

An amused huff comes from the doorway.

"Good to know you like it."

Chapter Twenty-Seven

LOUISA

Harry spins around, spoon in hand, finger between his lips. He looks like a kid caught with his hand in the cookie jar, and I have never loved him more. It is always a pleasure to see people enjoy my food, but this is next-level satisfying. Seeing him this besotted with my go-to, no-time-to-do-anything-fancy casserole is overwhelming. It almost makes me want to stay in this kitchen for the rest of my days, barefoot and cooking just for him.

Almost.

"You're back early," he says, standing.

His hair is damp from a shower, and he's shirtless.

It's more than I can take. I drop everything, not bothering to shut the door to keep out the cold, and am in his arms a beat later.

"Is everything alright, Lou?" he mumbles into my hair.

"It is now." I slide my arms around him, sinking my face into his chest and breathing him in. The last few hours were stressful, to say the least. The diner was my sure thing. But after this week, I have been let go. Darla got wind of me buying out the Mancinis and took it to heart, and not in a good way.

"I lost my job today, Harry." The words are muffled.

He simply hugs me tighter. Warm strength envelops me, holding steady. I can't think about what it means for my chances of scraping together the rest of the money to hand over to Mama when it's due. I can't see past the hurt in Darla's eyes as she sat me down after the lunch rush to hear the words from the horse's mouth.

"What's this I'm hearin' bout you buyin' Mama's Place?" Darla's eyes tighten, brows dropping. Worry mixes with hurt as she stares at me from her seat on the other side of the booth table.

I shift on my seat. I'd forgotten how small towns operate. God, I'm an idiot. Of course I should have considered her before making the offer. How this would impact my job.

I'm operating on Cali standards, logic and opportunistic thinking surpassing the village mentality that still runs strong and true through this little town.

"I'm sorry, I didn't even think. I'm used to people not caring either way. In Cali—"

"This is Lewistown, Montana, Louisa. We're all like family. You don't pull the rug out from under family. I guess you'll be wanting to open for lunch now, seein' as you have all that stored-up talent and nowhere to put it?"

The words sting. They may sound like a compliment, but they are the furthest thing from one.

"That's not how this is, Darla. I swear. I have no lunch plans. I mean—no plans to run a lunch service. All this is so new to me, but I needed some place to work and call my own. I'm stayin', and Mama's Place affords me that."

"I see." She leans back in the chair, folding her arms. She may as well have called it. The end of this conversation. The animosity is practically pouring off her peach uniform in unchecked waves.

"Mama's Place will maintain the same operating hours it has now. You can't possibly see this as a threat. Your diner is the best on Main Street."

"And there's a reason it is, Louisa. Hand in your uniform and apron after your Friday shift. Cynthia will cover for you from then on."

"Darla, no. What the hell?"

Heat prickles up my neck and engulfs my face in its hideous flames. I force air in and out of my lungs. Darla rises from the booth.

"This isn't California, Louisa. Folks around here take this sort of thing personal." She walks past the counter, disappearing into the back room. I sit there, staring. Any hope I had of funding the remaining payout for the restaurant just went up in smoke along with any goodwill I had here.

Not good.

Really, really not good.

"You needin' work couldn't have come at a better time," Harry whispers.

Confused, I frown, looking up into those blue eyes that are a mix of concern and wonder.

Heavens above, sometimes I can't get a read on my Harry.

"What d'you mean?" I study his face.

"Well, it so happens I am in desperate need of a ranch hand." He holds me at arm's length before turning me side to side, running an inspecting eye over my form. "Not bad. More than I can say for the pay. Which is none."

The biggest grin splits his face.

How can he be this happy about this?

"Harry, I needed that job to pay out the Mancinis. Unfortunately, I think Darla realized that."

His face falls instantly.

"That's fuckin' low, even for this small town."

"Yeah, well." I sigh. "What's done is done. I need another job that pays the same as the diner."

"How much an hour was Darla payin'?" he says, letting me go as he walks for the hearth.

"Two thirty an hour."

He glances back, the concern on his face deepening. "Lou, that's below minimum."

"Huh, should have known. Thought maybe she was taking the uniform allowance out."

He tosses logs onto the sooty bed of the fireplace and stuffs kindling underneath the darker hardwood before lighting it. He pushes back up to his feet, groaning, and heads for the sofa. I round the worn seat and flop down next to him. Swiveling on my seat, I drape my legs over his lap and rest my head on his shoulder.

"I'm not sure if I'll find anything else. Apparently, word travels fast in this tiny town. But maybe the grocer will take pity on me?" Even the words sound like defeat. Harry lays his head back, staring up at the ceiling.

"How much have you put down, percentage wise?"

"Around a quarter of the total now."

"You've done well, considering Darla underpaid you."

"Yeah well, might all be for nothing now."

"No, darlin'." He turns, his gaze meeting mine. "We will make this work. All of it."

I huff a small sound that sounds like amazement.

Hell, it is. He never ceases to amaze me.

"You know something, my love?" I say, almost a whisper.

"What?" He leans closer, his arm sliding behind me, tucking me into his side.

My heart all but explodes.

"You are something else, you know. There's never been a man on this earth who loves as hard, has so much faith in the people he loves, and—" I scrunch my nose up before drawing a long, steadying breath. "Who's believed in me so unconditionally."

His lips meet my forehead. "'Bout time you figured it out." A quiet chuckle shakes his body, now pressed to me.

I huff a breath and it hits his shoulder.

Smart ass.

But he's right. It took me way too long to learn who this man is to me. I'm done being clueless. If two people ever stood a chance to build something from nothing, it would be Harry and Louisa.

The ache in my legs and sore feet fade as I look up to an angled jaw and deep blue eyes. The five o'clock shadow claiming is face is sexy as hell. All I want to do is melt into him, pretend the rest of the world doesn't exist anymore.

Just for a while.

The early morning rays have only just splintered the horizon when I roll over to find the bed empty. Harry's spot is cold. Fragrant aromas of coffee and bacon waft down the hall and rouse me from the warmth of our bed.

I love that. Our bed. Like we are already doing this thing together. Like we are the only two people on God's green earth.

Out here, maybe we are.

I wander toward the kitchen to find a fully dressed and ready for a workday Harry. Socked feet slide across the hardwood floor as he scoots over to the stove, flipping the bacon sizzling on the heat.

"Hmm, he cooks."

Harry glances over his shoulder. "A little. Don't get used to it. It ain't my forte."

I chuckle and slide onto a stool at the counter. "Smells just fine."

"*Fine,* she says." He tosses three strips of bacon onto my plate and plucks a piece of toast from a pile on a plate to the one in his hand. "Here. Rancher's breakfast, for the newest ranch hand on this old place."

"You make all your new employees breakfast?" I raise a brow.

"Only the ones I can't get out of my head."

I take the plate in exchange for a warm smile. "You know, you should give this ranch a name." I pick a slice of bacon between two fingers and bite off the end. It's delicious.

"One day."

"One day, you need to give many things a name. Like poor old Horse. You can't possibly expect a girl to give it her all when she doesn't even have a name, Harry. That is the furthest thing from commitment."

He looks up at me and stills.

What'd I say?

Commitment?

His jaw feathers as he finally says, "You give her one. She's yours now."

My face lights up. "Really?"

He chuckles and shakes his head. "Really. Can't go expecting you to work a herd on foot now, can I?"

"What should I call her?"

"Lou, if I knew that, she'd have a name."

"Of course." I slip off the stool and head to the refrigerator for the butter and condiments. Back at the counter, I smother the toast in buttery goodness and take a bite.

Nothing beats butter. So simple, so satisfying.

"You and the butter need a minute?" Harry's voice breaks my savoring moment. I toss a bacon strip at him, and he throws two hands up, snatching it before it hits the ground. "Mine."

I finish my toast and set the knife on the plate. I round the counter and slide in front of him, between the counter with his food and where he stands. "Anything else you want, Harry?"

His jaw feathers, but he bites the last mouthful of his bacon and chews slowly. His eyes darken for a moment before he swallows, and his hands grip my hips. His stare breaks away only to rove over my tiny sleep tank and shorts.

"Yep, you on a horse in ten." He winks at me, literally *winks* at me, as he turns back, kills the stove, and walks back past on his way to the bathroom. Reaching the hall, he turns back.

He raises two fingers to his forehead and salutes me. The breath in my lungs stalls out, like I have any modicum of say in what just happened.

I clear up and get dressed. The only jeans I own will have to do. A pair of old boots sit at the foot of the bed with the old hat of Harry's I borrow. Sliding the boots on over my socks, I push the hat onto my head. It's a little big, but it'll do.

"Now you look like you're stayin'."

I spin back to find him leanin' on the doorframe. He pushes his hat on as his shoulder leaves the jamb. "Come on, this ranch ain't waitin' for no man." His lips curl into a smile. "Guess that should be no woman, this time 'round."

I close the distance between us. "Guess so."

He dips his head, his hands taking my face in a rough grip. "I can't promise you it won't be hard, only that it's worth fighting for."

A stone grows in my throat, lodging tight, but I manage a few syllables.

"The ranch or us, Harry?"

We both know what we're getting into. The intensity of what we've always had wasn't without its drama. His moodiness. My inability to let things go, the overthinking and worrying.

God, my stupid brain, I should take the statement back . . .

"I didn't—"

His kiss renders me speechless. The panicked thoughts screech to a halt.

When we part, breathless, he pants where he stands.

"Hell, woman. How we gonna get any work done when I can't keep my hands off you?"

"Commitment," I breathe.

A small smile pulls up on one side of his handsome face, sending my gut flipping like an overcooked pancake.

"We'll get to that part, darlin'." He releases me and nods toward the front door.

Damn you, Harry Rawlins, everything is always a double meaning.

I set my shoulders back and slip past his large frame in the doorway, heading for the front door. Footsteps fail to follow, so I glance back. "Come on Harry, wouldn't want to be caught slackin' off."

He shakes his head and is behind me a beat later.

By the time we get to the barn, his hands find my hips, his mouth on my neck.

"Dammit, Louisa May, watching you sway your way to the barn is pure fuckin' torture."

Inside the barn, I spin in his hold, walking backward as I look up to his darkened blues. "Work before play, sailor. I promise it'll be worth the wait."

"Yes, ma'am" is all he says.

I walk away, leaving him stalled out where he stands, and head for Horse.

Chapter Twenty-Eight

HARRY

Fine fingers brush over the trigger of my Winchester. I wrap my body around Louisa from behind. I can't send her up the mountain in good conscience, knowing what she'll find, without giving her a way to defend herself and Horse.

"Like this?" Lou asks softly, jaw set as she concentrates.

"Yup. Brace the butt of the rifle into the hollow between your shoulder and chest, raise the piece so you can look down the barrel, aim with the marker on the tip. See the tiny lug at the end?"

"I see it."

"Good, aim."

She sucks in a breath and holds it as she moves the rifle. It's an almost imperceptible movement. Precise and accurate. She's already good and hasn't let off a shot yet.

"Target acquired, sir." She gives me a cheeky sideways look.

Sir my ass.

"Somebody's been watching too many action films," I drawl and tighten my hold on her before stepping back. "Squeeze your finger over the trigger and be prepared for the kickback."

She gives me a subtle nod.

Another inhale, she stills, and . . .

Crack.

The small paint tin on the fence post yards away flings from its spot, crumpling as it falls into the grass.

Hot damn, woman.

Lou's eyes light up as she turns to me, pointing the rifle to the ground. "I did it!"

"You did. Good shot, little lady. Next one," I say, nodding to the next post along. The can is smaller, more like a soda can.

"Yes, sir."

She readjusts her position and aims.

Crack.

The can wobbles but doesn't fall.

Missed.

"Shit!" she growls.

A chuckle falls from my throat. The disappointment on her face forces it to fade out, and I give her a nod. "Again."

Brows lowered, she sets her jaw, fire growing in her eyes.

That's my girl.

"Time to meet your maker, Mr. Can," Lou hisses.

I rub a hand over my jaw to stifle my laugh. She's adorable pissed off. And absolutely fuckin' formidable as she is quick to aim.

Squeeze.

Crack.

The can flies off the post and into the air.

"Little fucker," she breathes.

Doubling over, I cackle at the face she pulls at the can before setting the rifle down. I lose it.

My Louisa May has a dark streak, who woulda knew?

"Any more targets you need taken out?" She's trying her best to tamp down the smile that's stretching her face.

I hold up a hand. "Just a minute."

I try for a breath, but the hysterics roll right back in. My hearty laugh has her giggle softly as I clamp a hand over my side, desperate to ward off the rising ache.

"Was it okay for a first time?" Lou's brows have fallen again.

I know she thinks the laughter is at her, not with her, now. That sobers me up, quick smart. I let the chuckle roll away and stand tall. "Darlin', remind me not to get on your bad side any time soon."

Delight drowns out the concern on her face. "So, that was good? How long should it take to learn to aim?"

"Louisa May, you can be my shooter any time."

"*Finally*, I have a talent," she says with a soft, huffy laugh.

"Woman, you are full of those."

"Oh yeah? Which one is your favorite?"

The space between us disappears. Good lord, we will never get a stitch of work done at this rate.

"How 'bout I show you when we get back at the end of the day?"

"Promise?" Green eyes study me suspiciously.

"Absolutely."

She beams as she walks back to the rifle, packing it away and disarming it like I taught her to less than an hour ago before she swings it over her back.

Watch out mountain, Louisa May is coming.

My chest expands with her here. On the ranch. By my side. She fits, like the last piece of a long-standing puzzle I have been working on my entire life.

"You comin', Harry?" Louisa calls from where she is, now halfway back to the barn.

"Yeah, darlin', I am."

Halfway across the field, I glance at the woman on the horse, Horse, beside me. This wasn't her plan. It occurs to me, despite her unending work ethic, her place of work is not limited to this ranch.

"What days do you need to be at the restaurant?" I ask.

"Wednesday through Saturday. From lunchtime 'til late, if I'm to start taking over from Mama."

Tomorrow she will have to be back in town. I get her for a total of three days a week. Selfishly, I wish she could be here every day. But the thought fades as fast as it formed when I see her focus is stuck on the distant horizon. The telltale signs of Louisa stuck in her thoughts are written all over her face.

"Good, then you'll be there. This old place will wait."

"I thought you needed help?"

She's staring at me now.

I ride along, letting the gelding swing his head low on the walk out.

Horse halts when I don't answer. "Harry?"

"This place needs more hands, but that's not an option at the moment."

"You mean we can't afford it."

It's a statement, not a question.

"No, we can't."

Her face crumbles with worry, and I regret sayin' anything. I will make this work. Every beast counts. Every season needs to be better than the last. We need to make the mortgage payment. We nee—

"What can I do to help? I mean . . . " She studies my face. "What are we going to do? We can't lose it, we just . . ."

Her breathing stutters out.

Fuck.

I rein the gelding to a halt and lean over, taking Horse's reins. She comes to a stop. I nudge the gelding sideways, and he obliges. My leg brushes against Lou's. Her hands grip the pommel tight.

I take her face in my hands. "Louisa May, you look at me."

She sank the last of her savings into this place. For me.

Hell will freeze over before I let her lose the one piece of security she has left.

Her shoulders rise and fall. The movement is too rapid.

"Hey! You listen here." I turn her face to mine. "We are not losin' this ranch."

Her green eyes are tight, tears welling in them. Shadowed from the sun by the brim of her hat, her eyes dilate, making her look so fragile. I know she's not.

I need her to understand that.

"What happens to you if this doesn't work out?" she finally says.

Me?

She is worried about me. My dreams, not hers or her life savings I have gambled with.

I slam my eyes shut, hands still wrapped around her face. My heart aches as it expands with her sentiment. Her unconditional love.

I don't deserve her.

Maybe I never have.

She could have been right the first time 'round. To walk away.

To find another life, far from the disaster I am. Thinking I could make something, something impressive, from dirt nothin'.

I'm a damn fool.

Now I have strung Louisa along with my foolishness.

I can't open my eyes and see the disappointment on her face. The realization that I don't have any of this figured out. That this could all turn bad inside of a few months.

"I'll sell my share of the restaurant."

My eyes snap open so fast, a wave of dizziness threatens as the gelding sways with my jerk. "Like hell."

Louisa sits taller in the saddle. "If it comes down to this place or the restaurant, I'm selling it."

"No, you fuckin' won't."

"Harry Rawlins, I thought you woulda realized by now there's no point in arguing."

Ma's words settle into my mind. *A good woman is the makin's of a man. There are some things you can't do in this life alone. Those things, essentially, mean the most . . . She's your captain. You, her first mate. You're mighty strong by yourself. With her, you'd be unstoppable.*

"Well, if you say so, Captain," I finally drawl.

"See . . . isn't it better when you listen to reason?" The widest grin splits her pretty face, the worry that twisted her face completely melted away, as if proving Ma's point, even now.

But there is no way in hell I'm lettin' Lou lose her dream.

Hell will freeze over before that day comes.

The restaurant is bustling when I pull up by the curb outside on Wednesday evening. I can see Lou through the oversized windows, talking to a couple at a table. Her smile tugs one onto my own face. She really is content here. Doin' what she loves, she's in her element.

I'm an hour early. But sittin' around home without her wasn't doin' me any favors, so here I am. Waitin'. Hangin' around like a lost pup.

Some things never change . . .

The truck's wheel is hot, sittin' in the sunny parking lot. Mid-May will do that. With the windows rolled down, I settle back into the seat as Louisa wanders from the doors as the end-of-day school bell rings. Her friend June walks with her as they chat, laughing at something Lou says.

She hasn't seen my truck yet. I wanted to surprise her.

She is almost done with her senior year.

Almost finishing one phase of her life, ready for the next.

I chew on the stalk of hay I plucked from the bale in the barn before I left. My life is all work—milkin' cows, chasing herds, building, hard labor—no play. I want more for Lou, but I want her by my side.

There's no other girl I can ever imagine having in my life.

She's it for me.

Leanin' over, I tug the glove compartment open, double-checking the small velvet box I picked up on my way here is still there. Like it could vanish.

I've been dreamin' about this since the day she agreed to go steady with me. Twelve months, three weeks, and six days ago.

I'm done for with this girl.

I take her in as she moves closer to the truck. Her gaze homes in on the old buckboard now, piercing the glass windshield, right through me. The passenger door cracks open as June waves a goodbye to the both of us. I offer up a small smile and nod. I like June. She's sensible, smart. Most importantly, a great friend. The two girls make a good pair.

"Well, hello," Louisa coos, sliding onto the seat. She tosses her satchel into the footwell and leans over, taking my face in her hands. "This is a nice surprise."

I crash my mouth to hers.

She wriggles over the seat and presses against me, and I drink *her in, wrapping her in my hold so she has no way out. I want in, coaxing her with my tongue. She relents, melting into me a little further.*

Out of breath and rock-hard, I force space between us.

Every inch of my body tingles with her this close.

We have talked about it, going all the way. God knows I'm willing.

Lou sets the pace in our relationship. Always has; hopefully, she always will.

With a shake of my head, I remind myself why I'm here.

"Ride with me a while?" I ask.

"Sure, Harry." She smiles and turns on the seat, buckling in.

I throw an arm over the back of the seat and push the old truck into reverse. Backward we roll until I spin the wheel and send her forward. Lou is quiet as we drive from the high school parking lot and through town. When I pull over at the lake, she still hasn't uttered a word, which is unusual for my Louisa. I suck in a breathe and shift the truck into park.

"Alright, spit it out, Lou."

She glances at the roof of the truck, her hands twisting her skirt through her fine fingers. Not helping my raging hard-on any as her chest rises and plummets, sending those perfect damn tits moving to the rhythm of my thundering heart.

She finally looks at me. "You haven't asked me."

Her face twists a little, and I can tell she's tryin' her best to hold it together.

I know what she's talking about. Prom.

It's two weeks away, and I still haven't had the balls to ask her.

Waitin' for some other guy to ask. Maybe I want to see if she turns him down, confirming this firestorm we have between us. Maybe I want her to choose someone else for that night, so I don't have to go through with my plan.

I'll be honest, I'm terrified.

I can't lose her.

"You want me to take you, Lou?" I say, softly, brows lowered as I run a hand over my jaw.

She huffs an incredulous laugh, eyes tightening. "Of course I do." Shaking her head, she unbuckles and pushes out the door. It slams a second later.

Dammit.

Opening my door, I slide from my seat and round the truck to the grill where she is leaning, arms folded, gaze set far in the distance. I step into her space and rub her arms. "I should have asked by now, I know. I'm sorry."

Her attention stays on the horizon, but her chin wobbles.

Fuck.

"Sometimes"—she shifts on her feet—"I think you don't understand how little it takes for you to tear me to pieces."

My gut sinks. My chest caves in on my heart as the beats slow. I fold her into me. That one line from her ripped a hole right through me. We are too much. Not enough. Live wires dancing in the lightning storm, barely missing each other as we dance in our own sparks.

I sink my mouth to her forehead, planting a kiss where I can show her how much I love her. "You and me . . . We're fire, darlin'. Smoldering some days, raging others. I'm so done for, it scares the hell out of me. The thought of you not in my life, however that could happen, feels like drownin'."

With a sniffle, she lifts her head, and those green eyes I adore flood with the same fire I just spoke about. "I'd drown with you any day, Harry Rawlins."

I chuckle, dotting another kiss to her forehead, and haul her into me, unwilling to ever let her go. "Good to know, Louisa May. Good to know."

I let my gaze wander down the street. Main Street is busy tonight. The tavern is bustling with a crowd, as is the community hall. Must be some function going on. The truck door creaks open, and I startle. Louisa chuckles. "Been here a while, my love?"

She slides into the truck and closes the door, like she's been doin' it every day for the past ten years. In a way—to me, at least—she has.

I smile at her, folding my hand over hers on the seat between us. "Something like that."

Chapter Twenty-Nine

LOUISA

It's been a long time since I have seen pure disbelief on Harry's face. Ten years, to be exact. But as we sit in the saddle barely a week after my last ride out with him, that's exactly what is etched all over his face.

Next comes rage, as he swings down from his horse.

He paces up and down the half-destroyed fence line toward the mutilated calf barely moving. Another beast down.

Wolves.

Heavens above.

At this rate, we won't have enough breeders left to make it through the next year. Let alone the longevity of the herd. Which is supposed to thrive and grow over the next decade. That was the plan, at least.

Now, with things so tight, each loss is a kick in the gut.

My installments on the restaurant are taking every last penny I have. We can't afford another setback. It's moments like these I wish Rosie was here. Her words always set Harry right. She knew him so well. Where his mind would take him.

He stalks back to the gelding and plucks his rifle from by the saddle. I swallow past the lump in my throat. Letting my eyes shutter closed, I grip the pommel, reins tightly woven through my fingers just in case Horse spooks.

Crack.

Dammit.

I set my jaw, grinding my molars to stem the emotion wanting out so bad my eyes burn. This is ranchin'. It's hard. It's Mother Nature versus us some days. And the damn wolves.

The saddle on the gelding creaks. I open my eyes to find Harry up on his horse, those blues trained on me.

"You good, darlin'?"

"Fine. Let's keep moving."

He nods and pushes the gelding into a lope. I fly off behind him. Horse catches up in no time, and we lope through the golden grasses at the base of the mountains. The low ground, where the wolves shouldn't be, this close to the homestead.

Supply and demand.

The colder weeks have chased them down. The diminishing feed in the higher pastures means the cattle are coming down from the mountain. It's not soon enough. We're losing too many of the smaller cattle.

Today we are bringing the cows and calves down off the mountain. The big roundup with the newer herd Harry brought on when he purchased the ranch roam free in the higher pastures. Hopefully they have fared better than his home lot.

Fingers crossed.

It isn't long until we find the old mob. And they are as familiar as the man beside me by now. The reddish cows graze the short green sprouts poking through the frosty ground. Their calves mill about, suckling, playing. They look content enough.

"Take the rear." Harry waves to the higher part of the slope. I trot Horse up to where he wants me and start rounding up.

Harry takes the lead, weaving back and forth on the gelding. It's automatic, a dance between the beast and man and his horse. Head down and haunches bunched, the gelding earns his keep, moving side to side as we slowly make our way down the side of the mountain. I push up the stragglers and keep an eye on the youngest of the calves. The cows are alert. Good mamas, they are.

That bond between them and their babies is heartwarming. I wonder if I will ever have it. A love so strong, so automatic. I sure hope so. My gaze drifts to the man on the horse beyond the herd. His dark hair pokes out from under his hat. His form on a horse is something else.

Collar up on his jacket, hat pulled down, strong legs wrapped around the gelding . . . It isn't until I hear a little bellow beside me that I realize my heart rate is exceptionally high, each breath too choppy. My panties, rocking in the saddle, are saturated.

Shit.

The calf by Horse stumbles, trying too hard to catch up. I pull Horse to a stop and let the little guy walk in front. "Hup-hup."

The calf bobs his head, hurrying for his mother. I can't help the smile growing over my face with his adorable awkward gait and the way she stops and looks back at him, patiently waiting for her son.

A small giggle slips past my lips as she nudges him forward with her muzzle. An unspoken reprimand, and a reminder to keep up.

We all know the price he will pay if he doesn't.

A few hours later, the cows and calves wander into the field behind the barn. Harry is visibly more relaxed, trotting around the herd, doing his recount.

Always with the numbers.

Me, on the other hand . . . Watching Harry ride, the sight of him working the gelding has me anything but relaxed. My body buzzes with the need to touch him, to have his hands on me. My panties have soaked through my jeans. My nipples rub on my cotton button-down shirt through my lacy bra. The breathlessness that claims me the moment the homestead comes into view all but sends me dizzy.

"What's got you all hot and bothered, darlin'?" Harry reins to a halt beside Horse. He's chewing on a grass stalk like he doesn't have a care in the world. Meanwhile, I'm set to implode.

When I don't respond, not taking my eyes from him as my breaths plummet and barely rise, he plucks the stalk from between his lips and nudges the gelding sideways. Our legs brush, my chest hitches, forgetting to fall, and his gaze darkens.

"Hell, Lou. Why didn't you say somethin' earlier?" His voice is gravel.

My breathing accelerates.

I'm embarrassed. I'm burning up for him. I'm desperate in the best—no, worst way possible.

Without a word, Harry leans over and slides the reins from my fingers. He clucks his tongue, and both horses walk for the barn, me a stunned passenger.

Inside, Harry dismounts and ties the gelding to the holding rail. He ties Horse next as I swing from the saddle. Harry stands below me, hands grabbing my ribs. I slide down his body, and his mouth claims me.

Starving for something to grab on to, I slide trembling digits into his hair, knocking his hat to the ground. He grabs mine, tossing it beside his. Crowding me against Horse, his hot, open-mouthed kisses run the length of my neck. I rest my head back on the fender. His rough touch traces the path of my neck, gripping my face as his mouth smashes over my lips.

God, I'm on fire.

Every stitch of clothing is driving me insane.

I tug at his shirt. He breaks away, taking my work shirt in his rough grip as he rips it open. Buttons fly onto the ground as he shoves the shirt from my back.

"I can't wait," I rasp.

My trembling fingers grab at his clothes. He grunts, tugging the shirt from his back and opening the buckle of his belt with one hand. I lean into Horse as he bends down, nipping at each hard peak through my lacy bra.

"Fuck me, darlin'," he growls, the sound vibrating around the nipple his lips have closed on.

I arch into him.

I'm drowning.

My throat is so thick. Each breath so wild it singes my lungs. I'm literally burning up from the inside.

"Too hot," I pant.

Harry tugs at my jeans, sending them over my hips. I falter, swaying into Horse. She shifts on her feet.

Harry sweeps me into his arms. Planting kisses to his jaw as he stalks to lord knows where, I close my eyes and breathe him in.

It's too much.

He always has been.

My ticket to heaven, dressed in boots and a hat. His blue eyes flicker to my face as he reaches the old workbench on the side of the barn. Tools, rope, saws, and axes line the wall. I'm deposited onto the rough, weathered surface. Caged in by strong arms a second later.

"Louisa May—" His face flinches as he leans into the bench, eliminating any space between us. His jaw feathers. A calloused hand slides behind my neck, pulling me up to him as he devours my mouth with his.

I open, just as desperate.

So damn hungry for him.

His hard length rubs at my center.

I need more.

I slide my hands over his on the bench beside my hips. With a low, raspy noise, he breaks from the kiss, resting his forehead on mine.

"I want to see how wet this sweet pussy is for me right now."

I lift my hips, pushing off the bench with both hands. His fingers scrape over my skin as he drags the jeans from my body. Not taking his gaze from me, he presses his hands to the inside of my knees, forcing my legs wide.

"Mine, darlin'."

"Yours," I breathe.

The ache in my clit is drowning out every other sensation. With every heaving breath, my breasts bounce. His dark eyes drop to them.

"See these, Louisa May?"

He nods to my chest.

"Uh huh."

"Mine," he says in a low voice. The sound sends a thrill through my chest.

He palms a breast and dips his head, taking a nipple between his teeth. The sting of the light bite is instantly soothed as he works his tongue over the hard peak. My legs fall open wider as I brace on my hands and arch into his touch. His tongue. His heat.

He loses the nipple with a pop, and I look back up.

No.

A smirk flickers over his face as he runs kisses down my belly, moving to my inner thighs, one then the other. A whimper falls as I open for him.

My panties are absolutely ruined.

My thighs are slick with the need I have for this man.

When he runs a finger under the side of my panties, I grab his hair, desperation contorting my face. "Ple— Harry . . . Oh god."

"Patience, Louisa May," he rasps.

God, I have none at all.

My implosion is imminent.

He tugs the panties from my hips, and I lift, wanting them gone.

Bare, I sit on the bench, spread for him. Heat rushes my neck and face. But when he swallows hard and meets my gaze, it fades. "Sweet Jesus, darlin'."

His finger traces the inside of my thigh as he drops his attention to my aching center.

"So fuckin' wet for me, Lou. This is what ranch work with me does to you?"

I nod.

Words are of no use to me now.

"Good." He leans to the side and grabs something from a hook behind me. He leans back, the rope in his hands, and my breathing shatters to nothing. "Day's not over."

"Harry," I gasp.

"Yeah?"

I glance at the rope in his hands.

"Trust, Louisa May."

I stare at him for a moment before I whisper, "Trust."

"Hands."

I press my hands together in front of my stomach. He binds the rope around and around before tying it off. A beat later, my arms are over my head, snagged on the hook above me. I can't get down. I can't touch him. I can't move from this bench.

"Right, now, this here . . . " He runs a thumb over my clit. My mouth gapes, a whimper tumbling out. "Mine. To do with whatever the hell I want."

Heat floods my face again as his finger falls away.

I want him to touch me.

I need him to touch me again.

The pounding throb in my clit is painful. The slightest touch would set me off. So worked up, I'm bound to come with the smallest mercy he could give me.

Harry picks up a set of fencing pliers. "This like your vibrator, Lou?"

He has to be joking.

I shake my head.

"I use these all the time. What I wouldn't do to have you all over these."

He tosses the tool in his hand, catching the gripping metal end in his palm. The handles ghost up my drenched center before he presses it into my clit. They're cold.

I arch against the small, frigid touch that sends me reeling.

"Cold, darlin'?"

"Too cold."

He runs the handle through my wet center. "Mine, remember?"

The mewl leaving my lips is ragged.

"More," I manage to gasp.

He raises one brow. "More?"

"Please . . ."

Fuck, please.

The pliers slide into me. So slow. Harry watches as the handle disappears, inch after inch.

I buck on the edge of the bench, not even caring I could slip off and hit the ground.

It's when the pliers slide from my center that I cry out. Harry's hand lands on my hip, his grip feral. His breathing is no better than my useless, ragged intakes.

Heat consumes his deep blues, turning them almost black.

"I need you," I pant, wishing I could grab for him.

The pliers fall from his hand and hit the ground with a thud. His hands wrap around one side of my face, squeezing a little. "Patience."

He studies me for a moment, then dips, bending down. His palms push into my thighs, his tongue sweeping through my center.

"Ah, oh my go—"

My hips leave the bench.

The heat of his tongue, his mouth . . . After the cold pliers, it's too much.

I tug at the binds. The rope burns into my wrists. Rocking my hips, every breath leaves with a strangled cry.

His lip close around my clit. Sparks litter my veins, and heat swells in my core. Two calloused fingers slide into my center, and I explode. He sucks hard, sliding the rough knuckles of bent fingers curling up toward my front. I shatter around his sinking fingers.

Twisting on the bench, the sound of my release echoes through the old barn.

"Fuck, Louisa May. I want you on my cock now, woman."

Not waiting for me to come down from sweet agony, he tugs the rope off the hook and over my head as he flips me over the bench. Nudging my legs apart, he leans over my back. "I'm gonna show you how much you're fuckin' mine. And why you'll never run from me again."

I cant my ass up, waiting. The zipper whines as he shoves his jeans down. His fat tip sweeps through my dripping center. I push back. Hands tied, all I can do is wriggle my hips in the hopes he gives in and shows me mercy.

His warm, tight grip lands on my hips, tugging me back toward him. He slams into me. The groan that follows is nothing short of feral. Seated to the base, he folds around me, brushing my hair from my face as his lips fall to my ear.

"This is for every night I had to go without you, Louisa May."

Oh god.

He stretches me, fills me up completely.

It's heaven, burning hot.

I can't breathe.

Emotion clouds my senses. Regret for all the days we missed together. The ridiculous need I have for him. Tangled together, they're a heady combination sending me higher. My legs tremble as he pulls out so slow, each inch feels like a mile.

I would take this walk with Harry, time and time again.

A hand leaves my hip to run up my spine. His fingers close around my hair and twist it around his wrist. I buck my hips.

God, more please.

He thunders into me, relentlessly.

Hard.

Fast.

Warm need runs down my thighs. Every time he rims my entrance with his fat tip, I almost buckle at the knees.

I move back a little, hunting for more, and he stills.

Hot breath hits the skin between my shoulder blades. "Mine, and I ain't askin'. You give in to me, you hear."

"Always," I rasp. "I will always be yours."

"Damn straight, woman."

He thrusts into me so hard I see stars. Unrecognizable sounds fall past my lips. Each damning stroke more blissful than the last.

The heat in my core builds, faster and faster, with his relentless rhythm. My body shakes as my release crests.

Lightning floods my veins.

The pressure mounts and spills over.

I detonate.

Chapter Thirty

HARRY

Louisa May bucks against the old workbench underneath me. Her sweet pussy milks my cock so fuckin' hard it takes all I have to stay upright and not succumb to the stars invading my vision.

Heat splashes up my lower spine, balls cinching tight as I shoot hot ropes of release deep inside her. I growl her name, gripping her hips in a bruising hold.

I meant every damn word I said. She is mine. Always has been, always fuckin' will be.

If she ever runs again, I'll drag her back here, kickin' and screaming, like the caveman she turns me into. Because without her I'm a man lost and wanderin', not seeing a way forward. No direction.

Hell, Ma was right.

She usually was.

My forehead meets Louisa's spine, me spent and

wantin' to be folded around her, and she turns her head. Green eyes flutter open, and it's in them I see something I have never seen before in her.

Contentment.

This may be the first moment of Louisa's life that she's not caught up in her head. Second-guessing every decision, every thought.

I did that for her. We did that.

"Satisfied looks good on you, darlin'."

She scoffs a light laugh. Her head hits the bench as her breathing slows. Still inside her, I don't want to pull out. If we could stay joined together for the rest of time, I'd take it.

"Harry?" My name is a breathy whisper.

"Yeah, Lou?"

"I need my hands."

I chuckle as she holds them up. I flick the knot loose and slide the rope from her reddened wrists. As she turns back to face me, I pluck them up, kissing the soreness on each one. Fuck. Hurtin' her wasn't my plan.

I don't think there was anywhere near enough blood in my head to think much through, to be honest. She rubs a thumb over the red area, and my brows fall.

"It's okay. I wanted it as much as you did," she offers.

"Somehow, I doubt that."

Her arms slide over my shoulders and curl around my neck as she pushes onto her tiptoes. Her nose brushes mine before she pecks a kiss to my lips. "I have no doubt about you. And for the record, Harrison Rawlins, I couldn't run from you again, even if I wanted to."

I can't respond. My throat is thickened to the point of strangulation.

She cups my face, hands on my jaw as she studies my face. A shiver shudders through her body.

"Come on, let's get you cleaned up." I take her hand, pulling my jeans up with a hand. Half-naked and shaking from the cold and the last twenty minutes, we head into the house. Down the hall, I turn on the shower and test the water. When it's hot, I usher Lou into the steaming water.

"You too," she says.

I lose the jeans and boxers and step into the stream. Instantly, she presses against my chest, her palms at my collarbones. I fold around her. This is how it is supposed to be. The two of us, building something incredible.

I will fight with every last breath I have to make sure she has the life she wants.

Every single one.

Sitting in the bank manager's office on Thursday morning, I tug at the collar of my shirt. Shoving my hat between my hand between my legs as I lean forward, I watch the man in front of me tally away. For the first month of winter, it's far too hot.

Maybe it's the fact we are about to receive the first mortgage repayment request. After the deposit, sale of two of the smaller blocks, and Louisa's installment, I managed to scrape together a minimal extra payment to prevent the shock of a larger quarterly payment.

Nothing prepares me for the figure typed onto the slip of paper the manager slides over the desk to me. If Lou wasn't sitting beside me, I would have stormed out, letting the frustration get the better of me.

But she is.

So, I don't.

She has a way of making me want to be a better man. This situation, as disheartening it is, is no different. I shift on my seat, hold my damn tongue, and take a deep breath.

"It's more than you thought?" Lou leans over, speaking softly.

"A little." My brows drop and I spin my hat between my fingers, sending the brim around.

"Interest rates have moved. This is in line with the current mortgage rates. If it's going to be a pro—"

"No. We'll be fine. How many days 'til it comes due?"

"Tomorrow fortnight. You have fourteen days to find the money, Rawlins."

Fucking hell.

Louisa's worried gaze swings between me and the

bank manager. His attention turns to her, a smirk on his ruddy face as he says, "Hear you're buyin' out the Mancinis. I know at least three investors wantin' a piece of that place. Play poker Thursdays with them, you see."

"Sounds like a boy's club. I wouldn't know anything about those," Lou says, her expression unreadable.

He shifts on his seat. "How New Age of you, Miss Masters."

It only takes a split second to recognize the sarcasm in his condescending tone. To my surprise, Lou rallies.

She gives him the most insincere smile I've ever seen bless her beautiful face. "Well, you know what they say, if you can't grow a pair. Outbid them."

I stifle a laugh, poorly disguising it with a cough. "Right, we must be done here."

I stand and offer Lou my hand. She pushes to her feet, but her heated stare weighing on the oversized bank manager doesn't waiver.

"Two weeks, Harry. Default, and we go to auct—"

I let the door slam behind us, cutting him off. Who kicked his fuckin' cat? Last time, when I was buying, he was all smiles and handshakes. Now, he's like the repo man turned mean.

Nice to know the coin can flip so quick. Not surprising, though, round these parts. People's demeanor changes with their loyalty. My bet is someone made him a better offer.

Over my dead body are they taking our future away.

The muted midmorning sun slaps me from my mental loathing. I take stock of the steady workings of Main Street, shoving my hat onto my head as Louisa's fine hand slides into mine.

"We'll figure this out. One way or another."

I flick my gaze to her worried face.

That right there, that look, is what I never wanted to see.

The last thing I want to do is give Louisa May another reason to fret. I'm supposed to be providing her with a good life.

Dammit.

This is not the start for us I imagined. Already on the back foot and having to make hard choices.

I freeze up on the sidewalk. All thoughts of grabbing some lunch fade with the last of my stupid hope.

She's wrapped around me a second later. I dip my head, my hat hiding us both away from the world. "We get through the next few weeks, do the best we can."

Her words are small comfort when I'm tryin' to build something that'll make her stay. For good.

Something she can't walk away from.

As if our relationship, my worth, is intricately tied to the life I can produce, the empire I can found. A scoff rattles up my throat.

The Rawlins Empire.

Hilarious.

One foot in the door on a run-down ranch and a half share of a tiny restaurant is no empire.

". . . Harry?"

"Hey, yeah?" I snap my gaze from the distance, where I wasn't even aware it drifted to. Louisa comes into focus, her face is close, warm hands cupping my jaw.

"Where did you go?" she says with a chuckle.

"Sorry, tryin' to figure this all out."

She tilts her head, as if reprimanding a small child. "Harry Rawlins, that is for the both of us to work out. You're not in this alone anymore. Or have you forgotten that singular detail?"

Her eyebrows are raised as she waits for me to respond.

"No, ma'am," is all I can manage.

I've gone from a one-man operation to the luckiest man on the planet in a matter of months. And I know she's here. And things are new. But what about when things are hard? When life seems impossible. Will she sta—

"Come on! Lunch, before I fade away to a shadow."

What else can I do but follow? A beat later, Lou opens the door to Darla's Diner. I hesitate, and she turns back. "You're not hungry?"

"I am, but—"

She smiles at me, the kind of smile to carry me through the worst of days just by remembering the warmth it brings to my chest. The noise of the busy diner filters through the half-open door.

"You sure, Lou?"

"Our money is good as any here. Besides, I don't hold grudges." She winks at me and disappears through the door. I tug it open and walk inside. Cynthia is chatting to Lou as she drops into the last booth on the left. My old spot.

I slide in opposite and remove my hat, tossing it to the seat. With a nod to Cynthia, I shift my eyes to Louisa's. Despite the bank and the hard week, and the fact she is scraping by with the restaurant, she's all sunshine.

We order and Darla brings out our food herself. She and Louisa have a short chat about menus and local gossip. It's all I can do to watch Lou in her element. Food, eating, cooking, talking about it, teaching it. That's her callin'. There's no denying it.

We get stuck into our lunch, and I'm done before too long. Leanin' back in the old booth seat, I slide a toothpick from the center container on the table. I bite down on it with my molars, mulling it over like a cow chewing its cud as I let the thoughts of what life could hold for Louisa and me run rampant.

For the umpteenth time since Ma passed, I grapple with the things she told me. What life will mean if I have this incredible woman by my side for the rest of my days. The long, hard days. The cold, dark nights. The moments of pure, unbridled pleasure we bring each other. How many of those we could make.

"What on earth are you thinking about, Harry Rawlins?" Louisa giggles.

My face falls. I must have had a ridiculous look on it. I clear my throat and lean over the booth. "Fencin'."

Louisa blushes instantly.

"There's so much of it we need to do. All that lost time to make up for," I say, each syllable a low, raspy noise.

Her lips part, eyes burning into mine.

I chuckle, plucking the toothpick from my teeth. I dump it to my empty plate. "That is, if we can make this work."

I'm not talkin' about us anymore. Or maybe I am. Still.

There is still a part of me waitin' for her to realize where she is. Who she's with. That tiny part of me expects her to hightail it outta this map-dot town as fast as she can. I'm yet to remove the last sliver of doubt.

God knows I want to.

I need to.

I'm just not there yet.

"Oh shoot!" Louisa jumps up, rounding the small booth table. "I'm late." She grabs her bag, dotting a peck to my temple. "I'll see you at home, okay?"

"Sure thing, darlin'."

I smile as she leaves, but when the diner door swooshes shut, it falls.

First the mortgage payment, then my stupid damaged heart attaching a financial outcome to the love of my damn life leavin'. I push to my feet and pay the bill, leaving Cynthia a good tip.

The trip home is too quiet.

Just the old truck and me. It's too familiar. A reminder of what my life was not so long ago.

Before Lou blew back into town.

I make the ranch and pull into the driveway, parkin' by the house. The soft glow of the kitchen lights Louisa leaves on tugs a smile to my lips. As if she is privy to how this mind of mine works, and this is her way of showing me she'll be back. Killing the engine, I make my way inside.

The warmth of our home lures me to a calmness I haven't felt in months. Not since before Ma passed. And my thoughts wander to her.

Before I realize, I'm standing in the doorway to her bedroom. Lights off, it's as if she's just out with Evelyn, and I'm due to head to town and pick her up.

It's when I flick the light switch and the room bursts with brightness that I see every detail that reminds me she ain't coming back. The brush and mirror on the dresser. Her nightgown folded and tucked under the pillow on her side of the bed. Her floppy hat, sitting on the old wooden chair that used to be in my room. The one I made in shop back in high school, all those years ago.

I step inside.

The neat space smells like her perfume, the cheap floral scent she always wore. Her ivory hair clip sits in a small, clear glass bowl. The tarnished mirror, edges decorated with some old-world ornate trim, leans against the wall. I catch a glimpse of my reflection before I spot two letters leaning against the right-hand side of it.

I lift the ivory stationery from its spot. Sliding them through my hands, I study Ma's elegant handwriting. The first envelope is addressed to me. The second, to Lou.

"Huh." I step back and sink onto the edge of the bed.

I open mine. Hands shaking, I stare at the paragraphs before reading a word.

What could she possibly say I hadn't already heard?

My darling Harry,

I know you would tell me it's morbid to write letters to people while you're still alive and well. But, just in case, because this is too important, I am doing it anyway.

I know you have worked yourself ragged to keep me housed and fed over the last decade. I also know you think it is expected of a son to do so for his mother. I disagree.

I have wished every day for things to change for the better.

I'd almost given up hope. Then, one morning,

as I trawled the aisles of the grocer, she appeared.

Your Louisa.

I can't tell you how happy that made this old lady's heart, my sweet boy.

Because her being here with you, I have a feeling about this, is the key to everything changing.

Everything.

Now, I can't promise I'll be here to see the two of you through it all, but I want you to know I have done everything in my power to make sure you stand a chance at this life you want so badly. So, you give it your best shot.

I'll be watching. Good things are coming your way, mark my words.

And I love you more than life itself. You are the best thing I have ever done.

Ma xx

P.S. You make sure Louisa gets my letter.

P.P.S. What you're needing is in the small velvet box, top right drawer. You'll know when it's time.

Moisture drops onto the page. The air in my lungs fights its way upward past the stone occluding my throat.

I swipe at my face as tears fall, drenching my stubbled jaw. I fold the paper in half and return it to the envelope. It slips from my hand onto the bed. Louisa's sits in my lap.

Staring at the wall, I slide off the end of the bed to the floor. I work a finger under the flap of Louisa's envelope. I shouldn't read it.

It's to her from Ma.

It's not for me.

But I can't help myself. It's the last bit of her left behind. Reading her words is like hearing her voice.

I flip the flap open and slide the letter out. I open the paper with a hand and skim over the curvy handwriting. I won't look at it properly. Just a quick look.

That's what I tell myself.

The quick skim screeches to a halt when I see my father's name.

That's the last person I thought Ma would be writing Lou about.

When I comprehend the sentence in full, the letter falls from my hand.

Fuckin' hell, Ma.

Chapter Thirty-One

LOUISA

"Honey, I'm home!" I coo as I slip in the front door and shut it quickly to stave off the winter chill. "Brr, it's damn cold outside."

I kick off my shoes and pad to the kitchen in my socks. I tug the refrigerator door open and pull out the sweet tea. God knows I could use some.

When nobody responds, I set the jug on the counter and wander down the hall. The light in Rosie's room is on. That's odd. We haven't ventured into her space since the funeral.

I stop in the doorway to find Harry sitting on the floor, leaning against the foot of the bed.

Shit.

Closing the distance, I sink to the floor by his side. I nudge his shoulder with mine, and he turns to face me. He's all tear-streaked cheeks, red eyes, and clenched jaw.

"Oh, Harry."

An ache swells in my chest. He moves his mouth like he's going to say something, but snaps it shut and snaps his gaze to the dresser. The way his stare burns into it, I'm surprised the old piece of furniture doesn't burst into flames.

He holds out an envelope to me. Another sits by his other side, open, the letter underneath the cream envelope. I take mine from his fingers.

"She wrote me?"

He barely nods.

Sucking in a breath, I turn the envelope over. It's not sealed. Maybe he read it. I don't mind. I slide the letter from its casing and unfold it. Harry doesn't move an inch as I read Rosie's pristine handwriting.

To my dearest Louisa,

I can call you that, can't I?

You are so precious to my Harry and me. And you have always felt like my daughter. I saw it, the connection between the two of you, the day you met. When we got home, I saw how my son lit up with the mention of you. Well, a mother knows these things.

The years you were gone were hard, I'm not gonna lie. And I understand why you left. Really, I do. More than you will ever understand. To be independent in this day and age as a woman, is truly admirable. Not everyone sees it that way, specially in these parts. I blame our mothers before us.

Enough of that.

I want to talk to you about Eddy.

And Harry.

I never told Harry about that night. Being a mother takes certain sacrifices. Some small and some much, much bigger. I have made my bed, and I'll lie in it when my time comes. But I don't regret dealing with Eddy, it needed to be done. It was the only thing I could give you two in the way of a real shot at a life together. He never would have allowed it. Well, you know the rest.

Now, to my darling Harry. He really is the most incredible man. I'm biased, as all mothers are, but I never could have asked for a kinder, harder working, more selfless son than our Harry. That man would give the air in his lungs for the people he loves. He's always been able to read what people need. So, promise me, when I'm gone, you will take care of him in the ways a good woman does for her husband.

Now, don't go getting all coy on me girl, we

both know that is where you two are heading. And, on the off chance I don't get to be there when you do, your something old, something new, something borrowed, and something blue are in my top left dresser drawer in a box for you. Only, don't look at them 'til that day. Do me that one little favor, sweetheart.

That's all for now.

Yours,

Rosie.

For now. Like she'd planned to tell me other things. Like we'd have time to bond, mother to daughter. My chin wobbles as I stare at the paper in my hand. It blurs, the pressure building behind my eyes.

I sniff, trying my best to hold it together, and look up to Harry. His jaw is set, and hurt and pain lance through his deep blues.

His jaw feathers. "You knew," he chokes.

Knew . . .

About Eddy.

That Rosie—

And Harry mustn't have.

Heavens above.

My heart cracks, and I reach for him as I nod.

The tears fall, warming my cheeks.

Before I can touch him, he jerks to his feet and stalks for the doorway.

"Harry," I plead.

He throws a hand up, not turning back, and disappears into the hallway.

I bolt from the floor and take off after him. "Where are you going?"

"Fencin'."

He shoves his hat on his head, tugging his coat from the hook. He slides his boots on. I slump against the corner of the hallway that meets the kitchen.

"Come on, you'll freeze out there. It's late. Too dark . . . Please stay."

He doesn't say a word.

The door slams, and the first sob tumbles from my twisted face. I slide down the wall and pull my knees to my chest. The pain that held him captive intensifies the ache in my chest. I choke on the slim wisp of air left in my lungs and rub my hands over my face.

Harry Rawlins.

My fire.

Always my ultimate demise.

We have always been strung too tight.

The crackling tension running between us has always been too much. We feel everything. We feel more than we should. Say things we don't mean. Do things that hurt, things we would take back if we could.

Like the incredible highs can only be balanced by the lowest of lows. We, stupidly, let them take us there.

Nope, not anymore.

I push to my feet, march for the front door, and pull on my coat. Boots and my dress will have to do. I shove my own hand-me-down hat onto my head to keep me warm.

I push out into the dark and follow the echoing clangs of tools being tossed into the back of the old buckboard.

I find him gripping the workbench, bent over, shoulders heaving, head hanging. His rough breaths are the only sound in the large, frigid space.

I fold my arms over my chest when I file in behind him.

"Fine. You want to fence, we do it together."

He turns back, arms hanging by his side. The fire in his eyes isn't something I've ever seen directed at me before. I set my shoulders back.

He homes in on me. "You're not coming."

"Yes. I am."

"I don't need you, Louisa." The second the words leave his mouth, his eyes dim, his body slacking. "I-I didn' . . ."

"I know."

My chin wobbles again. He's struggling with this. It's hurting him, and there is so little I can do.

Eliminating the distance between us, I brush a hand

over his jaw. "Yes, you do. You do need me. And I need you right back. So, we're fencin'. I *ain't* askin'."

His face crumples, but he schools it back. His hand takes mine from his face, and he puts space between us and paces by the bench. It's all I can do to watch him stew.

He stops and lifts the pliers from the bench. I follow the movement with the memory of the last time he held those stuck in my mind.

"You should have told me, Louisa May."

I snap my gaze from the tool in his hand to his eyes. "No, I shouldn't have."

"Why not? Hey?" His voice is rough, anger and torment twisting the tension in it until it warps. When I hesitate, he paces again. Lifting the hat from his head, he runs a hand through his hair.

"It wasn't my secret to tell, Harry," I say softly.

He spins toward me, fire in his eyes. "What the actual hell, Louisa!" he roars.

I flinch.

Harry's never raised his voice at me. He curses, sure. Loses his temper occasionally at some unsuspecting fence. But never before has his anger been directed at me.

The bridge of my nose prickles, tears burning the back of my eyes.

Ugh, not now.

I push a little taller and take a determined step toward where he seethes.

"You talk to me like that *ever again*, Harrison Rawlins, and they'll be the last words you ever say to me." Fire courses through my veins, tears burning still. I am his equal. His captain, if Rosie gets her way. This is *not* happening.

So, I say everything I've wanted to since the day Rosie defended me in their old living room when Eddy went rampant.

"He was hurting you, Harry. Hurting you both. Your mother did what she could to keep you safe. To keep us safe. She sacrificed everything so you would have what you want. She did this for *you!*"

He starts to shake.

His jaw slackens before he gasps on a breath he can't seem to capture.

Oh god.

His hands curl to fists before he turns away, closing in on the workbench. Both fists land with a bang. The heartbreaking groan that follows has the tears I've been fighting back spill over.

"Har—" I hold out a hand.

Wanting so badly to touch him. To take away the pain that the man who should have loved and protected his only son gave him in spades.

"She couldn't let him hurt you anymore," I whisper at his back.

He turns, so slowly. Silver lines his eyes.

"I know that!" The words are a mangled mess of

tortured emotions. "You think I don't know what he was capable of?"

His chest heaves. He rips the hat from his head, and it falls to the ground as he rakes both hands through his hair. "It should have been me! I should have knocked the old bastard off years ago. Hell, the whole town knew he was one drink away from a fatal accident. It wouldn't have even been hard. Instead, my frail goddamn mother who wouldn't hurt a fly had to do it. Because I couldn't."

A broken sob falls from my lips, and I press them together to stem the flow. Reaching for him with a shaking hand, I take a step.

He shakes his head and falters sideways.

"No, Lou. I wasn't man enough to do what had to be done to protect the both of us. Now, Ma's died with it on her fuckin' conscience."

My own body burns, each breath so choppy my chest aches. As if Harry's pain radiates through me.

He burns, I burn.

Hauling air in through clenched teeth, he falters backward and hits the bench. His legs buckle and I lunge for him, doing my best to hold him up. Grappling at his face, I try to rid his face of the tears streaming over his cheeks. He chokes, slumping against the lower shelf of the bench.

"No, you didn't do anything wrong. Harry." I'm shaking my head so fiercely, tears fly from my chin and soak into his jacket. "You hear me. Your parents made their own choices. Your father—"

Deep blues lift to my face.

"He was a monster." A faraway look descends over his gaze. "I should have done it. I should have saved her."

"Then you and I would be having this conversation through plate glass," I say, tilting my head, giving him a wry smile. The best I can force right now. Nowhere good enough for the pain he is in.

His breathing settles, and I shift onto his lap. Sliding my hands beneath his jacket, I huddle into his chest for warmth. With the tension dissipating, the chill is relentless, finding us instantly.

"You'd still be around if I went to prison, Lou?"

I huff a strangled laugh. "I don't think I have any choice at this point."

I lift my head to give him a cheeky smile.

His mouth comes down to mine before my lips even have the chance to tip up. Hands moving up his chest, I let my fingers travel over the pounding pulse points in his neck. Closing my palms over his jaw, I open for him.

Like I ever had a choice.

Dizzy from his heat, his kiss, I break away. His forehead rests against my own. We breathe heavily, the air from our lungs mingling like we could never be untangled ever again.

"Since we're makin' the most of things," Harry says, but swallows hard. "I want to name the ranch after Ma."

I nod, and the tears prickle the bridge of my nose again.

I couldn't think of a more fitting sentiment.

"What are you thinkin' we should call it, then?" I ask.

"Rosie's Ranch?"

I scrunch my nose up, and he loses a strained chuckle.

God, the sound is like coming up for air after the last hour.

"No, my love. That's not it."

"Alright, Captain, what do you think we should call it?" He raises a single brow.

I let my attention wander around the old, weathered barn, like the words will reveal themselves. It finally snags on the two sagging wooden doors. The tight grain of the hardwood that has stood the test of time speaks to me.

"Rosewood," I breathe.

Harry's gaze tracks to where mine stays stuck. "I like it. Rosewood Ranch."

"You're going to need a new sign," I say, shifting my focus back to those deep blues I love.

"*We* are gonna need a new sign."

"Oh yeah?"

"Louisa May, you were right the first time."

"I don't understand . . ."

"Neither of us have a choice at this point. So, your name is going to have to be on that sign somewhere, too."

I scoff a laugh. "Alright, if you say so."

"I do, woman."

The phrase takes my breath away.

I do.

Except this time, the thought of being tied to Harry Rawlins for the rest of my life feels like my greatest adventure to come. The thrill it brings is overwhelming.

He sighs, and it's exasperated.

"What is it?"

"Roundup in a few days. We're gonna have to make it count, or we won't get the chance to rename the ranch, let alone hang the sign."

I slump into his chest.

Right, the mortgage payment.

Dammit.

"We'll figure it out."

"I damn hope so," he says, letting his head fall back onto the lower shelf. His Adam's apple bobs as the veins in his neck pound away. The life force of Harry Rawlins.

We can't lose this place.

Not now.

That would break this man.

After everything he's been through, there is no way this ship can sink. It just can't.

Chapter Thirty-Two

LOUISA

M ara—or Horse, as she's formerly known as—is tense. She shifts on her feet as we wait, rifles strapped to our backs, hats pulled down low, and a pack horse between the two of us. Ned is late. And his buddy Mick, who apparently recently got out of service with the Navy and needed work.

"Here they come," Harry says, spitting the grass stalk from his mouth to the ground. The gelding, who I have dubbed Darby, shies as an old, busted pickup rolls into the driveway. Harry has their mounts saddled and a pack horse bundled up for them.

Ned parks and kills the engine. His megawatt smile finds me first before he waves to Harry. "Mornin'."

"You're late. Sun's rising higher by the minute, buddy."

He waves Harry off as Mick rounds the front of the truck. His short buzzed hair and muscly body look out of place on the ranch. To their credit, they have dressed appropriately and packed light.

"Mick, this is Harry Rawlins, and his missus, Louisa."

I stifle the laugh at him calling me the missus.

"You realize there's bad weather comin', right?" Mick's stare drills into Harry's.

"All the more reason to get these cattle off that mountain." Harry wastes no time, walking the gelding toward the far end of the barn. I cluck my tongue and push Mara after him. Ned swings into the saddle, tying his pack behind it. Mick does the same.

"Right. We take the northern end. You two the southern. Herd them down, camp out in the hollows to keep the herd together. Every beast counts. We meet on the flat in five days' time. Everyone on the same page?"

Ned nods. "Got it, boss."

Mick grunts, looking at the mountain like she's gonna eat him. He's probably not too far off with that assessment. There is no doubt it's going to be hard going. He flicks his gaze back to me and says, "You think you'll need that?"

He nods to the rifle at my back.

"Maybe. I ain't takin' any chances. Every beast counts," Harry answers before I can.

"Yeah, you said that already," the ex-sailor drawls,

looking about as interested in being here as a nun at a brothel's grand opening.

I slide the rifle from my back and hand it to Ned. "You two should have one."

I look to Harry, but he dips his hat and trots down the laneway heading for the fields flanking the mountains' base.

Here goes nothin'.

I take off after him on Mara.

When I glance back, Ned and Mick are riding for the southern fields. With Harry giving them the rundown a few days ago, going over the property lines on the map, they have a solid idea of where to ride and what to look for. The head count, after the wolves, is lighter than we hoped. If we can get them all down and sell off the calves, weaners, and any older cows who are calved out, we might make our first payment.

Might.

Harry's kept the finances close to his chest since our visit to the bank. It's eating at him. I have a feeling the next five days are going to be the hardest of my life. I glance back at the willows surrounding the house. The wind plays with their long green tendrils.

"A little help here, Ma," I whisper to the trees and push Mara faster to catch up to Harry.

I know she can hear me.

The bad weather rolls in on our second night. Harry and I have set up camp with a small herd in a narrow pocket nestled on the side of the mountain. As if the thunder rumbling in the distance isn't concern enough, the howls of a pack of wolves nearby have both the cattle and me spooked.

Harry sits on a fallen log, chewing on the stalk of grass he plucked from the ground earlier. He hasn't said a word since we stopped to set up camp. But the storm has found its way into his eyes.

Digging through our provisions for the trip, my fingers brush cold metal. Flat.

Round and modular.

I pull it from the satchel.

A flask, a larger one.

I didn't put that in there . . .

I unscrew the lid.

Whiskey fumes hit my senses, and I stifle a cough. I clear my throat and take a sip. It burns, almost producing another round of coughing.

It's a stark contrast to the snow-covered ground and crisp air that's smothered everything. Lightning flashes overhead. I move back to Harry's side and hand him the flask.

"That's for our last night on the mountain, darlin'."

"It is? You makin' plans for me?"

I narrow my eyes at him playfully.

A smile tugs at one corner of his mouth.

"Louisa May, I've always had plans for you."

"Is that so? What about when we first met?"

"Back in senior year?"

"*Your* senior year . . ."

"Yes, and yes."

"Really?" I can't help the smile stretching my face. It warms my heart to hear.

"Really, but right now, we should get some sleep. Tomorrow is going to be tough, little lady."

I stand and take another sip of the whiskey.

"What if I'm not tired?"

He chuckles. "You should be."

"Are you turning me down, Harry Rawlins?"

He looks up, pushing the brim of his hat up with one finger. "Woman, the day I say no to you is the day I stop breathin'."

I screw the flask cap back on tight and drop it to the log. Without taking my gaze from his, I straddle his lap. "Well then, in that case. I ain't askin'."

I knock his hat from his head as I push my fingers into his hair. Rough hands cup my face, dragging it down to his.

The fire crackles at my back. I roll my hips and find him hard.

I break from the kiss and tilt my face to the sky. Lightning tracks across it, quicker than my thundering heartbeat.

I don't think for as long as I live, I will ever forget this night.

Mara stumbles, her flank damp with sweat, her mouth and neck frothy with exertion. My back aches. My butt has been numb for hours now, and still, we trek across the unforgiving mountain in search of the rest of our half of the herd. Harry rides point, as usual, sometimes slowing the cattle, sometimes picking our path through the timber forest.

Snow covers everything now, and as pretty as it is, it is chafing my skin like there's no tomorrow. *Last night on the mountain,* I keep reminding myself every ten minutes. It's the only thing that keeps me moving forward.

"Hup, huh," I call with a dry, sore throat, flapping an arm up and down as I go, one hand still tight on the reins. The older cattle tire easily, and the little ones hang back. It's a constant job to push them up, trying to keep the herd together. Two more days of this.

Two more.

It's long, hard, boring, and tedious all rolled into one.

Nothing like the fast paced, high-octane thrill of a busy restaurant kitchen. Yet somehow, being here, in this magnificent place surrounded by Mother Nature, I long for nothing. There is nowhere else I'd rather be.

That makes me smile.

Getting a glimpse of the worn cream hat constantly bobbing and moving side to side with the gait of the gelding, my smile stretches further. And it hits me how far we have come.

With nothing else to occupy my mind, memories spring forward, mesmerizing me with their reminiscence. We were so young and free. Harry, always so gruff, stoic, and sweet when it was just the two of us. The only things we worried about were friends, grades, and each other.

God, we were on fire. It took him six months to ask me out, and another few weeks for me to say yes. It was hard to make plans when you could be up and movin' any time. With Dad's work, we seemed to be always moving around.

Mara's hoof hits a log and her head dips with a jerk. I lean back and brace for the rough ground I'm sending her over. It's only when I hear a bellow from behind that I realize I left somebody behind.

"Dammit."

I turn Mara back and pick our way through the trees toward the sound.

The wobbly little bellows rack up the closer I get.

Then they stop.

That's not good.

Clucking my tongue, I send Mara faster. A low branch rushes me, and I duck. Straightening, the air in my lungs freezes as it stalls out as I take in what stands in the small clearing.

Wolves.

Four of them.

The calf stands, rump against a tree, cornered.

I grab for the Winchester at my back and come up empty.

Fuck.

I gave it to Ned.

The calf pees, the rancid yellow coloring the snow, the acid tang scenting the air.

The wolves close in on the calf.

"Hey!" I wave at them ferociously, as if that will scare them off.

You idiot, Louisa.

Shaking, I wrap the reins around the pommel.

I shouldn't leave Mara's back, but they're not afraid of the horse, and we can't lose that little calf.

I clap my hands, and the sound cracks through the air.

Two of the wolves flinch, but none of them retreat.

I need that calf.

I need . . .

The calf bolts toward Mara.

A wolf lunges for it. I spur Mara forward, putting us between prey and predator.

They're so fuckin' game.

Starvation, no doubt, drives them to act this recklessly.

I twist in the saddle to see the calf scamper over the debris-littered ground. Two wolves take off after it.

"No! Fuck!"

I spin Mara around and break her into a rushed gait, desperate to get to the calf. To intercept before they take it down. Thunder growls overhead.

Snapping and hoofbeats close in on us. I'm screaming at the calf, the wolves.

Nothing helps.

I'm almost to the three animals when I catch a glimpse of a white hat and Darby's brown coat.

Crack!

The air ricochets with a shot fired.

The echo rings, over and over.

The wolves tear away from the calf, disappearing into the timber. Darby bursts through the trees, faster than I thought it was possible to go through this dense mountainside. Harry's off the gelding and manhandling the terrified calf a moment later.

He ropes his legs together and lifts him onto Darby in front of the pommel.

My heart flings against my rib cage.

"You good, Lou?" His glance is brief before he dashes back the way he came.

All I can do is nod to his retreating form. The herd is

most likely scattering with the shot. I shake my head, resetting my composure.

Right.

Good.

I push Mara back the way we came and follow Harry's too-quick pace.

That was too close for this girl's comfort.

The grumble of the storm overhead reminds me we are far from out of the woods. We still have to get down this mountain tomorrow. When Harry and I have the herd back under control and tracking along, the growly storm has turned to misty drizzle.

It's freezing.

We should have done this weeks ago.

In hindsight, it would have eased the burden, but we can't predict the weather any more than we can the mortgage rates.

This has to come out the way we planned. There isn't a plan B this time 'round. On the northernmost side of the mountain, we find a sheltered hollow and drive the cattle into it. With legs aching from riding all day and exhaustion that's started playing with my vision, I slide from Mara.

The cattle mill about, settling down for the night as I lean against Mara's side while Harry sets up camp. When I can feel my butt again, I pad to where he is rolling out our bedrolls under an overhanging ledge.

I pluck up any dry wood I find around the campsite

and start a pile for a fire. I turn back to find Harry watching me, something that takes all the exhaustion, every last aching muscle and weary bone, and sets it right.

"Come here, Louisa May." The low rumble of his voice moves me without thought.

The last of the daylight disappearing behind the mountain, I fold into the man I love.

"Whiskey time, darlin'."

Chapter Thirty-Three

HARRY

Amber liquid slips from the mouth of the bottle, dripping onto Lou's hard nipple. A man's never been this thirsty in the history of all mankind. Her silky skin is pure heaven under my calloused hands. One hand on her hip, the other bracing on the bedroll beside her, I dip my head and take the hard peak between my teeth.

She arches into me instantly, sending my cock impossibly hard.

Damn, this woman.

Lovin' her will never get old.

I lose the nipple with a pop and drench the next one with whiskey, repeating the process. This time, I'm rewarded with her drenched pussy pressing against my rigid cock. It's fuckin' heaven.

Her mouth opens, so fuckin' hungry for me.

I hook a thumb over her bottom lip. She clamps down, sucking it hard.

"Sweet Jesus," I growl.

At this rate, this will be over before it begins.

All blonde hair and green eyes, she lies on the bedroll, mine for the takin'. Fuck me if I ain't goin' to devour her like it's the first time I've tasted her.

She drives me wild.

Pretty sure those saturated panties are my fault.

"Fuckin' hell, Louisa May, you're damn beautiful, spread wide for me." I let a hand wander down her stomach, running two fingers through that soaked pussy of hers. "So wet, so needy, woman."

"Please, plea—"

"That's my girl. Beggin' for it."

I rub a thumb over her clit, and her hips buck off the bedroll, sending pressure against my cock. I groan at the touch.

"Makin' me wait ain't very sweet."

"Lou, nobody's ever accused me of bein' sweet."

She chuckles. "You're *my* sweet."

"Oh yeah, I taste sweet to you?"

"You're gonna have to remind me . . ."

She pushes on my shoulders and I'm leanin' back. Wriggling out from under me, she leans down, taking my throbbing cock into her mouth.

"Oh, fuck . . ." The words burn their way out.

One fine hand gripping the base of my cock, she takes me all the way to the hilt. With a long, torturous upward stroke, she sucks me hard. My balls tighten. I fist her hair and pull her head back. The tip of my cock falls from her lips.

"As good as this feels. Balls deep in your pretty pussy —" The words break off as the last of my air whooshes from my lungs at her doe-like green eyes, puffy pink lips, and breasts bouncing from dropping her ass to her heels.

Lord above.

Gripping her hips with more pressure than I should, I flip her over and pull her back to me, nudging her legs apart with my knees. In the firelight, she is stunning. Ass canted up to me. The long, slender curve of her back, the soft golden locks scattered around her shoulders. She's ethereal. Something sent from heaven for this man.

In this moment, I realize I have always thought of Louisa this way.

She has, in my mind, always been mine.

I have always been hers.

That will never change.

She turns her head, and green eyes study my face as I slide a hand under her stomach. With a tug backward, I nudge her entrance with my cock.

The campfire flames dance in her eyes.

My damn heart explodes.

I breathe through the emotion stuck in my airway.

"Harry . . ."

I slam into her. Her wild cry echoes over the mountainside. I pull out, slow and deliberate, like I want her to feel every inch of me inside her. Like I want her to understand that for every part I give her, she gives it back tenfold.

My fool of a heart wouldn't have it any other way.

Even if I'd known this woman would shatter my heart to splinters, I'd still love her anyway. Like I said, no choice.

Not for this man.

Never was.

Feeling too far from her, I wrap an arm around her and pull her up to me. Her arms wrap around my head instantly, her mouth hunting for my own. I thrust into her, wanting her to feel the pleasure I can give her.

This is the love I make for her.

Making her feel everything.

As much bliss as I can give her, I will.

In exchange for her holding my heart, taking care of it the way only Louisa can, I give her everything I have.

With each punishing, all-consuming stroke, I pull another whimper from her.

Her body trembles.

Mine follows a moment later.

Slick need drips down her thighs. The sound of each thrust tangles with the crackle of the fire.

When we get off this godforsaken mountain, I'm gonna make sure she gets every last day I have on this earth.

"Ha—Oh. God."

I slide a hand to her front, and with a steady rhythm, I circle her clit. Her breathing shatters, her back pushing against my chest as her hips roll and her tight little pussy clamps down around my cock, milking it.

I bite down on her soft shoulder. Sucking the spot to soothe it as she dances around my cock, her orgasm still rolling through her.

"Fuckin' mine, darlin'. That's it, strangle my damn cock."

Fine hands grope my neck and face, her mouth opening and closing like she's drowning.

God, we both are.

"Another one?" I ask.

She cries out.

I slam up into her and pinch her clit. I nibble her neck, and she shudders at the contact. Her slick drips down her thighs, soaking into the bedroll.

Utterly out of it, she drops a hand from my neck to her breast.

If that ain't the hottest thing I've ever seen. I keep up the rhythm, watching as she tugs her nipple and palms her soft flesh. The sight has liquid heat swelling low in my spine.

"Lou, fu-uck."

"Give in to me, Harry."

"Jesus," I rasp. "When you do."

Her head falls back onto my shoulder. I rub a thumb over her clit, coaxing her body into submission. Soon she explodes around my cock for the second time, and I let go, giving her what she wants. Hot ropes of release flood deep inside her.

She cries out as her pussy grips my cock, harder than before.

I growl into her ear, and a breathy whimper leaves those pretty lips.

So, I follow with, "I love you, Louisa May. Always have. Always damn well will."

A sob chokes out her next breath.

Hot, wet kisses find my four days' worth of stubble. The moment I pull away, she flies into my arms so fast, I almost topple backward. Her arms cradle my head as she wraps herself around me, and her fingers dig into my hair.

"I love you, too, Harry."

The last leg of the descent off this mountain is the hardest. I knew it would be. I slide back and forth with Darby. Head down, he reins from side to side as we hold the herd steady, heading down the slope. The storm from last night turned into a constant downpour.

Not the best-case scenario.

At all.

The stream marking the border between the flats and the mountains was already at full capacity. If it swells, we're stuck. And we do not have the provisions or the timeframe for that kind of delay.

Louisa's sweet little hup-hups have turned raspy over the last few days. She's exhausted. I can see it in her eyes, and the way she slumps over the saddle when she thinks I'm busy checking over the herd.

The sooner we get home, the better.

An hour later, we're riding toward the stream turned torrential river.

"Fuck!"

I pluck the hat from my head and run my hand through my soaked hair.

The rain washes away the muted sounds of the herd behind me. So when Lou appears on Mara, I startle.

"Can we cross downstream?" she asks.

"Maybe. We can't stay stranded on this side."

"I'll take a look." She reins the mare away, trotting on the muddy ground along the bank of the stream. In the downpour, she disappears into the gray sheet of weather.

My heart picks up pace.

With her out of sight, my gut ties into a bundle of knots.

I strain to hear her returning.

I hear nothing.

"Dammit."

With a quick glance over the herd, I trot off in the direction she went. The thunderstorm intensifies, and I shield my eyes like it's the sun I'm lookin' into, not cold, soaking rain.

Mara bursts through a scattering of trees up ahead, Louisa riding high. She waves when she sees me.

"Down here, it shallows out." She turns in her seat, pointing behind her.

"Right, I'll push them down. Wait here!" I shout over the hiss of the pelting drops.

She nods and pulls the mare to a halt.

I make my way around herd and send them down the bank toward Lou and Mara. She starts off, crossing the shallow part of the stream. The current buffers against the mare's legs. She snorts, plowing her way through the rapid current. Louisa looks back. I usher the cattle into the water. They, to my surprise, follow the lead with no hesitation.

The calves struggle, their lighter weight too easy for the current to drag away.

"Louisa! Watch the calves!"

She stands in the stirrups, twisting to look back. The cattle wade through the rapids, slowly. A calf stumbles and his head disappears under the turbulent surface. It comes up, startled, and bellows. Half of the herd rushes. Some move past Lou, some drift off downstream.

Hell.

Darby enters the water after the last beast is in the stream. I push him harder. Send the cattle at the rear faster. This could go sideways any second.

Louisa makes for the opposite bank. The tension in my gut unfurls a little.

A bellow makes both of us turn toward the sound.

A calf bobs, being carried by the current downstream. He's closer to the opposite side of the stream. Louisa turns Mara back, sending her into the water, fast. The mare obeys, despite shaking her head. Her tail twitches side to side.

The calf goes under.

"No!" Louisa yells.

The second she makes the spot the calf disappeared, Mara falters.

Both Mara and Louisa plummet into the current and vanish.

Fuck!

No!

"Ha!" I spur Darby forward, around the cattle.

God, no . . .

Heart between my teeth, my focus is homed in on the water, desperate to see horse and rider resurface. I slap the reins either side of Darby's neck, sending him faster.

"Louisa!" I call. "Fuck! Lou!"

Mara reappears, panicking, and scrambles up and out of the current. Froth flies from her muzzle as she slides and slips over the shallower section and up the bank.

No rider . . .

"LOUISA!"

Darby's head is high as he rushes through the water.

My blood thunders in my veins.

Goddammit, Louisa May.

Fear snaking through every inch of my veins, I make the other side and fly out of the saddle. I sprint along the bank, slipping on the slimy surface as I go, following the current. I jump over a fallen tree hanging over the raging water, scrambling as I almost lose my footing.

A gasp and a cry break from behind me.

I spin back to find Louisa grabbing for the fallen tree.

"Lou!" I drop to the ground, crawling out to her along the fallen trunk. She gasps for air. Her lips are already blue. Her hat gone, her teeth chattering. She looks up at me, pain twisting her face. I haul her up and out and settle her on the tree, folding her into my chest.

"I—" She shivers in my hold. "Lost." Her teeth smack together violently. "Him."

Oh god.

I pull her head into my neck. Rubbing her back with my hand, I watch with amazement as the half-drowned calf scrambles up the bank fifty feet away.

"Fuckin' Christ," I breathe. "He's fine, darlin'."

She moves her head, slow and shaky, to see the calf in question. A huffy laugh puffs from her blue lips.

"Let's get you home, Louisa May."

"Su-ure, I cou-ld use a h-hot ba-th."

She shakes against my body.

"Among other things."

She melts into me, and I hold her, herd forgotten for a moment.

Just for this small slice of time, this is all that matters.

Chapter Thirty-Four

LOUISA

Devastation is the only emotion I feel right now, watching Harry take stock of the miserably low numbers we brought down off the mountains. By the time we draft off the salable cattle, we'll be barely able to scrape together half of the mortgage payment.

He trots past on Darby, cursing under his breath, and I try to talk to him. He's closed off. Lost in worst-case-scenario mode.

"Harry?" I call after him.

He rounds the herd again. His hand points to the cattle as he roughly counts again.

Ned rides up beside me. "Something tells me he ain't happy."

"No, he's not."

My words are frail, like my hope at this point.

I adjust Mara's reins in my hands. If they aren't holding something right now, I think I will lose it.

My gut flips when Harry rips the hat from his head and shoves a hand through his hair. That one move tells me all I need to know.

After everything we went through, with buying the ranch, Ma, this roundup. This is a solid kick to the guts. Between the herd being too small, the wolves, and only being able to bring a portion of them down with the four of us, it's not good.

Not good at all.

"Best get to draftin' them out then, buddy," Ned calls to Harry.

He waves him off but starts pushing the herd toward the pound. Ned tips his hat at me and trots over to Harry.

Mick is already off his horse and opening the gate, letting the first few head into the round section to be drafted.

Harry trots in with them as Mick closes the gate behind him. Harry singles out the first beast, barking orders at Mick on which gate it's to go through. This is going to take a while. I'm exhausted, starving, and I'm betting the men are, too.

So, I walk Mara from the yards and tie her at the rail, heading for the house to do what I do best.

Feed the man I love.

In the kitchen, the food I left in the refrigerator a week ago looks more appealing than it should. I take out ingredients for a quick, hot meal and get to chopping. Instantly, it relaxes me. A thought hits me as I pause, knife hovering over the carrot under my persuasion. I could be happy here, cooking for the people I love.

Having long days with Harry.

The two of us working together. Working on something we build with our bare hands. And our hearts.

The knife slips from my hand.

If we don't make the payment, every dream Harry and I have attached to this place goes up in smoke.

If Rosie was right, and this is my ship to steer, there's one thing I can do that will make sure we stay afloat.

I push the veggies into a pile and wipe my hands on a tea towel. Plucking the phone from the receiver at the wall, I punch in Mama Mancini's number.

She picks up on the third ring.

"Hey Mrs. Mancini, it's Louisa. I need to talk to you about something. It's important. And it can't wait."

"Are you sure?" Mama's eyes are narrowed, her hands wrapped around one of mine.

I nod.

She leans forward. "Well, if this is what you want, and it's your choice, then I don't think we'll have any trouble finding an investor willing to buy both of us out. This place is a staple in this little old town."

"I have someone in mind. But . . ."

The thought of asking Brad for anything makes me cringe.

But his family owns many businesses in Lewistown. I guess it goes with the territory of being accountants. Good business is their bread and butter.

I only hope they are interested and their payment comes before the weeks end, otherwise Rosewood Ranch is going to be another thing Harry's lost.

"Well, you let me know what you find out. If nothing is settled by the week's end, I will telephone the real estate people." She gives me a soft smile. "For the record, despite your love of this old place, and the food, none of this will matter without the person you want to share it with. You're making the right choice, bambina. Other opportunities will come your way. Mark my words, hey."

"Thank you. And thank you for understanding. I realize you had everything planned."

She waves her hand and huffs a small sound. "Best laid plans, rotten things."

I chuckle at the face she pulls. She rises and wanders into the kitchen only to reappear. "You will be needing this. I meant what I said when I wanted you to have these recipes. As much as they are a family heirloom, they are no use to an old lady with no one to hand them down to. I couldn't think of a better cook to carry them on."

I stand, and she hands me the folder with the recipes we have cooked together, bound in the cream folder I scavenged from the restaurant's front counter. It's now bound with a large rubber band and is suspiciously fuller than the last time I saw it.

"You added more?" I ask.

"A few things to get you and Harry through the tougher times." She winks at me and pats my cheek like she's done since the day I turned up on her doorstep. "You know what they say about a man's heart. Intrinsically attached to his stomach."

I can't help the laugh bursting from me.

Mama's humor is always a little dry and a lot quirky, with her mismatched sayings and huge heart.

"Thank you, again. I can't say it enough."

"Go! Get that deal of yours done. Time waits for no woman."

With a smile to outshine the midday sun, I fly out of the restaurant, folder in hand, and rush my way to the only accounting office in town. The doorbell sings as I bust through it to find a small beige front counter.

I can't believe I've never been in here.

"Can I help you?" a young woman asks. I recognize her. She was with Brad at the restaurant a few weeks back.

Keeping it in-house, Brad.

How . . . convenient.

Bet his mother is pleased.

When I don't answer, she raises an eyebrow.

"Oh, sorry. Can I see Brad? It's kind of an emergency."

She drags her focus from me to her giant appointment book. Her finger runs down the page, and she sucks in a breath before saying, "He has five minutes 'til his next appointment. I suppose you could go in."

"Thanks!" I turn away from the desk. "Ah, which door is it?"

"Second on the left." She taps her wristwatch.

I nod and give her a tight wave before laying a knock onto Brad's door.

"Come."

Okay, here goes.

I open the door and the surprised look on his face is priceless. Well, I guess this time it has a price.

"Louisa?" He frowns and sits up taller in his chair.

"Hi, do you have a minute?"

"Ah, I guess. Have a seat."

"Thanks." I sit on the upholstered seat across the desk from him as I flip through ways to go about this. "I—"

"I'm seeing someone, if that's why you're here."

My mouth drops open, but I catch it before it can make this more awkward than it already is. I press my lips together and shift on the chair, clinging to the folder in my hands. "Actually, I have a proposition for you."

He leans back, and his frown deepens.

Not the best word choice.

Dammit.

How is this so hard?

"Okay, sorry, let me start again. I want you to buy Mama's Place."

He leans forward a little now. It's when his hands unfold from his chest and he mindlessly adjusts the stationery on his desk that I know I have him.

"I thought you had the contract on that place?"

"I do. I mean, I did. I need to sell my part. And the Mancinis need to retire."

"And you came to me?" The frown reappears.

"I know, we didn't have the best run in the relationship department. Mixed signals and all."

"Is that what you call your boyfriend punching me in the face?"

Now my mouth gapes open all the way.

Harry never told me he did . . .

What?

When?

As if reading the confusion on my face, Brad offers, "The night of the dance. He was pretty upset I didn't finish that dance with you."

His words sound incredulous, as if he'd conducted himself well and is shocked by the outcome. This is not where I want this conversation to go. I need it to go well. I need Brad to help me out.

"I'm sorry, I didn't—Harry, he—"

Brad holds up a hand. "I know all about the Rawlins family. Frankly, I don't see why you made the choice you did. But I've moved on. You should, too."

Now, the scoffing sound echoing around his office spills from my mouth.

Shut it down, Louisa.

"Good to know," I say, hoping that will placate him.

He simply nods. "The restaurant is a solid investment. Why do you want out?"

"I need the money for the ranch." The second the words leave my mouth, I realize I've made a mistake. He isn't likely to help Harry. Helping me was a stretch. But helping Harry after the drama at the dance, losing the girl to the guy who hit him in the face . . .

We're screwed.

A knock rattles the door that's still ajar.

"Louisa! I thought that was you." Mrs. Connors pokes her head inside the office.

"Hi," I offer, conjuring my brightest smile.

Maybe it's not all lost yet.

"What brings you to the office?" she asks, tilting her head while her glance bounces between me to her son.

"I'm just talking to Brad about selling my share of the restaurant."

"Oh, I love that old place. So many great memories for Mr. Connors and me there."

I twist on my seat and my expression is almost pleading, I'm sure. "Would you be interested in buying it? Brad was saying it's a solid investment."

"I can't believe Mama is selling. I never thought I'd see the day." Mrs. Connors sits on the corner of her son's desk.

"Well, she is. We are. And it's a quick sale. So no need to auction or negotiate, etc. No *competition*."

"You know what, you leave it with me. Can I get back to you in a day or two?"

"Absolutely." I shoot up from my seat and shake her hand like a goddamn idiot.

She chuckles. "I'll talk to you soon. Leave your number with reception."

"Will do." I back out of the office, not wanting to turn my back on the only lead I've got so far.

"Oh, and Louisa?" Mrs. Connors adds as I'm halfway out the door.

"It's so lovely to see you again." She shoots her son a pointed look.

"You too." I wave and hurry back to the reception counter. I scribble my number at the ranch and leave it with the receptionist.

Bursting with hope, and so stinkin' excited I could pass out, I walk through the accountant's front door. The milky sunshine barely warms my cheeks, but I don't care. After weeks of things going wrong, something finally has the potential to go right.

Now, all I need is for this deal to come through before

the week's out.

I glance up at the cold sky and the wispy clouds scudding across it. Crisp air whips at my face, sending my nose tingling.

Fingers crossed, Rosie.

Chapter Thirty-Five

HARRY

The slip of paper in Louisa's hand has me seein' red. None the wiser, the bank manager glances between us as my glare pierces Lou's soft expression.

"Nope." I jolt from the seat and walk out of his office.

"Harry," Lou pleads from behind me. She excuses herself politely, and fierce dainty steps close in behind me a heartbeat later. "Stop, please. This is how we keep Rosewood."

I don't stop.

I spill out onto the sidewalk and stalk my way down Main Street.

Dammit.

How does this woman always manage to send fire through my veins? Even when she's rooting for me, she drives me fuckin' crazy.

Now this.

A hand wraps around my bicep.

"Don't you walk away from me, Harry Rawlins."

I spin back so fast, I almost crash into her. "What did you do, hey?"

"I got the money we desperately needed."

Those green eyes may as well be made of flame, the way they burn into me. I grind my jaw shut. Chest heaving, I remove the space between us. People have started lookin'.

They can get fucked.

"What the hell did you go and do that for? That wasn't the plan. You pissin' your dreams away for me was *not* the fuckin' plan, Louisa May."

Her eyes soften, just the slightest.

She folds her arms over her chest. "I will have you know, I haven't pissed away anything. I'm fighting for this dream." One elegant arm breaks from its hostile hold and waves between us.

I pace a tight circle and come back to her. "And what happens when this is not enough? When you gave up everything for me. And I'm not enough?"

My throat closes over as my own words register.

Jaw feathering, I drag my hat backward before shoving it down tight.

"I didn't give up my dreams for you, Harry. I simply chose a new dream. Those plans I made, they were from a lifetime ago. Those goals were simply waypoints to what I thought success was supposed to look like. To make sure I never ended up like my own mother. Tied to some tiny town." A manic laugh spills through her lips. "God, I was an idiot. Dreams are just that, Harry. Dreams. They're not concrete. They're not unwavering devotion. They are not *reality*. And they most certainly are not *you*."

I jerk with her words as if she slapped my face.

Her face slips, her arms dropping to her sides as she steps closer. "You're not gettin' it." She shakes her head. "I don't want any of the other stuff if it means we don't get the life *we* want. The dreams I had don't come close to what I have with you."

Eliminating the remaining distance between us, she adds, "I don't want a moment of it if I don't have you with me. Plans change. So do dreams. I got a new one. And it's you and that crazy run-down ranch. With you on the horse next to me on mine."

I slam my hands over her jaw, dragging her mouth up, our lips almost touching.

I can barely breathe, but I can't get close enough to this woman who never ceases to stoke the fire in me, for good or for bad.

Hunger for her takes over and I dip, running my tongue over the seam of her lips. She opens instantly. Like it's the most natural thing in the world, her hands weave into my hair. My hat hits the sidewalk.

A voice clears.

We break apart.

The bank manager and a few of the townsfolk have crowded by the bank's front doors. Louisa's shy smile sends my heart into a flurry. I kiss her forehead and drop my own to it as I breathe, "Let's go save our ranch, darlin'."

"Heavens above, I thought you'd never ask."

The cheeky little smile she gives up warms me all the way to my bones. That, I'll circle back to later, without the audience. I lace my fingers through hers, and we walk back inside.

Bolstered by Lou's declaration and the fact we aren't losing the ranch today, I drop into the seat in the bank manager's office. He takes the check off the desk where Louisa must have left it. Tallying his book, he slides his glasses up his nose as we wait in silence.

Lou squeezes my hand, and I can't take my eyes off this woman.

Not only did she show up, she played her cards well. She loved me even though she was scared to. She found her true north, right where I knew it would be.

Captain.

My captain.

A good man is a great one with his captain by his side.

There is only one problem with this scenario. And I intend on fixin' that as soon as I'm able.

Next stop after this trip to town . . .

Top right drawer of Ma's dresser.

With the restaurant deal all wrapped up and Louisa now workin' with me on the ranch day after day, happiness has claimed this man. In ways I never knew possible. Every day we wake up making love. Every night, exhausted, she folds into my hold, drifting off to sleep.

And every single moment, I count my blessings. I thank my lucky stars Louisa May came home to me after all those years.

Life will never be easy for us. We're too emotional when it comes to the other. We fight for each other so hard some days, we lose sight of the fact we shouldn't be fightin' at all.

But it makes for fuckin' addictive make-up sex.

I swear that's the only reason she gives me attitude.

Despite the storm and the fury that drags us under from time to time, the dark lows are more than worth the millions of highs we live through every single day.

So, to make perfectly sure this woman of mine knows exactly where she damn belongs, I set out more fuckin' candles than should ever be lit in our small space. I toss them wildflowers she loves from our hilltops over the hardwoods. The food Mama Mancini made for tonight smells like something right outta old Italy. Lou's gonna love it.

I sent her on a wild-goose chase for a few cows and calves in the southern paddock while I unloaded the truck of hay that rolled in an hour ago. It took me twenty minutes to offload. I rushed through the shower and pulled on my best jeans, shirt, and the leather necklace she used to love when we were dating last time.

Running my hands through my hair, I pace the room. I sure I'm forgetting something.

Dammit.

Whiskey.

Wine.

Food.

I run a hand over my right pocket.

Small box. Check.

Fire. I forgot the fireplace.

I drop to a knee and start loading logs into the bed of the hearth. I shove kindling under the hardwood logs and light it up. It smokes and flickers to life as the front door opens, banging against the wall.

Fuck.

She's early.

"I couldn't find no—"

Her mouth gapes. Those gorgeous greens I love scan the candlelit room. After a moment, she closes her mouth, her gaze falling to where I'm kneeling by the fireplace.

"Harry," she whispers.

"Come here, Louisa May," I say, not moving off my knee.

She tugs off her long winter coat and places it on the hook on the wall with her hat. The new one she bought in town after losing her old one in the river. It looks good on her, a brown hat. Silver buckle.

Losing that train of thought as she steps in front of me, I take her hands in mine. Her eyes drop to where our hands are laced together.

"The day you blew back into town, Lou, I tried to tell myself this thing between us was just a passin' feeling. I realized, after a few weeks, I'd told myself that once before. Ten years ago. Yet not one day went past in those ten years that my heart ever thought of someone else. Not a single one."

Her chin wobbles.

She scrunches her nose up and her fingers move, squeezing tight.

"Ha—"

"No, woman, this is my turn to talk."

She scoffs a laugh and presses her lips together.

"You came home looking to find yourself, to build back what you thought you'd lost. But darlin', you never lost a thing. The girl I knew ten years ago has only been outshone by the woman you are today. And this man has no damn idea how to live without you. So, at the risk of bein' turned down twice . . . Louisa May Masters, will you marry me?"

I tug the box from my pocket and hold it up to her. Flipping the lid open, I wait for her to say something.

To move.

To stop staring at me like she's in shock.

She loses a shattered exhale.

My heart cinches in my chest. I clench my jaw shut, bracing for history to repeat itself.

She drops to her knees in front of me, and I lower the box.

"Lou?"

It's then I realize her breaths are too short. Her body trembles. She chokes through the next ragged inhale. The box drops from my hand, and I fold her into my arms.

"Breathe. Just breathe."

Her fingers grip my arms so tight, they whiten in the dim candlelight.

I rub a hand over her back. Whispering sweet nothings to steady her racing heart tapping a quick beat against my chest.

"You're okay. I got you, and I always will."

A sob smacks into my neck, and she pushes back a little. Her hands hunt for my face, as if feeling it over for the first time. Exploring, discovering, as she traces the lines, the angles. The shape of me.

Finally, she says, "North."

"Lou?"

I stop breathing.

My lungs ache.

Then her head dips, but her eyes stay homed to mine. "I didn't only find myself. I found what I needed. My true north."

Tears well in her eyes.

She scrunches her face, and they fall.

"Oh, Harry . . . I ran from you. I crossed the country, stayed away for far too long, searching for what I've wanted my whole life. Only to find it's here all along." She sobs out a cry. "You were here *all along*."

"Never left, Louisa May."

It takes a beat for her to steady herself. "Of course you didn't. North never does. That's what makes it so damn fine. It doesn't stray. It stays the course. You . . . You're mine, and my compass is never changing."

Now the tears that have been burning my eyes since she knelt on the floor slip over my face, sliding over my jaw.

"Don't make me ask you a third time, darlin'. 'Cause I ain't gonna."

She chuckles.

Actually laughs at me, her head tilting upward and the tears glistening over her gorgeous face. When she brings it back down, her smile lights a bonfire under my heart. "Yes, I will marry you, Harry."

"Damn straight, woman."

I tug her onto my lap. She leans back a little as I slide

the diamond ring on her finger. She doesn't pay it any heed, closing the space instantly, kisses dotting over my jawline. Her hands play with the opening of my shirt.

Louisa May Rawlins.

It has a nice ring to it—pun intended—if you ask this man.

Chapter Thirty-Six

LOUISA

SIX MONTHS LATER . . .

I slide the drawer to Rosie's dresser open. I know what I'm looking for, I only wish she'd been here to help me get ready. To see her life's work stand at the end of the aisle to wait for the love of his life.

There's a small white box at the back of the right-hand drawer. The lid is inscribed with the letter L. This one is for me.

Sliding it from the drawer, I flip the lid off.

Another handwritten note sits atop a bundle of items.

First, I open the note.

Louisa,

If there is one thing a mother is certain of about their child, it's the day they find the other half of their soul. It's not something to take lightly and must be treasured. It's as if that one person simply locks into place for them. They feel it. I saw the shift in my Harry, the day I first met you.

You remember the day, I'm sure. It's my guess you felt the same way my son did. Does. That's one thing I'm certain will never waiver in his brilliant mind, his commitment to you.

It never has.

On that note . . .

Something old - my crystal hair pin. It was my mother's and hers before. That's as old as anything has the right to get.

Something new - don't tell Harry but I splurged a little after we bought the ranch. I bought one for me and one for you. A silk hand-kerchief. I figured we'd need them in the near future.

I let the box slide from my lap and pluck out the pin and handkerchief. It's smooth and luscious, with an L embroidered in silver thread. The tears that welled in my eyes with the first half of the note slip over my cheeks. I sniff them back, desperate not to spoil my makeup, as basic as it is. Rosie was right, as she always was—I'm in need of a fine handkerchief today. And I'm yet to see Harry.

Sucking in a fortifying breath, I continue reading the note.

> *Something borrowed – well, this one was a little harder to come by, and it must be returned. Mama lent her finest cake slide to you and Harry for the cutting of the cake. And if it's a quiet little affair, like I suspect both of you will want, make my boy something sweet. He mentioned something about a chocolate cake you made him once? Maybe that.*

If I didn't know better, I'd say Rosie and Mama had exchanged the cake knife before I'd asked about buying the restaurant. Was that why they were so easy about the arrangement?

> *Something blue – ah, now this one might be my favorite. The best thing I have to give to you meeting this requirement is the long, steady gaze that will meet you at the end of the aisle. The shade varies with his mood, and we all know he has those in spades, but I promise you, they will always be yours.*

A sob chugs from my throat.

My makeup is absolutely ruined, tears flowing freely now. God, I wish she was here. To see Harry stand at the end of the aisle. To witness all her sacrifices blossom into a big, beautiful life. She founded this. Us. Without Rosie, her cooking lessons request—when I knew she clearly just wanted to find a way to have me in their life—her soul-deep faith in the two of us, her gumption 'til the very end, I wouldn't be sitting in this house that is about to be my home for the rest of my days. About to take her last name and stand beside her son.

She has handed over the helm.

I could never take her place. But I will make certain I live up to her legacy every day as Mrs. Harry Rawlins.

A soft knock snaps me from my reverie.

"Honey? You ready? The preacher is waiting. Harry's getting more fidgety with every minute."

My mother stands in the doorway to Rosie's room, her long, slightly silvered blonde hair tied up in a French knot. Her Sunday best still fits her like it did ten years ago, on the day of the last service I attended with her. Her green eyes, the exact replica of my own, travel my tear-stained face. She pushes off the frame and comes to sit beside me.

"I realize your father and I haven't been around much. But I am so glad you found your home here. I kind of always expected you to."

Her words only make my tears turn from a stemmed

smolder to a searing flow. I grip my face with both hands. I don't want to be puffy-eyed and splotchy on my wedding day. I don't want to look a mess for Harry.

"What's all this?" Mom asks.

I show her the note, and she reads it quickly. Her face pinches, and she scrunches her nose up. Her eyes line with silver as mine did.

"She was one hell of a woman, that Rosie Rawlins."

"Yeah?" I don't understand why the word comes out a question. I already know she was.

"Gosh, the woman was a saint. Putting up with that man. Raising a boy like Harry to the man he is today. I can tell you that was no accident. She gave up a lot."

"She did." More than my own mother, or anyone else, will ever know.

I take grounding breaths, straightening out my lacy dress and wiping my face dry. I channel my inner Rosie Rawlins and stand. Mom helps me fix the items in place and I do one last check in the old vintage mirror on her dresser before I crook my arm and escort my mother into the hallway.

"If I could be half the woman Rosie was, I would be happy. And you taught me well enough to make it happen." I kiss Mom's cheek, and she nudges my shoulder with hers.

"Well, let's get you married."

"Let's."

We walk through the back door to the yard. The old

willows sway in the breeze, stoically surrounding the handful of people in attendance. The way Harry and I wanted it. My parents, the preacher, Mama and Papa Mancini, Ned, and the girls from the diner rise from the cluster of wooden chairs when the single violin I commissioned from the town band plays the first note of the wedding march.

Everyone is dressed in their best. Dad meets me a few feet from the back door of the homestead, and Mom hurries to her seat at the front. But the only person I want to see stands, hands clasped behind his back and eyes burning into me, at the end of the aisle. And they are, in fact, the most brilliant shade of blue. Just as Rosie promised.

Harry stands in new dark jeans, a sport coat, and a tie, a new hat on his head, and the sweetest smile I think I've ever seen him crack.

Dad and I walk slowly toward the small gathering. The violin plays a steady tune that tangles through the green curtains of the willows. Harry stands by the preacher. I set my gaze to his and hold it there.

"You sure about this, Louisa?" Dad whispers.

I look up to see him wink.

I slap his arm that currently has mine woven around it. "It may have taken me a while to work it out, Dad, but I got here eventually."

He chuckles and dots a kiss to the crown of my head. "Yes, you did, my girl."

Is that what Rosie was talking about? Did my parents know all this time who Harry was to me?

A thought rocks me . . . Everyone in my life saw him and me as inevitable. I was the only one who needed a *second* look.

The next heartbeat finishes with me coming to a halt in front of Harry. Dad shakes his hand and sits by Mom.

When I look back at the man before me, his jaw is clenched, his eyes rimmed with silver. The rugged, rough, and moody Harry Rawlins has a soft spot.

And I am so grateful it's me. Even more that he waited for me to find my way home.

"We are gathered here today . . ." the preacher starts, his hands on the Bible.

Harry's jaw feathers.

My face curls with emotion. The preacher's words drown out. With our hands clasped together, we recite the words that will see us through the rest of our days together.

"Congratulations, sweetheart." Ma kisses my cheek and hugs Harry.

We stand holding hands as each person congratulates us in turn. It doesn't take long with our intimate gathering, and I'm grateful for the fact as my nerves and the day's emotions take their toll.

"Something you forgot to tell me, Lou?" Harry whispers into my ear as Brad steps through the back door, heading for the small crowd.

Oh my god.

What the hell?

"He your last-minute invite?" Harry's expression is playful.

"I—" My gaze swings between Harry and Brad. "No, he is not."

"Harry," Brad says in lieu of hello.

"Bradley. What are you doing here?"

"Sorry." He looks around suddenly realizing he has, in fact, intruded. "This came up. It's important. And I didn't want you to have to wait."

My husband—good lord, it feels good to call him that—braces, pulling me into his side. "What's more important than our wedding day, Connors?" His words have turned harsh.

Brad shifts on his feet and flicks his attention from the small crowd of people and the preacher back to us. "Sorry, if I'd known . . ."

"Spit it out." Harry's patience wears thinner.

Brad simply hands him an envelope.

Untangling himself from me, he opens it without a word. I glance at the paper, to Brad, and then back to

Harry as his mouth gapes, his breathing shortening as he runs a hand through his hair.

My stomach plummets.

But then, a smile grows over Harry's face.

"What? What is it?" I ask.

Harry hands me the paper. I skim it and then make myself read it from top to bottom.

Holy heavens above.

She did it.

Rosie, you will never cease to amaze me.

The paper is an account of bonds come due, for the sum of almost two hundred thousand dollars. The recipient in the case of her death, Harrison John Rawlins.

"This will tide us over for years," I breathe.

"Sure would . . ." His voice is far-off.

"Apparently, your mother had money invested on her behalf when she turned eighteen. Decades later, this is the outcome. It takes a few weeks for the paper trail to catch up. Otherwise, the funds are yours to do whatever you see fit." Brad gives a nod and smiles before turning to leave. A second later, he spins back. "Sorry for the intrusion. And . . . Congratulations."

"Thank you," I say softly.

He waves us off as he walks back through the house.

When the shock wears off, I turn to find Harry staring at me.

"What?"

He chuckles, hands resting on my face. "Nothing, Mrs. Rawlins."

"I like the sound of that." I drag his mouth down to my lips.

Harry wastes no time. His hunger for me never changes. I don't care that every person in our yard is watching. Cheers from the small crowd echo through the old trees guarding our home, and I smile against Harry's lips.

He leans back. "You're happy, darlin'."

"Of course I am. I'm home."

"'Bout damn time, woman."

I sigh a happy sound. "*Now*, Harry, you can walk me over that threshold."

So, he does. Sweeping my dress and skirts up, he strides around the side of the house until the front porch is at the toe of his boots. I slide my arms around his neck.

"Well, go on then."

"Yes, ma'am."

We walk over, and his mouth drops to mine the second we pass the imaginary line. The one I ran from once upon a time. All those years ago.

There life goes, giving me what I need. It just so happens, this time it's also what I want.

Chapter Thirty-Seven

HARRY

Everything has to be perfect.

Candles—check.

New drapes covering the restaurant's over-sized windows—Mama's input got that one over the line.

The old Italian lady's famous fettuccine—check.

And, as if she hadn't done enough for Louisa and me already, one Italian chocolate cake. Freshly baked, iced, and waiting for us to devour it, however we see fit.

After a bit of wrangling, I convinced Lou to return the Mancinis' cake slide this evening, claiming they needed to pack. Tomorrow, the Mancinis leave for Florida. After all they have done for Louisa and me, I'm glad I could help them out.

The front door opens, the small bell chiming. Louisa stops dead in her tracks. She smiles and studies me where

I stand, flowers in hand, dressed in the best clothes I own, behind the table set for two.

"What are you up to, Harry Rawlins?" She chuckles and takes off her coat. The cake slide sits in her hand.

"Sit, darlin'."

She pads to her side of the table, and I tug out her chair. She drops into it, and I hand her the bunch of flowers. Dusting a kiss onto her temple, I push her chair in.

"I'm just returning the cake slide. Did you set me up?" Her eyes narrow playfully.

"Actually, I think you were set up on many occasions. Apparently, the women in this town don't take runnin' off at the first sign of a proposal as an answer."

She rolls her eyes but laughs. I take the silver slide from her and place it by the chocolate cake. "We'll be needin' this later."

Her eyes darken, as if the memory of our last Italian chocolate cake found its way back. So, I lean down and pluck a thin folder from the ground and hand it to her before I lose the nerve.

She takes it, eyes never leavin' me. "What is this?"

"Part of *your* legacy."

She drops her gaze to the folder and opens it. Her face crumples as she takes in the contents of the document.

"Harry, no. I can't . . ."

I push out of my chair and squat by hers, taking the folder from her fingertips' grip. I rest it on her lap and take her hands. "There is only one thing I have to do in this life, and that's to take care of you. You have done the same for me, time and time again."

"But the ranch. The money's supposed to be for the ranch."

"It is. Most of it. But this place is special to you. I want you to have it. The Mancinis received a more than fair price for it from the Connors. I simply bought them out. I think Brad had a little sway there. The first and last time that guy gets a pass from me."

She huffs a small laugh. Her hands close over my jawline. "You, Harry Rawlins, are something else."

I don't respond. Not with words, at least, as I snatch that last thought up with a kiss. And I'm glad the new drapes are closed, because this man has zero control when it comes to this damn woman. I stand, my mouth still on hers. She reaches up, like I'm pulling away, likely to be lost forever.

Not this time.

Not ever again.

I sweep her out of her chair and deposit her on the edge of the table. Frantically, she shoves the food to one side. Turning back, her fingers make quick work of my shirt. It falls to the floor as I pull it over her head.

"Wait," she breathes.

"Darlin'. No one can see. Nobody's coming in here tonight."

"It's—" Each exhale crashes into my bare chest. She glances toward the kitchen before those green eyes meet mine. "What if I don't want it anymore . . ."

"Which part, Louisa May?" I ask, my gut flipping over. Some wounds will only ever be easily picked scabs.

Only this time, instead of giving up, I push through. 'Cause she's worth it.

"Working long hours. Spending so many hours in this old place," she finally says.

"Then you can own it. Someone else can work it."

Relief washes over her face.

Fuck.

"What is it you do want?" I cup her face with my palms and hold her eyes onto me. "*Really* want."

She swallows, and her arm moves behind her back. When cold, soft chocolate icing brushes over my bottom lip, she smiles. "I just want you." Her finger slips between my lips. "And one other thing."

I can't speak.

One other thing . . .

So, like any man with a raging hard-on for the woman in front of him would do, I grunt.

She giggles, sliding her finger from my mouth. "I want your babies. As many as you'll give me."

The air snaps from my lungs. Mouth gaping, my chest caves into an erratic cycle of useless pants.

Fuck me, Louisa May.

I don't respond.

"Say something, Harry."

I swallow past a boulder and rasp the first words that surge into my oxygen-deprived brain. "Yes, ma'am."

"I think you mean Captain?" She gives me the most ridiculous stern face I have ever seen before bursting into a laugh that echoes around the old restaurant.

"Woman, you can commandeer this man's ship any goddamn day."

"I was hoping you would say that," she says, slipping off the edge of the table and onto her feet. Her palms push my shoulders, and I sink onto the chair. Her weight settles over my lap as she straddles me, her skirt bunching up over her thighs. "Give me everything, 'cause I want it all. The husband, the ranch, the babies. Fill me up, Harry."

"You've already got the first two."

"The last one, then," she whispers, and her lips brush my ear, then skitter down my neck.

Oh, holy fuck, a man's never been harder in his life. Blood, red hot in my veins, rushes my body. I snap the clasp on her bra and dive right in, tongue, teeth, and mouth, loving this beautiful woman the only way I know how.

She arches into me, and I shift on the seat, freeing my cock. I move to the next breast, and she moans my name.

Heaven has nothin' on Louisa Rawlins.

With a quick sweep through her soaked center with two fingers, I have her vibrating in my lap. But this isn't some quick-release moment. I want to devour her. I want to savor her. Over and over again.

I push to my feet and spin to the table behind us. It's bare, save a small pot of napkins. They hit the floor as I swing a hand behind her and lay her down. The skirt and panties are comin' off.

"God, Harry. How do you always manage to set me on fire?"

"I could be askin' you the same thing."

I groan through a strangled breath as her skirt and panties hit the floor, and her legs fall open for me.

Sweet Jesus.

I drop to my knees, my rough grip spreading her further. Her hands slide over the table, getting purchase on the sides of it. Deciding to take this slow, I track kisses up one soft, creamy thigh before the other. She wriggles her hips. Always so impatient, my Louisa.

"Please . . ." she whimpers.

"Woman, a man could die of thirst looking at you like this."

"I'll be ashes first if you don't touch me soon."

I chuckle and side with putting her outta her misery, running my tongue through her center. Her grip turns white as she snaps up off the table. Goddamn, she tastes so fuckin' fine. The ache in my cock turns to a throb. The taste of her. The sight of her . . .

I lap her slick need as her legs begin to tremble with every suckle of her pretty little clit. As I press two fingers inside her, she stifles a cry, hips bucking off the hard surface. I curl them forward and take up a slow rhythm.

Hands leaving the table, she hunts for me. When she comes up short, she pushes up, bracing with one hand, her other running through my hair.

And damned if the sight isn't enough to see me come. I dive in, sucking hard, picking up the pace my fingers are giving. Louisa's mouth drops open, her breathing almost nonexistent when she tightens around me.

She's so close.

"Come for me, Louisa May. Let this sweet pussy grind all over my face."

Her eyes shutter closed, and she rocks her hips forward, doin' as I said. I add another finger, nipping at her clit. The mewl falling from her parted lips tightens my balls.

Sweet Jesus, woman.

I suck down hard, and she grinds against me in erratic waves. Her pussy clamps down over my fingers, and wetness coats my face and the table where she sits.

"Har—" Her hold in my hair turns to a fist. "God above."

I chuckle against her pussy, sending her feral. Her green eyes are burning when I look up to her. I'm not laughing at her. She delights me in ways I never expect. She always has.

Darkness clouds her gaze as she comes down from her high.

Still on my knees, I wipe my face and wait for her to come to me.

But she slips off the table and tugs me to my feet.

She says nothing as she sinks to her knees and tugs my cock free.

Jesus.

It's impossibly hard. Her mouth finds the tip, tongue swirling, teeth grazing the sensitive opening. A fine hand takes my balls, and I all but lose it in her goddamn mouth.

"Loui—"

"Mhmm?" The syllables vibrate all the way down my cock. My fingers tangle in her hair, tugging hard. She takes me all the way in, eyes homed in on my face.

Fuck me.

I can't control how she makes me feel.

I feel everything with this woman.

She pulls up, sucking hard. I groan.

"Fuck, no . . ."

The short, burnin' breaths I'm barely surviving on have my head spinning. Louisa May wants babies, then who am I to say no . . .

Reaching the tip, her pretty pink tongue tantalizes my cock. I lean down and pull her to her feet. Her hands automatically close around my jaw, pulling me down to her. I devour her, forcing my way in, like she isn't going to give in to me. She melts, and I sweep inside, tongues tangling, hungry and devastating.

I break away, and she stares up at me. Her lips puffy, gaze all doe-eyed. The best fuckin' view this man will ever get.

I drop my forehead to hers. "You want babies, wife? I'll give you babies."

I stand tall, spin her around, and bend her over the table. Her desperate eyes glance over her shoulder. Canting her ass up to me, she wriggles back.

So fuckin' needy.

So fuckin' mine.

"Everything is not nearly enough, Louisa May. Ask for more."

I slam into her. She arches, breasts bouncing as her nipples drag over the hard surface beneath her.

"More," she pants.

I pull back, slow, as I lean over and track hot, open-mouthed kisses up her spine. She turns her head, capturing my mouth when I make it past her shoulder. "More, Harry."

I slam into her.

Her cry rings through the empty, candlelit space.

"More . . ."

Her body trembles under my own. I send it harder, thrust after thrust, until she explodes around me, dragging me over the jagged edge with her. I give her everything I have. Stroke after stroke, hot ropey lengths of release dive deep inside her.

"This is only the beginning, darlin'." I lift her from the table and fold her back into my chest.

She grabs for me, her mouth hunting for a kiss. A heady, hungry need finds me as she slumps into me. "I know, my love."

Chapter Thirty-Eight

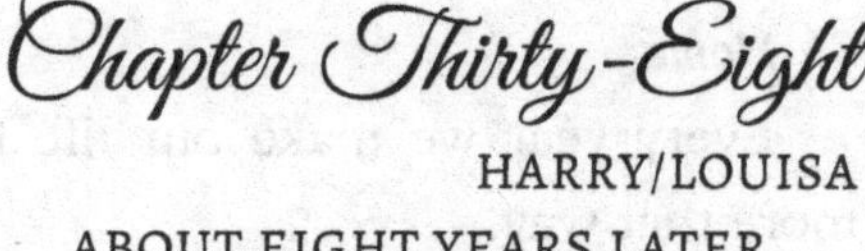

HARRY/LOUISA

ABOUT EIGHT YEARS LATER . . .

The old place doesn't look the same. The house isn't much different from the outside, but inside is a brand-new, state-of-the-art gourmet kitchen. The house yard now sports a brand-new white picket fence. Complete with an elegant white metal gate. Ned and Mick worked with me for a few days to get the wooden fence built and painted. We even managed to fix up the sign over the ranch.

And it's all a surprise.

Louisa is waitin' on me in the Lewistown hospital. Our firstborn arrived last week. A healthy, robust boy. If he ain't the spitting image of his daddy, I don't know what is.

I have been planning this little homestead makeover for nine damn months. The kitchen took a ton of covert planning. With secret calls to old Mrs. Mancini, I got the best we could afford and went with a better layout. Cabinetry that should see us out was a must. And I gotta say, they look mighty fine. Its orientation is slightly different to the old one, facing somewhere more meaningful.

I can't wait to see the look on her beautiful face when she comes home.

Home.

Every year we make our life here, it feels more and more that way.

The barn got a complete overhaul, and we built another. The old loading ramp and yards were the first fix. My ever-patient wife, after years of putting the ranch first, deserves homestead renovations. What better time than when we bring our first child home?

I will never be able to match what she's given me in this life. The sacrifices. The trust. The love.

Hell, I will spend every day I have on this earth makin' sure she has the life she wants. I used to think the bottom line was the most important thing to makin' a good life pan out.

Now, I understand bottom lines ain't got nothin' on the people in your life. We have built friendships. Taken on more investments, the new vet clinic in town being one. Mama's Place is a thriving eatin' spot, and Lou is in there every week, checking over menus, teaching her staff the things she's learned.

But long hours and the stress of working a business weighed on her when she found out she was pregnant.

So, when she told me before Hudson was born she was going silent on the restaurant, I knew she was making a good choice not only for her, but for us.

We spent the last eight years workin'. Lovin'. Making up for all those years we were apart. And when we were *finally* blessed with the chance at havin' a family, the way her face lit up when the stick turned and she realized she was with child . . . That memory, I'll never give up.

I thought I'd loved her in every way possible 'til that day.

That changed again a week ago when the strongest fuckin' woman I've ever known birthed me a son. The hours of agony she went through, only to come out smilin' when I bent over and cut the cord.

A man has never cried so hard in front of so many people.

So, a kitchen and a quaint white fence is the least I can give her today. I glance at the sky, of which the sun is halfway up. I still have one more errand before I head into town.

If I don't hurry, I'll be late.

Ain't no way that's happenin'. I promised to arrive at lunchtime. And I intend on keepin' my word and addin' some of those wildflowers she loves so much from our hills here on the ranch. I jump into the truck and poke toward the hills to the south.

Cresting the top of the first flower-covered hill, I park and gather as many flowers as I can manage. Once the cab is overflowing with the small yellow flowers on their raggedy stems, I slide back inside and track back toward the homestead.

An hour later, I have everything organized.

Flowers everywhere.

In vases.

Scattered over the floor and down the hall.

By our bed . . . Check.

Crib set up and baby things at the ready.

New kitchen all cleaned for use, food and utensils, pots and pans all stowed away. Check.

New white fence wrapping all the way round our homestead yard to raise our babies in. Check.

Shaved. Check.

Nervous as hell. Check.

Pining away, still, for the only woman I've ever loved.

Check and check.

The little hospital is quiet. I poke my head through the door to Louisa's room, and her wide smile and lit-up green eyes are the first thing I see. In her arms lies a small bundle. Throat workin' at the tiny sounds he makes, I drag my hat from my head.

I pad to Lou's side, brushing a kiss over her lips. "Hey, darlin'."

"Hey, Harry." Her words choke up. "Hey little man, daddy's here."

She lifts him up to me.

I drop my hat onto the bed and wrap my arms around him. He nestles into my hold. I make a promise to myself that he will know just how loved he is. And I decide right there that I will work every day to show him what it is to be a good man.

Leading by example.

So my wife never has to make a hard choice.

So she is never left alone.

So he grows up knowing the worth of a woman.

"Howdy, my boy. Bein' good for your mama?"

He pulls a face, his little mouth twisted, his brows down. And, I swear, he growls.

I chuckle. This little boy is a chip off the old block.

"About that . . ." Louisa looks up at me.

"Yeah, Lou?"

"Not Mama. Ma."

I know what she means.

Her face softens as she rises a little where she sits, leaning over as she pulls the swaddle blanket away from Hudson's small face. "Do you think she would mind?"

Hell.

A stone rises in my throat with her meaning, tamping down any words. I drop my gaze to Hudson, then shift it to Louisa. "She would be honored. And it sounds perfect to me."

Louisa smiles, a tear tracking down her cheek. She swipes it away as she whispers, "Ma."

A huffy breath snaps from her chest, and she slides from the bed. "Take us home, Harry."

"Yes, ma'am."

I pluck up the overnight bag, still cradling my son, and lead my wife home.

Louisa

Hudson rides on the bench seat between us, his small baby seat tethered to the lap belt. Harry drives slow. Almost too slow. He's been a father for five minutes and already outshines his own in every single way.

"How's things while I was away?" I ask, eyes searching the horizon as we get closer and closer to the ranch.

"Good. Same."

He glances at me, but those deep blues have a glint of something suspicious in them. *What are you up to, Harry Rawlins?*

His hands grip the wheel tight. His angled jaw and

dark hair still set the silhouette I adore. That stubble. The deep adoration burning right through me . . .

I'm more in love with this man than I've ever been.

Just when I think life can't get any better. That I can't love him more . . . Harry becomes a father, and that feeling, the invisible tug we've always had, infinitely grows. Fortified by this new adventure in our life together.

"I can hear the cogs turnin', Louisa May."

I smile at him, eyes shining with all the love I have for him. I don't respond. Instead, he turns into the ranch, but pulls up before the wide entrance.

"Welcome home, Mrs. Rawlins." He nods to the wide arch above us.

H J & L M Rawlins
Rosewood Ranch

My hand presses over my mouth. It's wonderful. We talked about this for so long. To see it, the new hardwood posts and the carved wooden entrance with our initials, it's something else.

"Oh, Harry . . ."

He gives me a wink. "Get used to sayin' that phrase."

What is he talkin' about?

We roll into the ranch, the barns flanking the driveway to the left, the homeste—

"Oh my god . . ." The words leave on puffy breaths.

A smile the size of Montana grows over his face as he

pulls up and kills the engine. A sweet white fence runs right 'round the house, the old trees—my favorite part of the homestead—encircled by it. The front yard is a large rectangle. It looks magnificent.

"Ain't even the best part," Harry rumbles softly beside me. Now his face is lit up and staring down at me at my open door. I didn't see him get out of the truck, let alone round it and open my door. Awe has me in its thrilling grip as I slip out of the truck, my hand in his. Harry leans inside and reappears with Hudson cradled safely in his arms.

"Welcome home, Lou."

I glance up at him and wander toward the small white gate. Its ornate iron top is the sweetest thing. I swing it open. Wide stone pavers are dotted along a curved path to the front porch, lining up perfectly with our front door.

"Harry . . . what did yo—When did you do all this?"

"I had a few days to get a couple things fixed up."

He leans around me and places his hand on the front doorknob. "Now, I realize you like your cookin' space a particular way, but I thought an upgrade was overdue for the most amazing woman I've ever known."

"Wha—" I flick my gaze to his face.

He swings the front door open, and I return my attention to inside the house.

To our home.

I cross the threshold and halt one step in.

The old ranch kitchen, with its sagging cabinet doors

and tiny stove, is nowhere to be found. Instead, a beautiful and massive kitchen sits in its place. I drift toward the wonder. My fingertips sweep over the new counter. The cabinets are gorgeous. The hardware . . .

My eyes burn.

A wide stove sits on the back wall, a long faucet hovering over it. A wide fridge, and is that . . . ?

"A wine fridge?" I gasp.

"You never know, with this family of ours growing, we're probably gonna take up drinkin'."

His grin is wide but falls when the sentiment hits home.

The memories of the little allotment outside Lewistown and the dim days Rosie and him lived there must have snagged in his mind.

I move into his space and push up on my tiptoes, planting a kiss on his lips. Hoping to remind him of what Harry, whiskey, and me have between us. Wanting to coax back every beautiful memory we have of whiskey kisses, and all the love we've made. "We will be just fine. A little whiskey never hurt a man."

Being careful not to disturb Hudson, I cup Harry's face and whisper my mouth over his. This hunger between us will never die. Of that, I'm sure now.

"Or a little fencin'," he rasps.

He caught on quick. Spinning back 'round, I take in all he's done for me, and emotion claims me. An arm slides around my waist, his stubbled cheek pressing against mine. "A captain needs a decent helm. Think this'll do, darlin'?"

It's all I can do to turn a little to the side and close my eyes, nestling my face into his neck. Hudson stirs in his arms, so I make my next words a whisper.

But their meaning is everything.

"It faces north. It's perfect, Harry."

Epilogue

LOUISA

THE SUMMER OF '96

Three out of four little boys asleep in their beds, I slide in beside my husband ever so slowly, like even the slightest move I make could disturb our youngest.

I just got him down.

I doubt he's asleep.

He's fussy.

Ain't that the understatement of the year.

Reed James Rawlins may be the last addition to our family, but he is the loudest. Every night of the past month has been the same.

Bedtime for the boys.

Washing up and sliding into my bed, exhausted, next to an equally as exhausted Harry.

Then we wait, in the darkness.

A cry pierces the warm summer air.

There he goes . . .

"Give him a minute, he'll right himself." Harry's weary rumble presses into my hair as he rolls over and drapes an arm over me. He's the king of wishful thinkin', my husband. The knot cinching in my chest with my youngest's cries pulls tighter every time.

His wail ebbs a little, only to split the air with new ferocity a moment later.

I sigh and turn my head to the side, planting a kiss to Harry's lips. God, I love this man.

So damn much.

When the cry ratchets up another ear-piercing level, I mutter my "I love you" to Harry's cheek and slip out of the soft bed.

I pull on my robe, its light cotton swaying mid-thigh as I trudge to the now well-worn path to Reed's room.

He is sitting up in his crib, his howl so much louder in his space. "Hey, little man. You're okay, my boy." I sweep him out of his crib and settle into the old rocking chair by the window.

The moon is high in the sky, lighting up this side of the house. I pop a button on my nightie, and he latches on to my nipple. He bites down hard, and I wince. But the soft, downy blond hair and those big green eyes lookin' right through me as he takes his fill . . . I can't find it in myself to feel anything but exhausted contentment.

Rosie was right. A mother will do anything for her child.

With my four babies tucked in safe and sound, and a man who loves his family more than anything, I can't even begin to imagine the loss she felt, having to raise her son without what I have.

What she's given Harry and me.

I lay my head back on the hardwood back of the rocking chair. My eyes drift shut as Reed suckles and fusses.

He pulls away, milk dribbling down his chin, and I fix my nightshirt before rising to my feet. Holding him, I pace the hallway, trying my best to get him to settle. Even after the feed, he whines softly.

So, I pace.

Back and forth.

Back and forth.

After I have lost count of the times the hallway has been traveled, my hand rubbing his small back, I look up to find Harry leaning in our doorway, boxers and a bare chest, his hair is ruffled to a mess, crooked smile and deep blue gaze fixed on his wife and son.

He's a sight for sore eyes, alright.

"Let me, Lou."

He pads to where I pace, taking Reed from my arms. Before he takes up the movement, he hovers, forehead pressing to my temple. "How can I ever repay you, darlin'?"

"What for, my love?"

"Givin' me this big, beautiful life. These four boys . . ."

"You don't owe me a thing," I whisper.

It's true. Where would I be without this man?

A captain is nothing without her ship.

He loses a small groan, as if being this close has him all worked up despite the fidgeting baby boy between us.

"When you figure it out, Louisa May, you let me know."

Dotting kisses to my cheek, he peels away, taking Reed on their first lap of the hallway, the small blond head poking over his shoulder. He leans his head to Reed's. His dark hair a stark contrast, even in this dim light. Father to son.

Imagine the things our boy will learn from this great man.

The milestones we will all travel together.

I decide, right in that moment, I want to make sure each one is marked somehow. A way to make sure our family takes stock every year. So nothing is overlooked, nothing is forgotten. And our bonds stay strong. Something only for us, not skewed by any other celebration.

Harry turns back and wanders toward me with a rhythmic sway in his step, quietly humming, I know what I want.

"I want a party, every year, for my birthday."

Harry raises an eyebrow. "That all? Isn't that a given?"

I breathe a small laugh. "I want everyone there. Every last person who is special to our family. Every year, to mark the milestones we have traveled. That's what I want."

"Then it shall be done." He winks at me and waves me away. "Back to bed, Louisa May. Us men need a moment."

With a soft laugh, I kiss his cheek as he passes by, making a U-turn back down the hall. The low rumble of his melody makes my heart swell.

"Lou?" he rasps, and I turn with a hand on our bedroom doorframe.

"Get some sleep, woman. I'm sure this lot will be mutinous in the mornin'."

I shake my head at him as he pretends to walk peg legged, one arm holding Reed tight.

"Let's hope so."

The smile blooming over my face is one part joy, one part adoration. And absolutely one hundred percent grateful this man waited.

Because lord above . . . he didn't have to.

Extended Epilogue

HARRY

ALMOST TWENTY-SIX YEARS LATER . . .

Louisa stands at the counter, kneading dough for biscuits, a chopping board loaded with prepped veggies by her side. I recognize the routine; it's the start of my favorite stew. Even now, she can still lure me in with her damn cookin'.

The back door slams as Hudson and the new vet, Dr. Howard, leave for the expecting mares. The instant the sound snaps down the hallway, Louisa's eyes find me. Those beautiful green eyes that held mine the first day we met still have a stranglehold over me to this day.

"What?" I ask, feigning innocence as I eliminate the space between me and her, only the kitchen counter separating us.

I know what she's thinkin'.

I felt it, too.

The way our son's face changed when he took Dr. Howard, *Addy*, in for the first time.

"She seems nice," is all Louisa says, but her eyes are lit up. I can tell she's tamping down a smile. Seein' her boys happy makes her heart swell. "Pity about that son of yours, chip off the old block."

Her words don't match the excited expression animating her face.

"I'll have you know, Louisa May Rawlins, this block is made of some hearty stuff."

She chuckles. "I'm aware."

"Besides, the boy needs to get there. It's been years."

Now, her smile fades. "He does."

I swipe the weekly paper from the counter and make my way to the kitchen table, dropping into the captain's seat at the head. The old chair groans, as it always does, but never folds. I shake the paper out, hunting for the business section, as small as it is in map-dot Lewistown. "A little help never hurt a man in the romance department."

The knife drops to the chopping board.

I peer over the paper to my wife's singular raised eyebrow.

"Just how are you plannin' on *helpin'* Hudson?"

"Easy. Find a way to shove them together." I put the paper down. "*Then* tell him he can't have her."

She pulls a mock warning face and plucks up the knife,

pointing it at me. "If this goes to hell in a handbasket, you're picking up the pieces."

"Don't I always?"

A chunk of carrot flies in my direction.

"Here we go again," she says with a sigh.

"Well, it took you two goes to get it right. Second time's the charm for Huddy, hey?"

I rarely use her nickname for our son, but after his last relationship, my heart goes out to the boy.

Her face softens, and she offers up a smile full of emotion. Because that's how my wife is wired. My Louisa May is the salt-of-the-earth kind of good, with a heart as big as this ranch.

What would have become of me without her?

A man is nothing without his captain. Sure, he might make some good choices, have success in its own right. But without someone to share it with, what was the point?

After all, you need something to fight for.

I want our boys to have the love and the life I found.

Sometimes, a little meddling is all it takes.

Hey, Ma.

As if she's listenin', as if she's proud of all Lou and I have built, the trees move with the breeze outside. It changes course and whips through the window behind me, ruffling the pages of the paper in my hands.

Ma would have been proud of Hudson.

Of all our sons.

Hell, I know I am.

And I have a good feelin' about this girl.

Need more Harry & Louisa?
Grab the BONUS SCENE now!
https://BookHip.com/BDGBSZX

Need more Rawlin men in your life?
Get ready to meet Lawson!
Pre-Order Sassy Love

Sign up to the newsletter to make sure you never miss an Alexandra Banks book!!

TRUE NORTH playlist 1982

- **BURNING LOVE**
  Elvis Presley

- **WORKING 9 TO 5**
  Dolly Parton

- **AM I OKAY?**
  Megan Moroney

- **I HAD SOME HELP**
  Post Malone (feat. Morgan Wallen)

- **STILL**
  Tim McGraw

TRUE NORTH
playlist
2024

SASSY Love

ALEXANDRA BANKS

Acknowledgments

Harry and Louisa's story was a long time coming. I just knew their start was going to be rocky. The highs and lows of loving someone that much never allows for plain sailing. But they fought for it, and eventually overcame their innermost fears to build something absolutely incredible. Even if it took a little while.

As always, thanks to my editors, Lindsey and Zainab. Your input and guidance is always wanted and appreciated.

To every ARC reader who volunteered to read this book, thank you!!

And lastly, but most certainly not least, my family for putting up with the endless country music playlist that I made them endure during the writing process to get into the zone ;)

Alex xx

Alexandra Banks is a romantic at heart, and an optimist down to her very bones. Her love for everything romance sees her writing HEAs all day long.

But don't be fooled, there will be angst along the way, possibly heartbreak. But her fierce heroines can handle just about anything!

For more heartwarming reads, follow her on socials and join the mailing list so you never miss another book boyfriend!

www.ingramcontent.com/pod-product-compliance
Lightning Source LLC
Chambersburg PA
CBHW010441170726
48283CB00011B/3326